中国人民大学2019年度“中央高校建设世界一流大学（学科）和特色发展引导专项资金”支持成果
“当代西方文艺批评理论要义”（2017）配套教材

Selected Readings of Contemporary Western Critical Theories

当代西方文艺批评理论选读

主　编 陈世丹
副主编 史岩林 张东芹 王小会 黄 贺

華中科技大學出版社
http://www.hustp.com
中国 · 武汉

图书在版编目(CIP)数据

当代西方文艺批评理论选读/陈世丹主编. —武汉:华中科技大学出版社,2021.2
ISBN 978-7-5680-4759-3

Ⅰ. ①当… Ⅱ. ①陈… Ⅲ. ①文艺批评-理论-西方国家 Ⅳ. ①I0

中国版本图书馆 CIP 数据核字(2021)第 058442 号

当代西方文艺批评理论选读 陈世丹 主编
Dangdai Xifang Wenyi Piping Lilun Xuandu

策划编辑:张馨芳
责任编辑:李文星
封面设计:刘 婷
责任监印:周治超

出版发行:华中科技大学出版社(中国·武汉) 电话:(027)81321913
武汉市东湖新技术开发区华工科技园 邮编:430223

录 排:华中科技大学出版社美编室
印 刷:武汉市金港彩印有限公司
开 本:787mm×1092mm 1/16
印 张:23.75 插页:1
字 数:588 千字
版 次:2021 年 2 月第 1 版第 1 次印刷
定 价:68.00 元

華中出版

前言

《当代西方文艺批评理论选读》(*Selected Readings of Contemporary Western Critical Theories*,以下简称《文论选读》)是高校英语语言文学专业文学、文化方向研究生专业基础课"当代西方文艺批评理论"教材。本书精选了当代18种文艺批评理论重要文论家的代表性著作篇章节选,配有文论家简介、节选内容简介,节选注释。本书是与*Main Ideas of Contemporary Western Critical Theories*(《当代西方文艺批评理论要义》,北京:中国人民大学出版社,2017年,以下简称《文论要义》)配套编写的。后者是对20世纪和21世纪初以来陆续出现的18种西方文艺批评理论的主要思想、观点的概述,可用作课堂教师的讲义。本书选读文献与《文论要义》概述的18种文艺批评理论对应,它们是:① 俄国形式主义;② 英美新批评;③ 马克思主义批评;④ 心理与精神分析批评;⑤ 神话与原型批评;⑥ 结构主义批评;⑦ 接受美学与读者反应理论;⑧ 后结构主义;⑨ 后现代主义;⑩ 女性主义批评;⑪ 新历史主义;⑫ 后殖民主义研究;⑬ 性别研究;⑭ 文化研究;⑭ 生态文学批评;⑮ 生态后现代主义;⑰ 后人文主义;⑱ 后现代文学伦理学批评。本书的文献节选可与理论讲解结合使用,对于研究生理解理论具有直接的重要意义。具体文献节选请见本书目录。

《文论要义》与《文论选读》旨在帮助青年读者、学者,特别是高校文学院、外国语学院从事文学批评、理论研究的硕士生、博士生系统地熟悉和掌握这18种西方文艺批评理论的核心观念和重要思想,恰当地选择理论作为自己学术研究立论的依据、观点的支撑和批判的武器,有助于青年学者在人文社会科学研究中处在学科前沿,不断探索,不断创新。

《文论要义》虽以专著的形式呈献给读者,但实际上它是以我自2004年秋季学期开始到现在一直在中国人民大学英语专业承担的研究生课程"当代西方文艺批评理论"讲义基础上,经过16年不断修改、不断扩展、不断充实而形成的,由最初的11种逐步扩展为现在的18种理论。逐步增加的理论包括：第九章——后现代主义；第十一章——新历史主义；第十二章——后殖民主义；第十五章——生态文学批评；第十六章——生态后现代主义；第十七章——后人文主义批评；第十八章——后现代文学伦理学批评。

此处对《文论要义》中"第十八章——后现代文学伦理学批评"做一个特殊的说明。对后现代主义文学的批评，国外学者多是从语言、叙事、哲学、政治学、社会学、文化、马克思主义、新历史主义、后殖民主义、女性主义、生态批评等理论视角展开，也有少数学者从伦理学视角讨论后现代主义文学作品。自20世纪90年代以来，国外虽也出现了齐格蒙特·鲍曼、伊曼纽尔·列维纳斯、雅克·德里达、让-吕克·南希等哲学家提出的后现代伦理学或后现代伦理思想，但一直未见有后现代文学伦理学批评的理论建构。我国学者聂珍钊教授在2004年首次提出了文学伦理学批评的理论构想，指出文学的价值就在于它的伦理教诲功能，文学批评不应该有伦理的缺失。他在2014年出版了专著《文学伦理学批评导论》，完成了文学伦理学批评理论的建构，产生了巨大影响。该书对我启发很大。我自1997年获得第一个国家社科基金青年项目"美国后现代主义小说主题与艺术手法论"（青年项目，97CWW004）以来，一直在从事英美后现代主义小说研究，出版了专著《美国后现代主义小说艺术论》（2002）、《虚构亦真实》（2005）、《美国后现代主义小说详解》（2010）等12部，发表核心期刊论文《论后现代主义小说之存在》（2005）、《代码》（2005）、《后现代文学中的媒介与"再现"和建构》（2012）、《在虚幻世界反思人类认知能力》（2016）、《戴维·洛奇小说〈好工作〉中后现代伦理的叙事手法》（2018）、《西方文论关键词：后人文主义》（2019）等80多篇。我在多年研究过程中发现，作为现代主义思想基础的现代性排斥、拒绝和否定差异，使一切"他者"成为不合法，通过不可能的真理、纯艺术、人性的普遍性来使本来不存在的形而上学的东西在场，把它强加给人们，从而使自己成为可能。现代性对中心性、普遍性、一致性、一元性和排他性的追求和强调，导致中心主义、主体中心主义、人类中心主义、普遍主义、绝对主义和一元主义的膨胀。而后现代性意指一种强大的变革冲动和创新精神，它要革除现代性对权威、中心和等级的维护，强调承认差异、尊重他者、主张多元性和包容性，是对现代性的批判、否定和颠覆。后现代性试图通过弘扬革新的思想观念，改变和超越现代性或现代精神，建立承认差异、尊重他者，主张多元性和包容性的合理的后现代社会秩序和后现代精神。后现代性是后现代主义的思想基础，也是后现代西方伦理学的思想基础。后现代主义文学消除作者的叙述权威、叙述中心，采用多角度观察、多叙述者、多声音（或复调）、多样杂糅的结构、多元变化的叙事技巧等构成的狂欢化叙事；用平行结构、戏仿、直接引用等构成的互文叙事，即用这种承认差异，尊重他者，主张多元性和包容性的后现代伦理学一致的后现代伦理的叙事，来表现文学文本中所表现的后现代伦理关系和道德秩序的变化及其引发的各种问题和产生的不同结果，为后现代人类文明进步提供经验和教诲。自2014年起，我根据聂珍钊教授文学伦理学批评的基本原理，系统研究了齐格蒙特·鲍曼、伊曼纽尔·列维纳斯、雅克·德里达、让-吕克·南希等哲学家提出的后现代西方伦理思想，在后现代主义文学研究基础上，尝试建构了“后现代文学伦理学批评理论”。从2015年开始，我在中国人民大学英语专业研究生课程“当代西方文艺批评理论”中增加了“后现代文学伦理学批评理论”一章。仅在2015—2016年、2016—2017年、2018—2019年三学年内，就有30多名本科生、20多名硕士生和10多名博士生用后现代文学伦理学批评理论为立论的依据和批判的武器，展开对英美后现代主义小说和戏剧的研究，撰写学位论文和在学术期刊上发表论文。

Selected Readings of Contemporary Western Critical Theories（《当代西方文艺批评理论选读》），可与 *Main Ideas of Contemporary Western Critical Theories*（《当代西方文艺批评理论要义》）配套使用，作为高校外国文学、比较文学和文艺理论研究方向研究生文学批评和理论研究课程教材，亦可作为文学、文化、文艺学研究生及从事文学批评和理论研究学者的工具书或参考书。

诚挚地欢迎广大读者批评指正！

陈世丹

2020年4月16日

CONTENTS

Volume 1

Volume 2

Volume 1

陈世丹 史岩林 张东芹 编

Chapter One **Russian Formalism**

俄国形式主义是一战前后在俄国兴起的一股新的批评思潮，成为20世纪西方文论的开端。俄国形式主义始于1914年，终于1930年，分别以什克洛夫斯基发表的文章《词语的复活》和《给科学上的错误立个纪念碑》为标志。主要的代表人物有：什克洛夫斯基(V. Shklovsky, 1893—1984)、埃亨鲍姆(B. Eichenbaum, 1886—1959)、托马舍夫斯基(B. Tomashevsky, 1890—1957)、雅各布森(R. Jakobsen)等。这一流派主要有两个理论中心：一是成立于1915年的"莫斯科语言学学会"，以雅各布森为代表的主要成员大多是莫斯科大学学生，他们将语言学最新成果运用于文学研究，从界定文学语言入手，注重研究文学语言的本质和文学语言规律，并据此对作品进行结构分析；二是成立于1916年的"彼得堡诗歌语言研究会"，以什克洛夫斯基、埃亨鲍姆为主要成员，从探讨诗歌语言和日常语言的差别入手，挖掘文学语言的基本特性，并据此总结出文学研究的总体思路和作品解读的基本方法，这些思路和方法成为形式主义的理论基础。

顾名思义，俄国形式主义的研究对象由文学作品为代表的内容(如社会现实、作者的生平、作品的主要思想)转为文学形式本身。形式主义批评的批评对象是当时批评界流行的传统文学批评方法：传记式的批评，根据作者的生活来解读文本；社会学的批评，把作品完全概括为社会思潮的反映；批评家借文学来阐述自己哲学思想的哲学批评。传统文学批评主要探讨文学所代表的内容。因此，它考察了作者的生平、与作品有关的社会事件以及作品孕育的主要思想，从而把文学的组织形式和文学作品成为文学的原因放在次要位置。俄国形式主义者把批评的重心转移到文本的形式和结构上，试图从科学的角度准确地描述作品叙事技巧的特点和功能。什克洛夫斯基在《作为技法的艺术》一文中明确表达了文学研究的对象不再是"文学"，而是文学之所以成为文学的东西，即"文学性"。"文学性"作为文学语言与日常语言的区分，成为俄国形式主义理论的核心。俄国形式主义者认为文学性在于普通语言的特殊使用。文学语言偏离和扭曲了普通语言。后者主要用于交流，前者没有这样的实际功能。因此，什克洛夫斯基提出文学性的基础在于"陌生化"，强调文学形象的感知过程，以延长审美过程，恢复读者感知的敏锐度。什克洛夫斯基认为诗歌的主要特征不是意象，而是用来处理和安排文字的技巧。诗歌意象与比较、重复、对称、夸张等手法具有相同的功能，都是用来提高人们对诗歌的直接体验，加深对读者的印象。使用这些技巧的目的是消除人们已经习惯的自动体验方式，延长和强化新的体验方式，并获得陌生化的效果。

叙事理论也是形式主义者探索的主要领域。他们最大的兴趣是找出构建故事的技巧，并研究将故事中所有事件联系起来的方法。俄国形式主义者严格区分"故事"和"情节"，认为故事是一系列按照事件发生的时间顺序和因果关系规律来展开的事件，而情节则使事件发生的时间顺序和因果关系规律陷入混乱。严格地说，只有情节才具有文学性，而故事仅仅是一套有待作者加工整理的原材料。

20 世纪 20 年代后期，俄国形式主义的主要代表纷纷流亡国外，30 年代之后，形式主义在苏联文坛销声匿迹。尽管这一文学批评流派仅仅存在了约 15 年，但仍为 20 世纪的西方文论提供了新的研究视角，布拉格学派成为它的理论延续，并对后来的符号学、叙事学和解构主义产生深远影响。

Viktor Borisovich Shklovsky

什克洛夫斯基(1893—1984)，俄国文学评论家和小说家，彼得堡诗歌语言研究会的核心人物，俄国形式主义美学的代表。什克洛夫斯基生于教师家庭，毕业于彼得堡大学历史语文系。什克洛夫斯基于 1914 年发表的题为《词语的复活》的论文，被认为是俄国形式主义文论的纲领性文献，标志着 20 世纪形式主义文艺理论思潮的开始。早期作品包括广受称赞的论文集《感伤的旅行：回忆录》(1923)，《关于散文理论》(1925)和《作家的精妙技巧》(1928)。20 世纪 30 年代受到批判以后，他发表了《给科学上的错误立个纪念碑》，逐渐放弃了俄国形式主义立场，转向社会主义现实主义的研究，50 年代重新从事文学批评工作，著有《艺术散文思考和分析》(1959)、《列夫·托尔斯泰》(1963)等。1984 年 12 月 6 日，什克洛夫斯基逝世于莫斯科。

Art as Technique

(Borisovich Shklovsky，Viktor. Art as Technique. 选自亚当斯、瑟尔主编，《柏拉图以来的批评理论(下册)》(第三版)，北京：北京大学出版社，2006 年，第 797 到 805 页。)

《作为技巧的艺术》(1917)是形式主义文论的重要文献。什克洛夫斯基在该文中提出了文学性、陌生化等著名的形式主义概念。他极力反对当时相当流行的"艺术即形象思维"观点——研究作品必须从形象入手。什克洛夫斯基认为诗歌的主要特征不是意象,而是用来处理和安排文字的技巧,艺术的目的不是提供认知的对象,而是提供感知的对象。他认为,文学绝对不是对生活的模仿,而是生活的变形。文学应以不寻常的新方法反映旧思想或世俗的经验,而迫使读者重新观看世界。诗歌意象与比较、重复、对称、夸张等手法具有相同的功能,都是用来提高人们对诗歌的直接体验,加深对读者的印象。使用这些技术的目的是消除人们已经习惯的自动体验方式,延长和强化新的体验方式,并获得陌生化的效果。

"Art is thinking in images." This maxim, which even high school students parrot, is nevertheless the starting point for the erudite philologist who is beginning to put together some kind of systematic literary theory. The idea, originated in part by Potebnya, has spread. "Without imagery there is no art, and in particular no poetry," Potebnya[1] writes. And elsewhere, "Poetry, as well as prose, is first and foremost a special way of thinking and knowing."

Poetry is a special way of thinking; it is precisely, a way of thinking in images, a way which permits what is generally called "economy of mental effort," a way which makes for "a sensation of the relative ease of the process." Aesthetic feeling is the reaction to this economy. This is how the academician Ovsyaniko-Kulikovsky[2], who undoubtedly read the works of Potebnya attentively, almost certainly understood and faithfully summarized the ideas of his teacher. Potebnya and his numerous disciples consider poetry a special kind of thinking—thinking by means of images; they feel that the purpose of imagery is to help channel various objects and activities into groups and to clarify the unknown by means of the known. Or, as Potebnya wrote:

> The relationship of the image to what is being clarified is that: (a) the image is the fixed predicate of that which undergoes change—the unchanging means of attracting what is perceived as changeable.... (b) the image is far clearer and simpler than what it clarifies.

In other words:

> Since the purpose of imagery is to remind us, by approximation, of those meanings for which the image stands, and since, apart from this, imagery is unnecessary for thought, we must be more familiar with the image than with what it clarifies.

It would be instructive to try to apply this principle to Tyutchev's[3] comparison of summer lightning to deaf and dumb demons or to Gogol's[4] comparison of the sky to the garment of God.

"Without imagery there is no art"—"Art is thinking in images." These maxims have led to far-fetched interpretations of individual works of art. Attempts have been made to evaluate even music, architecture, and lyric poetry as imagistic thought. After a quarter of a century of such attempts Ovsyaniko-Kulikovsky finally had to assign lyric poetry, architecture, and music to a special category of imageless art and to define them as lyric arts appealing directly to the emotions. And thus he admitted an enormous area of art which is not a mode of thought. A part of this area, lyric poetry (narrowly considered), is quite like the visual arts; it is also verbal. But, much more important, visual art passes quite imperceptibly into nonvisual art; yet our perceptions of both are similar.

Nevertheless, the definition "Art is thinking in images," which means (I omit the usual middle terms of the argument) that art is the making of symbols, has survived the downfall of the theory which supported it. It survives chiefly in the wake of Symbolism, especially among the theorists of the Symbolist movement.

Many still believe, then, that thinking in images—thinking, in specific scenes of "roads and landscape" and "furrows and boundaries"[5]—is the chief characteristic of poetry. Consequently, they should have expected the history of "imagistic art," as they call it, to consist of a history of changes in imagery. But we find that images change little; from century to century, from nation to nation, from poet to poet, they flow on without changing. Images belong to no one: they are "the Lord's." The more you understand an age, the more convinced you become that the images a given poet used and which you thought his own were taken almost unchanged from another poet. The works of poets are classified or grouped according to the new techniques that poets discover and share, and according to their arrangement and development of the resources of language; poets are much more concerned with arranging images than with creating them. Images are given to poets; the ability to remember them is far more important than the ability to create them.

Imagistic thought does not, in any case, include all the aspects of art nor even all the aspects of verbal art. A change in imagery is not essential to the development of poetry. We know that frequently an expression is thought to be poetic, to be created for aesthetic pleasure, although actually it was created without such intent—e. g., Annensky's[6] opinion that the Slavic languages are especially poetic and Andrey Bely's[7] ecstasy over the technique of placing adjectives after nouns, a technique used by eighteenth-century Russian poets. Bely joyfully accepts the technique as something artistic, or more exactly, as intended, if we consider intention as art. Actually, this reversal of the usual adjective-noun order is a peculiarity of the language (which had been influenced by Church Slavonic). Thus a work may be (1) intended as prosaic and accepted as poetic, or (2) intended as poetic and accepted as prosaic. This suggests that the artistry attributed to a given work results from the way we perceive it. By "works of art," in the narrow sense, we mean works created by special techniques designed to make the works as obviously artistic as possible.

Potebnya's conclusion, which can be formulated "poetry equals imagery," gave rise to the whole theory that "imagery equals symbolism," that the image may serve as the invariable predicate of various subjects. (This conclusion, because it expressed ideas similar to the theories of the Symbolists, intrigued some of their leading representatives—Andrey Bely, Merezhkovsky and his "eternal companions" and, in fact, formed the basis of the theory of Symbolism.) The conclusion stems partly from the fact that Potebnya did not distinguish between the language of poetry and the language of prose. Consequently, he ignored the fact that there are two aspects of imagery: imagery as a practical means of thinking, as a means of placing objects within categories; and imagery as poetic, as a means of reinforcing an impression. I shall clarify with an example. I want to attract the attention of a young child who is eating bread and butter and getting the butter on her fingers. I call, "Hey, butterfingers!" This is a figure of speech, a clearly prosaic trope. Now a different example. The child is playing with my glasses and drops them. I call, "Hey butterfingers!" This figure of speech is a poetic trope. (In the first example, "butterfinger" is metonymic; in the second, metaphoric—but this is not what I want to stress.)

Poetic imagery is a means of creating the strongest possible impression. As a method it is, depending upon its purpose, neither more nor less effective than other poetic techniques; it is neither more nor less effective than ordinary or negative parallelism, comparison, repetition, balanced structure, hyperbole, the commonly accepted rhetorical figures, and all those methods which emphasize the emotional effect of an expression (including words or even articulated sounds.) But poetic imagery only externally resembles either the stock imagery of fables and ballads or thinking in images—e. g. , the example in Ovsyaniko-Kulikovsky's *Language and Art* in which a little girl calls a ball a little watermelon. Poetic imagery is but one of the devices of poetic language. Prose imagery is a means of abstraction: a little watermelon instead of a lampshade, or a little watermelon instead of a head, is only the abstraction of one of the object's characteristics, that of roundness. It is no different from saying that the head and the melon are both round. This is what is meant, but it has nothing to do with poetry.

The law of the economy of creative effort is also generally accepted. [Herbert] Spencer wrote:

> On seeking for some clue to the law underlying these current maxims, we may see shadowed forth in many of them, the importance of economizing the reader's or the hearer's attention. To so present ideas that they may be apprehended with the least possible mental effort, is the desideratum towards which most of the rules above quoted point.... Hence, carrying out the metaphor that language is the vehicle of thought, there seems reason to think that in all cases the friction and inertia of the vehicle deduct from its efficiency; and that in composition, the chief, if not the sole thing to be done, is to reduce this friction and inertia to the smallest possible amount.

And R[ichard] Avenarius[8]:

> If a soul possess inexhaustible strength, then, of course, it would be indifferent to how much might be spent from this inexhaustible source; only the necessarily expended time would be important. But since its forces are limited, one is led to expect that the soul hastens to carry out the apperceptive process as expediently as possible—that is, with comparatively the least expenditure of energy, and, hence, with comparatively the best result.

Petrazhitsky[9], with only one reference to the general law of mental effort, rejects [William] James's theory of the physical basis of emotion, a theory which contradicts his own. Even Alexander Veselovsky[10] acknowledged the principle of the economy of creative effort, a theory especially appealing in the study of rhythm, and agreed with Spencer: "A satisfactory style is precisely that style which delivers the greatest amount of thought in the fewest words." And Andrey Bely, despite the fact that in his better pages he gave numerous examples of "roughened" rhythm and (particularly in the examples from Baratynsky) showed the difficulties inherent in poetic epithets, also thought it necessary to speak of the law of the economy of creative effort in his book—a heroic effort to create a theory of art based on unverified facts from antiquated sources, on his vast knowledge of the techniques of poetic creativity, and on Krayevich's high school physics text.

These ideas about the economy of energy, as well as about the law and aim of creativity, are perhaps true in their application to "practical" language; they were, however, extended to poetic language. Hence they do not distinguish properly between the laws of practical language and the laws of poetic language. The fact that Japanese poetry has sounds not found in conversational Japanese was hardly the first factual indication of the differences between poetic and everyday language. Leo Jakubinsky has observed that the law of the dissimilation of liquid sounds does not apply to poetic language. This suggested to him that poetic language tolerated the admission of hard-to-pronounce conglomerations of similar sounds. In his article, one of the first examples of scientific criticism, he indicates inductively, the contrast (I shall say more about this point later) between the laws of poetic language and the laws of practical language.

We must, then, speak about the laws of expenditure and economy in poetic language not on the basis of an analogy with prose, but on the basis of the laws of poetic language.

If we start to examine the general laws of perception, we see that as perception becomes habitual, it becomes automatic. Thus, for example, all of our habits retreat into the area of the unconsciously automatic; if one remembers the sensations of holding a pen or of speaking in a foreign language for the first time and compares that with his feeling at performing the action for the ten thousandth time, he will agree with us. Such habituation explains the principles by which, in ordinary speech, we leave phrases unfinished and words half expressed. In this process, ideally realized in algebra, things are replaced by symbols. Complete words are not expressed in rapid speech; their initial sounds are barely perceived. Alexander Pogodin offers the example of a boy considering the sentence "The Swiss mountains are beautiful" in the form of a series of letters: *T. S. m. a. b.*

This characteristic of thought not only suggests the method of algebra, but even prompts the choice of symbols (letters, especially initial letters). By this "algebraic" method of thought we apprehend objects only as shapes with imprecise extensions; we do not see them in their entirety but rather recognize them by their main characteristics. We see the object as though it were enveloped in a sack. We know what it is by its configuration, but we see only its silhouette. The object, perceived thus in the manner of prose perception, fades and does not leave even a first impression; ultimately even the essence of what it was is forgotten. Such perception explains why we fail to hear the prose word in its entirety (see Les Jakubinsky's article) and, hence, why (along with other slips of the tongue) we fail to pronounce it. The process of "algebrization," the over-automatization of an object, permits the greatest economy of perceptive effort. Either objects are assigned only one proper feature—a number, for example—or else they function as though by formula and do not even appear in cognition:

> I was cleaning a room and, meandering about, approached the divan and couldn't remember whether or not I had dusted it. Since these movements are habitual and unconscious, I could not remember and felt that it was impossible to remember—so that if I had dusted it and forgot—that is, had acted unconsciously, then it was the same as if I had not. If some conscious person had been watching, then the fact could be established. If, however, no one was looking, or looking on unconsciously, if the whole complex lives of many people go on unconsciously, then such lives are as if they had never been.

And so life is reckoned as nothing. Habitualization devours works, clothes, furniture, one's wife, and the fear of war. "If the whole complex lives of many people go on unconsciously, then such lives are as if they had never been." And art exists that one may recover the sensation of life; it exists to make one feel things, to make the stone *stony*. The purpose of art is to impart the sensation of things as they are perceived and not as they are known. The technique of art is to make objects "unfamiliar," to make forms difficult, to increase the difficulty and length of perception because the process of perception is an aesthetic end in itself and must be prolonged. *Art is a way of experiencing the artfulness of an object; the object is not important.*

The range of poetic (artistic) work extends from the sensory to the cognitive, from poetry to prose, from the concrete to the abstract; from Cervantes's Don Quixote—scholastic and poor nobleman, half consciously bearing his humiliation in the court of the duke—to the broad but empty Don Quixote of Turgenev[11]; from Charlemagne to the name "king" [in Russian "Charles" and "king" obviously derive from the same root, *korol*]. The meaning of a work broadens to the extent that artfulness and artistry diminish; thus a fable symbolizes more than a poem, and a proverb more than a fable. Consequently, the least self-contradictory part of Potebnya's theory is his treatment of the fable, which, from his point of view, he investigated thoroughly. But since his theory did not provide for "expressive" works of art, he could not finish his book. As we know, *Notes on the Theory of Literature* was published in 1905, thirteen years after Potebnya's death. Potebnya himself completed only the section on the fable.

After we see an object several times, we begin to recognize it. The object is in front of us and we know about it, but we do not see it—hence we cannot say anything significant about it. Art removes objects from the automatism of perception in several ways. Here I want to illustrate a way used repeatedly by Leo Tolstoy, that writer who, for Merezhkovsky at least, seems to present things as if he himself saw them, saw them in their entirety, and did not alter them.

Tolstoy makes the familiar seem strange by not naming the familiar object. He describes an object as if he were seeing it for the first time, an event as if it were happening for the first time. In describing something he avoids the accepted names of its parts and instead names corresponding parts of other objects. For example, in "Shame" Tolstoy "defamiliarizes" the idea of flogging in this way: "to strip people who have broken the law, to hurl them to the floor, and to rap on their bottoms with switches," and, after a few lines, "to lash about on the naked buttocks." Then he remarks:

> Just why precisely this stupid, savage means of causing pain and not any other—why not prick the shoulders or any part of the body with needles, squeeze the hands or the feet in a vise, or anything like that?

I apologize for this harsh example, but it is typical of Tolstoy's way of pricking the conscience. The familiar act of flogging is made unfamiliar both by the description and by the proposal to change its form without changing its nature. Tolstoy uses this technique of "defamiliarization" constantly. The narrator of "Kholstomer," for example, is a horse, and it is the horse's point of view (rather than a person's) that makes the content of the story seem unfamiliar. Here is how the horse regards the institution of private property:

> I understood well what they said about whipping and Christianity. But then I was absolutely in the dark. What's the meaning of "his own," "his colt"? From these phrases I saw that people thought there was some sort of connection between me and the stable. At the time I simply could not understand the connection. Only much later, when they separated me from the other horses, did I begin to understand. But even then I simply could not see what it meant when they called me "man's property." The words "my horse" referred to me, a living horse, and seemed as strange to me as the words "my land," "my air," "my water."
>
> But the words make a strong impression on me. I thought about them constantly, and only after the most diverse experiences with people did I understand, finally, what they meant. They meant this: In life people are guided by words, not by deeds. It's not so much that they love the possibility of doing or not doing something as it is the possibility of speaking with words, agreed on among themselves, about various topics. Such are the words "my" and "mine," which they apply to different things, creatures, objects, and even to land, people, and horses. They agree that only one may say "mine" about this, that, or the other thing. And the one who says "mine" about the greatest number of things is, according to the game which they've agreed to among themselves, the one they consider the most happy. I don't know the point of all this, but it's true. For a long time I tried to explain it to myself in terms of some kind of real gain, but I

had to reject that explanation because it was wrong. Many of those, for instance, who called me their own never rode on me—although others did. And so with those who fed me. Then again, the coachman, the veterinarians, and the outsiders in general treated me kindly, yet those who called me their own did not. In due time, having widened the scope of my observations, I satisfied myself that the notion "my," not only in relation to us horses, has no other basis than a narrow human instinct which is called a sense of or right to private property. A man says "this house is mine" and never lives in it; he only worries about its construction and upkeep. A merchant says "my shop," "my dry goods shop," for instance, and does not even wear clothes made from the better cloth he keeps in his own shop.

There are people who call a tract of land their own, but they never set eyes on it and never take a stroll on it. There are people who call others their own, yet never see them. And the whole relationship between them is that the so-called "owners" treat the others unjustly.

There are people who call women their own, or their "wives," but their women live with other men. And people strive not for the good in life, but for goods they can call their own.

I am now convinced that this is the essential difference between people and ourselves. And therefore, not even considering the other ways in which we are superior, but considering just this one virtue, we can bravely claim to stand higher than men on the ladder of living creatures. The actions of men, at least those with whom I have had dealings, are guided by *words* — ours, by deeds.

The horse is killed before the end of the story, but the manner of the narrative, its technique, does not change:

Much later they put Serpukhovsky's body, which had experienced the world, which had eaten and drunk, into the ground. They could profitably send neither his hide, nor his flesh, nor his bones anywhere.

But since his dead body, which had gone about in the world for twenty years, was a great burden to everyone, its burial was only a superfluous embarrassment for the people. For a long time no one had needed him; for a long time he had been a burden on all. But nevertheless, the dead who buried the dead found it necessary to dress this bloated body, which immediately began to rot, in a good uniform and good boots; to lay it in a good new coffin with new tassels at the four corners, then to place this new coffin in another of lead and ship it to Moscow; there to exhume ancient bones and at just that spot, to hide this putrefying body, swarming with maggots, in its new uniform and clean boots, and to cover it over completely with dirt.

Thus we see that at the end of the story Tolstoy continues to use the technique even though the motivation for it [the reason for its use] is gone.

注释:

1. 亚历山大·波捷布尼亚（1835—1891），俄罗斯著名语言学家，俄罗斯语言学心理学派奠基人。

2. 奥夫夏尼科-库利科夫斯基（1853—1920），俄罗斯文艺理论家、语言学家、文艺学心理学派的代表人物，俄罗斯科学院荣誉院士。他创立文学创作心理学理论，冲破了波捷布尼亚智力说的局限，将艺术分为形象艺术（雕塑、绘画、形象诗）和抒情艺术（音乐、建筑艺术、抒情诗）。

3. 费多尔·伊凡诺维奇·丘特切夫（1803—1873），19世纪俄罗斯著名抒情诗人。

4. 尼古拉斯·果戈理（1809—1852），俄国现实主义文学“自然派”奠基人，幽默讽刺大师，他的创作在俄罗斯文学中起了改变文风的作用。

5. 这里指的是俄罗斯作家、哲学家、象征主义理论家亚奇斯拉夫·伊凡诺夫（1866—1949）1916年的作品《犁沟和田边》。

6. 伊那肯蒂·费多洛维奇（1855—1909），俄罗斯诗人、评论家和翻译家，俄罗斯第一次象征主义浪潮的代表人物。

7. 安德鲁·贝利（1880—1934），鲍里斯·尼古拉耶维奇·布加耶夫（Boris Nikolayevich Bugayev）的笔名，俄罗斯象征主义诗人、小说家和散文家。

8. 理查德·阿芬那留斯（1843—1896），19世纪德国哲学家、经验批判主义创始人之一。

9. 利奥·彼得拉日斯基（1867—1931），俄罗斯批评家、诗人。

10. 亚历山大·维塞洛夫斯基（1838—1906），俄罗斯文学学者。

11. 伊万·谢尔盖耶维奇·屠格涅夫（1818—1883），俄罗斯现实主义小说家、诗人和剧作家。他的主要作品有《罗亭》《贵族之家》《前夜》《父与子》《烟》《处女地》等。

Boris Eichenbaum

埃亨鲍姆(1886—1959),苏联文学学者,俄罗斯文学史学家,文献学博士,曾在彼得格勒(现圣彼得堡)各高等院校任教,俄国形式主义的代表人物。1912年,埃亨鲍姆毕业于圣彼得堡大学历史与文献系。1918年,他加入了诗歌语言研究会,成为其主要代表。埃亨鲍姆在文学研究中关注文本结构、节奏和风格问题的探讨,如《果戈理的"大衣"是如何塑造的》(1919)和《俄罗斯抒情诗的旋律》(1922),深受形式主义研究方法的影响。他后期致力于文学史研究,在广泛的历史、社会和文化背景下分析作家的作品,大量使用传记、文献和档案材料,放弃了其早期的单一的结构主义论述模式。他是列夫·托尔斯泰、茹科夫斯基、列斯科夫、阿赫玛托娃和许多其他俄罗斯以及苏联作家的研究专家。代表作有《诗句的旋律构造》《透视文学》《形式方式的理论》《文学》《列夫·托尔斯泰》,以及《论诗歌》《论散文》等。他曾发表过数百篇有关俄国重要作家作品著述的评论,成为苏联最重要的文本批评家之一。埃亨鲍姆的作品以尖锐的文学问题、独到的见解和优雅的论述而闻名。1959年,埃亨鲍姆在彼得格勒去世,享年73岁。

The Theory of the "Formal Method"

(Eichenbaum, Boris. The Theory of the "Formal Method". 选自亚当斯、瑟尔主编,《柏拉图以来的批评理论》(下册)(第三版),北京:北京大学出版社,2006年,第867到884页。)

1925年,埃亨鲍姆发表论文《形式方式的理论》,总结了俄国形式主义的主要论点,这是了解俄国形式主义文论的一份重要文献。他指出,文学批评可以不依赖于社会环境、艺术家的生活经历和创作心理对文学作品的影响,以及艺术作品对读者心理产生的作用的传记式考察,而是力图为文学批评建立独立的规则,强调文学研究的对象是文学性,以科学实证主义态度看待文学,努力保卫文学研究的自主性和具体性。文学的发展具有其自身的必然规律性,存在着一条从作品到作品、从风格到风格、从派别到派别、从一个主要结构成分到另一个主要结构成分的发展道路。努力清除社会意识形态和现实生活对文学素材的影响,以保证纯艺术形式的探讨。努力在纯粹的和封闭的文学系列内部揭示出艺术形式发展的内在规律性。该文在俄国形式主义学派发展史上具有里程碑的意义。

The worst, in my opinion, are those who describe science as if it were settled.

A. DE CANDOLLE

The so-called formal method grew out of a struggle for a science of literature that would be both independent and factual; it is not the outgrowth of a particular methodology. The notion of a method has been so exaggerated that it now suggests too much. In principle the question for the Formalist is not how to study literature, but what the subject matter of literary study actually is. We neither discuss methodology nor quarrel about it. We speak and may speak only about theoretical principles suggested to us not by this or that ready-made methodology, but by the examination of specific material in its specific context. The Formalists' works in literary theory and literary history show this clearly enough, but during the past ten years so many new questions and old misunderstandings have accumulated that I feel it advisable to try to summarize some of our work—not as a dogmatic system but as a historical summation. I wish to show how the work of the Formalists began, how it evolved, and what it evolved into.

The evolutionary character of the development of the formal method is important to an understanding of its history; our opponents and many of our followers overlook it. We are surrounded by eclectics and latecomers who would turn the formal method into some kind of inflexible formalistic system in order to provide themselves with a working vocabulary, a program, and a name. A program is a very handy thing for critics, but not at all characteristic of our method. Our scientific approach has had no such prefabricated program or doctrine, and has none. In our studies we value a theory only as a working hypothesis to help us discover and interpret facts; that is, we determine the validity of the facts and use them as the material of our research. We are not concerned with definitions, for which the latecomers thirst; nor do we build general theories, which so delight eclectics. We posit specific principles and adhere to them insofar as the material justifies them. If the material demands their refinements or change, we change or refine them. In this sense we are quite free from our own theories—as science must be free to the extent that theory and conviction are distinct. There is no ready-made science; science lives not by settling on truth, but by overcoming error.

This essay is not intended to argue our position. The initial period of scientific struggle and journalistic polemics is past. Such attacks as that in *The Press and the*

Revolution (with which I was honored) can be answered only by new scientific works. My chief purpose here is to show how the formal method, by gradually evolving and broadening its field of research, spread beyond the usual "methodological" limits and became a special science of literature, a specific ordering of facts. Within the limits of this science, the most diverse methods may develop, if only because we focus on the empirical study of the material. Such study was, essentially, the aim of the Formalists from the very beginning, and precisely that was the significance of our quarrel with the old traditions. The name *formal method*, bestowed upon the movement and now firmly attached to it, may be tentatively understood as a historical term; it should not be taken as an accurate description of our work. Neither *Formalism* as an aesthetic theory nor *methodology* as a finished scientific system characterizes us; we are characterized only by the attempt to create an independent science of literature which studies specifically literary material. We ask only for recognition of the theoretical facts of literary art as such.

Representatives of the formal method were frequently reproached by various groups for their lack of clarity or for the inadequacy of their principles—for indifference to general questions of aesthetics, sociology, psychology, and so on. These reproofs, despite their varying merit, are alike in that they correctly grasp that the chief characteristic of the Formalists is indeed their deliberate isolation both from "aesthetics from above" and from all ready-made or self-styled general theories. This isolation (particularly from aesthetics) is more or less typical of all contemporary studies of art. Dismissing a whole group of general problems (problems of beauty, the aims of art, etc.), the contemporary study of art concentrates on the concrete problems of aesthetics [*Kunstwissenschaft*]. Without reference to socio-aesthetic premises, it raises questions about the idea of artistic form and its evolution. It thereby raises a series of more specific theoretical and historical questions. Such familiar slogans as Wölfflin's "history of art without names" [*Kunstgeschichte ohne Nahmen*] characterized experiments in the empirical analysis of style and technique (like Voll's[1] "experiment in the comparative study of paintings"). In Germany especially the study of the theory and history of the visual arts, which had had there an extremely rich history of tradition and experiment, occupied a central position in art studies and began to influence the general theory of art and its separate disciplines—in particular, the study of literature. In Russia, apparently for local historical reasons, literary studies occupied a place analogous to that of the visual arts in Germany.

The formal method has attracted general attention and become controversial not, of course, because of its distinctive methodology, but rather because of its characteristic attitude towards the understanding and the study of technique. The Formalists advocated principles which violated solidly entrenched traditional notions, notions which had appeared to be axiomatic not only in the study of literature, but in the study of art generally. Because they adhered to their principles so strictly, they narrowed the distance between particular problems of literary theory and general problems of aesthetics. The ideas and principles of the Formalists, for all their concreteness, were pointedly directed towards a general theory of aesthetics. Our creation of a radically unconventional poetics, therefore, implied more than a simple reassessment of particular problems; it had an impact on the study of art generally. It had its impact because of a series of historical developments, the most important of which were the crisis in philosophical aesthetics and the startling innovations in art (in Russia most abrupt and most clearly defined in poetry). Aesthetics seemed barren and art deliberately denuded—in an entirely primitive condition. Hence, Formalism and Futurism seemed bound together by history.

But the general historical significance of the appearance of Formalism comprises a special theme; I must speak of something else here because I intend to show how the principles and problems of the formal method evolved and how the Formalists came to their present position.

Before the appearance of the Formalists, academic research, quite ignorant of theoretical problems, made use of antiquated aesthetic, psychological, and historical axioms and had so lost sight of its proper subject that its very existence as a science had become illusory. There was almost no struggle between the Formalists and the Academicians, not because the Formalists had broken in the door (there were no doors), but because we found an open passageway instead of a fortress. The theoretical heritage which Potebnya and Veselovsky left to their disciples seemed to lie like dead capital—a treasure which they were afraid to touch, the brilliance of which they had allowed to fade. In fact, authority and influence had gradually passed from academic scholarship to the "scholarship" of the journals, to the work of the Symbolist critics and theoreticians. Actually, between 1907 and 1912 the books and essays of Vyacheslav Ivanov, Bryusov[2], Merezhkovsky[3], Chukovsky[4], and others, were much more influential than the scholarly studies and dissertations of the university professors. This journalistic scholarship, with all its subjectivity and tendentiousness, was supported by the theoretical principles and slogans of the new artistic movements and their propagandists. Such books as Bely's *Simvolizm* (1910) naturally meant much more to the younger generation than the monographs on the history of literature which sprang up from no set of principles and which showed that the authors completely lacked both a scientific temperament and a scientific point of view.

The historical battle between the two generations [the Symbolists and the Formalists]—a battle which was fought over principles and was extraordinarily intense—was therefore resolved in the journals, and the battle line was drawn over Symbolist theory and Impressionistic criticism rather than over any work being done by the Academicians. We entered the fight against the Symbolists in order to wrest poetics from their hands—to free it from its ties with their subjective philosophical and aesthetic theories and to direct it toward the scientific investigation of facts. We were raised on their works, and we saw their errors with the greatest clarity. At this time, the struggle became even more urgent because the Futurists (Khlebnikov[5], Kruchenykh[6], and Mayakovsky[7]), who were on the rise, opposed the Symbolist poetics and supported the Formalists.

The original group of Formalists was united by the idea of liberating poetic diction from the fetters of the intellectualism and moralism which more and more obsessed the symbolists. The dissension among the Symbolist theoreticians (1910—11) and the appearance of the Acmeists prepared the way for our decisive rebellion. We knew that all compromises would have to be avoided, that history demanded of us a really revolutionary attitude—a categorical thesis, merciless irony, and bold rejections of whatever could not be reconciled with our position. We had to oppose the subjective aesthetic principles espoused by the Symbolists with an objective consideration of the facts. Hence our Formalist movement was characterized by a new passion for scientific positivism—a rejection of philosophical assumptions of psychological and aesthetic interpretations, etc. Art, considered apart from philosophical aesthetics and ideological theories, dictated its own position on things. We had to turn to facts and, abandoning general systems and problems, to begin "in the middle," with the facts which art forced upon us. Art demanded that we approach it closely; science, that we deal with the specific.

The establishment of a specific and factual literary science was basic to the organization of the formal method. All of our efforts were directed toward disposing of the earlier position which, according to Alexander Veselovsky, made of literature an abandoned thing [a *res nullius*]. This is why the position of the Formalists could not be reconciled with other approaches and was so unacceptable to the eclectics. In rejecting these other approaches, the Formalists actually rejected and still reject not the methods, but rather the irresponsible mixing of various disciplines and their problems. The basis of our position was and is that the object of literary science, as such, must be the study of those specifics which distinguish it from any other material. (The secondary, incidental features of such material, however, may reasonably and rightly be used in a subordinate way by other scientific disciplines.) Roman Jakobson formulated this view with perfect clarity:

> The object of the science of literature is not literature, but literariness—that is, that which makes a given work a work of literature. Until now literary historians have preferred to act like the policeman who, intending to arrest a certain person, would, at any opportunity, seize any and all persons who chanced into the apartment, as well as those who passed along the street. The literary historians used everything—anthropology, psychology, politics, philosophy. Instead of a science of literature, they created a conglomeration of homespun disciplines. They seemed to have forgotten that their essays strayed into related disciplines—the history of philosophy, the history of culture, of psychology, etc.—and that these could rightly use literary masterpieces, only as defective, secondary documents.

To apply and strengthen this principle of specificity and to avoid speculative aesthetics, we had to compare literary facts with other kinds of facts, extracting from a limitless number of important orders of fact that order which would pertain to literature and would distinguish it from the others by its function. This was the method Leo Jakubinsky followed in his essays in the first *Opoyaz* collection, in which he worked out the contrast between poetic and practical language that served as the basic principle of the Formalists' work on key problems of poetics. As a result, the Formalists did not look, as literary students usually had, towards history, culture, sociology, psychology, or aesthetics, etc., but toward linguistics, a science bordering on poetics and sharing material with it, but approaching it from a different perspective and with different problems. Linguistics, for its part, was also interested in the formal method in that what was discovered by comparing poetic and practical language could be studied as a purely linguistic problem, as part of the general phenomena of language. The relationship between linguistics and the formal method was somewhat analogous to that relation of mutual use and delimitation that exists, for example, between physics and chemistry. Against this background, the problems posed earlier by Potebnya and taken for granted by his followers were reviewed and reinterpreted.

Leo Jakubinsky's first essay, *On the Sounds of Poetic Language*, compared practical and poetic language and formulated the difference between them:

> The phenomena of language must be classified from the point of view of the speaker's particular purpose as he forms his own linguistic pattern. If the pattern is formed for the purely practical purpose of communication, then we are dealing with a system of *practical language* (the language of thought) in which the linguistic pattern (sounds, morphological features, etc.) have no independent value and are merely a *means* of communication. But other linguistic systems, systems in which the practical purpose is in the background (although perhaps not entirely hidden) are conceivable; they exist, and their linguistic patterns acquire *independent value*.

The establishment of this distinction was important both for the construction of a poetics and for understanding the Futurist's preference for nonsense language as revealing the furthest extension of the sheer independent value of words, the kind of value partially observed in the language of children, in the glossolalia of religious sects, and so on. The Futurist experiments in nonsense language were of prime significance as a demonstration against Symbolism which, in its theories, went no further than to use the idea of instrumentation to indicate the accompaniment of meaning by sound and so to deemphasize the role of sound in poetic language. The problem of sound in verse was especially crucial because it was on this point that the Formalists and Futurists united to confront the theorists of Symbolism. Naturally, the Formalists gave battle at first on just that issue; the question of sound had to be disposed of first if we were to oppose the aesthetic and philosophical tendencies of the

Symbolists with a system of precise observations and to reach the underlying scientific conclusions. This accounts for the content of the first volume of *Opoyaz*, a content devoted entirely to the problem of sound and nonsense language.

Victor Shklovsky, along with Jakubinsky, in *On Poetry and Nonsense Language*, cited a variety of examples which showed that "even words without meaning are necessary." He showed such meaninglessness to be both a widespread linguistic fact and a phenomenon characteristic of poetry. "The poet does not decide to use the meaningless word; usually 'nonsense' is disguised as some kind of frequently delusive, deceptive content. Poets are forced to acknowledge that they themselves do not understand the content of their own verses." Shklovsky's essay, moreover, transfers the question from the area of pure sound, from the acoustical level (which provided the basis for impressionistic interpretations of the relation between sound and the description of objects or the emotion represented) to the level of pronunciation and articulation. "In the enjoyment of a meaningless 'nonsense word,' the articulatory aspect of speech is undoubtedly important. Perhaps generally a great part of the delight of poetry consists in pronunciation, in the independent dance of the organs of speech." The question of meaningless language thus became a serious scientific concern, the solution of which would help to clarify many problems of poetic language in general. Shklovsky also formulated the general question:

> If we add to our demand of the word as such that it serve to clarify understanding, that it be generally meaningful, then of course "meaningless" language, as a relatively superficial language, falls by the wayside. But it does not fall alone; a consideration of the facts forces one to wonder whether words always have a meaning, not only in meaningless speech, but also in simple poetic speech—or whether this notion is only a fiction resulting from our inattention.

The natural conclusion of these observations and principles was that poetic language is not only a language of images, that sounds in verse are not at all merely elements of superficial euphony, and that they do not play a mere "accompaniment" to meaning, but rather that they have an independent significance. The purpose of this work was to force a revision of Potebnya's general theory, which had been built on the conviction that poetry is "thought in images." Potebnya's analysis of poetry, the analysis which the Symbolists had adopted, treated the sound of verse as expressive of something behind it. Sound was merely onomatopoetic, merely "aural description." The works of Andrey Bely (who discovered the complete sound picture that champagne makes when poured from a bottle into a glass in two lines from Pushkin[8], and who also discovered the "noisomeness of a hangover" in Blok's repetition of the consonantal cluster *rdt*) were quite typical.[9] Such attempts to explain alliteration, bordering on parody, required a rebuff and an attempt to produce concrete evidence showing that sounds in verse exist apart from any connection with imagery, that they have an independent oral function.

Leo Jakubinsky, in his essays, provided linguistic support for [our arguments in favor of] the independent value of sound in verse. Osip Brik's[10] essay on *Sound Repetitions* illustrated the same point with quotations from Pushkin and Lermontov[11] arranged to present a variety of models. Brik doubted the correctness of the common opinion that poetic language is a language of images:

> No matter how one looks at the interrelationship of image and sound, there is undoubtedly only one conclusion possible—the sounds, the harmonies, are not only euphonious accessories to meaning; they are also the result of an independent poetic purpose. The superficial devices of euphony do not completely account for the instrumentation of poetic speech. Such instrumentation represents on the whole an intricate product of the interaction of the general laws of harmony. Rhyme, alliteration, etc., are only obvious manifestations, particular cases, of the basic laws of euphony.

In opposing the work of Bely, Brik, in the same essay, made no comment at all on the meaning of this or that use of alliteration, but merely affirmed that repetition in verse is analogous to tautology in folklore—that is, that repetition itself plays something of an aesthetic role: "Obviously we have here diverse forms of one general principle, the principle of simple combination, by which either the sounds of the words or their meanings, or now one and now the other, serve as the material of the combination." Such an extension of one device to cover the various forms of poetic material is quite characteristic of the work of the Formalists during their initial period. After the presentation of Brik's essay the question of sound in verse lost something of its urgency, and the Formalists turned to questions of poetics in general.

The Formalists began their work with the question of the sounds of verse—at that time the most controversial and most basic question. Behind this particular question of poetics stood more general theses which had to be formulated. The distinction between systems of poetic and practical language, which defined the work of the Formalists from the very beginning, was bound to result in the formulation of a whole group of basic questions. The idea of poetry as "thought by means of images" and the resulting formula, poetry = imagery, clearly did not coincide with our observations and contradicted our tentative general principles. Rhythm, sound, syntax—all of these seemed secondary from such a point of view; they seemed uncharacteristic of poetry and necessarily extraneous to it. The Symbolists accepted Potebnya's general theory because it justified the supremacy of the image-symbol; yet they could not rid themselves of the notorious theory of the "harmony of form and content" even though it clearly contradicted their bent for formal experimentation and discredited it by making it seem mere aestheticism. The Formalists, when they abandoned Potebnya's point of view, also freed themselves from the traditional correlation of form and content and from the traditional idea of form as an envelope, a vessel into which one pours a liquid (the content). The facts of art demonstrate that art's uniqueness consists not in the parts which enter into it but in their original *use*. Thus the notion of form was changed; the new notion of form required no companion idea, no correlative.

注释:

1. 卡尔·沃尔（1867—1917），德国艺术史学家，专攻荷兰文艺复兴和巴洛克艺术。

2. 瓦莱里·布吕索夫（1873—1924），俄国诗人、散文作家、剧作家、翻译家、评论家和历史学家，俄国象征主义运动的主要成员之一。

3. 迪米特里·梅日科夫斯基（1866—1941），俄国小说家、诗人、宗教思想家和文学评论家。

4. 科尼·楚科夫斯基（1882—1969），俄语中最受欢迎的儿童诗人之一，他的诗歌节奏朗朗上口，押韵富有创意，人物形象荒诞。

5. 韦勒米尔·赫列布尼科夫（1885—1922），俄国诗人和剧作家，俄国未来主义运动的代表人物。

6. 阿列克西·克鲁奇尼赫（1886—1968），俄国"白银时代"的著名诗人，俄国未来主义最激进的诗人。

7. 弗拉基米尔·马雅可夫斯基（1893—1930），俄国未来主义诗人、剧作家、艺术家和演员。

8. 亚历山大·谢尔盖耶维奇·普希金（1799—1837），俄国著名文学家、诗人、小说家，现代俄国文学的创始人，19世纪俄国浪漫主义文学的主要代表，现实主义文学的奠基人，现代标准俄语的创始人。

9. 亚历山大·亚历山德罗维奇·勃洛克（1880—1921），俄国诗人、作家、剧作家、翻译家和文学评论家。

10. 奥西普·布里克（1888—1945），俄国先锋派作家、文学批评家，俄国形式主义学派的重要成员之一。

11. 米哈伊尔·尤里耶维奇·莱蒙托夫（1814—1841），俄国浪漫主义作家、诗人和画家，其诗歌和散文奠定了俄国心理小说的传统。

Chapter Two **Anglo-American New Criticism**

20世纪四五十年代,英美新批评在美国盛极一时,强调文学文本尤其是诗歌的细读,试图发现一部文学作品是如何作为一个独立的、自我参照的对象发挥作用的。英美新批评大致分为以下三个时期:① 启蒙时期(1910—1930年),20世纪20年代,是英国的托马斯·斯特恩斯·艾略特(Thomas Stearns Eliot)、艾弗·阿姆斯特朗·理查兹(Ivor Armtrong Richards)和威廉·燕卜逊(William Empson),美国的约翰·克罗·兰塞姆(John Crowe Ransom)和艾伦·泰特(Allen Tate)开始提出新批评的一些基本观点并付诸实践的时期。② 形成时期(1930—1945年),20世纪三四十年代,在这个时期,赞成和支持新批评的人数大量增加,新批评的观点得到迅速传播,直接影响到文学杂志、高校教学和课程设置。除上述五位代表外,主要代表还有理查德·布莱克默(Richard P. Blackmur)、克林斯·布鲁克斯(Cleanth Brooks)、雷内·韦勒克(Rene Wellek)、威廉·威姆萨特(William K. Wimsatt)和沃伦(Robert Penn Warren),后四位由于长期在耶鲁大学同事,人称"耶鲁集团"(Yale Group)。③ 主导时期(1945—1957年),从20世纪40年代末持续到50年代末,新批评在这一时期占据了主流地位。它形成了一种制度化的批评模式,但失去了革命的味道;批评家的作品大多阐述新批评的原则,但缺乏独创性。20世纪50年代末,新批评失去了生命力,虽然仍在大学教学中应用,但许多人认为它已经过时,开始用新的理论观念对其进行批判和超越。

新批评与俄国形式主义有许多相似之处,二者的主要目的都是探究其独特的文学性在何处,但新批评也有其特殊性。布鲁克斯将新批评的特点概括为五点:① 将文学批评与起源研究分开,使批评失去与社会背景、思想史、政治和社会影响的联系,寻求一种不考虑"外在"因素的纯文学批评,只关注文学对象本身;② 专注于作品结构的探讨,忽略作者的思想或读者的反应;③ 坚持"有机统一"的文学理论,不同意区分形式和内容的二分法概念,强调探讨作品中的词语与整个作品的语境之间的关系,认为每一个词语对特定语境都有自己的影响,并根据其在语境中的地位产生意义;④ 它强调对一部作品的细读,特别注意词与词、修辞方式、意义之间的细微差别,试图具体阐释作品的语境与意义的统一;⑤ 它把文学与宗教、道德区分开来,主要是因为许多新批评的支持者都有自己明确的宗教观念,不想抛弃它,也不想用它来代替道德或文学。

在新批评中,“意义”的概念极其重要。新批评认为,作品的价值不在于内容,而在于结构。在诗歌中寻找内容,总结或阐释文本,都违反了新批评的原则,因为这样做会使“意义”变成观点或陈述,形式失去内容,文学与哲学、政治发生冲突。在新批评看来,“意义”是结构的一个方面,阅读的任务是综合考察和评价由语言学、修辞学、语义学、哲学、心理学等要素构成的结构,从而使结构成为最重要的批评概念。新批评认为,意义是结构的一个从属范畴,是结构中不可分割的要素;统一的文学结构既不参与生成和接受,也不被认为是可以解释的要素和可以推论的观点;意义陈述至多起到框架的作用。根据新批评的观点,在阅读中,只有找到结构上的统一、平衡与和谐,阅读才能完成。要找出文本中的含混、悖论、隐喻、反讽、象征,以及由此形成的张力和统一结构,一个批评家或读者必须采取文本细读的阅读方式。

新批评寻求结构的有机统一,使其对意义的理解受到极大的限制;新批评寻求专业性的批评,使其范围也受到限制。因此,它既不能提供真正科学的批评,也不能提供精确的解释性批评。因此,在 20 世纪 50 年代末,新批评开始衰落,随着 60 年代其他新理论的出现,新批评几乎完全失去了生命力。

—— W. K. Wimsatt, Jr., and Monroe C. Beardsley ——

威廉·维姆萨特(1907—1975),美国英语教授、文学理论家和评论家。他出生于华盛顿,就读于乔治敦大学,后来又在耶鲁大学获得博士学位。1939 年,维姆萨特进入耶鲁大学英语系任教,直到 1975 年去世。他以研究 18 世纪文学而闻名,出版多部文学批评理论著作,如《塞缪尔·约翰逊的散文风格》(1941)和《哲学词汇:塞缪尔·约翰逊的“漫谈者”和“词典”的风格和意义研究》(1948)。他的主要作品还包括《言语符号:诗歌意义研究》(1954)、《仇恨的对立》(1965)和《文学批评:一段短暂的历史》(1957,与克林斯·布鲁克斯合著)。维姆萨特通常被认为是英美新批评的关键人物,也是康涅狄格艺术与科学学院的成员。

门罗·柯蒂斯·伯兹里(1915—1985)是美国艺术哲学家。他生于康涅狄格州的布里奇波特,后就读于耶鲁大学(1936 年获得学士学位,1939 年获得博士学位)。他曾在一些学院和大学任教,包括蒙特霍利克学院和耶鲁大学,但他的大部分职业生涯都是在斯沃斯莫尔学院(22 年)和坦普尔大学(16 年)度过的。他的美学作品以其对工具主义艺术理论和审美经验概念的推崇而闻名。比尔兹利于1956年当选为美国美学学会主席。他还写了一篇关于美学的介绍性文章，并编辑了一本颇受好评的哲学概论集。他的作品还包括《实用逻辑》(1950)、《美学》(1958)和《美学：一段短暂的历史》(1966)。1976年，他被选为美国艺术与科学学院院士。

The Intentional Fallacy

(W. K. Wimsatt, Jr., and Monroe C. Beardsley. The Intentional Fallacy. *The Sewanee Review*, Vol. 54, No. 3 (Jul.-Sep., 1946), pp. 468-488.)

维姆萨特和伯兹里在1946年和1949年共同发表了两篇重要文章《意图谬见》和《情感谬见》。这两篇论文成为英美新批评的重要文本，《意图谬见》旨在从文学批评中去除作者，《情感谬见》则去除了读者，使批评对象只剩下文本自身。他们指出对诗歌的任何分析都必须以文本本身为中心，强调用科学客观的方法来进行文学批评，如果文学批评只考虑作者的"意图"或者作品对于读者的"效果"，必然带来"谬见"。《意图谬见》反对的是文学批评中的作者决定论，即从作者的写作意图推导批评的标准，维姆萨特和伯兹里认为作者的创作意图或个人生平决定不了作品的价值，研究文学不等同于研究个人，因为作品是日常事件、个人经历经过文学技巧重新加工之后的产物。他们强调作品的意义存在于其内在模式，主张对诗歌本身的风格和技巧进行全面而深入的研究。

He owns with toil he wrote the following scenes;
But, if they're naught, ne'er spare him for his pains;
Damn him the more; have no commiseration
For dullness on mature deliberation.

William Congreve, Prologue to
The Way of the World

I

THE claim of the author's "intention" upon the critic's judgment has been challenged in a number of recent discussions, notably in the debate entitled *The Personal Heresy*, between Professors Lewis[1] and Tillyard[2], and at least implicitly in periodical essays like those in the "Symposium" of 1940 in the *Southern* and *Kenyon*

Reviews. But it seems doubtful if this claim and most of its romantic corollaries are as yet subject to any widespread questioning. The present writers, in a short article entitled "Intention" for a *Dictionary* of literary criticism, raised the issue but were unable to pursue its implications at any length. We argued that the design or intention of the author is neither available nor desirable as a standard for judging the success of a work of literary art, and it seems to us that this is a principle which goes deep into some differences in the history of critical attitudes. It is a principle which accepted or rejected points to the polar opposites of classical "imitation" and romantic expression. It entails many specific truths about inspiration, authenticity, biography, literary history and scholarship, and about some trends of contemporary poetry, especially its allusiveness. There is hardly a problem of literary criticism in which the critic's approach will not be qualified by his view of "intention."

"Intention," as we shall use the term, corresponds to *what he intended* in a formula which more or less explicitly has had wide acceptance. "In order to judge the poet's performance, we must know *what he intended*." Intention is design or plan in the author's mind. Intention has obvious affinities for the author's attitude toward his work, the way he felt, what made him write.

We begin our discussion with a series of propositions summarized and abstracted to a degree where they seem to us axiomatic, if not truistic.

1. A poem does not come into existence by accident. The words of a poem, as Professor Stoll has remarked, come out of a head, not out of a hat. Yet to insist on the designing intellect as a *cause* of a poem is not to grant the design or intention as a *standard*.

2. One must ask how a critic expects to get an answer to the question about intention. How is he to find out what the poet tried to do? If the poet succeeded in doing it, then the poem itself shows what he was trying to do. And if the poet did not succeed, then the poem is not adequate evidence, and the critic must go outside the poem—for evidence of an intention that did not become effective in the poem. "Only one *caveat* must be borne in mind," says an eminent intentionalist in a moment when his theory repudiates itself; "the poet's aim must be judged at the moment of the creative act, that is to say, by the art of the poem itself."

3. Judging a poem is like judging a pudding or a machine. One demands that it work. It is only because an artifact works that we infer the intention of an artificer. "A poem should not mean but be." A poem can *be* only through its *meaning* —since

its medium is words—yet it *is*, simply *is*, in the sense that we have no excuse for inquiring what part is intended or meant. Poetry is a feat of style by which a complex of meaning is handled all at once. Poetry succeeds because all or most of what is said or implied is relevant; what is irrevelant has been excluded, like lumps from pudding and "bugs" from machinery. In this respect poetry differs from practical messages, which are successful if and only if we correctly infer the intention. They are more abstract than poetry.

4. The meaning of a poem may certainly be a personal one, in the sense that a poem expresses a personality or state of soul rather than a physical object like an apple. But even a short lyric poem is dramatic, the response of a speaker (no matter how abstractly conceived) to a situation (no matter how universalized). We ought to impute the thoughts and attitudes of the poem immediately to the dramatic *speaker*, and if to the author at all, only by a biographical act of inference.

5. If there is any sense in which an author, by revision, has better achieved his original intention, it is only the very abstract, tautological, sense that he intended to write a better work and now has done it. (In this sense every author's intention is the same.) His former specific intention was not his intention. "He's the man we were in search of, that's true," says Hardy's rustic constable, "and yet he's not the man we were in search of. For the man we were in search of was not the man we wanted."

"Is not a critic," asks Professor Stoll, "... a judge, who does not explore his own consciousness, but determines the author's meaning or intention, as if the poem were a will, a contract, or the constitution? The poem is not the critic's own." He has diagnosed very accurately two forms of irresponsibility, one which he prefers. Our view is yet different. The poem is not the critic's own and not the author's (it is detached from the author at birth and goes about the world beyond his power to intend about it or control it). The poem belongs to the public. It is embodied in language, the peculiar possession of the public, and it is about the human being, an object of public knowledge. What is said about the poem is subject to the same scrutiny as any statement in linguistics or in the general science of psychology or morals. Mr. Richards has aptly called the poem a *class* —"a class of experiences which do not differ in any character more than a certain amount... from a standard experience." And he adds, "We may take as this standard experience the relevant experience of the poet when contemplating the completed composition." Professor

Wellek in a fine essay on the problem has preferred to call the poem "a system of norms," "extracted from every individual experience," and he objects to Mr. Richards' deference to the poet as reader. We side with Professor Wellek in not wishing to make the poet (outside the poem) an authority.

A critic of our *Dictionary* article, Mr. Ananda K. Coomaraswamy[3], has argued that there are two kinds of enquiry about a work of art: (1) whether the artist achieved his intentions; (2) whether the work of art "ought ever to have been undertaken at all" and so "whether it is worth preserving." Number (2), Mr. Coomaraswamy maintains, is not "criticism of any work of art *qua* work of art," but is rather moral criticism; number (1) is artistic criticism. But we maintain that (2) need not be moral criticism: that there is another way of deciding whether works of art are worth preserving and whether, in a sense, they "ought" to have been undertaken, and this is the way of objective criticism of works of art as such, the way which enables us to distinguish between a skillful murder and a skillful poem. A skillful murder is an example which Mr. Coomaraswamy uses, and in his system the difference between the murder and the poem is simply a "moral" one, not an "artistic" one, since each if carried out according to plan is "artistically" successful. We maintain that (2) is an inquiry of more worth than (1), and since (2) and not (1) is capable of distinguishing poetry from murder, the name "artistic criticism" is properly given to (2).

Ⅱ

It is not so much an empirical as an analytic judgment, not a historical statement, but a definition, to say that the intentional fallacy is a romantic one. When a rhetorician, presumably of the first century A. D., writes: "Sublimity is the echo of a great soul," or tells us that "Homer enters into the sublime actions of his heroes" and "shares the full inspiration of the combat," we shall not be surprised to find this rhetorician considered as a distant harbinger of romanticism and greeted in the warmest terms by so romantic a critic as Saintsbury. One may wish to argue whether Longinus[4] should be called romantic, but there can hardly be a doubt that in one important way he is.

Goethe's[5] three questions for "constructive criticism" are "What did the author set out to do? Was his plan reasonable and sensible, and how far did he succeed in carrying it out?" If one leaves out the middle question, one has in effect the system of Croce—the culmination and crowning philosophic expression of romanticism. The beautiful is the successful intuitionexpression, and the ugly is the unsuccessful; the intuition or private part of art is *the* aesthetic fact, and the medium or public part is not the subject of aesthetic at all. Yet aesthetic reproduction takes place only "if all the other conditions remain equal."

> Oil-paintings grow dark, frescoes fade, statues lose noses... the text of a poem is corrupted by bad copyists or bad printing.

> The Madonna of Cimabue is still in the Church of Santa Maria Novella; but does she speak to the visitor of today as to the Florentines of the thirteenth century?

> *Historical interpretation* labours... to reintegrate in us the psychological conditions which have changed in the course of history. It... enables us to see a work of art (a physical object) as its *author saw it* in the moment of production.

The first italics are Croce's, the second ours. The upshot of Croce's system is an ambiguous emphasis on history. With such passages as a point of departure a critic may write a close analysis of the meaning or "spirit" of a play by Shakespeare or Corneille[6]—a process that involves close historical study but remains aesthetic criticism—or he may write sociology, biography, or other kinds of non-aesthetic history. The Crocean system seems to have given more of a boost to the latter way of writing.

"What has the poet tried to do," asks Spingarn in his 1910 Columbia Lecture from which we have already quoted, "and how has he fulfilled his intention?" The place to look for "insuperable" ugliness, says Bosanquet, in his third *Lecture* of 1914, is the "region of insincere and affected art." The seepage of the theory into a non-philosophic place may be seen in such a book as Marguerite Wilkinson's inspirational *New Voices*, about the poetry of 1919 to 1931—where symbols "as old as the ages... retain their strength and freshness" through "Realization." We close this section with two examples from quarters where one might least expect a taint of the Crocean. Mr. I. A. Richards' fourfold distinction of meaning into "sense," "feeling,""tone," "intention" has been probably the most influential statement of intentionalism in the past fifteen years, though it contains a hint of self-repudiation:"This function [intention]," says Mr. Richards, "is not on all fours with the others." In an essay on "Three Types of Poetry" Mr. Allen Tate writes as follows:

> We must understand that the lines
> Life like a dome of many-colored glass
> Stains the white radiance of eternity
> are not poetry; they express the *frustrated will*
> trying to compete with science. The *will* asserts
> a rhetorical proposition about the whole of life,
> but the *imagination* has not seized upon the materials
> of the poem and made them into a whole. Shelley's
> simile is imposed upon the material from
> above; it does not grow out of the material.

The last sentence contains a promise of objective analysis which is not fulfilled. The reason why the essay relies so heavily throughout on the terms "will" and "imagination" is that Mr. Tate is accusing the romantic poets of a kind insincerity (romanticism in reverse) and at the same time is trying to describe something mysterious and perhaps indescribable, an "imaginative whole of life," a "wholeness of vision at a particular moment of experience," something which "yields us the quality of the experience." If a poet had a toothache at the moment of conceiving a poem, that would be part of the experience, but Mr. Tate of course does not mean anything like that. He is thinking about some kind of "whole" which in this essay at least he does not describe, but which doubtless it is the prime need of criticism to describe—in terms that may be publicly tested.

Ⅲ

> I went to the poets; tragic, dithyrambic, and all sorts. . . . I took them some of the most elaborate passages in their own writings, and asked what was the meaning of them. . . . Will you believe me?. . . there is hardly a person present who would not have talked better about their poetry than

they did themselves. Then I knew that not by wisdom do poets write poetry, but by a sort of genius and inspiration.

That reiterated mistrust of the poets which we hear from Socrates[7] may have been part of a rigorously ascetic view in which we hardly wish to participate, yet Plato's Socrates saw a truth about the poetic mind which the world no longer commonly sees—so much criticism, and that the most inspirational and most affectionately remembered, has proceeded from the poets themselves.

Certainly the poets have had something to say that the analyst and professor could not say; their message has been more exciting: that poetry should come as naturally as leaves to a tree, that poetry is the lava of the imagination, or that it is emotion recollected in tranquillity. But it is necessary that we realize the character and authority of such testimony. There is only a fine shade between those romantic expressions and a kind of earnest advice that authors often give. Thus Edward Young[8], Carlyle[9], Walter Pater[10]:

> I know two golden rules from *ethics*, which are no less golden in *Composition*, than in life. 1. *Know thyself*; 2dly, *Reverence thyself*.

> This is the grand secret for finding readers and retaining them: let him who would move and convince others, be first moved and convinced himself. Horace's rule, *Si vis me flere*, is applicable in a wider sense than the literal one. To every poet, to every writer, we might say: Be true, if you would be believed.

> Truth! there can be no merit, no craft at all, without that. And further, all beauty is in the long run only *fineness* of truth, or what we call expression, the finer accommodation of speech to that vision within.

And Housman's little handbook to the poetic mind yields this illustration:

> Having drunk a pint of beer at luncheon—beer is a sedative to the brain, and my afternoons are the least intellectual portion of my life—I would go out for a walk of two or three hours. As I went along, thinking of nothing in particular, only looking at things around me and following the

progress of the seasons, there would flow into my mind, with sudden and unaccountable emotion, sometimes a line or two of verse, sometimes a whole stanza at once....

This is the logical terminus of the series already quoted. Here is a confession of how poems were written which would do as a definition of poetry just as well as "emotion recollected in tranquillity"—and which the young poet might equally well take to heart as a practical rule. Drink a pint of beer, relax, go walking, think on nothing in particular, look at things, surrender yourself to yourself, search for the truth in your own soul, listen to the sound of your own inside voice, discover and express the *vraie vérité*.

It is probably true that all this is excellent advice for poets. The young imagination fired by Wordsworth and Carlyle is probably closer to the verge of producing a poem than the mind of the student who has been sobered by Aristotle or Richards. The art of inspiring poets, or at least of inciting something like poetry in young persons, has probably gone further in our day than ever before. Books ofcreative writing such as those issued from the Lincoln School are interesting evidence of what a child can do if taught how to manage himself honestly. All this, however, would appear to belong to an art separate from criticism, or to a discipline which one might call the psychology of composition, valid and useful, an individual and private culture, yoga, or system of selfdevelopment which the young poet perhaps does well to notice, but different from the public science of evaluating poems.

Coleridge and Arnold were better critics than most poets have been, and if the critical tendency dried up the poetry in Arnold and perhaps in Coleridge, it is not inconsistent with our argument, which is that judgment of poems is different from the art of producing them. Coleridge has given us the classic "anodyne" story, and tells what he can about the genesis of a poem which he calls a "psychological curiosity," but his definitions of poetry and of the poetic quality "imagination" are to be found elsewhere and in quite other terms.

The day may arrive when the psychology of composition is unified with the science of objective evaluation, but so far they are separate. It would be convenient if the passwords of the intentional school, "sincerity," "fidelity," "spontaneity," "authenticity," "genuineness," "originality," could be equated with terms of analysis such as "integrity," "relevance," "unity," "function"; with "maturity," "subtlety," and "adequacy," and other more precise axiological terms—in short, if "expression" always meant aesthetic communication. But this is not so.

"Aesthetic" art, says Professor Curt Ducasse, an ingenious theorist of expression, is the conscious objectification of feelings, in which an intrinsic part is the critical moment. The artist corrects the objectification when it is not adequate, but this may mean that the earlier attempt was not successful in objectifying the self, or "it may also mean that it was a successful objectification of a self which, when it confronted us clearly, we disowned and repudiated in favor of another." What is the standard by which we disown or accept the self? Professor Ducasse does not say. Whatever it may be, however, this standard is an element in the definition of art which will not reduce to terms of objectification. The evaluation of the work of art remains public; the work is measured against something outside the author.

注释:

1. 克莱夫·斯特普尔斯·刘易斯（1898—1963），英国文学家、批评家，20 世纪最重要的基督教作者之一。

2. 蒂利亚德（1889—1962），英国古典文学学者，1945 年至 1959 年在剑桥大学耶稣学院获得硕士学位。

3. 库马拉斯瓦米（1877—1947），印度艺术的先驱和哲学家，印度文化在西方的早期阐释者。

4. 卡西乌斯·朗吉努斯（213—273），修辞学家和哲学批评家，通常被认为是文学批评著作《论崇高》的作者。

5. 约翰·沃尔夫冈·冯·歌德（1749—1832），德国作家、政治家、思想家、科学家，魏玛的古典主义最著名的代表人物。著有《葛兹·冯·伯利欣根》《少年维特的烦恼》《浮士德》等作品。

6. 皮埃尔·高乃依（1606—1684），法国悲剧家，他与莫里哀和拉辛一起被公认为 17 世纪法国三大剧作家。

7. 苏格拉底（公元前 470—前 399 年），古希腊（雅典）哲学家，被认为是西方哲学的奠基人之一，也是西方伦理思想传统的第一位道德哲学家。

8. 爱德华·杨（约 1683—1765），英国诗人、批评家、哲学家和神学家。

9. 托马斯·卡莱尔（1795—1881），英国历史学家、讽刺作家、散文家、翻译家、哲学家、数学家和教师。

10. 沃尔特·霍雷肖·帕特（1839—1894），英国散文家、文艺评论家、小说家和文体家。

I. A. Richards

艾弗·阿姆斯特朗·理查兹(1893—1979),英国文学评论家、修辞学家、诗人和教育家。理查兹1915年毕业于剑桥大学后留校担任讲师,1922年开始在剑桥大学讲授英国文学和心理学,1930年曾到中国清华大学任教,1931年后长期在美国哈佛大学任教,1944年起任教授,1963年退休后任荣誉教授。他是英美新批评的创始人之一,语义学发展的先驱者,也是将科学方法引入文学批评的先锋。他在研究文学时强调文本和心理上的细微差别和模糊性,试图用现代语义学和心理学的原理阐释文学阅读。著有《意义的意义》(与C. K.奥格登合著,1923)、《文学批评原理》(1924)、《实用批评》(1929)和《修辞哲学》(1936)等。理查兹还与奥格登一起创立了"基础英语"。他的其他作品包括《孟子论心智》(1932)、《解读教学》(1934)、《基础英语及其应用》(1943)、《其他》(1974)、《告别土地》(1958)、《屏幕》(1960)、《内心交流》(1971)。

Practical Criticism: The Four Kinds of Meaning from Chapter Ⅰ

(Richards, I. A. Practical Criticism: The Four Kinds of Meaning from Chapter I. 选自亚当斯、瑟尔主编,《柏拉图以来的批评理论》(下册)(第三版),北京:北京大学出版社,2006年,第863到866页。)

20世纪20年代,理查兹曾在剑桥大学做了一项著名的阅读实验,他选取十三首诗歌,不注明题目和作者,让学生阅读后做出评论。在《实用批评》中,他分析了学生们在实际阅读过程中的理解偏差,并力求找出错误的原因。他借助阅读实验证实文本存在一个"统一"的意义,这个意义是可以认知的,而且存在一个统一的评价体系。他试图以这种方法让学生阅读和理解诗歌本身。同时,他通过对学生的阅读结果进行评估后认为,一般语言(包括诗歌语言)可以行使四种语言功能:观念(sense)、感情(feeling)、语气(tone)和意图(intention)。在实际语言运用中,可能会由于语言使用情况的不同使以上部分功能得到突出而掩盖住其他功能,从而使语言具有四种不同的意义类型。同期,理查兹撰写了多部著作,系统地阐述了他的批评理论,试图以现代语义学和心理学的原理来阐释文学阅读,对新批评后来的发展产生了巨大的影响。

The all-important fact for the study of literature—or any other mode of communication—is that there are several kinds of meaning. Whether we know and intend it or not, we are all jugglers when we converse, keeping the billiard balls in the air while we balance the cue on our nose. Whether we are active, as in speech or writing, or passive, as readers or listeners, the total meaning we are engaged with is, almost always, a blend, a combination of several contributory meanings of different types. Language—and preeminently language as it is used in poetry—has not one but several tasks to perform simultaneously, and we shall misconceive most of the difficulties of criticism unless we understand this point and take note of the differences between these functions. For our purposes here a division into four types of function, four kinds of meaning, will suffice.

It is plain that most human utterances and nearly all articulate speech can be profitably regarded from four points of view. Four aspects can be easily distinguished. Let us call them *sense*, *feeling*, *tone*, and *intention*.

Ⅰ. *Sense*

We speak *to say something*, and when we listen we expect something to be said. We use words to direct our hearers' attention upon some state of affairs, to present to them some items for consideration and to excite in them some thoughts about these items.

Ⅱ. *Feeling*

But we also, as a rule, have some feelings *about these items*, about the state of affairs we are referring to. We have an attitude towards it, some special direction, bias, or accentuation of interest towards it, some personal flavor or coloring of feeling; and we use language to *express* these feelings, this nuance of interest. Equally, when we listen we pick it up, rightly or wrongly; it seems inextricably part of what we receive; and this whether the speaker be conscious himself of his feelings towards what he is talking about or not. I am, of course, here describing the normal situation; my reader will be able without difficulty to think of exceptional cases (mathematics for example) where no feeling enters.

Ⅲ. *Tone*

Furthermore, the speaker has ordinarily *an attitude to his listener*. He chooses or arranges his words differently as his audience varies, in automatic or deliberate *recognition of his relation to them*. The tone of his utterance reflects his awareness of this relation, his sense of how he stands towards those he is addressing. Again the exceptional case of dissimulation, or instances in which the speaker unwittingly reveals an attitude he is not consciously desirous of expressing, will come to mind.

Ⅳ. *Intention*

Finally, apart from what he says (sense), his attitude to what he is talking about (feeling), and his attitude to his listener (tone), there is the speaker's intention, his aim, *conscious or unconscious*, the effect he is endeavoring to promote. Ordinarily he speaks for a purpose, and his purpose modifies his speech. The understanding of it is part of the whole business of apprehending his meaning. Unless we know what he is trying to do, we can hardly estimate the measure of his success. Yet the number of readers who omit such considerations might make a fainthearted writer despair. Sometimes, of course, he will purpose no more than to state his thoughts (Ⅰ), or to express his feelings about what he is thinking of, e. g. Hurrah! Damn! (Ⅱ), or to express his attitude to his listener (Ⅲ). With this last case we pass into the realm of endearments and abuse.

Frequently his intention operates through and satisfies itself in a combination of the other functions. Yet it has effects not reducible to their effects. It may govern the stress laid upon points in an argument for example, shape the arrangement, and even call attention to itself in such phrases as *for contrast's sake or lest it be supposed*. It controls the plot in the largest sense of the word, and is at work whenever the author is "hiding his hand." And it has especial importance in dramatic and semidramatic literature. Thus the influence of his intention upon the language he uses is additional to, and separable from, the other three influences, and its effects can profitably be considered apart.

We shall find in the protocols instances, in plenty, of failure on the part of one or other of these functions. Sometimes all four fail together; a reader garbles the sense, distorts the feeling, mistakes the tone and disregards the intention; and often a partial collapse of one function entails aberrations in the others. The possibilities of human misunderstanding make up indeed a formidable subject for study, but something more can be done to elucidate it than has yet been attempted. Whatever else we may do by the light of nature it would be folly to maintain that we should read by it. But before turning back to scrutinize our protocols some further explanation of these functions will be in place.

If we survey our uses of language as a whole, it is clear that, at times, now one now another of the functions may become predominant. It will make the possible situations clearer if we briefly review certain typical forms of composition. A man writing a scientific treatise, for example, will put the sense of what he has to say first, he will subordinate his feelings about his subject or about other views upon it and be careful not to let them interfere to distort his argument or to suggest bias. His tone will be settled for him by academic convention; he will, if he is wise, indicate respect for his readers and a moderate anxiety to be understood accurately and to win acceptance for his remarks. It will be well if his intention, as it shows itself in the work, be on the whole confined to the clearest and most adequate statement of what he has to say (function 1, sense). But, if the circumstances warrant it, further relevant aims—an intention to reorientate opinion, to direct attention to new aspects, or to encourage or discourage certain methods of work or ways of approach—are obviously fitting. Irrelevant aims—the acceptance of the work as a thesis for a Ph. D., for example—come in a different category.

Consider now a writer engaged upon popularizing some of the results and hypotheses of science. The principles governing his language are not nearly so simple, for the furtherance of his intention will properly and inevitably interfere with the other functions.

In the first place, precise and adequate statement of the sense may have to be sacrificed, to some degree, in the interests of general intelligibility. Simplifications and distortions may be necessary if the reader is to "follow." Secondly, a much more lively exhibition of feelings on the part of the author towards his subject matter is usually appropriate and desirable, in order to awaken and encourage the reader's interest. Thirdly, more variety of tone will be called for; jokes and humorous illustrations, for example, are admissible, and perhaps a certain amount of cajolery. With this increased liberty, tact, the subjective counterpart of tone, will be urgently required. A human relation between the expert and his lay audience must be created, and the task, as many specialists have discovered, is not easy. These other functions will interfere still more with strict accuracy of statement; and if the subject has a "tendency," if political, ethical or theological implications are at all prominent, the intention of the work will have further opportunities to intervene.

This leads us to the obvious instance of political speeches. What rank and precedence shall we assign to the four language functions if we analyze public utterances made in the midst of a General Election? Function 4, the furtherance of intentions (of all grades of worthiness) is unmistakably predominant. Its instruments are function 2, the expression of feelings about causes, policies, leaders and opponents, and function 3, the establishment of favorable relations with the audience ("the great heart of the people"). Recognizing this, ought we to be pained or surprised that function 1, the presentation of facts (or of objects of thought to be regarded as facts are regarded), is equally subordinated? But further consideration of this situation would lead us into a topic that must be examined later, that of *sincerity*, a word with several important meanings. (See Chapter 7.)

In conversation, perhaps, we get the clearest examples of these shifts of function, the normal verbal apparatus of one function being taken over by another. Intention, we have seen, may completely subjugate the others; so, on occasion, may feeling or tone express themselves through sense, translating themselves into explicit statements about feelings and attitudes towards things and people—statements sometimes belied by their very form and manner. Diplomatic formulae are often good examples, together with much of the social language (Malinowski's[1] "phatic communion"), the *thank you so very muches*, and *pleased to meet yous*, that help us to live amicably with one another. (But see Appendix A, note 1.)

Under this head, too, may be put the psychological analyses, the introspective expatiations that have recently flourished so much in fiction as well as in sophisticated conversation. Does it indicate a confusion or a tenuousness in our feelings that we should now find ourselves so ready to make statements about them, to translate them into disquisitions, instead of expressing them in more direct and natural ways? Or is this phenomenon simply another result of the increased study of psychology? It would be rash to decide as yet. Certainly some psychologists lay themselves open to a charge of emptiness, of having so dealt with themselves that they have little left within them to talk about. "Putting it into words," if the words are those of a psychological textbook, is a process which may well be damaging to the feelings. I shall be lucky if my reader does not murmur *de te fabula* at this point.

But feeling (and sometimes tone) may take charge of and operate through sense in another fashion, one more constantly relevant in poetry. (If indeed the shift just dealt with above might not be better described as sense interfering with and dominating feeling and tone.)

When this happens, the statements which appear in the poetry are there for the sake of their effects upon feelings, not for their own sake. Hence to challenge their truth or to question whether they deserve serious attention *as statements claiming truth*, is to mistake their function. The point is that many, if not most, of the statements in poetry are there *as a means* to the manipulation and expression of feelings and attitudes, not as contributions to any body of doctrine of any type whatever. With narrative poetry there is little danger of any mistake arising, but with "philosophical" or meditative poetry there is great danger of a confusion which may have two sets of consequences.

On the one hand there are very many people who, if they read any poetry at all, try to take all its statements seriously—and find them silly. "My soul is a ship in full sail," for example, seems to them a very profitless kind of contribution to psychology. This may seem an absurd mistake but, alas! It is nonetheless common. On the other hand there are those who succeed too well, who swallow "Beauty is truth, truth beauty...., "[2] as the quintessence of an aesthetic philosophy, not as the expression of a certain blend of feelings, and proceed into a complete stalemate of muddle-mindedness as a result of their linguistic naivety. It is easy to see what those in the first group miss; the losses of the second group, though the accountancy is more complicated, are equally lamentable.

A temptation to discuss here some further intricacies of this shift of function must be resisted. An overflow into Appendix A, which may serve as a kind of technical workshop for those who agree with me that the matter is important enough to be examined *with pains*, will be the best solution. I am anxious to illustrate these distinctions from the protocols before tedium too heavily assails us. It will be enough here to note that this subjugation of statement to emotive purposes has innumerable modes. A poet may distort his statements which have logically nothing to do with the subject under treatment; he may, by metaphor and otherwise, present objects for thought which are logically quite irrelevant; he may perpetrate logical nonsense, be as trivial or as silly, logically, as it is possible to be; all in the interests of the other functions of his language—to express feeling or adjust tone or further his other intentions. If his success in these other aims justify him, no reader (of the kind at least to take his meaning as it should be taken) can validly say anything against him.

But these indirect devices for expressing feeling through logical irrelevance and nonsense, through statements not to be taken strictly, literally or seriously, though preeminently apparent in poetry, are not peculiar to it. A great part of what passes for criticism comes under this head. It is much harder to obtain statements about poetry, than expressions of feelings towards it and towards the author. Very many apparent statements turn out on examination to be only these disguised forms, indirect expressions, of feeling, tone and intention. Dr. Bradley's[3] remark that *poetry is a spirit*, and Dr. Mackail's[4] that it is *a continuous substance or energy whose progress is immortal* are eminent examples that I have made use of elsewhere, so curious that I need no apology for referring to them again. Remembering them, we may be more ready to apply to the protocols every instrument of interpretation we possess. May we avoid if possible in our own reading of the protocols those errors of misunderstanding which we are about to watch being committed towards the poems.

注释:

1. 马林诺夫斯基（1884—1942），英国社会人类学家，功能学派创始人之一。他推崇田野调查，提出了新的民族志写作方法，强调“抢救人类学”的重要性。

2. “美就是真，真就是美”出自英国诗人约翰·济慈（1795—1821）的《希腊瓮颂》。

3. A. C. 布拉德利（1851—1935），19 世纪末 20 世纪初的文学评论家和杰出的莎士比亚研究学者。

4. J. W. 麦凯尔（1859—1945），牛津大学的苏格兰学者，英国教育体系的改革者。

Chapter Three **Myth and Archetypal Criticism**

“原型”(archetype)一词在拉丁语中由“初始”(arche)和“形式”(typos)组成。这一词语古来有之,曾在古代著名哲学家柏拉图的著述中出现。原型是文学中常用的符号,但它又不同于符号。它主要是指一种“原始形象”,即早期人类利用图腾崇拜、梦、神话、传说来表达的形象,如太阳象征光明、水象征圣洁。由于原型研究实际上包含了神话的内容,所以常用原型批评指代神话原型批评。加拿大批评家和理论家诺思洛普·弗莱(Northrop Frye)说,原型是一种反复出现的类型或形象。他用原型来表示符号。原型把一首诗与其他诗歌联系起来。每个诗人都有自己独特的意象。然而,当许多诗人,特别是千年前远在万里之外的诗人,不约而同地使用相同的意象时,人们会产生疑问。例如,自古以来,许多国家把太阳和山看作是男性形象,而把月亮和水与女性形象联系起来。古罗马诗人维吉尔的田园诗,西德尼的《阿卡迪亚》、斯宾塞的《仙女皇后》、圣经中关于羊群的宗教暗示、莎士比亚的森林喜剧都充满了田园意象。符号或意象,通过一代又一代的文学作品,已经延伸到文学整体的原型符号。它已经成为一个可以交换的神秘符号。十字架象征着基督教和耶稣基督的死亡,它已经成为一个普遍接受的形象。原型可以是:① 形象;② 细节描述(如四季更替、生、老、病、死等);③ 情节(如善恶之争、灵肉之争、灰姑娘型的好运);④ 性格类型。例如,人物类型可分为两种:善的和恶的。好人又可分为两类:一类是拯救灵魂的人,如上帝和牧师;另一类是救人于危难之中的英雄和勇士,如英国文学中的罗宾汉、中国文学中的梁山好汉等。原型积累了一代又一代人的智慧和心理能量。在纵向上,它使现代人与原始人、我们的祖先直接接轨;在横向上,它使一个种族或民族与其他种族或民族相联系。这是文学艺术的奥秘所在,也是原型批评的价值所在。

探讨“原型批评”必然涉及心理分析批评的传统。弗洛伊德所谓的“俄狄浦斯情结”,实际上正是体现了一种普遍的、跨文化的原型。瑞士心理学家荣格(C. G. Jung)以“集体无意识”解释不同时代、不同文化中相似的神话和原型,为神话原型批评做了开创性的工作。荣格的“集体无意识”理论,被较早运用于鲍德金(M. Bodkin)的《诗歌中的原型模式》(1934),其中将柯尔律治的《古舟子咏》与《旧约》中约拿的故事相比,归之于“再生”的原型。对原型批评的重要研究始于弗雷泽(J. Frazer),到 20 世纪 50 年代由弗莱发展成熟。《金枝:巫术与宗教研究》是弗雷泽的代表作,研究内容是对世界各文化中艺术、宗教和神话的相互关联进行穷尽性研究。其研究对象之一就是金枝王国里“老国王被新国王、新国王又被后来的新国王所杀”的循环模式,这也是书名的由来。此类“模式”通过不同的文学叙述凝聚在“民族记忆”之中,便是荣格的“集体无意识”。1957 年,加拿大批评家弗莱出版《批评的解剖》一书,借用了荣格作品中的“原型”一词,使原型批评理论得到更为系统的阐发。弗莱常说,他的原型批评理论是在荣格的集体无意识理论的启发下形成的。因此,他将自己的原型批评理论称为荣格的批评理论。《批评的解剖》将文学归纳为五种叙述模式和四种基本原型。五种叙述模式指神话、罗曼司(浪漫故事)、高级摹仿(悲剧)、低级摹仿(现实主义文学)和反讽(现代文学)。四种基本原型依据四季更迭归纳出分别与之相应的喜剧、传奇、悲剧和讽刺文学。弗莱使“原型批评”真正确立了地位,结束了新批评的统治。

Northrop Frye

诺思洛普・弗莱(1912—1991),加拿大文学批评家、文学理论家和神学家。他出生于魁北克的舍布鲁克,曾在多伦多大学维多利亚学院攻读本科学位,并在此编辑了学院文学期刊《维多利亚学报》,后在埃曼纽尔学院学习神学。在萨斯喀彻温省做了短暂的学生牧师后,他被任命为加拿大联合教会的牧师。然后他在牛津大学莫顿学院学习,之后又回到维多利亚学院,在那里他度过了职业生涯的剩余时间。1947 年,弗莱出版了第一本书《可怕的对称》,对威廉・布莱克的诗歌进行了重新解读,在国际上崭露头角。1957 年,弗莱因《批评的剖析》一书而闻名,认为文学批评既是艺术也是科学,应具有方法论原则和自然科学的连续性,真正确立了原型批评理论在文论领域的地位。

Archetypal Criticism: Theory of Myths

(Frye, Northrop. Archetypal Criticism: Theory of Myths. *Anatomy of Criticism*. Princeton: Princeton University Press, 2000, pp. 131-239.)

弗莱在《批评的剖析》一书中试图对完全源于文学的文学批评的范围、理论、原则和技巧形成一个整体的观点。弗莱有意识地忽略了所有具体和实际的批评,提供了模式、符号、神话和流派的经典启发理论，他称之为"一组相互联系的建议"。该书共分为六部分，除了"争论性的导论"和"试探性的结论"之外，四篇论文的题目分别是"历史批评：模式论"、"伦理批评：符号论"、"原型批评：神话论"和"修辞批评：流派论"。其中，"原型批评：神话论"将人物塑造的要素和前两篇文章中所呈现的五个象征阶段有机地结合在一起。弗莱将神话模式与神话、罗曼司（浪漫故事）、高级摹仿（悲剧）、低级摹仿（现实主义文学）和反讽（现代文学）分别加以类比。高级摹仿占据了其他四种模式的中心。这种顺序使弗莱能够将模式置于圆形结构中，并指向神话和原型的循环性质。在这一背景下，文学代表了出生、成长、成熟、衰落、死亡、复活、重生的自然循环。"原型批评：神话论"将讨论四季更迭分别对应于喜剧（春）、传奇（夏）、悲剧（秋）和讽刺文学（冬）。

INTRODUCTION

IN THE ART of painting it is easy to see both structural and representational elements. A picture is normally a picture "of" something: it depicts or illustrates a "subject" made up of things analogous to "objects" in sense experience. At the same time there are present certain elements of pictorial design: what a picture represents is organized into structural patterns and conventions which are found only in pictures. The words "content" and "form" are often employed to describe these complementary aspects of painting. "Realism" connotes an emphasis on what the picture represents; stylization, whether primitive or sophisticated, connotes an emphasis on pictorial structure. Extreme realism of the illusive or *trompe l'œil* type is about as far as the painter can go in one kind of emphasis; abstract, or, more strictly, non-objective painting is about as far as he can go in the other direction. (The phrase "non-representational painting" seems to me illogical, a painting being itself a representation.) The illusive painter however cannot escape from pictorial conventions, and non-objective painting is still an imitative art in Aristotle's sense, and so we may say without much fear of effective contradiction that the whole art of painting lies within a combination of pictorial "form" or structure and pictorial "content" or subject.

For some reason the traditions of both practice and theory in Western painting have weighed down heavily on the imitative or representational end. Even from Classical painting we have inherited a number of depressing stories, of birds pecking painted grapes and the like, suggesting that Greek painters took their greatest pride in concocting *trompe l'œil* puzzles. The development of perspective painting in the

Renaissance gave a great prestige to such skills, the suggesting of three dimensions in a two-dimensional medium being essentially a *trompe l'œil* device. An eavesdropper in a modern art gallery may easily discover the strength and persistence of the feeling that to achieve recognizable likeness in a subject, and to make this likeness the primary thing in his picture, is a moral obligation on the painter. A good deal of the freakishness of experimental movements in painting during the last half-century or so has been due to the energy of its revolt against the tyranny of the representational fallacy.

An original painter knows, of course, that when the public demands likeness to an object, it generally wants the exact opposite, likeness to the pictorial conventions it is familiar with. Hence when he breaks with these conventions, he is often apt to assert that he is nothing but an eye, that he merely paints what he sees as he sees it, and the like. His motive in talking such nonsense is clear enough: he wishes to say that painting is not merely facile decoration, and involves a difficult conquest of some very real spatial problems. But this may be freely admitted without agreeing that the formal cause of a picture is outside the picture, an assertion which would destroy the whole art if it were taken seriously. What he has actually done is to obey an obscure but profound impulse to revolt against the conventions established in his own day, in order to rediscover convention on a deeper level. By breaking with the Barbizon school[1], Manet[2] discovered a deeper affinity with Goya[3] and Velasquez[4]; by breaking with the impressionists, Cézanne[5] discovered a deeper affinity with Chardin[6] and Masaccio[7]. The possession of originality cannot make an artist unconventional; it drives him further into convention, obeying the law of the art itself, which seeks constantly to reshape itself from its own depths, and which works through its geniuses for metamorphosis, as it works through minor talents for mutation.

Music affords a refreshing contrast to painting in its critical theory. When perspective was discovered in painting, music might well have gone in a similar direction, but in fact the development of representational or "program" music has been severely restricted. Listeners may still derive pleasure from hearing external sounds cleverly imitated in music, but no one asserts that a composer is being a decadent or a charlatan if he fails to produce such imitations. Nor is it believed that these imitations are prior in importance to the forms of music itself, still less that they constitute those forms. The result is that the structural principles of music are clearly understood, and can be taught even to children.

Suppose, for example, that the present book were an introduction to musical theory instead of poetics. Then we could begin by isolating, from the range of audible sounds, the interval of the octave, and explain that the octave is divided into twelve theoretically equal semitones, forming a scale of twelve notes which contains potentially all the melodies and harmonies that the reader of the book will ordinarily hear. Then we could abstract the two points of repose in this scale, the major and minor common chords, and explain the system of twenty-four interlocking keys and the conventions of tonality which require that a piece should normally open and close in the same key. We could describe the basis of rhythm as an accentuation of every second or every third beat, and so on through the whole list of rudiments.

Such an outline would give a rational account of the structure of Western music from 1600 to 1900, and, in a qualified and more flexible but not essentially different form, of everything that the user of the book would be accustomed to call music. If we chose, we could lock up all the music outside the Western tradition in the solitary confinement of a prefatory chapter, before we got down to serious business. Someone might object that the system of equal temperament, in which C♯ and Db are the same note, is an arbitrary fiction. Another might object that a composer ought not to be tied down to so rigidly conventionalized a set of musical elements, and that the resources of expression in music ought to be as free as the air. A third might object that we are not talking about music at all: that while the Jupiter Symphony is in C major and Beethoven's Fifth is in C minor, explaining the difference between the two keys will give nobody any real notion of the difference between the two symphonies. All these objectors could be quite safely ignored. Our handbook would not give the reader a complete musical education, nor would it give an account of music as it exists in the mind of God or the practice of angels—but it would do for its purposes.

In this book we are attempting to outline a few of the grammatical rudiments of literary expression, and the elements of it that correspond to such musical elements as tonality, simple and compound rhythm, canonical imitation, and the like. The aim is to give a rational account of some of the structural principles of Western literature in the context of its Classical and Christian heritage. We are suggesting that the resources of verbal expression are limited, if that is the word, by the literary equivalents of rhythm and key, though that does not mean, any more than it means in music, that its resources are artistically exhaustible. We doubtless have objectors similar to those just imagined for music, saying that our categories are artificial, that they do not do justice to the variety of literature, or that they are not relevant to their own experiences in reading. However, the question of what the structural principles of literature actually are seems important enough to discuss; and, as literature is an art of words, it should be at least as easy to find words to describe them as to find such words as sonata or fugue in music.

In literature, as in painting, the traditional emphasis in both practice and theory has been on representation or "lifelikeness." When, for instance, we pick up a novel of Dickens[8], our immediate impulse, a habit fostered in us by all the criticism we know, is to compare it with "life," whether as lived by us or by Dickens's contemporaries. Then we meet such characters as Heep or Quilp, and, as neither we nor the Victorians have ever known anything much "like" these curious monsters, the method promptly breaks down. Some readers will complain that Dickens has relapsed into "mere" caricature (as though caricature were easy); others, more sensibly, simply give up the criterion of lifelikeness and enjoy the creation for its own sake.

The structural principles of painting are frequently described in terms of their analogues in plane geometry (or solid, by a further reach of analogy). A famous letter of Cézanne speaks of the approximation of pictorial form to the sphere and the cube, and the practice of abstract painters seems to confirm his point. Geometrical shapes are analogous only to pictorial forms, not by any means identical with them; the real structural principles of painting are to be derived, not from an external analogy with something else, but from the internal analogy of the art itself. The structural principles of literature, similarly, are to be derived from archetypal and anagogic criticism, the only kinds that assume a larger context of literature as a whole. But we saw in the first essay that, as the modes of fiction move from the mythical to the low mimetic and ironic, they approach a point of extreme "realism" or representative likeness to life. It follows that the mythical mode, the stories about gods, in which characters have the greatest possible power of action, is the most abstract and conventionalized of all literary modes, just as the corresponding modes in other arts—religious Byzantine painting, for example—show the highest degree of stylization in their structure. Hence the structural principles of literature are as closely related to mythology and comparative religion as those of painting are to geometry. In this essay we shall be using the symbolism of the Bible, and to a lesser extent Classical mythology, as a grammar of literary archetypes.

In the Egyptian tale of The Two Brothers, thought to be the source of the Potiphar's wife story in the Joseph legend, an elder brother's wife attempts to seduce an unmarried younger brother who lives with them, and, when he resists her, accuses him of attempting to rape her. The younger brother is then forced to run away, with the enraged elder brother in pursuit. So far, the incidents reproduce more or less credible facts of life. Then the younger brother prays to Ra for assistance, pleading the justice of his cause; Ra places a large lake between him and his brother, and, in a burst of divine exuberance, fills it full of crocodiles. This incident is no more a fictional episode than anything that has preceded it, nor is it less logically related than any other episode to the plot as a whole. But it has given up the external analogy to "life": this, we say, is the kind of thing that happens only in stories. The Egyptian tale has acquired, then, in its mythical episode, an abstractly literary quality; and, as the story-teller could just as easily have solved his little problem in a more "realistic" way, it appears that literature in Egypt, like the other arts, preferred a certain degree of stylization.

Similarly, a medieval saint with a huge decorated halo around his head may look like an old man, but the mythical feature, the halo, both imparts a more abstract structure to the painting and gives the saint the kind of appearance that one sees only in pictures. In primitive societies, a flourishing development in myth and folk tale usually accompanies a taste for geometrical ornament in the plastic arts. In our tradition we have a place for verisimilitude, for human experience skillfully and consistently imitated. The occasional hoaxes in which fiction is presented, or even accepted, as fact, such as Defoe's[9] *Journal of the Plague Year* or Samuel Butler's[10] *The Fair Haven*, correspond to *trompe l'œil* illusions in painting. At the other extreme we have myths, or abstract fictional designs in which gods and other such beings do whatever they like, which in practice means whatever the story-teller likes. The return of irony to myth that we noted in the first essay is contemporary with, and parallel to, abstraction, expressionism, cubism, and similar efforts in painting to emphasize the self-contained pictorial structure. Sixty years ago, Bernard Shaw[11] stressed the social significance of the themes in Ibsen's plays and his own. Today, Mr. Eliot calls our attention to the Alcestis archetype in *The Cocktail Party*, to the Ion archetype in *The Confidential Clerk*. The former is of the age of Manet and Degas; the latter of the age of Braque and Graham Sutherland.

We begin our study of archetypes, then, with a world of myth, an abstract or purely literary world of fictional and thematic design, unaffected by canons of plausible adaptation to familiar experience. In terms of narrative, myth is the imitation of actions near or at the conceivable limits of desire. The gods enjoy beautiful women, fight one another with prodigious strength, comfort and assist man, or else watch his miseries from the height of their immortal freedom. The fact that myth operates at the top level of human desire does not mean that it necessarily presents its world as attained or attainable by human beings. In terms of meaning or *dianoia*, myth is the same world looked at as an area or field of activity, bearing in mind our principle that the meaning or pattern of poetry is a structure of imagery with conceptual implications. The world of mythical imagery is usually represented by the conception of heaven or Paradise in religion, and it is apocalyptic, in the sense of that word already explained, a world of total metaphor, in which everything is potentially identical with everything else, as though it were all inside a single infinite body.

Realism, or the art of verisimilitude, evokes the response "How like that is to what we know!" When what is written is *like* what is known, we have an art of extended or implied simile. And as realism is an art of implicit simile, myth is an art of implicit metaphorical identity. The word "sun-god," with a hyphen used instead of a predicate, is a pure ideogram, in Pound's terminology, or literal metaphor, in ours. In myth we see the structural principles of literature isolated; in realism we see the *same* structural principles (not similar ones) fitting into a context of plausibility. (Similarly in music, a piece by Purcell and a piece by Benjamin Britten may not be in the least *like* each other, but if they are both in D major their tonality will be the same.) The presence of a mythical structure in realistic fiction, however, poses certain technical problems for making it plausible, and the devices used in solving these problems may be given the general name of *displacement*.

Myth, then, is one extreme of literary design; naturalism is the other, and in between lies the whole area of romance, using that term to mean, not the historical mode of the first essay, but the tendency, noted later in the same essay, to displace myth in a human direction and yet, in contrast to "realism," to conventionalize content in an idealized direction. The central principle of displacement is that what can be metaphorically identified in a myth can only be linked in romance by some form of simile: analogy, significant association, incidental accompanying imagery, and the like. In a myth we can have a sun-god or a tree-god; in a romance we may have a person who is significantly associated with the sun or trees. In more realistic modes the association becomes less significant and more a matter of incidental, even coincidental or accidental, imagery. In the dragon-killing legend of the St. George and Perseus family, of which more hereafter, a country under an old feeble king is terrorized by a dragon who eventually demands the king's daughter, but is slain by the hero. This seems to be a romantic analogy (perhaps also, in this case, a descendant) of a myth of a waste land restored to life by a fertility god. In the myth, then, the dragon and the old king would be identified. We can in fact concentrate the myth still further into an Oedipus fantasy in which the hero is not the old king's son-in-law but his son, and the rescued damsel the hero's mother. If the story were a private dream such identifications would be made as a matter of course. But to make it a plausible, symmetrical, and morally acceptable story a good deal of displacement is necessary, and it is only after a comparative study of the story type has been made that the metaphorical structure within it begins to emerge.

In Hawthorne's[12] *The Marble Faun* the statue which gives the story that name is so insistently associated with a character named Donatello that a reader would have to be unusually dull or inattentive to miss the point that Donatello "is" the statue. Later on we meet a girl named Hilda, of singular purity and gentleness, who lives in a tower surrounded by doves. The doves are very fond of her; another character calls her his "dove," and remarks indicating some special affinity with doves are made about her by both author and characters. If we were to say that Hilda is a dove-goddess like Venus, identified with her doves, we should not be reading the story quite accurately in its own mode; we should be translating it into straight myth. But to recognize how close Hawthorne is to myth here is not unfair. That is, we recognize that *The Marble Faun* is not a typical low mimetic fiction: it is dominated by an interest that looks back to fictional romance and forward to the ironic mythical writers of the next century—to Kafka, for instance, or Cocteau. This interest is often called allegory, but probably Hawthorne himself was right in calling it romance. We can see how this interest tends toward abstraction in character-drawing, and if we know no other canons than low mimetic ones, we complain of this.

Or, again, we have, in myth, the story of Proserpine, who disappears into the underworld for six months of every year. The pure myth is clearly one of death and revival; the story as we have it is slightly displaced, but the mythical pattern is easy to see. The same structural element often recurs in Shakespearean comedy, where it has to be adapted to a roughly high mimetic level of credibility. Hero in *Much Ado* is dead enough to have a funeral song, and plausible explanations are postponed until after the end of the play. Imogen in *Cymbeline* has an assumed name and an empty grave, but she too gets some funeral obsequies. But the story of Hermione and Perdita is so close to the Demeter and Proserpine myth that hardly any serious pretence of plausible explanations is made. Hermione, after her disappearance, returns once as a ghost in a dream, and her coming to life from a statue, a displacement of the Pygmalion myth, is said to require an awakening of faith, even though, on one level of plausibility, she has not been a statue at all, and nothing has taken place except a harmless deception. We notice how much more abstractly mythical a thematic writer can be than a fictional one: Spenser's Florimell, for instance, disappears under the sea for the winter with no questions asked, leaving a "snowy lady" in her place and returning with a great outburst of spring floods at the end of the fourth book.

In the low mimetic, we recognize the same structural pattern of the death and revival of the heroine when Esther Summerson gets smallpox, or Lorna Doone is shot at her marriage altar. But we are getting closer to the conventions of realism, and although Lorna's eyes are "dim with death," we know that the author does not really mean death if he is planning to revive her. Here again it is interesting to compare *The Marble Faun*, where there is so much about sculptors and the relation of statues to living people that we almost expect some kind of denouement like that of *The Winter's Tale*. Hilda mysteriously disappears, and during her absence her lover, the sculptor Kenyon, digs out of the earth a statue that he associates with Hilda. After that Hilda returns, with a plausible reason eventually assigned for her absence, but not without some rather pointed and petulant remarks from Hawthorne himself to the effect that he has no interest in concocting plausible explanations, and that he wishes his reading public would give him a bit more freedom. Yet Hawthorne's inhibitions seem to be at least in part self-imposed, as we can see if we turn to Poe's *Ligeia*, where the straight mythical death and revival pattern is given without apology. Poe is clearly a more radical abstractionist than Hawthorne, which is one reason why his influence on our century is more immediate.

This affinity between the mythical and the abstractly literary illuminates many aspects of fiction, especially the more popular fiction which is realistic enough to be plausible in its incidents and yet romantic enough to be a "good story," which means a clearly designed one. The introduction of an omen or portent, or the device of making a whole story the fulfillment of a prophecy given at the beginning, is an example. Such a device suggests, in its existential projection, a conception of ineluctable fate or hidden omnipotent will. Actually, it is a piece of pure literary design, giving the beginning some symmetrical relationship with the end, and the only ineluctable will involved is that of the author. Hence we often find it even in writers not temperamentally much in sympathy with the portentous. In *Anna Karenina*, for instance, the death of the railway porter in the opening book is accepted by Anna as an omen for herself. Similarly, if we find portents and omens in Sophocles, they are there primarily because they fit the structure of his type of dramatic tragedy, and prove nothing about any clear-cut beliefs in fate held by either dramatist or audience.

We have, then, three organizations of myths and archetypal symbols in literature. First, there is undisplaced myth, generally concerned with gods or demons, and which takes the form of two contrasting worlds of total metaphorical identification, one desirable and the other undesirable. These worlds are often identified with the existential heavens and hells of the religions contemporary with such literature. These two forms of metaphorical organization we call the apocalyptic and the demonic respectively. Second, we have the general tendency we have called romantic, the tendency to suggest implicit mythical patterns in a world more closely associated with human experience. Third, we have the tendency of "realism" (my distaste for this inept term is reflected in the quotation marks) to throw the emphasis on content and representation rather than on the shape of the story. Ironic literature begins with realism and tends toward myth, its mythical patterns being as a rule more suggestive of the demonic than of the apocalyptic, though sometimes it simply continues the romantic tradition of stylization. Hawthorne, Poe, Conrad, Hardy and Virginia Woolf all provide examples.

In looking at a picture, we may stand close to it and analyze the details of brush work and palette knife. This corresponds roughly to the rhetorical analysis of the new critics in literature. At a little distance back, the design comes into clearer view, and we study rather the content represented: this is the best distance for realistic Dutch pictures, for example, where we are in a sense reading the picture. The further back we go, the more conscious we are of the organizing design. At a great distance from, say, a Madonna, we can see nothing but the archetype of the Madonna, a large centripetal blue mass with a contrasting point of interest at its center. In the criticism of literature, too, we often have to "stand back" from the poem to see its archetypal organization. If we "stand back" from Spenser's *Mutabilitie Cantoes*, we see a background of ordered circular light and a sinister black mass thrusting up into the lower foreground—much the same archetypal shape that we see in the opening of the Book of Job. If we "stand back" from the beginning of the fifth act of *Hamlet*, we see a grave opening on the stage, the hero, his enemy, and the heroine descending into it, followed by a fatal struggle in the upper world. If we "stand back" from a realistic novel such as Tolstoy's[13] *Resurrection* or Zola's[14] *Germinal*, we can see the mythopoeic designs indicated by those titles. Other examples will be given in what follows.

We proceed to give an account first of the structure of imagery, or *dianoia*, of the two undisplaced worlds, the apocalyptic and the demonic, drawing heavily on the Bible, the main source for undisplaced myth in our tradition. Then we go on to the two intermediate structures of imagery, and finally to the generic narratives or *mythoi* which are these structures of imagery in movement.

注释:

1. 巴比松画派，法国19世纪三四十年代兴起的乡村风景画派，是法国浪漫主义画派转向写实与现代主义的一个起点。

2. 埃杜阿尔·马内特（1832—1883），法国现代派画家。他是19世纪最早描绘现代生活的艺术家之一，也是从现实主义向印象主义过渡的关键人物。

3. 弗朗西斯科·何塞·德·戈雅-卢西恩特斯（1746—1828），西班牙浪漫主义画家和版画家，他被认为是18世纪末19世纪初最重要的西班牙艺术家。

4. 迭戈·罗德里格斯·德·席尔瓦·委拉斯凯兹（1599—1660），17世纪巴洛克时期西班牙画家。

5. 保罗·塞尚（1839—1906），印象派到立体主义之间的重要画家，后印象主义画派的代表人物。

6. 让·巴蒂斯特·西梅翁·夏尔丹（1699—1779），法国画家，法国18世纪市民艺术的杰出代表。

7. 马萨乔（1401—1428），意大利佛罗伦萨画派画家，其对线性透视法的革命性运用和对光影的掌握深刻地影响了文艺复兴时期的绘画。

8. 查尔斯·约翰·赫芬姆·狄更斯（1812—1870），19世纪英国最伟大的作家，作品以反映现实生活见长。

9. 丹尼尔·笛福（1660—1731），英国作家，英国启蒙时期现实主义小说的奠基人，被誉为“英国现实主义小说之父”。

10. 塞缪尔·巴特勒（1835—1902），英国著名作家，戏剧大师萧伯纳赞誉巴特勒是“19世纪后半期英国最伟大的作家”。

11. 乔治·伯纳德·萧（1856—1950），爱尔兰剧作家，评论家，曾获得诺贝尔文学奖。

12. 纳撒尼尔·霍桑（1804—1864），美国心理分析小说的开创者，也是美国文学史上首位写作短篇小说的作家，被称为美国19世纪最伟大的浪漫主义小说家。

13. 列夫·尼古拉耶维奇·托尔斯泰（1828—1910），19世纪中期俄国批判现实主义作家、思想家和哲学家，代表作有《战争与和平》《安娜·卡列尼娜》《复活》等。

14. 爱弥尔·左拉（1840—1902），法国著名自然主义小说家和理论家，自然主义文学流派创始人和领袖。

Chapter Four **Structuralism**

20 世纪 60 年代中后期和 70 年代，继俄国形式主义和英美新批评之后出现的结构主义批评理论极为盛行。瑞士语言学家费尔迪南·德·索绪尔（Ferdinand de Saussure）是现代语言学的重要奠基者，也是结构主义的开创者之一。索绪尔去世后，其学生根据课堂和讲座笔记整理成书，以他的名义出版了《普通语言学教程》，该书对结构主义的兴起起到极大作用。《普通语言学教程》是索绪尔的代表性著作，集中体现了他的基本语言学思想，对 20 世纪的现代语言学研究产生了深远的影响。同时，由于其研究视角和方法论所具有的一般性和深刻性，书中的思想也成为 20 世纪重要的哲学流派结构主义的主要思想来源。结构主义批评就是将索绪尔所倡导的现代结构主义语言学的研究方法和原则运用到文学批评中。索绪尔指出语言是一个独立的、自给自足的系统，意义不是由说话人的主观意图决定的，而是由整个语言系统决定的。语言学家的任务不是研究个别的演讲，而是研究整个语言系统。与此类似，文学结构主义者认为，个体作品应该被看作是一种话语，它充满了文学语言的规律。按照这一思路，列维-斯特劳斯（Levi-Strauss）将索绪尔的语言理论引入文化人类学。他对美洲大陆原始居民的神话、亲属关系和烹调技巧的结构分析表明，这些神话、亲属关系和烹调技巧与语言一样，都是有结构的系统。它们各自的组件元素之所以有意义，仅仅是因为它们是一个完整系统的一部分。在他的分析中，神话被分解成基本单位（神话元素），就像语言的基本语音单位（音素）。

罗兰·巴特（Roland Barthes）的符号学批评是结构主义的重要组成部分。他在作品《神话》（1957）、《符号学基础》（1965）、《文本的快乐》（1973）等中，对当代社会文化现象进行了广泛的分析。在他的分析中渗透着这样一个理念：在服装和谈话的背后，有一个赋予服装或谈话以意义的系统。他将这些社会行为解释为各种符号系统，它们按照语言模式运行。任何社会行为都受一套规则体系的支配。巴尔特的结构主义符号学批评对早期英语研究产生了很大的影响，是文化研究批判实践的重要理论来源。

当代结构主义批评代表人物还包括法国的热拉尔·热奈特(Gerard Genette)、路易·阿尔都塞(Louis Althusser)、雅克·拉康(Jacques Lacan),让·皮亚杰(Jean Piaget)、A. J. 格雷马斯(Algirdas Julien Greimas),俄罗斯的罗曼·雅各布森(Roman Jakobson)、巴赫金(M. M. Bakhtin),美国的皮尔斯(C. S. Peirce)、爱德华·萨丕尔(Edward Sapir)、诺姆·乔姆斯基(Noam Chomsky)等。

与传统批评相比,结构主义批评最具革命性的本质在于赋予了语言一个极其重要的地位:语言本身不仅成为结构主义批评的对象,而且被视为非语言学科的研究模式。但由于结构主义批评过于关注文本本身,脱离了文学作品赖以产生的历史和社会语境,常常机械地运用语言模式,证明过程显得琐碎复杂,它得出的结论往往是矛盾的,其科学性和客观性也值得怀疑。对于后结构主义来说,结构主义只是一种解释行为,而不是一门以探索其所研究领域的内在结构为己任的科学。随着后结构主义和解构主义的兴起,巴尔特等结构主义者开始转向后结构主义,结构主义时代逐渐成为过去。

Ferdinand de Saussure

费尔迪南·德·索绪尔(1857—1913),瑞士语言学家,现代语言学的重要奠基者,结构主义的开创者之一,被后人称为现代语言学之父、结构主义的鼻祖。索绪尔出生于瑞士日内瓦,曾在日内瓦大学学习物理学和化学,后进入德国莱比锡大学学习历史语言学并获得博士学位。1878 年,21 岁的索绪尔发表了他的成名作《论印欧系语言元音的原始系统》,被誉为"历史语言学中杰出的篇章"。他把原始印欧语的语音系统看成一个有规则的整体结构,因此从语言结构的不规则处着眼,拟测原始印欧语的元音系统,该论文奠定了索绪尔当时在语言学界的学术地位。1881—1891 年,他在法国巴黎高等研究学院任教,讲授历史比较语法,对法国的一代语言学家有着深远的影响。1907—1911 年,他在日内瓦大学讲授普通语言学课程,首创这一学科,但没有写成讲义。他去世之后,其学生根据同学们的笔记整理成《普通语言学教程》一书。

From

Course in General Linguistics
Part One
General Principles
Chapter I
Nature of the Linguistic Sign

(de Saussure, Ferdinand. Course in General Linguistics: Part One General Principles Chapter I Nature of the Linguistic Sign. 选自亚当斯、瑟尔主编,《柏拉图以来的批评理论》(下册)(第三版),北京:北京大学出版社, 2006 年,第 786 到 795 页。)

1916 年,索绪尔去世三年后,他的两名学生查尔斯·巴里(Charles Bally)和阿尔伯特·谢海伊(Albert Sechehaye)根据课堂和讲座笔记整理成书,以他的名义出版了《普通语言学教程》,这是一部具有划时代意义的著作,提出了全新的语言理论、原则和概念,为语言的研究和语言学的发展奠定了科学的基础,成为语言学史乃至学术史上一部重要的经典著作。索绪尔普通语言学的核心观念是语言的任意性、关系性和系统性。他提出语言由一系列符号组成,存在于一个具体、自足的系统中,起支配作用的是符号间的相互关系。他反对历时语言学探索语言变化的研究方法,主张通过具体的言语行为对语言进行共时分析,挖掘语言潜在的支配系统。他阐释了言语和语言的重要区别:言语是社会成语对语言的个别使用;语言是支配具体言语的规则体系,是社会集团为个人行使言语机能而采用的规约,得到社会成员的一致认可。他反对语言符号和现实世界的一一对应联系,认为语言是一种符号系统,符号是由能指(语言符号)和所指(与符号相对应的东西)两部分构成。意义的产生是符号之间相互区别的结果,也就是说,词的意义不是根据现实产生的。

1. *Sign*, *Signified*, *Signifier*

Some people regard language, when reduced to its elements, as a naming-process only—a list of words, each corresponding to the thing that it names. For example:

ARBOR

EQUOS

etc. etc.

This conception is open to criticism at several points. It assumes that ready-made ideas exist before words; it does not tell us whether a name is vocal or psychological in nature (*arbor*, for instance, can be considered from either viewpoint); finally, it lets us assume that the linking of a name and a thing is a very simple operation—an assumption that is anything but true. But this rather naive approach can bring us near the truth by showing us that the linguistic unit is a double entity, one formed by the associating of two terms.

We have seen in considering the speaking-circuit that both terms involved in the linguistic sign are psychological and are united in the brain by an associative bond. This point must be emphasized.

The linguistic sign unites, not a thing and a name, but a concept and a sound-image. The latter is not the material sound, a purely physical thing, but the psychological imprint of the sound, the impression that it makes on our senses. The sound-image is sensory, and if I happen to call it "material," it is only in that sense, and by way of opposing it to the other term of the association, the concept, which is generally more abstract.

The psychological character of our sound-images becomes apparent when we observe our own speech. Without moving our lips or tongue, we can talk to ourselves or recite mentally a selection of verse. Because we regard the words of our language as sound-images, we must avoid speaking of the "phonemes" that make up the words. This term, which suggests vocal activity, is applicable to the spoken word only, to the realization of the inner image in discourse. We can avoid that misunderstanding by speaking of the *sounds* and *syllables* of a word provided we remember that the names refer to the sound-image.

The linguistic sign is then a two-sided psychological entity that can be represented by the drawing:

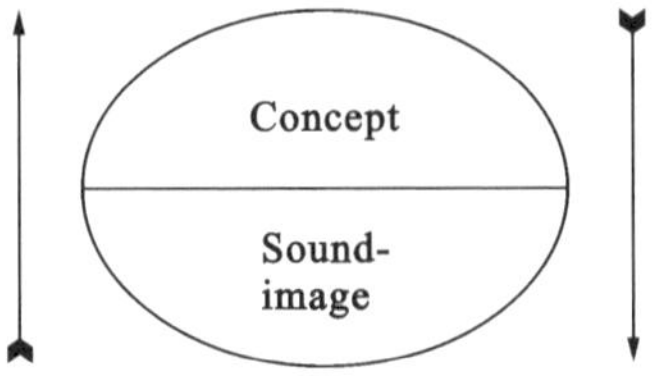

The two elements are intimately united, and each recalls the other. Whether we try to find the meaning of the Latin word *arbor* or the word that Latin uses to designate the concept "tree," it is clear that only the associations sanctioned by that language appear to us to conform to reality, and we disregard whatever others might be imagined.

Our definition of the linguistic sign poses an important question of terminology. I call the combination of a concept and a sound-image a *sign*, but in current usage the term generally designates only a sound-image, a word, for example (*arbor*, etc.). One tends to forget that *arbor* is called a sign only because it carries the concept "tree," with the result that the idea of the sensory part implies the idea of the whole.

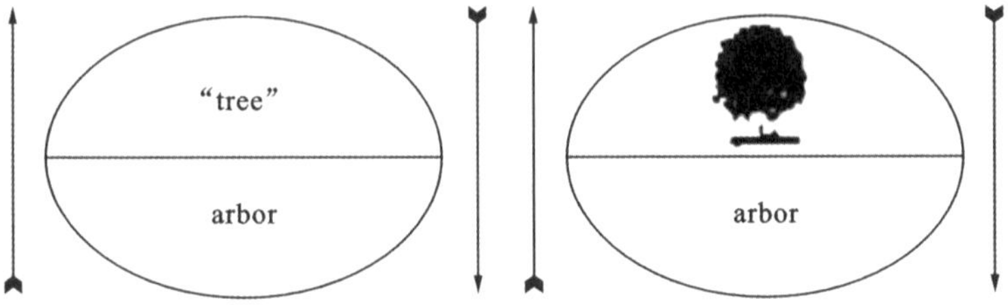

Ambiguity would disappear if the three notions involved here were designated by three names, each suggesting and opposing the others. I propose to retain the word *sign* [*signe*] to designate the whole and to replace *concept* and *sound-image* respectively by *signified* [*signifié*] and *signifier* [*signifiant*]; the last two terms have the advantage of indicating the opposition that separates them from each other and from the whole of which they are parts. As regards *sign*, if I am satisfied with it, this is simply because I do not know of any word to replace it, the ordinary language suggesting no other.

The linguistic sign, as defined, has two primordial characteristics. In enunciating them I am also positing the basic principles of any study of this type.

2. *Principle I: The Arbitrary Nature of the Sign*

The bond between the signifier and the signified is arbitrary. Since I mean by sign the whole that results from the associating of the signifier with the signified, I can simply say: *the linguistic sign is arbitrary*.

The idea of "sister" is not linked by any inner relationship to the succession of sounds *s-ö-r* which serves as its signifier in French; that it could be represented equally by just any other sequence is proved by differences among languages and by the very existence of different languages: the signified "ox" has as its signifier *b-ö-f* on one side of the border and *o-k-s* (*Ochs*) on the other.

No one disputes the principle of the arbitrary nature of the sign, but it is often easier to discover a truth than to assign to it its proper place. Principle I dominates all the linguistics of language; its consequences are numberless. It is true that not all of them are equally obvious at first glance; only after many detours does one discover them, and with them the primordial importance of the principle.

One remark in passing: when semiology[1] becomes organized as a science, the question will arise whether or not it properly includes modes of expression based on completely natural signs, such as pantomime[2]. Supposing that the new science welcomes them, its main concern will still be the whole group of systems grounded on the arbitrariness of the sign. In fact, every means of expression used in society is based, in principle, on collective behavior or—what amounts to the same thing—on convention. Polite formulas, for instance, though often imbued with a certain natural expressiveness (as in the case of a Chinese who greets his emperor by bowing down to the ground nine times), are nonetheless fixed by rule; it is this rule and not the intrinsic value of the gestures that obliges one, to use them. Signs that are wholly arbitrary realize better than the others the ideal of the semiological process; that is why language, the most complex and universal of all systems of expression, is also the most characteristic; in this sense linguistics can become the master-pattern for all branches of semiology although language is only one particular semiological system.

The word *symbol* has been used to designate the linguistic sign, or more specifically, what is here called the signifier. Principle I in particular weighs against the use of this term. One characteristic of the symbol is that it is never wholly arbitrary; it is not empty, for there is the rudiment of a natural bond between the signifier and the signified. The symbol of justice, a pair of scales, could not be replaced by just any other symbol, such as a chariot.

The word *arbitrary* also calls for comment. The term should not imply that the choice of the signifier is left entirely to the speaker (we shall see below that the individual does not have the power to change a sign in any way once it has become established in the linguistic community); I mean that it is unmotivated, i. e. arbitrary in that it actually has no natural connection with the signified.

In concluding let us consider two objections that might be raised to the establishment of Principle I:

1) *Onomatopoeia* might be used to prove that the choice of the signifier is not always arbitrary. But onomatopoeic formations are never organic elements of a linguistic system. Besides, their number is much smaller than is generally supposed. Words like French *fouet* 'whip' or *glas* 'knell' may strike certain ears with suggestive sonority, but to see that they have not always had this property we need only examine their Latin forms (*fouet* is derived from *fāgus* 'beech-tree,' *glas* from *classicum* 'sound of a trumpet'). The quality of their present sounds, or rather the quality that is attributed to them, is a fortuitous result of phonetic evolution.

As for authentic onomatopoeic words (e. g. *glug-glug*, *tick-tock*, etc.), not only are they limited in number, but also they are chosen somewhat arbitrarily, for they are only approximate and more or less conventional imitations of certain sounds (cf. English *bow-bow* and French *ouaoua*). In addition, once these words have been introduced into the language, they are to a certain extent subjected to the same evolution—phonetic, morphological, etc.—that other words undergo (cf. *pigeon*, ultimately from Vulgar Latin *pīpiō*, derived in turn from an onomatopoeic formation): obvious proof that they lose something of their original character in order to assume that of the linguistic sign in general, which is unmotivated.

2) *Interjections*, closely related to onomatopoeia, can be attacked on the same grounds and come no closer to refuting our thesis. One is tempted to see in them spontaneous expressions of reality dictated, so to speak, by natural forces. But for most interjections we can show that there is no fixed bond between their signified and their signifier. We need only compare two languages on this point to see how much such expressions differ from one language to the next (e. g. the English equivalent of French *aïe*! is *ouch*!). We know, moreover, that many interjections were once words with specific meanings (cf. French *diable*! 'darn!' *mordieu*! 'golly!' from *mort Dieu* 'God's death.' etc.).

Onomatopoeic formations and interjections are of secondary importance, and their symbolic origin is in part open to dispute.

3. *Principle* Ⅱ: *The Linear Nature of the Signifier*

The signifier, being auditory, is unfolded solely in time from which it gets the following characteristics: (a) it represents a span, and (b) the span is measurable in a single dimension; it is a line.

While Principle Ⅱ is obvious, apparently linguists have always neglected to state it, doubtless because they found it too simple; nevertheless, it is fundamental, and its consequences are incalculable. Its importance equals that of Principle Ⅰ: the whole mechanism of language depends upon it. In contrast to visual signifiers (nautical signals, etc.) which can offer simultaneous groupings in several dimensions, auditory signifiers have at their command only the dimension of time. Their elements are presented in succession; they form a chain. This feature becomes readily apparent when they are represented in writing and the spatial line of graphic marks is substituted for succession in time.

Sometimes the linear nature of the signifier is not obvious. When I accent a syllable, for instance, it seems that I am concentrating more than one significant element on the same point. But this is an illusion; the syllable and its accent constitute only one phonational act. There is no duality within the act but only different oppositions to what precedes and what follows.

注释:

1. 符号学，是研究事物符号的本质、符号的发展变化规律、符号的各种意义以及符号与人类多种活动之间的关系。索绪尔是现代符号学的创始人之一。

2. 哑剧，该词源于希腊语，意思是“模仿者”。哑剧是不用台词而凭借形体动作和表情表达剧情的戏剧形式。

Roland Barthes

罗兰·巴特(1915—1980)，法国符号学家、文学批评家、思想家和社会学家，是最早把结构主义运用到文学研究中的批评家之一。巴特早期的著作关注语言结构的随意性及大众文化现象，后来关注起读者对文本的主观反应，很快转向后结构主义批评方法，发表后结构主义作品《作者之死》(1968)，但他拒绝把自己纳入任何一个批评流派。巴特研究兴趣广泛，对结构主义、社会理论、设计理论、人类学和后结构主义均有涉猎，其思想体系影响了人们对文学和文化的看法。其作品对文学批评和著名文学人物的传统学术观点提出了许多挑战。其主要作品有《写作的零度》(1953)、《神话学》(1957)、《论拉辛》(1963)、《符号学基础》(1965)、《批评与真理》(1966)、《符号帝国》(1970)、《S/Z》(1970)、《文本的快乐》(1973)等等。1976年，巴特在法兰西学院担任文学符号学讲座教授，成为这个讲座的第一位学者。

The Structuralist Activity

(Barthes, Roland. The Structuralist Activity. *Critical Essays*. Evanston: Northwestern University Press, 1972, pp. 213-220.)

20世纪60年代初期，巴特开始对符号学与结构主义进行探索，主要是对传统学院文学理论观点以及大众文学类型的论述。其思想独特，不墨守成规，引起法国思想家的不满，他们认为巴尔特漠视且不尊重文化中的文学根源。《结构主义活动》这篇文章就展示了巴尔特独特的结构主义论述。他指出：结构主义本质上是一种活动，是一定数量的受到控制的思维活动过程；一切结构主义活动的目标都是对一个客体进行重建，从而揭示该客体运作的规律；结构其实是对客体进行的有目的的模仿活动，该活动具有分割和明确表达这两种典型做法。

What is structuralism? Not a school, nor even a movement (at least, not yet), for most of the authors ordinarily labeled with this word are unaware of being united by any solidarity of doctrine or commitment. Nor is it a vocabulary. *Structure* is already an old word (of anatomical and grammatical provenance), today quite overworked: all the social sciences resort to it abundantly, and the word's use can distinguish no one, except to polemicize about the content assigned to it; *functions*, *forms*, *signs* and *significations* are scarcely more pertinent: they are, today, words of common usage, from which one asks (and obtains) whatever one wants, notably the camouflage of the old determinist schema of cause and product; we must doubtless resort to pairings like those of *signifier / signified* and *synchronic / diachronic* in order to approach what distinguishes structuralism from other modes of thought: the first because it refers to the linguistic model as originated by Saussure and because, along with economics, linguistics is, in the present state of affairs, the true science of structure; the second, more decisively, because it seems to imply a certain revision of the notion of history, insofar as the idea of the synchrony (although in Saussure this is a pre-eminently operational concept) accredits a certain immobilization of time, and insofar as diachrony tends to represent the historical process as a pure succession of forms. This second pairing is all the more distinctive in that the chief resistance to structuralism today seems to be of Marxist origin and in that it focuses on the notion of history (and not of structure); whatever the case, it is probably the serious recourse to the nomenclature of signification (and not to the word itself, which is, paradoxically, not at all distinctive) which we must ultimately take as structuralism's spoken sign: watch who uses *signifier* and *signified*, *synchrony* and *diachrony*, and you will know whether the structuralist vision is constituted.

This is valid for the intellectual metalanguage, which explicitly employs methodological concepts. But since structuralism is neither a school nor a movement, there is no reason to reduce it a priori, even in a problematical way, to the activity of philosophers; it would be better to try and find its broadest description (if not its definition) on another level than that of reflexive language. We can in fact presume that there exist certain writers, painters, musicians, in whose eyes a certain exercise of structure (and no longer merely its thought) represents a distinctive experience, and that both analysts and creators must be placed under the common sign of what we might call *structural man*, defined not by his ideas or his languages, but by his imagination—in other words, by the way in which he mentally experiences structure.

So the first thing to be said is that in relation to all its users, structuralism is essentially an *activity*, i. e., the controlled succession of a certain number of mental operations: we might speak of structuralist activity as we once spoke of surrealist activity (surrealism, moreover, may well have produced the first experience of structural literature, a possibility which must some day be explored). But before seeing what these operations are, we must say a word about their goal.

The goal of all structuralist activity, whether reflexive or poetic, is to reconstruct an "object" in such a way as to manifest thereby the rules of functioning (the "functions") of this object. Structure is therefore actually a *simulacrum* of the object, but a directed, *interested* simulacrum, since the imitated object makes something appear which remained invisible, or if one prefers, unintelligible in the natural object. Structural man takes the real, decomposes it, then recomposes it; this appears to be little enough (which makes some say that the structuralist enterprise is "meaningless," "uninteresting," "useless," etc.). Yet from another point of view, this "little enough" is decisive: for between the two objects, or the two tenses, of structuralist activity, there occurs something new, and what is new is nothing less than the generally intelligible: the simulacrum is intellect added to object, and this addition has an anthropological value, in that it is man himself, his history, his situation, his freedom and the very resistance which nature offers to his mind.

We see, then, why we must speak of a structuralist *activity* : creation or reflection are not, here, an original "impression" of the world, but a veritable fabrication of a world which resembles the primary one, not in order to copy it but to render it intelligible. Hence one might say that structuralism is essentially *an activity of imitation*, which is also why there is, strictly speaking, no *technical* difference between structuralism as an intellectual activity, on the one hand, and literature in particular, art in general, on the other: both derive from a *mimesis*, based not on the analogy of substances (as in so-called realist art), but on the analogy of functions (what Lévi-Strauss[1] calls *homology*). When Troubetskoy[2] reconstructs the phonetic object as a system of variations; when Dumézil[3] elaborates a functional mythology; when Propp[4] constructs a folk tale resulting by structuration from all the Slavic tales he has previously decomposed; when Lévi-Strauss discovers the homologic functioning of the totemic imagination, or Granger the formal rules of economic thought, or Gardin[5] the pertinent features of prehistoric bronzes; when Richard decomposes a poem by Mallarmé[6] into its distinctive vibrations—they are all doing nothing different from what Mondrian[7], Boulez[8] or Butor[9] are doing when they articulate a certain object—what will be called, precisely, a *composition* —by the controlled manifestation of certain units and certain associations of these units. It is of little consequence whether the initial object submitted to the simulacrum activity is given by the world in an already assembled fashion (in the case of the structural analysis made of a constituted language or society or work) or is still dispersed (in the case of the structural "composition"); whether this initial object is drawn from a social reality or an imaginary reality. It is not the nature of the copied object which defines an art (though this is a tenacious prejudice in all realism), it is the fact that man adds to it in reconstructing it: technique is the very being of all creation. It is therefore to the degree that the goals of structuralist activity are indissolubly linked to a certain technique that structuralism exists in a distinctive fashion in relation to other modes of analysis or creation: we recompose the object in order to make certain functions appear, and it is, so to speak, the way that makes the work; this is why we must speak of the structuralist activity rather than the structuralist work.

The structuralist activity involves two typical operations: dissection and articulation. To dissect the first object, the one which is given to the simulacrum-activity, is to find in it certain mobile fragments whose differential situation engenders a certain meaning; the fragment has no meaning in itself, but it is nonetheless such that the slightest variation wrought in its configuration produces a change in the whole; a *square* by Mondrian, a *series* by Pousseur[10], a *versicle* of Butor's *Mobile*, the "mytheme" in Lévi-Strauss, the phoneme in the work of the phonologists, the "theme" in certain literary criticism—all these units (whatever their inner structure and their extent, quite different according to cases) have no significant existence except by their frontiers: those which separate them from other actual units of the discourse (but this is a problem of articulation) and also those which distinguish them from other virtual units, with which they form a certain class (which linguistics calls a *paradigm*); this notion of a paradigm is essential, apparently, if we are to understand the structuralist vision: the paradigm is a group, a reservoir—as limited as possible—of objects (of units) from which we summon, by an act of citation, the object or unit we wish to endow with an actual meaning; what characterizes the paradigmatic object is that it is, vis-à-vis other objects of its class, in a certain relation of affinity and of dissimilarity: two units of the same paradigm must resemble each other somewhat in *order* that the difference which separates them be indeed evident: *s* and *z* must have both a common feature (dentality) and a distinctive feature (presence or absence of sonority) so that we cannot, in French, attribute the same meaning to *poisson* and *poison*; Mondrian's squares must have both certain affinities by their shape as squares, and certain dissimilarities by their proportion and color; the American automobiles (in Butor's *Mobile*) must be constantly regarded in the same way, yet they must differ each time by both their make and color; the episodes of the Oedipus myth (in Lévi-Strauss's analysis) must be both identical and varied—in order that all these languages, these works may be intelligible. The dissection-operation thus produces an initial dispersed state of the simulacrum, but the units of the structure are not at all anarchic: before being distributed and fixed in the continuity of the composition, each one forms with its own virtual group or reservoir an intelligent organism, subject to a sovereign motor principle: that of the least difference.

Once the units are posited, structural man must discover in them or establish for them certain rules of association: this is the activity of articulation, which succeeds the summoning activity. The syntax of the arts and of discourse is, as we know, extremely varied; but what we discover in each work of structural enterprise is the submission to regular constraints whose formalism, improperly indicted, is much less important than their stability; for what is happening, at this second stage of the simulacrum-activity, is a kind of battle against chance; this is why the constraint of recurrence of the units has an almost demiurgic value: it is by the regular return of the units and of the associations of units that the work appears constructed, i. e., endowed with meaning; linguistics calls these rules of combination *forms*, and it would be advantageous to retain this rigorous sense of an overtaxed word: form, it has been said, is what keeps the contiguity of units from appearing as a pure effect of chance: the work of art is what man wrests from chance. This perhaps allows us to understand on the one hand why so-called nonfigurative works are nonetheless to the highest degree works of art, human thought being established not by the analogy of copies and models but by the regularity of assemblages; and on the other hand why these same works appear, precisely, fortuitous and thereby useless to those who discern in them no form: in front of an abstract painting, Khrushchev is certainly wrong to see only the traces of a donkey's tail whisked across the canvas; at least he knows in his way, though, that art is a certain conquest of chance (he simply forgets that every rule must be learned, whether one wants to apply or interpret it).

The simulacrum, thus constructed, does not render the world as it has found it, and it is here that structuralism is important. First of all, it manifests a new category of the object, which is neither the real nor the rational, but the *functional*, thereby joining a whole scientific complex which is being developed around information theory and research. Subsequently and especially, it highlights the strictly human process by which men give meaning to things. Is this new? To a certain degree, yes; of course the world has never stopped looking for the meaning of what is given it and of what it produces; what is new is a mode of thought (or a "poetics") which seeks less to assign completed meanings to the objects it discovers than to know how meaning is possible, at what cost and by what means. Ultimately, one might say that the object of structuralism is not man endowed with meanings, but man fabricating meanings, as if it could not be the *content* of meanings which exhausted the semantic goals of humanity, but only the act by which these meanings, historical and contingent variables, are produced. *Homo significans* : such would be the new man of structural inquiry.

According to Hegel[11], the ancient Greek was amazed by the natural in nature; he constantly listened to it, questioned the meaning of mountains, springs, forests, storms; without knowing what all these objects were telling him by name, he perceived in the vegetal or cosmic order a tremendous shudder of meaning, to which he gave the name of a god: *Pan*. Subsequently, nature has changed, has become social: everything given to man is already human, down to the forest and the river which we cross when we travel. But confronted with this social nature, which is quite simply culture, structural man is no different from the ancient Greek: he too listens for the natural in culture, and constantly perceives in it not so much stable, finite, "true" meanings as the shudder of an enormous machine which is humanity tirelessly undertaking to create meaning, without which it would no longer be human. And it is because this fabrication of meaning is more important, to its view, than the meanings themselves, it is because the function is extensive with the works, that structuralism constitutes itself as an activity, and refers the exercise of the work and the work itself to a single identity: a serial composition or an analysis by Lévi-Strauss are not objects except insofar as they have been made: their present being *is* their past act: they are *having-been-mades*; the artist, the analyst recreates the course taken by meaning, he need not designate it: his function, to return to Hegel's example, is a *manteia*; like the ancient soothsayer, he speaks the locus of meaning but does not name it. And it is because literature, in particular, is a mantic activity that it is both intelligible and interrogating, speaking and silent, engaged in the world by the course of meaning which it remakes with the world, but disengaged from the contingent meanings which the world elaborates: an answer to the man who consumes it yet always a question to nature, an answer which questions and a question which answers.

How then does structural man deal with the accusation of "unreality" which is sometimes flung at him? Are not forms in the world? are not forms responsible? Was it really his Marxism that was revolutionary in Brecht[12]? Was it not rather the decision to link to Marxism, in the theater, the placing of a spotlight or the deliberate fraying of a costume? Structuralism does not withdraw history from the world: it seeks to link to history not only certain contents (this has been done a thousand times) but also certain forms, not only the material but also the intelligible, not only the ideological but also the esthetic. And precisely because all thought about the historically intelligible is also a participation in that intelligibility, structural man is scarcely concerned to last; he knows that structuralism, too, is a certain form of the world, which will change with the world; and just as he experiences his validity (but not his truth) in his power to speak the old languages of the world in a new way, so he knows that it will suffice hat a new language rise out of history, a new language which speaks *him* in his turn, for his task to be done.

注释:

1. 克洛德·列维-斯特劳斯(1908—2009),生于比利时的法国作家、哲学家、人类学家和民族学家,结构主义人类学创始人,推动了结构主义和结构人类学理论的发展。

2. 尼古拉·谢尔盖耶维奇·特鲁贝茨科伊(1890—1938),俄罗斯语言学家和历史学家。

3. 乔治·杜梅齐尔(1898—1986),法国比较语言学家,以分析原始印欧宗教和社会中的主权与权力而闻名。

4. 弗拉基米尔·雅可夫列维奇·普洛普(1895—1970),当代著名的语言学家、民俗学家、民间文艺学家、艺术理论家,苏联民间创作问题研究的杰出代表。

5. 让-克劳德·加尔丁(1925—2013),法国考古学家,考古计算的奠基人之一。

6. 斯特芳·马拉美(1842—1898),法国象征主义诗人和散文家。

7. 彼埃·蒙德里安(1872—1944),荷兰画家,抽象风格派核心人物,风格派运动幕后艺术家和非具象绘画的创始者之一。

8. 皮埃尔·布列兹(1925—2016),法国指挥家、作曲家和音乐理论家,以准确清晰地诠释20世纪音乐而著称。

9. 米歇尔·布托尔(1926—2016),法国作家。

10. 亨利·普瑟(1929—2009),比利时作曲家、教师和音乐理论家。

11. 格奥尔格·威廉·弗里德里希·黑格尔(1770—1831),德国19世纪唯心论哲学的代表人物之一。

12. 贝托尔特·布莱希特(1898—1956),德国戏剧家、诗人。

Chapter Five Psycho-Analytical Criticism

精神分析批评始于19世纪末，是一种出现较早、影响深远的批评模式。它将西格蒙德·弗洛伊德(Sigmund Freud)的精神分析学和其他心理学理论应用到文学批评中。追溯其百年的发展历程可以看出，精神分析批评在其发展的不同阶段的观点也有所不同。① 以弗洛伊德为代表的传统精神分析批评主要研究作者本人(或作品中的人物)的无意识心理，文学作品被视为作者的心理标志。② 后弗洛伊德时代的自我精神分析批评开始分析读者对文本的心理反应，突出了读者与文本的互动关系。③ 在卡尔·古斯塔夫·荣格(Carl Gustav Jung)的原型精神分析批评中，文学作品不是体现作者心理特征的场所，也不是满足读者个人无意识中隐藏的幻想的渠道，而是对集体无意识的再现。④ 雅克·拉康(Jacques Lacan)等人将传统精神分析批评与结构主义语言学联系起来，对传统精神分析批评中的许多概念进行了重新阐释和改造。之后，精神分析批评仍有一定发展，逐渐包含了马克思主义、解构主义和女性主义等多重视角，兼容了心理学、叙事学、接受理论和读者反应批评等多种元素。后期代表人物还包括吉尔·德勒兹(Gilles Deleuze)和皮埃尔·菲利克斯·加塔利(Pierre Felix Guattari)等人。

弗洛伊德把个人心理学分为意识、前意识和无意识三部分。他在后来提出的心理结构模式中，又将心理的无意识和非理性部分称为本我(id)，将心理的理性和意识部分称为自我(ego)。自我的主要任务是把本我控制在一定范围内。本我遵循所谓的"享乐原则"，自我遵循"现实原则"，超我(superego)则代表着社会道德，与自我合作，牢牢地控制着社会道德所不允许的一切无意识的思想和本能冲动。弗洛伊德指出，为本我提供能量的是本能(instincts)，两种最基本的本能是爱和死。他将爱的本能称为力比多(libido)。在弗洛伊德看来，婴儿期产生的、憎恨同性父母的隐性情感，是无意识的重要组成部分。在男孩的无意识中，他把父亲当作敌人，在希望与母亲结合的同时，有一种被父亲阉割的恐惧感。弗洛伊德把这种情感情结称为"俄狄浦斯情结"。此外，弗洛伊德认为梦是对被压抑的欲望的虚假满足。人的许多欲望由于没有得到社会道德的认可，被排除在意识层面之外，往往不得不以变相的形象出现，以迂回的方式出现在梦中。弗洛伊德梦的解析本身并不是目的,从"非常态的精神活动"推及人类的心灵世界才是目的。

霍兰德吸收弗洛伊德的人格学说,发展出一套读者心理反应理论,即"防卫-期待-幻想-改造"(defence-expectation-fantasy-transformation),简称 DEFT 机制。在他看来,读者对文本的不同解读实际上是他们投射到文本中的恐惧、防御、需要和欲望的产物。霍兰德成功地将超我、自我和本我"移植"到文学阅读行为上,为文本阐释提供了一个心理学模型。

荣格倡导的原型批评,与传统的精神分析批评和读者的反应精神分析批评完全不同,他认为文学作品源于人类的集体无意识,作家的创作往往受到集体无意识的控制。集体无意识的概念是荣格理论的基石。集体无意识的内容是原型。荣格在他的论文《论分析心理学与诗歌的关系》中称原型为原始意象。荣格自己的文学批评著作并不多,但他的理论启发了神话和原型批评这一重要的文学批评流派。

拉康的精神分析学则是在结构主义人类学和语言学的一些重要文献的基础上建立起来的。他把语言学研究引入精神分析。他认为,与语言一样,无意识也有一个潜在的结构。他从结构主义语言学的角度阐释了俄狄浦斯情结的形成过程。他还用"隐喻"和"转喻"取代了弗洛伊德的"凝聚"和"置换",认为口误、笑话、梦境等各种无意识的表现都是由"隐喻""转喻"等语言机制控制的。此外,他提出镜像阶段的理论,又从镜像阶段的理论引出了关于个性或人格的想象、象征和现实三个层次的学说。

Sigmund Freud

西格蒙德·弗洛伊德(1856—1939),犹太人,医学博士,奥地利神经学家,也是精神分析学的奠基人,20 世纪最伟大的心理学家之一。弗洛伊德提出意识体验的三层结构(意识、前意识、无意识)、人格的三重结构(本我、自我、超我)、"俄狄浦斯情结"、"力比多"、"心理防卫机制"等概念。著有《梦的解析》(1899)、《日常生活之精神病学》(1901)、《图腾与禁忌》(1913)、《超越快乐原则》(1920)、《自我与本我》(1923)、《幻象之未来》(1927)、《文明及其不满》(1929)、《精神分析概要》(1940)等。弗洛伊德开创的精神分析学是一种通过病人和精神分析师之间的对话来治疗精神病理学的临床方法。尽管后来精神分析学被认为想象推断多于实证,并非有效的临床治疗方法,但它在临床心理学的发展史上具有重要意义,在心理学、精神病学、心理治疗和人文学科中仍然具有影响力。

Creative Writers and Daydreaming

（Freud，Sigmund. Creative Writers and Daydreaming. *The Freud Reader*. Peter Gay ed. New York：W. W. Norton & Company，1995，pp. 436-442.）

西方文论史上关于艺术创造活动的最早记载，大都强调“灵感”，突出艺术过程的某种神秘意味。而经过弗洛伊德的心理学分析，艺术活动中的心理状态却得到了完全不同的解释。弗洛伊德把文学作品看作是作者无意识的表现，把文学文本看作符号或梦，把作者看作梦想家，而写作则可以满足一种在童年形成并隐藏在潜意识中的难以言喻的欲望。弗洛伊德在《作家与白日梦》一文中将创造性作家的创作与白日梦做了比较，指出作家从现实走向幻想，将自己的情感投射到主人公身上，通过创作加工和改造自己的白日梦，使之为他人所接受，使自己暂时摆脱压抑，获得快乐。作家的想象活动就像孩子们玩游戏时的心理想象，一部创造性的文学作品就像一个白日梦，成为作者童年游戏的延续或替代。

Sigmund Freud

Creative Writers and Daydreaming

（Freud，Sigmund. Creative Writers and Daydreaming. From *The Freud Reader*. Edited by Peter Gay. New York：W. W. Norton & Company，1995，pp. 436-442.）

The informal diction Freud employed in this paper is agood instance of his capacity for adjusting his style to his audience. He delivered the paper to about ninety laymen，brought together by one of his publishers，Hugo Heller，late in 1907. The English title misses the main psychoanalytic point of the paper，which connects the play of children with the *fantasies* of “creative writers”（Freud uses the economical，untranslatable German word “Dichter，” which embraces story-tellers，novelists，poets，and playwrights）. It is interesting to note that Freud gives to aesthetic pleasure the name of “fore-pleasure，”which links it to sexual pleasure. Altogether，the paper，however casual its tone，is a serious contribution to the psychology of creativity，and hence part of Freud's effort at constructing a general psychology.

We laymen have always been intensely curious to know—like the Cardinal who put a similar question to Ariosto[1]—from what sources that strange being，the creative writer，draws his material，and how he manages to make such an impression on us with it and to arouse in us emotions of which, perhaps, we had not even thought ourselves capable. Our interest is only heightened the more by the fact that, if we ask him, the writer himself gives us no explanation, or none that is satisfactory; and it is not at all weakened by our knowledge that not even the clearest insight into the determinants of his choice of material and into the nature of the art of creating imaginative form will ever help to make creative writers of *us*.

If we could at least discover inourselves or in people like ourselves an activity which was in some way akin to creative writing! An examination of it would then give us a hope of obtaining the beginnings of an explanation of the creative work of writers. And, indeed, there is some prospect of this being possible. After all, creative writers themselves like to lessen the distance between their kind and the common run of humanity; they so often assure us that every man is a poet at heart and that the last poet will not perish till the last man does.

Should we not look for the first traces of imaginative activity as early as in childhood? The child's best-loved and most intense occupation is with his play or games. Might we not say that every child at play behaves like a creative writer, in that he creates a world of his own, or, rather, re-arranges the things of his world in a new way which pleases him? It would be wrong to think he does not take that world seriously; on the contrary, he takes his play very seriously and he expends large amounts of emotion on it. The opposite of play is not what is serious but what is real. In spite of all the emotion with which he cathects his world of play, the child distinguishes it quite well from reality; and he likes to link his imagined objects and situations to the tangible and visible things of the real world. This linking is all that differentiates the child's 'play' from 'phantasying'.

The creative writer does the same as the child at play. He creates a world of phantasy which he takes very seriously—that is, which he invests with large amounts of emotion—while separating it sharply from reality. Language has preserved this relationship between children's play and poetic creation. It gives [in German] the name of '*Spiel*' ['play'] to those forms of imaginative writing which require to be linked to tangible objects and which are capable of representation. It speaks of a '*Lustspiel*' or '*Trauerspiel*' ['comedy' or 'tragedy': literally, 'pleasure play' or 'mourning play'] and describes those who carry out the representation as '*Schauspieler*' ['players': literally 'show-players']. The unreality of the writer's imaginative world, however, has very important consequences for the technique of his art; for many things which, if they were real, could give no enjoyment, can do so in the play of phantasy, and many excitements which, in themselves, are actually distressing, can become a source of pleasure for the hearers and spectators at the performance of a writer's work.

There is another consideration for the sake of which we will dwell a moment longer on this contrast between reality and play. When the child has grown up and has ceased to play, and after he has been labouring for decades to envisage the realities of life with proper seriousness, he may one day find himself in a mental situation which once more undoes the contrast between play and reality. As an adult he can look back on the intense seriousness with which he once carried on his games in childhood; and, by equating his ostensibly serious occupations of today with his childhood games, he can throw off the too heavy burden imposed on him by life and win the high yield of pleasure afforded by *humour*.

As people grow up, then, they cease to play, and they seem to give up the yield of pleasure which theygained from playing. But whoever understands the human mind knows that hardly anything is harder for a man than to give up a pleasure which he has once experienced. Actually, we can never give anything up; we only exchange one thing for another. What appears to be a renunciation is really the formation of a substitute or surrogate. In the same way, the growing child, when he stops playing, gives up nothing but the link with real objects; instead of *playing*, he now *phantasies*. He builds castles in the air and creates what are called *day-dreams*. I believe that most people construct phantasies at times in their lives. This is a fact which has long been overlooked and whose importance has therefore not been sufficiently appreciated.

People's phantasies are less easy to observe than the play of children. The child, it is true, plays by himself or forms a closed psychical system with other children for the purposes of a game; but even though he may not play his game in front of the grown-ups, he does not, on the other hand, conceal it from them. The adult, on the contrary, is ashamed of his phantasies and hides them from other people. He cherishes his phantasies as his most intimate possessions, and as a rule he would rather confess his misdeeds than tell anyone his phantasies. It may come about that for that reason he believes he is the only person who invents such phantasies and has no idea that creations of this kind are widespread among other people. This difference in the behaviour of a person who plays and a person who phantasies is accounted for by the motives of these two activities, which are nevertheless adjuncts to each other.

A child's play is determined by wishes: in point of fact by a single wish—one that helps in his upbringing—the wish to be big and grown up. He is always playing at being 'grown up', and in his games he imitates what he knows about the lives of his elders. He has no reason to conceal this wish. With the adult, the case is different. On the one hand, he knows that he is expected not to go on playing or phantasying any longer, but to act in the real world; on the other hand, some of the wishes which give rise to his phantasies are of a kind which it is essential to conceal. Thus he is ashamed of his phantasies as being childish and as being unpermissible.

But, you will ask, if people make such a mystery of their phantasying, how is it that we know such a lot about it? Well, there is a class of human beings upon whom, not a god, indeed, but a stern goddess—Necessity—has allotted the task of telling what they suffer and what things give them happiness.[2] These are the victims of nervous illness, who are obliged to tell their phantasies, among other things, to the doctor by whom they expect to be cured by mental treatment. This is our best source of knowledge, and we have since found good reason to suppose that our patients tell us nothing that we might not also hear from healthy people.

Let us now make ourselves acquainted with a few of the characteristics of phantasying. We may lay it down that a happy person never phantasies, only an unsatisfied one. The motive forces of phantasies are unsatisfied wishes, and every single phantasy is the fulfilment of a wish, a correction of unsatisfying reality. These motivating wishes vary according to the sex, character and circumstances of the person who is having the phantasy; but they fall naturally into two main groups. They are either ambitious wishes, which serve to elevate the subject's personality; or they are erotic ones. In young women the erotic wishes predominate almost exclusively, for their ambition is as a rule absorbed by erotic trends. In young men egoistic and ambitious wishes come to the fore clearly enough alongside of erotic ones. But we will not lay stress on the opposition between the two trends; we would rather emphasize the fact that they are often united. Just as, in many altar-pieces, the portrait of the donor is to be seen in a corner of the picture, so, in the majority of ambitious phantasies, we can discover in some corner or other the lady for whom the creator of the phantasy performs all his heroic deeds and at whose feet all his triumphs are laid. Here, as you see, there are strong enough motives for concealment; the well-brought-up young woman is only allowed a minimum of erotic desire, and the young man has to learn to suppress the excess of self-regard which he brings with him from the spoilt days of his childhood, so that he may find his place in a society which is full of other individuals making equally strong demands.

We must not suppose that the products of this imaginative activity—the various phantasies, castles in the air and day-dreams—are stereotyped or unalterable. On the contrary, they fit themselves in to the subject's shifting impressions of life, change with every change in his situation, and receive from every fresh active impression what might be called a 'date-mark'. The relation of a phantasy to time is in general very important. We may say that it hovers, as it were, between three times—the three moments of time which our ideation involves. Mental work is linked to some current impression, some provoking occasion in the present which has been able to arouse one of the subject's major wishes. From there it harks back to a memory of an earlier experience (usually an infantile one) in which this wish was fulfilled; and it now creates a situation relating to the future which represents a fulfilment of the wish. What it thus creates is a day-dream or phantasy, which carries about it traces of its origin from the occasion which provoked it and from the memory. Thus past, present and future are strung together, as it were, on the thread of the wish that runs through them.

A very ordinary example may serve to make what I have said clear. Let us take the case of apoor orphan boy to whom you have given the address of some employer where he may perhaps find a job. On his way there he may indulge in a day-dream appropriate to the situation from which it arises. The content of his phantasy will perhaps be something like this. He is given a job, finds favour with his new employer, makes himself indispensable in the business, is taken into his employer's family, marries the charming young daughter of the house, and then himself becomes a director of the business, first as his employer's partner and then as his successor. In this phantasy, the dreamer has regained what he possessed in his happy childhood—the protecting house, the loving parents and the first objects of his affectionate feelings. You will see from this example the way in which the wish makes use of an occasion in the present to construct, on the pattern of the past, a picture of the future.

There is a great deal more that could be said about phantasies; but I will only allude as briefly as possible to certain points. If phantasies become over-luxuriant and over-powerful, the conditions are laid for an onset of neurosis or psychosis.

Phantasies, moreover, are the immediate mental precursors of the distressing symptoms complained of by our patients. Here a broad by-path branches off into pathology.

I cannot pass over the relation of phantasies to dreams. Our dreams at night are nothing else than phantasies like these, as we can demonstrate from the interpretation of dreams. Language, in its unrivalled wisdom, long ago decided the question of the essential nature of dreams by giving the name of 'day-dreams' to the airy creations of phantasy. If the meaning of our dreams usually remains obscure to us in spite of this pointer, it is because of the circumstance that at night there also arise in us wishes of which we are ashamed; these we must conceal from ourselves, and they have consequently been repressed, pushed into the unconscious. Repressed wishes of this sort and their derivatives are only allowed to come to expression in a very distorted form. When scientific work had succeeded in elucidating this factor of *dream-distortion*, it was no longer difficult to recognize that night-dreams are wish-fulfilments in just the same way as day-dreams—the phantasies which we all know so well.

So much for phantasies. And now for the creative writer. May we really attempt to compare the imaginative writer with the 'dreamer in broad daylight', and his creations with day-dreams? Here we must begin by making an initial distinction. We must separate writers who, like the ancient authors of epics and tragedies, take over their material readymade, from writers who seem to originate their own material. We will keep to the latter kind, and, for the purposes of our comparison, we will choose not the writers most highly esteemed by the critics, but the less pretentious authors of novels, romances and short stories, who nevertheless have the widest and most eager circle of readers of both sexes. One feature above all cannot fail to strike us about the creations of these story-writers: each of them has a hero who is the centre of interest, for whom the writer tries to win our sympathy by every possible means and whom he seems to place under the protection of a special Providence. If, at the end of one chapter of my story, I leave the hero unconscious and bleeding from severe wounds, I am sure to find him at the beginning of the next being carefully nursed and on the way to recovery; and if the first volume closes with the ship he is in going down in a storm at sea, I am certain, at the opening of the second volume, to read of his miraculous rescue—a rescue without which the story could not proceed. The feeling of security with which I follow the hero through his perilous adventures is the same as the feeling with which a hero in real life throws himself into the water to save a drowning man or exposes himself to the enemy's fire in order to storm a battery. It is the true heroic feeling, which one of our best writers has expressed in an inimitable phrase: 'Nothing can happen to *me*!'[3] It seems to me, however, that through this revealing characteristic of invulnerability we can immediately recognize His Majesty the Ego, the hero alike of every day-dream and of every story.

Other typical features of these egocentric stories point to the same kinship. The fact that all the women in the novel invariably fall in love with the hero can hardly be looked on as a portrayal of reality, but it is easily understood as a necessary constituent of a day-dream. The same is true of the fact that the other characters in the story are sharply divided into good and bad, in defiance of the variety of human characters that are to be observed in real life. The 'good' ones are the helpers, while the 'bad' ones are the enemies and rivals, of the ego which has become the hero of the story.

We are perfectly aware that very many imaginative writingsare far removed from the model of the naïve day-dream; and yet I cannot suppress the suspicion that even the most extreme deviations from that model could be linked with it through an uninterrupted series of transitional cases. It has struck me that in many of what are known as 'psychological' novels only one person—once again the hero—is described from within. The author sits inside his mind, as it were, and looks at the other characters from outside. The psychological novel in general no doubt owes its special nature to the inclination of the modern writer to split up his ego, by self-observation, into many part-egos, and, in consequence, to personify the conflicting currents of his own mental life in several heroes. Certain novels, which might be described as 'eccentric', seem to stand in quite special contrast to the type of the daydream. In these, the person who is introduced as the hero plays only a very small active part; he sees the actions and sufferings of other people pass before him like a spectator. Many of Zola's later works belong to this category. But I must point out that the psychological analysis of individuals who are not creative writers, and who diverge in some respects from the so-called norm, has shown us analogous variations of the daydream, in which the ego contents itself with the role of spectator.

If our comparison of the imaginative writer with the day-dreamer, and of poetical creation with the day-dream, is to be of any value, it must, above all, show itself in some way or other fruitful. Let us, for instance, try to apply to these authors' works the thesis we laid down earlier concerning the relation between phantasy and the three periods of time and the wish which runs through them; and, with its help, let us try to study the connections that exist between the life of the writer and his works. No one has known, as a rule, what expectations to frame in approaching this problem; and often the connection has been thought of in much too simple terms. In the light of the insight we have gained from phantasies, we ought to expect the following state of affairs. A strong experience in the present awakens in the creative writer a memory of an earlier experience (usually belonging to his childhood) from which there now proceeds a wish which finds its fulfilment in the creative work. The work itself exhibits elements of the recent provoking occasion as well as of the old memory.

Do not be alarmed at the complexity of this formula. I suspect that in fact it will prove to be too exiguous a pattern. Nevertheless, it may contain a first approach to the true state of affairs; and, from some experiments I have made, I am inclined to think that this way of looking at creative writings may turn out not unfruitful. You will not forget that the stress it lays on childhood memories in the writer's life—a stress which may perhaps seem puzzling—is ultimately derived from the assumption that a piece of creative writing, like a day-dream, is a continuation of, and a substitute for, what was once the play of childhood.

We must not neglect, however, to go back to the kind of imaginative works which we have to recognize, not as original creations, but as the re-fashioning of ready-made and familiar material. Even here, the writer keeps a certain amount of independence, which can express itself in the choice of material and in changes in it which are often quite extensive. In so far as the material is already at hand, however, it is derived from the popular treasure-house of myths, legends and fairy tales. The study of constructions of folk-psychology such as these is far from being complete, but it is extremely probable that myths, for instance, are distorted vestiges of the wishful phantasies of whole nations, the *secular dreams* of youthful humanity.

You will say that, although I have put the creative writer first in the title of my paper, I have told you for less about him than about phantasies. I am aware of that, and I must try to excuse it by pointing to the present state of our knowledge. All I have been able to do is to throw out some encouragements and suggestions which, starting from the study of phantasies, lead on to the problem of the writers choice of his literary material. As for the other problem—by what means the creative writer achieves the emotional effects in us that are aroused by his creations—we have as yet not touched on it at all. But I should like at least to point out to you the path that leads from our discussion of phantasies to the problems of poetical effects.

You will remember how I have said that the day-dreamer carefully conceals his phantasies from other people because he feels he has reasons for being ashamed of them. I should now add that even if he were to communicate them to us he could give us no pleasure by his disclosures. Such phantasies, when we learn them, repel us or at least leave us cold. But when a creative writer presents his plays to us or tells us what we are inclined to take to be his personal day-dreams, we experience a great pleasure, and one which probably arises from the confluence of many sources. How the writer accomplishes this is his innermost secret; the essential *ars poetica* lies in the technique of overcoming the feeling of repulsion in us which is undoubtedly connected with the barriers that rise between each single ego and the others. We can guess two of the methods used by this technique. The writer softens the character of his egoistic day-dreams by altering and disguising it, and he bribes us by the purely formal—that is, aesthetic—yield of pleasure which he offers us in the presentation of his phantasies. We give the name of an *incentive bonus*, or a *fore-pleasure*, to a yield of pleasure such as this, which is offered to us so as to make possible the release of still greater pleasure arising from deeper psychical sources. In my opinion, all the aesthetic pleasure which a creative writer affords us has the character of a forepleasure of this kind, and our actual enjoyment of an imaginative work proceeds from a liberation of tensions in our minds. It may even be that not a little of this effect is due to the writer's enabling us thenceforward to enjoy our own day-dreams without self-reproach or shame. This brings us to the threshold of new, interesting and complicated enquiries; but also, at least for the moment, to the end of our discussion.

Notes

1. Cardinal Ippolito d'Este was Aristotle's first patron, whom he dedicated to *Orlando Furioso*. The poet's only reward was the question "Where did you find so many stories, Lodovico?"

2. This sentence, as the editors note, is an allusion (unmistakable to any educated German or Austrian) to Goethe's Torquato Tasso: in the concluding scene, the troubled hero of the play exclaims, "Und wenn der Mensch in seiner Qual verstummt, Gab mir ein Gott zu sagen, wie ich leide—And when a man fells silent in

his torment / A godgranted me to tell how I suffer."

3. 'Es kann dir nix g'schehen!' This phrase from Anzengruber, the Viennese dramatist, was a favourite one of Freud's.

Jacques Lacan

雅克·拉康(1901—1981),法国哲学家、精神分析学家和精神病学家,被称为自弗洛伊德以来最具争议性的精神分析学家,也是结构主义代表人物。1953 年起,拉康在巴黎的研究班正式向公众开放,到 1980 年止,其间从未间断,共举办大型研究班 26 个。拉康的讲座吸引了大量青年、精神分析学家和哲学家,特别是当时法国思想界众多名家的参加与支持,影响了法国 20 世纪六七十年代大批知识分子,尤其是与后结构主义研究相关的知识分子。拉康的主要成就是从结构主义语言学角度对弗洛伊德的观点进行重新阐释。他为心理分析理论引入了语言学的范式,认为无意识的结构犹如语言,将"无意识"的结构与"语言"的结构相并列,使其直接导入一种关于"无意识"的语言和结构研究。拉康的著作神秘、隐晦、富于技巧而有诗意,读来艰涩难懂。他的思想对后结构主义、批判理论、语言学、20 世纪法国哲学、电影理论和临床精神分析都产生了重大影响。

Desire and the Interpretation of Desire in *Hamlet*

(Lacan, Jacques. Desire and the Interpretation of Desire in *Hamlet*. *Yale French Studies*, No. 55/56, Literature and Psychoanalysis. The Question of Reading: Otherwise, 1977, pp. 11-52)

1958—1959 年,拉康在巴黎圣安娜医院以《欲望及其阐释》为题做研究班讲座,每周一次。《欲望及对〈哈姆雷特〉中欲望的阐释》就是该系列讲座中的第六个。这篇作品在 20 世纪 70 年代由拉康的继承人雅克-阿莱茵·米勒整理后,于 1977 年在美国耶鲁大学的《耶鲁法国研究》杂志第 55、56 期先行刊出,一时间风行英语世界。文中,拉康用精神分析式的语言学构架对《哈姆雷特》全剧进行全面分析,哈姆雷特的欲望结构被化作了语言结构。他认为,哈姆雷特迟疑不决,不能实行复仇行动不是偶然的,根本原因在于他处于一个心理-语言结构之中，他没有本人行动的自由，只能遵守“他人”的规则。拉康把精神分析与索绪尔结构主义语言学结合为一，用语言学概念改造精神分析，用后精神理论为争论已久的“哈姆雷特行动之谜”提出了一种新的诠释。

The Object Ophelia

As a sort of come-on, I announced that I would speak today about that piece of bait named Ophelia, and I'll be as good as my word.

Our purpose, as you remember, is to show the tragedy of desire as it appears in *Hamlet*, human desire, that is, such as we are concerned with in psychoanalysis.

We distort this desire and confuse it with other terms if we fail to locate it in reference to a set of co-ordinates that, as Freud showed, establish the subject in a certain position of dependence upon the signifier. The signifier is not a reflection, a product pure and simple of what are called interhuman relationships—all psychoanalytic experience indicates the contrary. To account for the presuppositions of this experience, we must refer to a topological system without which all the phenomena produced in our domain would be indistinguishable and meaningless. The illustration shows the essential co-ordinates of this topology[1].

The story of *Hamlet* (and this is why I chose it) reveals a most vivid dramatic sense of this topology, and this is the source of its exceptional power of captivation. Shakespeare's poetic skill doubtless guided him along the way, step by step, but we can also assume that he introduced into the play some observations from his own experience, however indirectly.

Shakespeare's play contains one shift in the plot that distinguishes it from previous treatments of the story, including both the narratives of Saxo Grammaticus[2] and Belleforest[3] and the other plays of which we possess fragments. This shift involves the character Ophelia.

Ophelia is present, to be sure, from the beginning of the legend on. She appears in the early versions, as I've said, as the bait in the trap that Hamlet doesn't fall into, first because he's warned in advance, and then because Ophelia herself refuses to have any part of it, having long been in love with the prince, according to Belleforest's version. Perhaps Shakespeare merely extended her function in the plot, which is to capture Hamlet's secret by surprise. But she thus becomes one of the innermost elements in Hamlet's drama, the drama of Hamlet as the man who has lost the way of his desire. She provides an essential pivot in the hero's progress toward his mortal rendezvous with his act—an act that he carries out, in some sense, in spite of himself. There is a level in the subject on which it can be said that his fate is expressed in terms of a pure signifier, a level at which he is merely the reverse-side of a message that is not even his own. Well, Hamlet is the very image of this level of subjectivity, as we shall see even more clearly in what follows.

1

Our first step in this direction was to express the extent to which the play is dominated by the Mother as Other [*Autre*][4], i. e., the primordial subject of the demand [*la demande*]. The omnipotence of which we are always speaking in psychoanalysis is first of all the omnipotence of the subject as subject of the first demand, and this omnipotence must be related back to the Mother.

The principal subject of the play is beyond all doubt Prince Hamlet. The play is the drama of an individual subjectivity, and the hero is always present on stage, more than in any other play. How is the desire of the Other manifested in the very perspective of this subject, Prince Hamlet? This desire, of the mother, is essentially manifested in the fact that, confronted on one hand with an eminent, idealized, exalted object—his father—and on the other with the degraded, despicable object Claudius, the criminal and adulterous brother, Hamlet does not choose.

His mother does not choose because of something present inside her, like an instinctive voracity. The sacrosanct genital object that we recently added to our technical vocabulary appears to her as an object to be enjoyed [*objet d'une jouissance*] in what is truly the direct satisfaction of a need, and nothing else. This is the aspect that makes Hamlet waver in his abjuration of his mother. Even when he transmits to her—in the crudest, cruellest terms—the essential message with which the ghost, his father, has entrusted him, he still first appeals to her to abstain. Then, a moment later, his appeal fails, and he sends her to Claudius' bed, into the arms of the man who once again will not fail to make her yield.

This fall, this abandon, gives us a model that enables us to conceive how it is that Hamlet's desire—his zeal with respect to an act that he so longs to carry out that the whole world becomes for him a living reproach for his perpetual inadequacy to his own will—how this zeal always flags. The dependence of his desire on the Other subject forms the permanent dimension of Hamlet's drama.

To get a better grip on the problem we must go into a psychological detail that would remain utterly enigmatic if it were not placed in the total orientation that determines the direction and meaning of the tragedy: how this permanent dimension touches the very nerve and sinew of Hamlet's will—which would appear in my diagram as the hook, the question mark, of the *Che vuoi?* of subjectivity constituted and articulated in the Other.

The end-term that buttresses this model of the subject and his question, is symbolized on our graph by the barred subject ($) in the presence of the object *a* [5]—in the economic system of the psyche we call this the fantasy. Desire, which can be situated on the line A [$◊D] at a variable indeterminate point, finds in the fantasy its reference, its substratum, its precise tuning in the imaginary register.

There is something mysterious about the fantasy; indeed, it's ambiguous and paradoxical. It is on one hand the end-term of desire, and on the other hand, if we approach it from one of its aspects, it's actually located in the conscious: ambiguous indeed. Insofar as the fantasy marks every human passion with those traits which we call perverse, it appears in a sufficiently paradoxical form to have long ago motivated the rejection of the phantasmatic dimension as being on the order of the absurd. In this respect an essential step was taken in the present age when psychoanalysis undertook the interpretation of the fantasy in its very perversity. This interpretation was made possible only by placing the fantasy in an economy of the unconscious—this is what you see in the graph.

On this graph the fantasy is hooked up on the circuit of the unconscious, a very different one from the circuit commanded by the subject, which I call the level of the demand [*demande*]. In the normal state of affairs, nothing from the unconscious circuit is carried over to the level of the message, of the signified of the Other, which is the sum and module of the significations acquired by the subject in human discourse. The fantasy is not communicated to the message level: it remains separate and unconscious. When, on the other hand, it does cross over to the level of the message, we find ourselves in an atypical situation. The phases in which the fantasy makes this crossover are of a more or less pathological order. We shall give a name to these moments of crossover, of communication, which, as the diagram indicates, can take place only in one direction. I underscore this essential statement, because our purpose here is to refine our understanding and application of this apparatus.

For now, let us consider only how the moment in which Hamlet's desire becomes distracted and deflected functions in Shakespeare's tragedy, insofar as this moment must be related back to the precise adjustments of his imaginary register. Ophelia's place in this constellation is on the level of the letter *a* as it appears in our representation of the fantasy. [....]

With respect to the object *a*, at once image and pathos, the subject feels himself to be in an imaginary situation of otherness. This object satisfies no need and is itself already relative, i. e., placed in relation to the subject. It is obvious from simple phenomenology (and this is something to which I shall return in a few moments) that the subject is present in the fantasy. And the object is the object of desire only by virtue of being the end-term of the fantasy. The object takes the place, I would say, of what the subject is—symbolically—deprived of.

This may seem a bit abstract to those who have not accompanied us along the road that has led up to this point. What is it that the subject is deprived of? The phallus; and it is from the phallus that the object gets its function in the fantasy, and from the phallus that desire is constituted with the fantasy as its reference.

The object of the fantasy, image and pathos, is that other element that takes the place of what the subject is symbolically deprived of. Thus the imaginary object is in a position to condense in itself the virtues or the dimension of being and to become that veritable delusion of being [*leurre de l'être*] that Simone Weil[6] treats when she focuses on the very densest and most opaque relationship of a man to the object of his desire: the relationship of Molière's[7] Miser to his strongbox. This is the culmination of the fetish character of the object of human desire. Indeed all objects of the human world have this character, from one angle at least. [....]

The opaque character of the object *a* in the imaginary fantasy determines it in its most pronounced forms as the pole of perverse desire. It is the structural element of perversions, insofar as perversion is characterized by the complete emphasis in the fantasy on the strictly imaginary term, *a*. In parentheses with it we also encounter *a* plus *b* plus *c* and so forth: the most elaborate combinations of sequelae, of lingering traces combined by chance, by means of which a fantasy has crystallized and functions in a perverse desire. But however bizarre the fantasy of perverse desire may appear to you, never forget that the subject is always in some way present and involved in that fantasy. In the fantasy the subject always stands in some relationship to the pathos of existence—to the suffering of existing itself or that of existing as a term in a sexual configuration. For a sadistic fantasy to endure, the subject's interest in the person who suffers humiliation must obviously be due to the possibility of the subject's being submitted to the same humiliation himself. This is the phenomenological point to which I was alluding a few moments ago. It's a wonder indeed that people could ever think of avoiding this dimension and could treat the sadistic tendency as an instance of primal aggression pure and simple.

2

The time has come to articulate the true opposition between perversion and neurosis.

Perversion is indeed something articulate, interpretable, analyzable, and on precisely the same level as neurosis. In the fantasy, as I have said, an essential relationship of the subject to his being is localized and fixed. Well, whereas in the perversion, the accent is on the object *a*, the neurosis can be situated as having its accent on the other term of the fantasy, the $.

The fantasy is located at the extreme tip, the end-point of the subject's question, as if it were its buttress [*butée* : lit., abutment], just as the subject tries to get control of himself in the fantasy, in the space beyond the demand. This is because he must find again in the very discourse of the Other what was lost for him, the subject, the moment he entered into this discourse. What ultimately matters is not the truth but the hour [*l'heure*] of truth.

This is what permits us to specify the factor that most profoundly distinguishes the fantasy of neurosis from the fantasy of perversion.

The fantasy of perversion is namable. It is in space. It suspends an essential relationship. It is not atemporal but rather outside of time. In neurosis, on the contrary, the very basis of the relationships of subject to object on the fantasy level, is the relationship of the subject to time. The object is charged with the significance sought in what I call the hour of truth, in which the object is always at another hour, fast or slow, early or late.

I have said before that hysteria is characterized by the function of an unsatisfied desire and obsession by the function of an impossible desire. But beyond these two terms the two cases are distinguished by inverse relationships with time: the obsessive neurotic always repeats the initial germ of his trauma, i. e., a certain precipitancy, a fundamental lack of maturation.

This is at the base of neurotic behavior, in its most general form: the subject tries to find his sense of time [*lire son heure*] in his object, and it is even in the object that he will learn to tell time [*lire l'heure*]. This is where we get back to our friend Hamlet, to whom everyone can attribute at will all the forms of neurotic behavior, as far as you want to go, i. e., up to character neurosis. The first factor that I indicated to you in Hamlet's structure wash is situation of dependence with respect to the desire of the Other, the desire of his mother. Here now is the second factor that I ask you to recognize: Hamlet is constantly suspended in the time of the Other, throughout the entire story until the very end.

Do you remember one of the first turning-points we focussed on when we were beginning to decipher the text of *Hamlet*? During the play scene the king becomes unsettled and visibly reveals his own guilt, incapable of viewing the dramatization of his own crime. Hamlet relishes his triumph and mocks the king. But on the way to the meeting he has already arranged with his mother, he comes upon his stepfather in prayer: Claudius is shaken to the depths of his being by the scene that has just shown him the very countenance and program of his deed. Hamlet stands before this Claudius, who by every indication is not only in no state to defend himself but also does not even see the threat that hangs over his head. And Hamlet stops, because it's not time. It's not the hour of the Other: not time for the Other to render his "audit" to heaven. That would be too kind, from one point of view, or too cruel, from another. That might not avenge his father properly, because prayer, being a gesture of repentance, might open up the way to salvation for Claudius. In any case, one thing is sure: Hamlet, who has just managed to "catch the conscience of the king" as planned—stops. Not for a moment does he think that his time has come. Whatever may happen later, this is not the hour of the Other, and he suspends his action. Whatever Hamlet may do, he will do it only at the hour of the Other.

Hamlet accepts everything. Let's not forget that at the beginning, in the state of disgust he was already in (even before his meeting with the ghost) because of his mother's remarriage, he thought only of leaving for Wittenberg. A recent commentary on a certain practicality that is becoming more and more typical of present-day life, used this as an illustration, noting that Hamlet was the best example of the fact that many dramatic crises can be avoided by the prompt issuance of passports. If Hamlet had been given his papers to travel to Wittenberg, there would have been no drama.

When he stays on, it is the hour of his parents. When he suspends his crime, it is the hour of the others. When he leaves for England, it is the hour of his stepfather. It's the hour of Rosencrantz and Guildenstern when he sends them on ahead to death—with a casualness that amazed Freud—by means of a bit of hocus-pocus that he brings off not half badly. And it is the hour of Ophelia, the hour of her suicide, when the tragedy will run its course, in a moment when Hamlet has just realized that it's not hard to kill a man, the time to say "one"... he won't know what hit him.

He receives word of an event that in no way seems to promise an opportunity to kill Claudius: a tournament, the rules of which have been worked out to the last detail. They tempt him with the stakes—all precious objects, swords, fittings, and other things that have value only as luxuries; this should be followed in the text, for these are the nuances of the world of the collector. Hamlet's sense of rivalry and honor is aroused by the assumption that Laertes is the more skillful swordsman and by the handicap thus granted to Hamlet in the terms of the wager. This complicated ceremony is a trap for him to fall into, laid by his stepfather and his friend Laertes: we know this, but Hamlet does not. For him, going along with the wager will be a lark, like playing hookey. Still, he feels a slight warning signal in the region of his heart: something troubles him. For a moment here the dialectic of foreboding brings its special accent to the play. But, all in all, it is still at the hour of the Other, and what's more, for the sake of the Other's wager (for it is Claudius, not Hamlet, whose possessions are at stake), wearing the king's colors, for his stepfather's sake, that Hamlet enters into this supposedly friendly combat with a man considered to be a better swordsman than he. Thus Claudius and Laertes have aroused his sense of rivalry and honor, as part of a trap that is calculated to be foolproof.

Thus he rushes into the trap laid by the Other. All that's changed is the energy and fire with which he rushes into it. Until the last term, until the final hour, Hamlet's hour, in which he is mortally wounded before he wounds his enemy, the tragedy follows its course and attains completion at the hour of Other: this is the absolutely essential framework for our conception of what is involved here.

This is the sense in which Hamlet's drama has the precise meta-physical resonance of the question of the modern hero. Indeed, something has changed since classical antiquity in the relationship of the hero to his fate.

As I have said, the thing that distinguishes Hamlet from Oedipus is that Hamlet *knows*. This characteristic explains, for example, Hamlet's madness. In the tragedies of antiquity, there are mad heroes, but, to the best of my knowledge, there are no heroes—in tragedy, I say, not in legends—no heroes who feign madness. Hamlet, however, does.

I am not saying that everything in his madness comes down to feigning, but I do underscore the fact that the essential characteristic in the original legend, i. e. , in the versions of Saxo Grammaticus and Belleforest, is that the hero feigns madness because he knows that he is in a position of weakness. And from that moment on, everything hinges on the question of what's going on in his mind.

However superficial this characteristic may seem to you, it's still the thing that Shakespeare seized on for his *Hamlet*. He chose the story of a hero who is forced to feign madness in order to follow the winding paths that lead him to the completion of his act. The person who knows is indeed in such a perilous position, marked for failure and sacrifice, that he is led to feign madness, and even, as Pascal says, to be mad along with everyone else. Feigning madness is thus one of the dimensions of what we might call the strategy of the modern hero.

Thus we arrive at the point at which Ophelia must fulfill her role. If the structure of the play is really as complex as I have just portrayed it as being, you may be wondering, what is the point of the character Ophelia? Ophelia is obviously essential. She is linked forever, for centuries, to the figure of Hamlet.

Some people have reproached me for the timidity with which they feel I've been proceeding. I don't think that's the case. I wouldn't want to encourage you to produce the sort of hogwash that psychoanalytic texts are full of. I'm just surprised that nobody's pointed out that Ophelia is *Ophallos*, because you find other things equally gross, flagrant, extravagant, if you just open the *Papers on Hamlet*, which Ella Sharp[8] unfortunately left unfinished and which it was perhaps a mistake to publish after her death.

Since it's getting late, I just want to stress what happens to Ophelia in the course of the play.

We first hear Ophelia spoken of as the cause of Hamlet's sad state. This is Polonius' psychoanalytic wisdom: Hamlet is sad, and that's because he's not happy, and if he's not happy, it's because of my daughter. You don't know her—

she's the very finest there is—and I, of course, as a father, could never permit her to. . . .

We first encounter Ophelia—and this makes her quite a remarkable figure already—in the context of a clinical observation. She indeed has the good fortune to be the first person Hamlet runs into after his unsettling encounter with the ghost, and she reports his behavior in terms that are worth noting.

> My lord, as I was sewing in my closet,
> Lord Hamlet, with his doublet all unbraced,
> No hat upon his head, his stockings fouled,
> Ungartered, and down-gyvèd to his ankle,
> Pale as his shirt, his knees knocking each other,
> And with a look so piteous in purport
> As if he had been loosèd out of hell
> To speak of horrors—he comes before me.
> … … … … … … … … … … … … … …
> He took me by the wrist and held me hard.
> Then goes he to the length of all his arm,
> And with his other hand thus o'er his brow
> He falls to such perusal of my face
> As'a would draw it. Long stayed he so.
> At last, a little shaking of mine arm
> And thrice his head thus waving up and down,
> He raised a sigh so piteous and profound
> As it did seem to shatter all his bulk
> And end his being. That done, he lets me go,
> And with his head over his shoulder turned
> He seemed to find his way without his eyes,
> For out o' doors he went without their helps
> And to the last bended their light on me.

(Act Ⅱ, Sc. Ⅰ)

And Polonius cries out: This is love!

This distance from the object that Hamlet takes in order to move on to whatever new and henceforth difficult identification, his vacillation in the presence of what has been until now the object of supreme exaltation, gives us the first stage, which is, to use the English word, one of "estrangement."

That's all we can say. Nevertheless, I don't believe that it's excessive to designate this moment as pathological, related to those periods of irruption, of subjective disorganization which occur when something in the fantasy wavers and makes the components of the fantasy appear. This experience, called depersonalization, in the course of which the imaginary limits between subject and object change, leads us to what is called in the strict sense the fantastic dimension [*le fantastique*].

This dimension arises when something from the imaginary structure of the fantasy is placed in communication with something that normally reaches the level of the message, i. e., the image of the other subject, in the case in which that image is my own ego. Moreover, some authors like Federn[9] note with great precision the necessary correlation between the feeling of the subject's own body and the strangeness of that which arises in a certain crisis, a certain rupture, when the object as such is attained.

I may have forced things here a bit for the purpose of interesting you by showing you how this episode is related to certain types of clinical experience. But I assure you that without reference to this pathological schema it is impossible to locate what Freud was the first to elevate to the level of analysis under the name of *das Unheimliche*, the uncanny, which is linked not, as some believed, to all sorts of irruptions from the unconscious, but rather to an imbalance that arises in the fantasy when it decomposes, crossing the limits originally assigned to it, and rejoins the image of the other subject.

In the case of Hamlet, Ophelia is after this episode completely null and dissolved as a love object. "I did love you once," Hamlet says. Henceforth his relations with Ophelia will be carried on in that sarcastic style of cruel aggression which makes these scenes—and particularly the scene that occupies the middle of the play—the strangest in all of classical literature.

In this attitude we find a trace of what I mentioned a moment ago, the perverse imbalance of the fantasmatic relationship, when the fantasy is tipped toward the object. Hamlet no longer treats Ophelia like a woman at all. She becomes in his eyes the childbearer to every sin, a future "breeder of sinners," destined to succumb to every calumny. She is no longer the reference-point for a life that Hamlet condemns in its essence. In short, what is taking place here is the destruction and loss of the object. For the subject the object appears, if I may put it this way, on the outside. The subject is no longer the object: he rejects it with all the force of his being and will not find it again until he sacrifices himself. It is in this sense that the object is here the equivalent of, assumes the place of, indeed is—the phallus.

This is the second stage in the relationship of the subject to the object. Ophelia is at this point the phallus, exteriorized and rejected by the subject as a symbol signifying life.

What is the indication of this? There's no need to resort to the etymology of "Ophelia." Hamlet speaks constantly of one thing: child-bearing. "Conception is a blessing," he tells Polonius, but keep an eye on your daughter. And all of his dialogue with Ophelia is directed at woman conceived as the bearer of that vital swelling that he curses and wishes dried up forever. The use of the word "nunnery" in Shakespeare's time indicates that it can also refer to a brothel. And isn't the relationship of the phallus and the object of desire also indicated in Hamlet's attitude during the play scene? In Ophelia's presence he says of her to his mother, "Here's metal more attractive," and wants to place his head between the girl's legs: "Lady, shall I lie in your lap?"

Considering the great interest of iconographers in the subject, I don't think it excessive to note that the list of flowers in the midst of which Ophelia drowns herself, explicitly includes "dead men's fingers." The plant in question is the *Orchis mascula*, which is related to the mandrake and hence to the phallic element. You'll find "dead men's fingers" in the *Oxford English Dictionary*, both under "finger" and in an entry of its own under "D," where Shakespeare's allusion is duly cited.

The third stage, to which I have already directed your attention several times, is the graveyard scene, in the course of which Hamlet is finally presented with the possibility of winding things up, of rushing to his fate. The whole scene is directed toward that furious battle at the bottom of the tomb, which I have stressed repeatedly, and which is entirely of Shakespeare's own invention. Here we see something like a reintegration of the object *a*, won back here at the price of mourning and death.

I should be able to finish up next time.

(15 April 1959)

注释：

1. 拓扑学。拉康从1956年开始在教学中使用拓扑学图形。

2. 萨克索·格拉玛提库斯（1160—1220），丹麦历史学家、神学家和作家。他是《丹麦人的业绩》的作者，这本书是第一部丹麦通史，莎士比亚笔下的哈姆雷特的故事可以追溯至此。

3. 弗朗索瓦·德·贝勒福雷斯特（1530—1583），法国文艺复兴时期的作家、诗人和翻译家。

4. 大写的他者。

5. 小写的客体。

6. 西蒙内·威尔（1909—1943），法国哲学家、神秘主义者和政治活动家。

7. 莫里哀（1622—1673），法国剧作家、演员和诗人，法语和世界文学中最伟大的作家之一，法国芭蕾舞喜剧的创始人。莫里哀是艺名，原名为让·巴蒂斯特·波克兰（Jean Baptiste Poquelin）。

8. 埃拉·弗里曼·夏普（1875—1947），英国早期精神分析学发展的领军人物，英国最有影响力的首批培训分析师之一。

9. 保罗·费德恩（1871—1950），奥地利精神分析学家，也是弗洛伊德理论的早期追随者和坚定支持者之一。

Chapter Six Reception Aesthetics and Reader's Response Theory

纵观古希腊以来西方批评理论的发展状况，关注读者并不是当代批评理论所独有的。柏拉图、亚里士多德、贺拉斯、朗吉努斯等古典批评家讨论文学时，主要是从文学对受众的影响开始的，但读者批评理论的兴起主要针对形式主义文论的文本自足论，代表的是一个批评思维范式的转变，不仅仅是批评视角的转移。在20世纪初的批评理论中，美国新批评主张关注"诗歌本身"和"具体作品"，反对从心理效应入手研究诗歌，认为读者的兴趣多种多样，反应各异，对于一部作品的意义，他们很难得出相同的结论，并谴责这种批评是"情感谬论"。艾弗·阿姆斯特朗·理查兹(Ivor Armstrong Richards)和威廉·燕卜逊(William Empson)作为美国新批评的重要理论提倡者，却强调读者对诗歌的情感反应。此外，在读者理论兴起之前，符号学研究已经注意到读者的重要作用。例如，安伯托·艾柯(Umberto Eco)认为有些文本(如1939年詹姆斯·乔伊斯的《芬尼根守灵夜》)是"开放式的"，其意义的产生需要读者的合作；但有些文本(如侦探小说)是"封闭式的"，读者对作品的反应是可以预测的。

一般来说，文学阐释的会话实践是力图揭示文本中隐藏的深层意义；读者导向理论认为文本的意义不是由自身产生的，而是文本与读者相互交流的结果。文本中总是有许多空白等待着读者在阅读时用他的想象力去填补。审美对象的建构只有通过读者的理解才能完成，也就是说，文本的完整意义是读者期待的结果。虽然以读者为中心的理论中有太多的学派，他们对阅读过程的问题持有不同的看法，但他们一致认为读者在理解过程中的作用不可忽视，读者不是被动地接受文本所呈现的意义，而是积极地参与到阅读过程中文本意义的建构。

从20世纪70年代以来兴起的许多以读者为中心的理论中，汉斯·罗伯特·姚斯(Hans Robert Jauss)的接受美学理论和沃尔夫冈·伊瑟尔(Wolfgang Iser)的读者反应理论是最具原创性和影响力的。姚斯在文学文本的阅读活动中强调伽达默尔在诠释学意义上的“期待视野”，使得“视野融合”成为意义产生的关键；伊瑟尔在1974年的论文《隐含读者》中提出“隐含读者”概念，突出读者对文本的积极参与。具有辉煌成就的读者反应评论家还包括诺曼·霍兰德(Norman Holland)和斯坦利·费什(Stanley Fish)等人。霍兰德主要从心理学的角度研究读者的反应。早期费什提倡一种“情感文体学”的研究方法，强调文学文本是时间的存在，即文学文本是在阅读时形成的思维，而不是空间形式存在的对象。费什认为，作品的意义是在阅读过程中实现的，是读者的期待、心理投射、结论和判断相互作用的结果。这种批判性的实践往往仔细地逐字逐句地分析文本，考察一些因素对读者阅读心理的影响。进入20世纪80年代后，费什再次提出了“阐释群体”的概念。他认为，使用相同解释策略的读者形成了一个解释共同体，读者对文学作品的主观反应实际上是受到所属解释共同体影响的结果。

Hans Robert Jauss

汉斯·罗伯特·姚斯(1921—1997)，德国文艺理论家、美学家，接受美学的主要创立者和代表人物。他深受老师伽达默尔的影响，从阐释学角度对文学和文学史进行研究。姚斯在批判前人的基础上，力图建立较完善的文学史科学，批判将文学与社会历史分裂、对立的倾向，重建对文学的美学思考与历史思考，解决“文学史悖论”。姚斯后期转向了对接受与接受史的审美经验的研究，认为只有深入研究审美经验，才能推进接受美学的发展。主要著作有《文学史作为向文学理论的挑战》《文学范式的改变》《审美经验小辩》《审美经验与文学阐释学》等。

Literary History as a Challenge to Literary Theory

(Jauss, Hans Robert. Literary History as a Challenge to Literary Theory. *New Literary History*, Vol. 2, No. 1, A Symposium on Literary History, 1970, pp. 7-37.)

1967年，姚斯被聘为康斯坦茨大学教授时，在就职典礼上发表一篇演说——《研究文学史的意图是什么？为什么？》，后来这篇演讲稿发表出版时更名为《文学史作为向文学理论的挑战》，得到欧洲和美国批评界的认可，一般认为是接受美学的诞生宣言。以伽达默尔的阐释学哲学和美学为基础，姚斯在《文学史作为向文学理论的挑战》中指出文学史应以读者为中心，文学史是由“作者、作品、读者”共同构成的创作与审美历史，是作家与文学接受者共同的理想史与艺术史。他的理论具有浓厚的阐释学色彩，强调对文本意义的解读，认为文本的意义要通过过去与现在的关系来把握，文本的解读在很大程度上是一个重构读者“期待视野”的过程。《文学史作为向文学理论的挑战》首次全面地提到接受美学的基本观点，特别是向传统文学史的研究对象、重心、方法提出了有力的挑战，引起了欧美文学理论批评界和美学界的广泛注意。姚斯把文学活动视为一种审美接受和生产的过程，认为作家（生产）、作品（文本）和读者（接受）作为文学活动的三个环节是一个动态的实现过程，打破了孤立地研究作家或作品的传统思路，建立了一种总体性动态研究的新思路。把读者提到一个突出重要的地位，把文学看成文学效果的历史，从读者接受的角度探讨文学的社会功能，开创了一种富有启发性的文学和文学史研究的新思路。

LITERARY history may be seen as challenging literary theory to take up once again the unresolved dispute between the Marxist and formalist schools. My attempt to bridge the gap between literature and history, between historical and aesthetic approaches, begins at the point at which both schools stop. Their methods understand the literary fact in terms of the circular aesthetic system of production and of representation. In doing so, they deprive literature of a dimension which unalterably belongs to its aesthetic character as well as to its social function: its reception and impact. Reader, listener and spectator—in short, the audience—play an extremely limited role in both literary theories. Orthodox Marxist aesthetics treats the reader—if at all—the same way as it does the author; it inquires about his social position or describes his place within the structure of the society. The formalist school needs the reader only as perceiving subject who follows the directions in the text in order to perceive its form or discover its techniques of procedure. It assumes that the reader has the theoretical knowledge of a philologist sufficiently versed in the tools of literature to be able to reflect on them. The Marxist school, on the other hand, actually equates the spontaneous experience of the reader with the scholarly interest of historical materialism, which seeks to discover relationships between the economic basis of production and the literary work as part of the intellectual superstructure. However, as Walther Bulst[1] has stated, "no text was ever written to be read and interpreted philologically by philologists," nor, may I add, historically by historians. Neither approach recognizes the true role of the reader to whom the literary work is primarily addressed, a role as unalterable for aesthetic as for historical appreciation.

For the critic who judges a new work, the writer who conceives of his work in light of positive or negative norms of an earlier work and the literary historian who classifies a work in his tradition and explains it historically are also readers before their reflex relationship to literature can become productive again. In the triangle of author, work and reading public the latter is no passive part, no chain of mere reactions, but even history-making energy. The historical life of a literary work is unthinkable without the active participation of its audience. For it is only through the process of its communication that the work reaches the changing horizon of experience in a continuity in which the continual change occurs from simple reception to critical understanding, from passive to active reception, from recognized aesthetic norms to a new production which surpasses them. The historicity of literature as well as its communicative character presupposes a relation of work, audience and new work which takes the form of a dialogue as well as a process, and which can be understood in the relationship of message and receiver as well as in the relationship of question and answer, problem and solution. The circular system of production and of representation within which the methodology of literary criticism has mainly moved in the past must therefore be widened to include an aesthetics of reception and impact if the problem of understanding the historical sequence of literary works as a continuity of literary history is to find a new solution.

The perspective of the aesthetics of reception mediates between passive reception and active understanding, norm-setting experience and new production. If the history of literature is viewed in this way as a dialogue between work and public, the contrast between its aesthetic and its historical aspects is also continually mediated. Thus the thread from the past appearance to the present experience of a work, which historicism had cut, is tied together.

The relationship of literature and reader has aesthetic as well as historical implications. The aesthetic implication is seen in the fact that the first reception of a work by the reader includes a test of its aesthetic value in comparison with works which he has already read. The obvious historical implication of this is that the appreciation of the first reader will be continued and enriched through further "receptions" from generation to generation; in this way the historical significance of a work will be determined and its aesthetic value revealed. In this process of the history of reception, which the literary historian can only escape at the price of ignoring his own principles of comprehension and judgment, the repossession of past works occurs simultaneously with the continual mediation of past and present art and of traditional evaluation and current literary attempts. The merit of a literary history based on an aesthetics of reception will depend upon the degree to which it can take an active part in the continual integration of past art by aesthetic experience. This demands on the one hand—in opposition to the objectivism of positivist literary history—a conscious attempt to establish canons, which, on the other hand—in opposition to the classicism of the study of traditions—presupposes a critical review if not destruction of the traditional literary canon. The criterion for establishing such a canon and the ever necessary retelling of literary history is clearly set out by the aesthetics of reception. The step from the history of the reception of the individual work to the history of literature has to lead us to see and in turn to present the historical sequence of works in the way in which they determine and clarify our present literary experience.

Literary history can be rewritten on this premise, and the following remarks suggest seven theses that provide a systematic approach to such rewriting.

I

If literary history is to be rejuvenated, the prejudices of historical objectivism must be removed and the traditional approach to literature must be replaced by an aesthetics of reception and impact. The historical relevance of literature is not based on an organization of literary works which is established *post factum* but on the reader's past experience of the "literary data." This relationship creates a dialogue that is the first condition for a literary history. For the literary historian must first become a reader again himself before he can understand and classify a work; in other words, before he can justify his own evaluation in light of his present position in the historical progression of readers.

R. G. Collingwood's[2] criticism of the prevailing ideology of objectivity in history—"History is nothing but the re-enactment of past thought in the historian's mind"—is even more valid for literary history. For the positivistic view of history as the "objective" description of a series of events in an isolated past neglects the artistic quality as well as the specific historical relevance of literature. A literary work is not an object which stands by itself and which offers the same face to each reader in each period. It is not a monument which reveals its timeless essence in a monologue. It is much more like an orchestration which strikes ever new chords among its readers and which frees the text from the substance of the words and makes it meaningful for the time: "words which must, at the same time that they speak to him, create an interlocutor capable of listening." A literary work must be understood as creating a dialogue, and philological scholarship has to be founded on a continuous re-reading of texts, not on mere facts. Philological scholarship is continuously dependent upon interpretation, which must have as its goal, along with learning about the object, the reflection upon and description of the perfection of this knowledge as an impulse to new understanding.

History of literature is a process of aesthetic reception and production which take place in realization of literary texts on the part of the receptive reader, the reflective critic and the author in his continued creativity. The continuously growing "literary data" which appear in the conventional literary histories are merely left over from this process; they are only the collected and classified past and therefore not history at all, but pseudo-history. Anyone who considers such literary data as history confuses the eventful character of a work of art with that of historical matter-of-factness. *Perceval* by Chrétien de Troyes[3], a literary event, is not historical in the same sense as the Third Crusade, which was occurring at the same time. It is not a "fact" which could be explained as caused by a series of situational preconditions and motives, by the intent of an historical action as it can be reconstructed, and by the necessary and secondary results of this deed as an eventful turning point. The historical context in which a literary work appears is not a factual, independent series of events which exists apart from the reader. *Perceval* becomes a literary event only for the reader who reads this last work of Chrétien in light of his earlier works and who recognizes its individuality in comparison with these and other works which he has already read, so that he gains a new criterion for evaluating works. In contrast to a political event, a literary event has no lasting results which succeeding generations cannot avoid. It can continue to have an effect only if future generations still respond to it or rediscover it—if there are readers who take up the work of the past again or authors who want to imitate, outdo, or refute it. The organization of literature according to events is primarily integrated in the artistic standards of contemporary and succeeding readers, critics, and authors. Whether it is possible to comprehend and present the history of literature in its specific historicity depends on whether these standards can be objectified.

Ⅱ

The analysis of the literary experience of the reader avoids the threatening pitfalls of psychology if it describes the response and the impact of a work within the definable frame of reference of the reader's expectations: this frame of reference for each work develops in the historical moment of its appearance from a previous understanding of the genre, from the form and themes of already familiar works, and from the contrast between poetic and practical language.

My thesis is opposed to a widespread skepticism that doubts that an analysis of the aesthetic impact can approach the meaning of a work of art or can produce at best more than a plain sociology of artistic taste. René Wellek[4] directs such doubts against the literary theory of I. A. Richards[5]. Wellek argues that neither the individual consciousness, since it is immediate and personal, nor a collective consciousness, as J. Mukarovsky[6] assumes the effect of an art work to be, can be determined by empirical means. Roman Jakobson[7] wanted to replace the "collective consciousness" by a "collective ideology." This he thought of as a system of values which exists for each literary work as *langue* and which becomes *parole* for the respondent—although incompletely and never as a whole. This theory, it is true, limits the subjectivity of the impact, but it leaves open the question of which data can be used to interpret the impact of a unique work on a certain public and to incorporate it into a system of values. In the meantime there are empirical means which had never been thought of before—literary data which give for each work a specific attitude of the audience (an attitude that precedes the psychological reaction as well as the subjective understanding of the individual reader). As in the case of every experience, the first literary experience of a previously unknown work demands a "previous knowledge which is an element of experience itself and which makes it possible that anything new we come across may also be read, as it were, in some context of experience."

A literary work, even if it seems new, does not appear as something absolutely new in an informational vacuum, but predisposes its readers to a very definite type of reception by textual strategies, overt and covert signals, familiar characteristics or implicit allusions. It awakens memories of the familiar, stirs particular emotions in the reader and with its "beginning" arouses expectations for the "middle and end," which can then be continued intact, changed, re-oriented or even ironically fulfilled in the course of reading according to certain rules of the genre or type of text. The psychical process in the assimilation of a text on the primary horizon of aesthetic experience is by no means only a random succession of merely subjective impressions, but the carrying out of certain directions in a process of directed perception which can be comprehended from the motivations which constitute it and the signals which set it off and which can be described linguistically. If, along with W. D. Stempel, one considers the previous horizon of expectations of a text as paradigmatic isotropy, which is transferred to an immanent syntactical horizon of expectations to the degree to which the message grows, the process of reception becomes describable in the expansion of a semiological procedure which arises between the development and the correction of the system. A corresponding process of continuous horizon setting and horizon changing also determines the relation of the individual text to the succession of texts which form the genre. The new text evokes for the reader (listener) the horizon of expectations and rules familiar from earlier texts, which are then varied, corrected, changed or just reproduced. Variation and correction determine the scope, alteration and reproduction of the borders and structure of the genre. The interpretative reception of a text always presupposes the context of experience of aesthetic perception. The question of the subjectivity of the interpretation and the taste of different readers or levels of readers can be asked significantly only after it has been decided which transsubjective horizon of understanding determines the impact of the text.

The ideal cases of the objective capability of such literary frames of reference are works which, using the artistic standards of the reader, have been formed by conventions of genre, style, or form. These purposely evoke responses so that they can frustrate them. This can serve not only a critical purpose but can even have a poetic effect. Thus Cervantes in *Don Quixote* fosters the expectations of the old tales of knighthood, which the adventures of his last knight then parody seriously. Thus Diderot in the beginning of *Jacques le Fataliste* evokes the expectations of the popular journey novel along with the (Aristotelian) convention of the romanesque fable and the providence peculiar to it, so that he can then confront the promised journey and love novel with a completely unromanesque "verité de l'histoire": the bizarre reality and moral casuistry of the inserted stories in which the truth of life continually denies the lies of poetic fiction. Thus Nerval in *Chimères* cites, combines, and mixes a quintessence of well-known romantic and occult motives to produce the expectation of a mythical metamorphosis of the world only in order to show his renunciation of romantic poetry. The mythical identification and relationships which are familiar to the reader dissolve in the unknown to the same degree as the attempted private myth of the lyrical "I" fails; the law of sufficient information is broken and the darkness which has become expressive gains a poetic function.

There is also the possibility of objectifying the expectations in works which are historically less sharply delineated. For the specific reception which the author anticipates from the reader for a particular work can be achieved, even if the explicit signals are missing, by three generally acceptable means: first, by the familiar standards or the inherent poetry of the genre; second, by the implicit relationships to familiar works of the literary-historical context; and third, by the contrast between fiction and reality, between the poetic and the practical function of language, which the reflective reader can always realize while he is reading. The third factor includes the possibility that the reader of a new work has to perceive it not only within the narrow horizon of his literary expectations but also within the wider horizon of his experience of life. I shall return to this horizon structure and its ability to be objectivized by means of the hermeneutics of question and answer in the discussion of the relationship between literature and practical life(see Ⅶ).

Ⅲ

If the horizon of expectations of a work is reconstructed in this way, it is possible to determine its artistic nature by the nature and degree of its effect on a given audience. If the "aesthetic distance" is considered as the distance between the given horizon of expectations and the appearance of a new work, whose reception results in a "horizon change" because it negates familiar experience or articulates an experience for the first time, this aesthetic distance can be measured historically in the spectrum of the reaction of the audience and the judgment of criticism (spontaneous success, rejection or shock, scattered approval, gradual or later understanding).

The way in which a literary work satisfies, surpasses, disappoints, or disproves the expectations of its first readers in the historical moment of its appearance obviously gives a criterion for the determination of its aesthetic value. The distance between the horizon of expectations and the work, between the familiarity of previous aesthetic experiences and the "horizon change" demanded by the response to new works, determines the artistic nature of a literary work along the lines of the aesthetics of reception: the smaller this distance, which means that no demands are made upon the receiving consciousness to make a change on the horizon of unknown experience, the closer the work comes to the realm of "culinary" or light reading. This last phrase can be characterized from the point of view of the aesthetics of reception in this way: it demands no horizon change but actually fulfills expectations, which are prescribed by a predominant taste, by satisfying the demand for the reproduction of familiar beauty, confirming familiar sentiments, encouraging dreams, making unusual experiences palatable as "sensations" or even raising moral problems, but only to be able to "solve" them in an edifying manner when the solution is already obvious. On the other hand, if the artistic character of a work is to be measured by the aesthetic distance with which it confronts the expectations of its first readers, it follows that this distance, which at first is experienced as a happy or distasteful new perspective, can disappear for later readers to the same degree to which the original negativity of the work has become self-evident and, as henceforth familiar expectation, has even become part of the horizon of future aesthetic experience. Especially the classic nature of so-called masterworks belongs to this second horizon change; their self-evident beauty and their seemingly unquestionable "eternal significance" bring them, from the point of view of the aesthetics of reception, into dangerous proximity with the irresistable convincing and enjoyable "culinary" art, and special effort is needed to read them "against the grain" of accustomed experience so that their artistic nature becomes evident again (compare with Ⅳ).

The relationship between literature and the public encompasses more than the fact that every work has its specific, historically and sociologically determined audience, that every writer is dependent upon the milieu, views and ideology of his readers and that literary success requires a book "which expresses what the group expects, a book which presents the group with its own portrait. . . . " The objectivist determination of literary success based on the congruence of the intent of a work and the expectation of a social group always puts literary sociology in an embarrassing position whenever it must explain later or continuing effects. This is why R. Escarpit[8] wants to presuppose a "collective basis in space or time" for the "illusion of continuity" of a writer, which leads to an astonishing prognosis in the case of Molière: he "is still young for the Frenchman of the 20th century because his world is still alive and ties of culture, point of view and language still bind us to him... but the ties are becoming ever weaker and Molière will age and die when the things which our culture has in common with the France of Molière die"(p. 117). As if Molière had only reflected the manners of his time and had only remained successful because of this apparent intention! Where the congruence between work and social group does not exist or no longer exists, as for example in the reception of a work by a group which speaks a foreign language, Escarpit is able to help himself by resorting to a "myth": "myths which are invented by a later period which has become estranged from the reality which they represent"(p. 111). As if all reception of a work beyond the first socially determined readers were only "distorted echoes," only a consequence of "subjective myths"(p. 111) and did not have its objective *a priori* in the received work which sets boundaries and opens possibilities for later understanding! The sociology of literature does not view its object dialectically enough when it determines the circle of writers, work and readers so one-sidedly. The determination is reversible: there are works which at the moment of their publication are not directed at any specific audience, but which break through the familiar horizon of literary expectations so completely that an audience can only gradually develop for them. Then when the new horizon of expectations has achieved more general acceptance, the authority of the changed aesthetic norm can become apparent from the fact that readers will consider previously successful works as obsolete and reject them. It is only in view of such a horizon change that the analysis of literary effect achieves the dimension of a literary history of readers and provides the statistical curves of the historical recognition of the bestseller.

A literary sensation from the year 1857 may serve as an example of this. In this year two novels were published: Flaubert's[9] *Madame Bovary*, which has since achieved world-wide fame, and *Fanny* by his friend Feydeau[10], which is forgotten today. Although Flaubert's novel brought with it a trial for obscenity, *Madame Bovary* was at first overshadowed by Feydeau's novel: *Fanny* had thirteen editions in one year and success the likes of which Paris had not seen since Chateaubriand's[11] *Atala*. As far as theme is concerned, both novels fulfilled the expectations of the new audience, which—according to Baudelaire's analysis—had rejected anything romantic and scorned grand as well as naive passion. They treated a trivial subject—adultery—

the one in a bourgeois and the other in a provincial milieu. Both authors understood how to give a sensational twist to the conventional, rigid triangle which in the erotic scenes surpassed the customary details. They presented the worn-out theme of jealousy in a new light by reversing the expected relationship of the three classic roles. Feydeau has the youthful lover of the "femme de trente ans" becoming jealous of his lover's husband, although he has already reached the goal of his desires, and perishing over this tormenting situation; Flaubert provides the adulteries of the doctor' s wife in the provinces, which Baudelaire presents as a sublime form of "dandysme," with a surprising ending, so that the ridiculous figure of the deceived Charles Bovary takes on noble traits at the end. In official criticism of the time there are voices which reject *Fanny* as well as *Madame Bovary* as a product of the new school of "réalisme," which they accuse of denying all ideals and attacking the ideas on which the order of the society in the Second Empire was based.[25] The horizon of expectations of the public of 1857, here only sketched in, which did not expect anything great in the way of novels after the death of Balzac[12], explains the differing success of the two novels only when the question of the effect of their narrative form is posed. Flaubert' s innovation in form, his principle of "impersonal telling" *impassibilité* which Barbey d'Aurevilly[13] attacked with this comparison: if a story-telling machine could be made of English steel, it would function the same as Monsieur Flaubert), must have shocked the same audience which was offered the exciting contents of *Fanny* in the personable tone of a confessional novel. It could also have found in Feydeau's descriptionspopular ideals and frustrations of the level of society which sets the style, and it could delight unrestrainedly in the lascivious main scene in which Fanny (without knowing that her lover is watching from the balcony) seduces her husband—for their moral indignation was forestalled by the reaction of the unfortunate witness. However, as *Madame Bovary*, which was understood at first only by a small circle of knowledgeable readers and called a turning point in the history of the novel, became a world-wide success, the group of readers who were formed by this book sanctioned the new canon of expectations, which made the weaknesses of Feydeau—his flowery style, his modish effects, his lyrical confessional clichés—unbearable and relegated *Fanny* to the class of bestsellers of yesterday.

注释：

1. 沃尔特·布尔斯特（1899—1986），海德堡大学中世纪拉丁语教授。

2. R. G. 柯林伍德（1889—1943），英国哲学家、历史学家和考古学家。

3. 克雷蒂安·德·特鲁瓦（1135—1183），12 世纪后期法国游吟诗人，其作品标志着传奇文学的繁荣和成熟。在美国，他是继普鲁斯特之后读者最多的法国作家。

4. 勒内·韦勒克（1903—1995），美国比较文学批评家。

5. 艾弗·阿姆斯特朗·理查兹（1893—1979），英国著名教育家、文学评论家和修辞学家。

6. 穆卡洛夫斯基（1891—1975），捷克文学、语言和美学理论家，布拉格结构主义学派中最重要的理论家之一，被认为是俄国形式主义传统的继承者。

7. 罗曼·雅各布森（1896—1982），俄国杰出的语言学家，诗学家，莫斯科语言小组的领袖。

8. 罗伯特·埃斯卡皮特（1918—2000），法国学者、作家和记者。

9. 古斯塔夫·福楼拜（1821—1880），法国小说家，法国现实主义文学的主要代表人物。

10. 乔治·费多（1862—1921），19 世纪晚期 20 世纪初期法国著名喜剧作家。

11. 弗朗索瓦·雷内·德·夏多布里昂（1768—1848），法国作家、政治家、外交家和历史学家，是法国早期浪漫主义的代表作家。

12. 奥诺雷·德·巴尔扎克（1799—1850），法国小说家、剧作家，被称为现代法国小说之父、欧洲批判现实主义文学奠基人。

13. 巴尔贝·多尔维利（1808—1889），法国小说家。

Wolfgang Iser

沃尔夫冈·伊瑟尔（1926—2007），德国美学家、文学批评家，联邦德国康斯坦茨大学英国文学和比较文学教授，接受美学的创始人与重要理论家，也是康斯坦茨学派的代表人物之一。伊瑟尔生于德国马林堡，曾先后就读于莱比锡大学、图宾根大学、海德堡大学，获哲学博士学位。伊瑟尔 1969 年的力作《本文的召唤结构》与姚斯的《文学史作为向文学理论的挑战》一同被认为是美学的奠基之作，引起强烈反响，奠定了他接受美学主要理论家的地位。伊瑟尔主要受英伽登的现象学美学的影响，深入研究了文学本文与读者的相互作用和关系，着重揭示了文学阅读的心理过程。主要著作有《亨利·菲尔丁的艺术世界》（1952）、《隐含读者：从班扬到贝克特散文小说的交流模式》（1974）、《阅读活动：审美反应理论》（1976）等。

The Reading Process: A Phenomenological Approach

（Wolfgang Iser. The Reading Process: A Phenomenological Approach. *New*

Literary History, Vol. 3, No. 2, On Interpretation: I (Winter, 1972), pp. 279-299)

伊瑟尔在《阅读过程:一种现象学方法》这篇文章中,以现象学美学和接受美学的观点对文本的阅读过程进行了阐释。文章着重分析了读者在阅读过程中的重要意义,将人们的注意力从单纯关注作者的意图转移到了读者反应。伊瑟尔认为文学作品是由文本和读者接受这两极构成的,文学作品研究除了关注文本之外,还应探索读者阅读过程中对文本所做出的反应。他同时提出文本的召唤结构理论,认为文学文本的召唤结构由"空白""空缺""否定"三个要素构成,它们共同激发、召唤、诱导读者在阅读中发挥创造性的想象来填补作者的文字和自己的理解之间的缺口。

I

THE PHENOMENOLOGICAL THEORY of art lays full stress on the idea that, in considering a literary work, one must take into account not only the actual text but also, and in equal measure, the actions involved in responding to that text. Thus Roman Ingarden[1] confronts the structure of the literary text with the ways in which it can be *konkretisiert* (realized). The text as such offers different "schematised views" through which the subject matter of the work can come to light, but the actual bringing to light is an action of *Konkretisation*. If this is so, then the literary work has two poles, which we might call the artistic and the aesthetic: the artistic refers to the text created by the author, and the aesthetic to the realization accomplished by the reader. From this polarity it follows that the literary work cannot be completely identical with the text, or with the realization of the text, but in fact must lie halfway between the two. The work is more than the text, for the text only takes on life when it is realized, and furthermore the realization is by no means independent of the individual disposition of the reader—though this in turn is acted upon by the different patterns of the text. The convergence of text and reader brings the literary work into existence, and this convergence can never be precisely pinpointed, but must always remain virtual, as it is not to be identified either with the reality of the text or with the individual disposition of the reader.

It is the virtuality of the work that gives rise to its dynamic nature, and this in turn is the precondition for the effects that the work calls forth. As the reader uses the various perspectives offered him by the text in order to relate the patterns and the "schematised views" to one another, he sets the work in motion, and this very process results ultimately in the awakening of responses within himself. Thus, reading causes the literary work to unfold its inherently dynamic character. That this is no new discovery is apparent from references made even in the early days of the novel. Laurence Sterne[2] remarks in *Tristram Shandy* : "... no author, who understands the just boundaries of decorum and good-breeding, would presume to think all: The truest respect which you can pay to the reader's understanding, is to halve this matter amicably, and leave him something to imagine, in his turn, as well as yourself. For my own part, I am eternally paying him compliments of this kind, and do all that lies in my power to keep his imagination as busy as my own." Sterne's conception of a literary text is that it is something like an arena in which reader and author participate in a game of the imagination. If the reader were given the whole story, and there were nothing left for him to do, then his imagination would never enter the field, the result would be the boredom which inevitably arises when everything is laid out cut and dried before us. A literary text must therefore be conceived in such a way that it will engage the reader's imagination in the task of working things out for himself, for reading is only a pleasure when it is active and creative. In this process of creativity, the text may either not go far enough, or may go too far, so we may say that boredom and overstrain form the boundaries beyond which the reader will leave the field of play.

The extent to which the "unwritten" part of a text stimulates the reader's creative participation is brought out by an observation of Virginia Woolf's[3] in her study of *Jane Austen*: "Jane Austen is thus a mistress of much deeper emotion than appears upon the surface. She stimulates us to supply what is not there. What she offers is, apparently, a trifle, yet is composed of something that expands in the reader's mind and endows with the most enduring form of life scenes which are outwardly trivial. Always the stress is laid upon character.... The turns and twists of the dialogue keep us on the tenterhooks of suspense. Our attention is half upon the present moment, half upon the future.... Here, indeed, in this unfinished and in the main inferior story, are all the elements of Jane Austen's greatness." The unwritten aspects of apparently trivial scenes, and the unspoken dialogue within the "turns and twists," not only draw the reader into the action, but also lead him to shade in the many outlines suggested by the given situations, so that these take on a reality of their own. But as the reader's imagination animates these "outlines," they in turn will influence the effect of the written part of the text. Thus begins a whole dynamic process: the written text imposes certain limits on its unwritten implications in order to prevent these from becoming too blurred and hazy, but at the same time these implications, worked out by the reader's imagination, set the given situation against a background which endows it with far greater significance than it might have seemed to possess on its own. In this way, trivial scenes suddenly take on the shape of an "enduring form of life." What constitutes this form is never named, let alone explained, in the text, although in fact it is the end product of the interaction between text and reader.

Ⅱ

The question now arises as to how far such a process can be adequately described. For this purpose a phenomenological analysis recommends itself, especially since the somewhat sparse observations hitherto made of the psychology of reading tend mainly to be psychoanalytical, and so are restricted to the illustration of predetermined ideas concerning the unconscious. We shall, however, take a closer look later at some worthwhile psychological observations.

As a starting point for a phenomenological analysis we might examine the way in which sequent sentences act upon one another. This is of especial importance in literary texts in view of the fact that they do not correspond to any objective reality outside themselves. The world presented by literary texts is constructed out of what Ingarden has called *intentionale Satzkorrelate* (intentional sentence correlatives):

> Sentences link up in different ways to form more complex units of meaning that reveal a very varied structure giving rise to such entities as a short story, a novel, a dialogue, a drama, a scientific theory.... In the final analysis, there arises a particular world, with component parts determined in this way or that, and with all the variations that may occur within these parts—all this as a purely intentional correlative of a complex of sentences. If this complex finally forms a literary work, I call the whole sum of sequent intentional sentence correlatives the 'world presented' in the work.

This world, however, does not pass before the reader's eyes like a film. The sentences are "component parts" insofar as they make statements, claims, or observations, or convey information, and so establish various perspectives in the text. But they remain only "component parts" they are not the sum total of the text itself. For the intentional correlatives disclose subtle connections which individually are less concrete than the statements, claims, and observations, even though these only take on their real meaningfulness through the interaction of their correlatives.

How is one to conceive the connection between the correlatives? It marks those points at which the reader is able to "climb aboard" the text. He has to accept certain given perspectives, but in doing so he inevitably causes them to interact. When Ingarden speaks of intentional sentence correlatives in literature, the statements made, or information conveyed in the sentence are already in a certain sense qualified: the sentence does not consist solely of a statement—which, after all, would be absurd, as one can only make statements about things that exist—but aims at something beyond what it actually says. This is true of all sentences in literary works, and it is through the interaction of these sentences that their common aim is fulfilled. This is what gives them their own special quality in literary texts. In their capacity as statements, observations, purveyors of information, etc., they are always indications of something that is to come, the structure of which is foreshadowed by their specific content.

They set in motion a process out of which emerges the actual content of the text itself. In describing man's inner consciousness of time, Husserl[4] once remarked: "Every originally constructive process is inspired by pre-intentions, which construct and collect the seed of what is to come, as such, and bring it to fruition." For this bringing to fruition, the literary text needs the reader's imagination, which gives shape to the interaction of correlatives foreshadowed in structure by the sequence of the sentences. Husserl's observation draws our attention to a point that plays a not insignificant part in the process of reading. The individual sentences not only work together to shade in what is to come; they also form an expectation in this regard. Husserl calls this expectation "pre-intentions." As this structure is characteristic of *all* sentence correlatives, the interaction of these correlatives will not be a fulfilment of the expectation so much as a continual modification of it.

For this reason, expectations are scarcely ever fulfilled in truly literary texts. If they were, then such texts would be confined to the individualization of a given expectation, and one would inevitably ask what such an intention was supposed to achieve. Strangely enough, we feel that any confirmative effect—such as we implicitly demand of expository texts, as we refer to the objects they are meant to present—is a defect in a literary text. For the more a text individualizes or confirms an expectation it has initially aroused, the more aware we become of its didactic purpose, so that at best we can only accept or reject the thesis forced upon us. More often than not, the very clarity of such texts will make us want to free ourselves from their clutches. But generally the sentence correlatives of literary texts do not develop in this rigid way, for the expectations they evoke tend to encroach on one another in such a manner that they are continually modified as one reads. One might simplify by saying that each intentional sentence correlative opens up a particular horizon, which is modified, if not completely changed, by succeeding sentences. While these expectations arouse interest in what is to come, the subsequent modification of them will also have a retrospective effect on what has already been read. This may now take on a different significance from that which it had at the moment of reading.

Whatever we have read sinks into our memory and is foreshortened. It may later be evoked again and set against a different background with the result that the reader is enabled to develop hitherto unforeseeable connections. The memory evoked, however, can never reassume its original shape, for this would mean that memory and perception were identical, which is manifestly not so. The new background brings to light new aspects of what we had committed to memory; conversely these, in turn, shed their light on the new background, thus arousing more complex anticipations. Thus, the reader, in establishing these interrelations between past, present and future, actually causes the text to reveal its potential multiplicity of connections. These connections are the product of the reader's mind working on the raw material of the text, though they are not the text itself—for this consists just of sentences, statements, information, etc.

This is why the reader often feels involved in events which, at the time of reading, seem real to him, even though in fact they are very far from his own reality. The fact that completely different readers can be differently affected by the "reality" of a particular text is ample evidence of the degree to which literary texts transform reading into a creative process that is far above mere perception of what is written. The literary text activates our own faculties, enabling us to recreate the world it presents. The product of this creative activity is what we might call the virtual dimension of the text, which endows it with its reality. This virtual dimension is not the text itself, nor is it the imagination of the reader: it is the coming together of text and imagination.

As we have seen, the activity of reading can be characterized as a sort of kaleidoscope of perspectives, preintentions, recollections. Every sentence contains a preview of the next and forms a kind of viewfinder for what is to come; and this in turn changes the "preview" and so becomes a "viewfinder" for what has been read. This whole process represents the fulfilment of the potential, unexpressed reality of the text, but it is to be seen only as a framework for a great variety of means by which the virtual dimension may be brought into being. The process of anticipation and retrospection itself does not by any means develop in a smooth flow. Ingarden has already drawn attention to this fact, and ascribes a quite remarkable significance to it:

> Once we are immersed in the flow of *Satzdenken* (sentence-thought), we are ready, after completing the thought of one sentence, to think out the 'continuation,' also in the form of a sentence—and that is, in the form of a sentence that connects up with the sentence we have just thought through. In this way the process of reading goes effortlessly forward. But if by chance the following sentence has no tangible connection whatever with the sentence we have just thought through, there then comes a blockage in the stream of thought. This hiatus is linked with a more or less active surprise, or with indignation. This blockage must be overcome if the reading is to flow once more.

The hiatus that blocks the flow of sentences is, in Ingarden's eyes, the product of chance, and is to be regarded as a flaw; this is typical of his adherence to the classical idea of art. If one regards the sentence sequence as a continual flow, this implies that the anticipation aroused by one sentence will generally be realized by the next, and the frustration of one's expectations will arouse feelings of exasperation. And yet literary texts are full of unexpected twists and turns, and frustration of expectations. Even in the simplest story there is bound to be some kind of blockage, if only for the fact that no tale can ever be told in its entirety. Indeed, it is only through inevitable omissions that a story will gain its dynamism. Thus whenever the flow is interrupted and we are led off in unexpected directions, the opportunity is given to us to bring into play our own faculty for establishing connections—for filling in the gaps left by the text itself.

These gaps have a different effect on the process of anticipation and retrospection, and thus on the "gestalt" of the virtual dimension, for they may be filled in different ways. For this reason, one text is potentially capable of several different realizations, and no reading can ever exhaust the full potential, for each individual reader will fill in the gaps in his own way, thereby excluding the various other possibilities; as he reads, he will make his own decision as to how the gap is to be filled. In this very act the dynamics of reading are revealed. By making his decision he implicitly acknowledges the inexhaustibility of the text; at the same time it is this very inexhaustibility that forces him to make his decision. With "traditional" texts this process was more or less unconscious, but modern texts frequently exploit it quite deliberately. They are often so fragmentary that one's attention is almost exclusively occupied with the search for connections between the fragments; the object of this is not to complicate the "spectrum" of connections, so much as to make us aware of the nature of our own capacity for providing links. In such cases, the text refers back directly to our own preconceptions—which are revealed by the act of interpretation that is a basic element of the reading process. With all literary texts, then, we may say that the reading process is selective, and the potential text is infinitely richer than any of its individual realizations. This is borne out by the fact that a second reading of a piece of literature often produces a different impression from the first. The reasons for this may lie in the reader's own change of circumstances, still, the text must be such as to allow this variation. On a second reading familiar occurrences now tend to appear in a new light and seem to be at times corrected, at times enriched.

In every text there is a potential time-sequence which the reader must inevitably realize, as it is impossible to absorb even a short text in a single moment. Thus the reading process always involves viewing the text through a perspective that is continually on the move, linking up the different phases, and so constructing what we have called the virtual dimension. This dimension, of course, varies all the time we are reading. However, when we have finished the text, and read it again, clearly our extra knowledge will result in a different time-sequence; we shall tend to establish connections by referring to our awareness of what is to come, and so certain aspects of the text will assume a significance we did not attach to them on a first reading, while others will recede into the background. It is a common enough experience for a person to say that on a second reading he noticed things he had missed when he read the book for the first time, but this is scarcely surprising in view of the fact that the second time he is looking at the text through a different perspective. The time-sequence that he realized on his first reading cannot possibly be repeated on a second reading and this unrepeatability is bound to result in modifications of his reading experience. This is not to say that the second reading is "truer" than the first—they are, quite simply, different: the reader establishes the virtual dimension of the text by realizing a new time-sequence. Thus even on repeated viewings a text allows and, indeed, induces innovative reading.

In whatever way, and under whatever circumstances, the reader may link the different phases of the text together, it will always be the process of anticipation and retrospection that leads to the formation of the virtual dimension, which in turn transforms the text into an experience for the reader. The way in which this experience comes about through a process of continual modification is closely akin to the way in which we gather experience in life. And thus the "reality" of the reading experience can illuminate basic patterns of real experience:

> We have the experience of a world, not understood as a system of relations which wholly determine each event, but as an open totality the synthesis of which is inexhaustible.... From the moment that experience—that is, the opening on to our de facto world—is recognized as the beginning of knowledge, there is no longer any way of distinguishing a level of a priori truths and one of factual ones, what the world must necessarily be and what it actually is.

The manner in which the reader experiences the text will reflect his own disposition, and in this respect the literary text acts as a kind of mirror; but at the same time, the reality which this process helps to create is one that will be *different* from his own (since, normally, we tend to be bored by texts that present us with things we already know perfectly well ourselves). Thus we have the apparently paradoxical situation in which the reader is forced to reveal aspects of himself in order to experience a reality which is different from his own. The impact this reality makes on him will depend largely on the extent to which he himself actively provides the unwritten part of the text, and yet in supplying all the missing links, he must think in terms of experiences different from his own; indeed, it is only by leaving behind the familiar world of his own experience that the reader can truly participate in the adventure the literary text offers him.

注释:

1. 罗曼·英伽登（1893—1970），当代波兰现象学哲学家和美学家，现象学美学的主要代表人物。

2. 劳伦斯·斯特恩（1713—1768），爱尔兰小说家和英国圣公会牧师。

3. 弗吉尼亚·伍尔夫（1882—1941），英国作家、文学批评家和文学理论家，意识流文学代表人物。

4. 埃德蒙德·古斯塔夫·阿尔布雷希特·胡塞尔（1859—1938），20世纪奥地利著名作家、哲学家，现象学的创始人。

Wolfgang Iser

The Role of the Reader: In Fielding's *Joseph Andrews* and *Tom Jones*

(Iser, Wolfgang. *The Implied Reader: Patterns of Communication in Prose Fiction from Bunyan to Beckett*. Baltimore and London: The Johns Hopkins University Press, 1974, pp. 29-56.)

伊瑟尔在《论菲尔丁〈约瑟夫·安德鲁斯〉中读者的作用》这篇文章中以菲尔丁的小说《约瑟夫·安德鲁斯》为例，指出该小说的创新之处就在于关注读者的阅读过程和反应，借此详述了读者的作用。文本是固定的，意义是通过阅读的行为以及读者如何将文本的结构与自己的经验联系起来实现的。小说的意义不再是文本中可以找到的一个独立的客观实在，而是某种必须由读者去建构的事物。作品的意义不确定性和意义空白需要读者靠想象力去填补，小说的意义最终在读者的反应中得以具体化。文本的空白唤起读者的敏锐性，刺激读者产生对作品的看法，使得读者参与作品审美潜能的实现和作品艺术的再创造，这样，有限的文本便有了意义生成的无限可能性。

I

"A new province of writing": this is what Fielding[1] called his novels. In what way new? Innovations as such in literature are very difficult to perceive; it is only when they are set against a familiar background that we can get some idea of their novelty. Once the new is distinguished from the old, there arises a certain tension, because we have lost the security of the familiar without knowing for sure the precise nature of the innovation. For what is new comes into being through changes in the reader's mind—the casting aside of old assumptions and preconceptions. It is difficult for Fielding as an author to define these changes, since he is concerned with presenting the new and not with merely changing the old.

For innovation itself to be a subject in a novel, the author needs direct cooperation from the person who is to perceive that innovation—namely, the reader. This is why it is hardly surprising that Fielding's novels, and those of the eighteenth century in general, are so full of direct addresses to the reader, which certainly have a rhetorical function, though this is by no means their only function. John Preston's book *The Created Self* is the first full-length study of these apostrophies, which he interprets in terms of rhetoric only: "I make no attempt to provide a 'rhetoric of reading', though no doubt this would be worth doing. Rather I trust that the rhetorical principles in question will provide a unifying point of view for these four novels (i. e. *Moll Flanders*, *Clarissa*, *Tom Jones*, and *Tristram Shandy*), and yet not seem unduly arbitrary or restrictive. And I should be glad to feel that such an approach might prompt other more radical enquiries into the nature of the reader's role in fiction."

This recommendation for a more radical enquiry can be taken as a starting-point for our discussion. The role which the Fielding novel assigns to its readers is not confined to awillingness to be persuaded. In the act of reading, we are to undergo a kind of transformation, such as W. Booth[2] has described in connection with fiction in general: "The author creates, in short, an image of himself and another image of his reader; he makes his reader, as he makes his second self, and the most successful reading is one in which the created selves, author and reader, can find complete agreement." But this transformation of the reader into the image created by the author does not take place through rhetoric alone. The reader has to be stimulated into certain activities, which may be guided by rhetorical signposts, but which lead to a process that is not merely rhetorical. Rhetoric, if it is to be successful, needs a clearly formulated purpose, but the "new province of writing" that Fielding is trying to open up to his readers is in the nature of a promise, and it can only rouse the expectations necessary for its efficacy if it is not set out in words. The reader must be made to feel for himself the new meaning of the novel. To do this he must actively participate in bringing out the meaning and this participation is an essential precondition for communication between the author and the reader. Rhetoric, then, may be a guiding influence to help the reader produce the meaning of the text, but his participation is something that goes far beyond the scope of this influence. Northrop Frye[3] has referred to an attack on Jakob Böhme[4] which aptly describes the conditions leading to the reader's act of production: "It has been said of Boehme that his books are like a picnic to which the author brings the words and the reader the meaning. The remark may have been intended as a sneer at Boehme, but it is an exact description of all works of literary art without exception."

Eighteenth-century novelists were deeply conscious of this interplay with the reader. Richardson once wrote—admittedly in a letter, and not in the novel itself—that the story must leave something for the reader to do. Laurence Sterne, in *Tristram Shandy*, describes this vital process with the same unmistakable clarity with which he disclosed the principles of fiction as practiced in the novel during the first half of the eighteenth century. He writes in Ⅱ, 11: "no author, who understands the just boundaries of decorum and good-breeding, would presume to think all: The truest respect which you can pay to the reader's understanding, is to halve this matter amicably, and leave him something to imagine, in his turn, as well as yourself. For my own part, I am eternally paying him compliments of this kind, and do all that lies in my power to keep his imagination as busy as my own." The participation of the reader could not be stimulated if everything were laid out in front him. This means that the formulated text must shade off, through allusions and suggestions, into a text that is unformulated though nonetheless intended. Only in this way can the reader' s imagination be given the scope it needs; the written text furnishes it with indications which enable it to conjure up what the text does not reveal.

Fielding, too, often speaks of the offer of participation that must be made to the reader, if he is to learn to fulfill the promise of the novel. There is a clear reference to this in *Tom Jones* :

> Bestir thyself therefore on this occasion; for, though we will always lend thee proper assistance in difficult places, as we do not, like some others, expect thee to use the arts of divination to discover our meaning, yet we shall not indulge thy laziness where nothing but thy own attention is required; for thou art highly mistaken if thou dost imagine that we

intended, when we began this great work, to leave thy sagacity nothing to do; or that, without sometimes exercising this talent, thou wilt be able to travel through our pages with any pleasure or profit to thyself.

This typical appeal to the reader's "sagacity" aims at arousing a sense of discernment. This is to be regarded as a pleasure, because in this way the reader will be able to test his own faculties. It also promises to be profitable, because the need for discernment stimulates a process of learning in the course of which one's own sense of judgment may come under scrutiny. Here we have a clear outline of the role of the reader, which is fulfilled through the continual instigation of attitudes and reflections on those attitudes. As the reader is maneuvered into this position, his reactions—which are, so to speak, prestructured by the written text—bring out the meaning of the novel; it might be truer to say that the meaning of the novel only materializes in these reactions, since it does not exist per se.

Ⅱ

This rough outline of the reader's role is something we can elaborate on in more detail with reference to *Joseph Andrews* and *Tom Jones*, so that we can see more clearly the nature of the activity required of the reader as he produces the meaning of the novel. In the very first sentence of *Joseph Andrews*, the author mentions the fact that the "mere English reader" will certainly have different conceptions and also different expectations regarding the reading that lies ahead of him. For his reading habits are conditioned by epics, tragedies, and comedies, the underlying principles of which are called to mind so that the enterprise of our own author can be separated from them. Certainly the association of this novel with the hallowed forms of traditional literature was intended by Fielding, primarily, to raise the status of his tale in prose; but just as clear is the intention underlying his description of his work as a "comic epic poem in prose." By listing his deviations from the classical models, he is drawing attention to the unique features of his enterprise. And so the "classical reader" will find pleasure in the "parodies or burlesque imitations" precisely because they conjure up the very 'genre' which they set out to transform.

This process can be linked with what Gombrich[5] terms in esthetics 'schema and correction'. Fielding calls to mind a whole repertoire of familiar literary 'genres', so that these allusions will arouse particular expectations from which his novel then proceeds to diverge. These subsequent divergences are the first step toward innovation.

In the preface, Fielding specifies the differences between his novel and classical predecessors, but these informative indications gradually disappear as the reader begins to fall in with the book. In the first of the initial essays of the novel, again he makes use of a familiar repertoire. But here the starting-point is contemporary rather than ancient literature. It is true that he alludes to classical and medieval Lives, but his main concern here is with Colley Cibber's[6] *Autobiography* and Richardson's[7] *Pamela*, which both fit in perfectly with Fielding's intentions, since they each present a life-story. But here it is no longer a question of Fielding showing the differences between his work and the models alluded to. Instead they are shown to be exemplary in a way that Fielding pretends he wants to emulate with his *Joseph Andrews* —and this regardless of the fact that one biography is fictitious and the other real, though it is ironically pointed out that there is much fiction in the real one, and in the fictitious much that presumes to be exemplary for real life.

If the beginning of the introduction emphasized the divergences from the established repertoire, now the stress is laid on the similarities, so that the reader is left to discover the differences for himself—though these always remain clearly visible thanks to the ever-present irony. *Joseph Andrews* is not to be read, then, as a glorification of the hero—in the mould of the Cibber *Autobiography* —or as a moral vade mecum for worldly success, like Richardson's novel. Here, too, schemata are corrected, though the correction is never formulated. As a result there appears a gap between the familiar repertoire in the novel and one's own observation of it.

These gaps heighten our awareness, and their effectiveness lies in the fact that they conceal something of vital importance. As we have seen, the reader is forced to discover for himself the divergences from the established repertoire, and, at first sight this seems simple enough. The ironic style is sufficient to show us that the text means the opposite of what it says; but the situation becomes rather more complicated when we ask, "What will the opposite of Richardson's *Pamela* and Colley Cibber's *Autobiography* look like?" The answer to this is far from obvious, and so the ironic allusions can no longer be regarded as a mere reversal of the written statement.

By negating the familiar, the irony indicates that now something is to be communicated of which hitherto there has been no proper conception. Our attention is drawn to the difficulty of deducing the exemplary from the private. Consequently, this negating irony drives us to seek the proper conception beyond the confines of the familiar models; and in this way, the nonfulfillment of those expectations aroused by the presence of the familiar, becomes the spur that pricks our imagination into action.

The repertoire of the familiar in *Joseph Andrews* is not confined to established literary patterns; it also incorporates various norms that were generally accepted in Fielding's day. The transplanting of these norms into the novel results in their transformation, for here they are presented in a different light from that in which they appeared at the time within the "collective consciousness" we call society. This esthetic arrangement of social norms has certain consequences for the reader which can best be illustrated through the character of Abraham Adams, the real hero of the novel. The list of virtues that Fielding unfolds contains nearly all the qualities that would make up the perfect man. And yet it is his very possession of all these qualities that makes Adams totally incapable of dealing with this world, as Fielding actually points out. The list of virtues is not seen from a Christian or a Platonic stand-point now, but from a worldly one, and from this totally different perspective the virtues appear to lose all their validity; they seem to belong to the past, for they are no longer capable of inspiring sensible conduct in the present. The question now arises as to whether this means that amoral conduct is best suited to this world. Or does it mean that we have to find a compromise relationship between norm and world? If this were so, surely any such compromise would be an intolerable strain, since the two factors—contemporary norms and worldly demands—would forever be tugging us in opposite direction. Virtues cannot be contemplated separated from the world, and the world cannot be viewed without the background of virtue. Is the conflict to be resolved? If so, how and why? The answers are not given us. They are the gaps in the text. They give the reader the motivation and the opportunity to bring the two poles meaningfully together for himself.

Here, then, we have our first insight into the nature of the reader's active participation, as mobilized by the novel. The repertoire of the familiar—whether it be literary tradition, contemporary 'Weltanschauung', or social reality—forms the background of the novel. The familiar is reproduction in the text, but in its reproduction it seems different, for its component parts have been altered, its frame of reference has changed, its validity has, to a degree, been negated. But if the starting-point of the novel is a set of negation, then the reader is impelled to counterbalance these negations by seeking their positive potential, the alternate fulfillment of which we shall henceforth call the realization of the text.

Fielding's preoccupation with this aspect of the reader's role can be traced from the remarks in the preface right through the initial essays in the novel. After drawing distinctions between his own novel and traditional writings, he continues: "Having thus distinguished Joseph Andrews from the productions of romance writers on the one hand and burlesque writers on the other, and given some few very short hints (for I intended no more) of this species of writing, which I have affirmed to be hitherto unattempted in our language; I shall leave to my good-natured reader to apply my piece to my observations." The reader, then, must apply the author's remarks to his novel, but the text will not tell him how to do this. The application will coincide largely with the realization. In the preface, however, Fielding does outline the sphere in which this application is to take place, for he promises that the reader will have revealed to him the sources of the ridiculous which, he says, spring from the discovery of affectation and hypocrisy. The intention of the novel, then, is not the presentation of affectation and hypocrisy, but the uncovering of their ridiculousness, which always occurs with the penetration of those false appearances that mask all social vices.

However, a discovery of this nature does not end with the unmasking of vice. Fielding simply says that the veil will fall from the ridiculous, without saying that this absurdity might carry with it some indication as to the proper way to conduct oneself. So far the reaction of the reader will signify no more than a feeling of superiority, and the question arises as to what lies behind this superiority evinced by our laughter. At best it is an awareness of the potential presence of what proper conduct should be, although we cannot discount the possibility that our superiority is also based on a misunderstanding. The reader, therefore, must not only see through the original false appearances; he must also set out even more intensively to discover the preconditions for model conduct, to make sure that this superiority, obtained through the unmasking of absurd vices, does not in its turn become a false appearance. In this process, ridicule performs a very different function from its function in the literature of the past: it ceases to stigmatize the lower classes and instead stimulates the reader's mind into trying to formulate the potential morality contained in the unmasking. In order to set such a mental process into operation, the intention of the novel cannot be the subject of narration, for it is only by reconstructing for himself the unformulated part of the text—in this case, the correct mode of conduct—that the reader can experience this intention as a reality.

How this reality is constituted is indicated about half-way through *Joseph Andrews* in Fielding's final theoretical essay(Ⅲ,1). He would like to feel that the novel is a kind of mirror, in which the reader can see himself, as it were, through the characters he has been laughing at in apparent superiority. It is his purpose "not to expose one pitiful wretch to the small and contemptible circle of his acquaintance; but to hold the glass to thousands in their closets, that they may contemplate their deformity, and endeavour to reduce it, and thus by suffering private mortification may avoid public shame."

If looking in the glass gives the reader the opportunity for self-correction, then the role assigned to him is clear. In taking this opportunity, he is bound to encounter sides of himself that he had not known about or—worse still—had not wanted to know about; only then can he see that the correct mode of conduct first involves shaking off the familiar. However, it is obvious that correct conduct as such is only a potential thing, which will come into being in as many different ways as there are situations. Fielding makes his characters react almost mechanically and invariably, following the straight and narrow path of their own habits, and in this way the reader is called upon to replace the motivation presented by a motivation that will remove the imbalance of the characters' conduct.

The text, however, leaves out this corrective motivation, although it is not difficult to find. These omissions are repaired by the reader's own imagination. As the text invites him to imagine for himself what would be the right reaction to the given situation, he is bound to make the necessary adjustments consciously, and this process must in turn make him conscious of himself, of his own conduct, and of the customs and prejudices that condition it. This new awareness, Fielding hopes, will make the reader suddenly see himself as he really is, and so the role that he is to play in uncovering the hidden reality of the text will lead ultimately to his uncovering and correcting the hidden reality of himself.

注释:

1. 亨利·菲尔丁(1707—1754),英国小说家、戏剧家,英国现实主义小说的奠基人。

2. 韦恩·布斯（1921—2005），美国芝加哥大学教授，文学批评家，“芝加哥学派”（又称“新亚里士多德学派”）第二代领军人物。

3. 诺思洛普·弗莱（1912—1991），加拿大文学评论家和文学理论家，以《批评的剖析》一书而闻名。

4. 雅各布·布赫姆（1575—1624），德国哲学家、基督教神秘主义者和路德新教神学家。

5. E. H. 贡布里希（1909—2001），奥地利裔艺术史学家，后加入英国国籍。

6. 科利·西伯（1671—1757），英国演员兼经理、剧作家和桂冠诗人。

7. 塞缪尔·理查逊（1689—1761），18 世纪英国著名小说家，保守派作家。

Chapter Seven Western Marxist Literary Theory

马克思主义批评，一种以历史和社会为主要关注对象的理论，是20世纪视野最广的重要理论流派。它的政治批评立场贯穿于一切带有激进文化色彩和政治色彩的理论和批评实践之中。在一二十年后突如其来的后殖民主义、新历史主义、文化研究等新理论中，仍然有马克思主义批评的影子。纵观整个20世纪的理论图景，我们可以发现马克思主义的批评通常是以对话者的身份与其他理论一起出现的，它往往填补了一些偏颇和狭隘的理论命题的空白。批评家曾经总结过，当读者的反应批评预设是一名普通读者时，马克思主义批评从阶级角度描述读者间的差异；当形式主义致力于研究文学本身的风格时，马克思主义批评对不同形式策略背后的意识形态内涵提出质疑；当心理学批评想要探求作品中的个人心理意义时，马克思主义批评考察社会权力与整体深层心理结构的关系；当解构主义批评家关注破坏中心思想或意义的修辞手法时，马克思主义批评利用这一策略指出，某个特殊的主导意识形态或思维模式潜伏在作品中，认为这一作品鼓励这种意识形态或思维方式。马克思主义理论的介入无疑给文学批评增添了浓重的忧患意识。在与其他理论的对话过程中，当代马克思主义批评也吸收了其他理论的丰富内容，使其更加丰富和完善。现象学、解释学、符号学和结构主义精神分析学都为马克思主义批评所用。当代马克思主义批评已经超越了传统的局限性，似乎已经成为所有批评方法的综合。

马克思主义文论按照时间顺序划分为传统马克思主义文论、早期西方马克思主义文论和当代西方马克思主义文论三部分。传统马克思主义文论，即自马克思(Karl Heinrich Marx)、恩格斯(Friedrich Engels)直到20世纪中叶这段历史时期的马克思主义批评理论，源于马克思和恩格斯的政治经济著作。马克思和恩格斯没有提出任何系统的文艺美学理论，他们对文艺的评论往往是支离破碎的。马克思对古希腊艺术的永恒魅力的阐述和恩格斯的文学书信的论述，是后来马克思主义批评家经常引用的文献。他们对经济基础与上层建筑、意识形态关系的论述，成为马克思主义批评中的新课题。早期西方马克思主义批评严格遵循经济基础决定上层建筑的公式，把文学作品视为现实的反映，认为这是社会经济力量直接决定的。这种批评通常被认为是庸俗的马克思主义经济决定论。除了马克思、恩格斯之外，传统马克思主义批评家还有德国的梅林（Franz Mehring）、俄国的普列汉诺夫（Georgi Valentinovich Plekhanov）和列宁（Vladimir Ilich Lenin）。

西方马克思主义批评因对文化的重视和对哲学的青睐而有别于传统马克思主义。早期的马克思主义批评家认为艺术与社会经济有着直接的对应关系，艺术的任务是用生动的语言和形象反映社会生活，艺术的消亡与社会经济的兴衰相呼应。他们从经济学的角度探讨文学的起源，支持经济基础决定上层建筑，具体社会制度决定具体文学的公式。早期西方马克思主义代表人物有卢卡奇（Georg Lukács）、柯尔施（Karl Korsch）、葛兰西（Gramsci Antonio）等。西方马克思主义者逐渐意识到马克思主义是一门不断发展的科学，既包括马克思本人的学说，以及由此产生的种种理论体系，也包括在一定时期占主导地位的马克思主义。当代西方马克思主义文论，以詹明信（Fredric Jameson）为代表，指出不同的社会经济制度、政治制度、社会环境产生不同的思维观念，不同的社会历史境况也会产生不同的马克思主义。当代西方马克思主义批评从哲学的角度将马克思主义批评转向文化批判。西方马克思主义代表人物还包括德国的瓦尔特·本雅明（Whalter Benjamin）、英国的雷蒙·威廉斯（Raymond Williams）和特里·伊格尔顿（Terry Eagleton）、法兰克福学派的马克斯·霍克海默（Max Hirkheimer）、西奥多·阿多诺（Theodor Adorno）、赫伯特·马尔库塞（Herbert Marcuse）、结构主义马克思主义者路易·阿尔都塞（Louis Althusser）、吕西安·戈德曼（Lucien Goodmann）、皮埃尔·马舍雷（Pierre Macherey）等人。

Louis Althusser

路易·阿尔都塞（1918—1990），法国著名哲学家、结构主义马克思主义的奠基人。1918年，阿尔都塞生于阿尔及利亚，其父是一家法国银行的经理。1939年，他被巴黎高师录取，同年9月被征入伍，法军溃败后在德国的集中营度过了5年的时光。1945年到1948年，他重回高师攻读哲学，毕业后直到1980年，一直担任高师的哲学辅导教师。1948年，他加入了法国共产党。阿尔都塞结构主义思潮，运用结构主义方法阐释马克思的著作，对经验主义、历史主义和人道主义进行了批判，构成了有别于正统马克思主义的结构主义马克思主义思想体系，并在法国形成了一个学派。1990

年10月22日，因心脏病突发辞世。主要著作有《政治和历史：孟德斯鸠、卢梭、黑格尔和马克思》(1959)、《保卫马克思》(1965)、《阅读〈资本论〉》(1965)、《列宁和哲学》(1968)、《自我批评》(1974)。

Ideology and Ideological State Apparatuses: On Ideology

(Althusser, Louis. Ideology and Ideological State Apparatuses: On Ideology. 选自亚当斯、瑟尔主编，《柏拉图以来的批评理论》(下册)(第三版)，北京：北京大学出版社，2006年，第1298到1308页。)

《意识形态和意识形态国家机器》1970年6月发表于法国的《思想》(*La Pensée*)杂志第151期，是阿尔都塞从《论生产关系的再生产》手稿中抽取的一些片段合成的，这部手稿由法国大学出版社以《论再生产》为题于1995年整理出版。该文章中，阿尔都塞对国家上层建筑结构与意识形态进行了分析，提出强制性国家机器与意识形态国家机器的概念，认为国家机器通过使用强制手段和意识形态这两种方式进行运作，完成了劳动力的意识形态的再生产和现存生产关系的再生产。该文章一经面世，就产生了巨大且深远的影响，迄今为止仍是阿尔都塞最重要的文章之一。

When I put forward the concept of an Ideological State Apparatus, when I said that the ISAs 'function by ideology,' I invoked a reality which needs a little discussion: ideology.

It is well known that the expression 'ideology' was invented by Cabanis[1], Destutt de Tracy[2] and their friends, who assigned to it as an object the (genetic) theory of ideas. When Marx took up the term fifty years later, he gave it a quite different meaning, even in his Early Works. Here, ideology is the system of the ideas and representations which dominate the mind of a man or a social group. The ideologico-political struggle conducted by Marx as early as his articles in the *Rheinische Zeitung* inevitably and quickly brought him face to face with this reality and forced him to take his earliest intuitions further.

However, here we come upon a rather astonishing paradox. Everything seems to lead Marx to formulate a theory of ideology. In fact, *The German Ideology* does offer us, after the 1844 *Manuscripts*, an explicit theory of ideology, but... it is not Marxist (we shall see why in a moment). As for *Capital*, although it does contain many hints towards a theory of ideologies (most visibly, the ideology of the vulgar economists), it does not contain the theory itself, which depends for the most part on a theory of ideology in general.

I should like to venture a first and very schematic outline of such a theory. The theses I am about to put forward are certainly not off the cuff, but they cannot be sustained and tested, i. e. confirmed or rejected, except by much thorough study and analysis.

Ideology Has No History

One word first of all to expound the reason in principle which seems to me to found, or at least to justify, the project of a theory of ideology *in general*, and not a theory of particular ideologies, which, whatever their form (religious, ethical, legal, political), always express *class positions*.

It is quite obvious that it is necessary to proceed towards a theory of ideologi*es* in the two respects I have just suggested.[3] It will then be clear that a theory of ideologi*es* depends in the last resort on the history of social formations, and thus of the modes of production combined in social formations, and of the class struggles which develop in them. In this sense it is clear that there can be no question of a theory of ideologi*es in general*, since ideologi*es* (defined in the double respect suggested above: regional and class) have a history, whose determination in the last instance is clearly situated outside ideologies alone, although it involves them.

On the contrary, if I am able to put forward the project of a theory of ideology *in general*, and if this theory really is one of the elements on which theories of ideologi*es* depend, that entails an apparently paradoxical proposition which I shall express in the following terms: *ideology has no history*.

As we know, this formulation appears in so many words in a passage from *The German Ideology*. Marx utters it with respect to metaphysics, which, he says, has no more history than ethics (meaning also the other forms of ideology).

In *The German Ideology*, this formulation appears in a plainly positivist context. Ideology is conceived as a pure illusion, a pure dream, i. e. as nothingness. All its reality is external to it. Ideology is thus thought as an imaginary construction whose status is exactly like the theoretical status of the dream among writers before Freud. For these writers, the dream was the purely imaginary, i. e. null, result of 'day's residues,' presented in an arbitrary arrangement and order, sometimes even 'inverted,' in other words, in 'disorder.' For them, the dream was the imaginary, it was empty, null and arbitrarily 'stuck together' (*bricolé*), once the eyes had closed, from the residues of the only full and positive reality, the reality of the day. This is exactly the status of philosophy and ideology (since in the book philosophy is ideology *par excellence*) in *The German Ideology*.

Ideology, then, is for Marx an imaginary assemblage (*bricolage*), a pure dream, empty and vain, constituted by the 'day's residues' from the only full and positive reality, that of the concrete history of concrete material individuals materially producing their existence. It is on this basis that ideology has no history in *The German Ideology*, since its history is outside it, where the only existing history is, the history of concrete individuals, etc. In *The German Ideology*, the thesis that ideology has no history is therefore a purely negative thesis, since it means both:

1. ideology is nothing insofar as it is a pure dream(manufactured by who knows what power: if not by the alienation of the division of labour, but that, too, is a *negative* determination);

2. ideology has no history, which emphatically does not mean that there is no history in it (on the contrary, for it is merely the pale, empty and inverted reflection of real history) but that it has no history *of its own*.

Now, while the thesis I wish to defend formally speaking adopts the terms of *The German Ideology* ('ideology has no history'), it is radically different from the positivist and historicist thesis of *The German Ideology*.

For on the one hand, I think it is possible to hold that ideologi*es have a history of their own* (although it is determined in the last instance by the class struggle); and on the other, I think it is possible to hold that ideology *in general has no history*, not in a negative sense (its history is external to it), but in an absolutely positive sense.

This sense is a positive one if it is true that the peculiarity of ideology is that it is endowed with a structure and a functioning such as to make it a non-historical reality, i. e. an *omni-historical* reality, in the sense in which that structure and functioning are immutable, present in the same form throughout what we can call history, in the sense in which the *Communist Manifesto* defines history as the history of class struggles, i. e. the history of class societies.

To give a theoretical reference-point here, I might say that, to return to our example of the dream, in its Freudian conception this time, our proposition: ideology has no history, can and must (and in a way which has absolutely nothing arbitrary about it, but, quite the reverse, is theoretically necessary, for there is an organic link between the two propositions) be related directly to Freud's proposition that the *unconscious is eternal*, i. e. that it has no history.

If eternal means, not transcendent to all (temporal) history, but omnipresent, trans-historical and therefore immutable in form throughout the extent of history, I shall adopt Freud's expression word for word, and write *ideology is eternal*, exactly like the unconscious. And I add that I find this comparison theoretically justified by the fact that the eternity of the unconscious is not unrelated to the eternity of ideology in general.

That is why I believe I am justified, hypothetically at least, in proposing a theory of ideology *in general*, in the sense that Freud presented a theory of the unconscious *in general*.

To simplify the phrase, it is convenient, taking into account what has been said about ideologies, to use the plain term ideology to designate ideology in general, which I have just said has no history, or, what comes to the same thing, is eternal, i. e. omnipresent in its immutable form throughout history (the history of social formations containing social classes). For the moment I shall restrict myself to 'class societies' and their history.

Ideology Is a 'Representation' of the Imaginary Relationship of Individuals to Their Real Conditions of Existence

In order to approach my central thesis on the structure and functioning of ideology, I shall first present two theses, one negative, the other positive. The first concerns the object which is 'represented' in the imaginary form of ideology, the second concerns the materiality of ideology.

THESIS I: Ideology Represents the Imaginary Relationship of Individuals to Their Real Conditions of Existence

We commonly call religious ideology, ethical ideology, legal ideology, political ideology, etc., so many 'world outlooks.' Of course, assuming that we do not live one of these ideologies as the truth (e. g. 'believe' in God, Duty, Justice, etc....), we admit that the ideology we are discussing from a critical point of view, examining it as the ethnologist examines the myths of a 'primitive society,' that these 'world outlooks' are largely imaginary, i. e. do not 'correspond to reality.'

However, while admitting that they do not correspond to reality, i. e. that they constitute an illusion, we admit that they do make allusion to reality, and that they need only be 'interpreted' to discover the reality of the world behind their imaginary representation of that world (ideology = *illusion* / *allusion*).

There are different types of interpretation, the most famous of which are the *mechanistic* type, current in the eighteenth century (God is the imaginary representation of the real King), and the '*hermeneutic*' interpretation, inaugurated by the earliest Church Fathers, and revived by Feuerbach[3] and the theologico-philosophical school which descends from him, e. g. the theologian Barth[4] (to Feuerbach, for example, God is the essence of real Man). The essential point is that on condition that we interpret the imaginary transposition (and inversion) of ideology we arrive at the conclusion that in ideology 'men represent their real conditions of existence to themselves in an imaginary form.'

Unfortunately, this interpretation leaves one small problem unsettled: why do men 'need' this imaginary transposition of their real conditions of existence in order to 'represent to themselves' their real conditions of existence?

The first answer (that of the eighteenth century) proposes a simple solution: Priests or Despots are responsible. They 'forged' the Beautiful Lies so that, in the belief that they were obeying God, men would in fact obey the Priests and Despots, who are usually in alliance in their imposture, the Priests acting in the interests of the Despots or *vice versa*, according to the political positions of the 'theoreticians' concerned. There is therefore a cause for the imaginary transposition of the real conditions of existence: that cause is the existence of a small number of cynical men who base their domination and exploitation of the 'people' on a falsified representation of the world which they have imagined in order to enslave other minds by dominating their imaginations.

The second answer (that of Feuerbach, taken over word for word by Marx in his Early Works) is more 'profound,' i. e. just as false. It, too, seeks and finds a cause for the imaginary transposition and distortion of men's real conditions of existence, in short, for the alienation in the imaginary of the representation of men's conditions of existence. This cause is no longer Priests or Despots, nor their active imagination and the passive imagination of their victims. This cause is the material alienation which reigns in the conditions of existence of men themselves. This is how, in *The Jewish Question* and elsewhere, Marx defends the Feuerbachian idea that men make themselves an alienated (=imaginary) representation of their conditions of existence because these conditions of existence are themselves alienating (in the 1844 *Manuscripts*: because these conditions are dominated by the essence of alienated society—'*alienated labour*').

All these interpretations thus take literally the thesis which they presuppose, and on which they depend, i. e. that what is reflected in the imaginary representation of the world found in an ideology is the conditions of existence men, i. e. their real world.

Now I can return to a thesis which I have already advanced: it is not their real conditions of existence, their real world, that 'men' 'represent to themselves' in ideology, but above all it is their relation to those conditions of existence which is represented to them there. It is this relation which is at the centre of every ideological, i. e. imaginary, representation of the real world. It is this relation that contains 'cause' which has to explain the imaginary distortion of the ideological representation of the real world. Or rather, to leave aside the language of causality it is necessary to advance the thesis that it is the *imaginary nature of this relation* which underlies all the imaginary distortion that we can observe (if we do not live in its truth) in all ideology.

To speak in a Marxist language, if it is true that the representation of the real conditions of existence of the individuals occupying the posts of agents of production, exploitation, repression, ideologization and scientific practice, does in the last analysis arise from the relations of production, and from relations deriving from the relations of production, we can say the following: all ideology represents in its necessarily imaginary distortion not the existing relations of production (and the other relations that derive from them), but above all the (imaginary) relationship of individuals to the relations of production and the relations that derive from them. What is represented in ideology is therefore not the system of the real relations which govern the existence of individuals, but the imaginary relation of those individuals to the real relations in which they live.

If this is the case, the question of the 'cause' of the imaginary distortion of the real relations in ideology disappears and must be replaced by a different question: why is the representation given to individuals of their (individual) relation to the social relations which govern their conditions of existence and their collective and individual life necessarily an imaginary relation? And what is the nature of this imaginariness? Posed in this way, the question explodes the solution by a 'clique' by a group of individuals (Priests or Despots) who are the authors of the great ideological mystification, just as it explodes the solution by the alienated character of the real world. We shall see why later in my exposition. For the moment I shall go no further.

THESIS Ⅱ: *Ideology Has a Material Existence*

I have already touched on this thesis by saying that the 'ideas' or 'representations,' etc., which seem to make up ideology do not have an ideal (*idéale* or *idéelle*) or spiritual existence, but a material existence. I even suggested that the ideal (*idéale* / *idéelle*) and spiritual existence of 'ideas' arises exclusively in an ideology of the 'idea' and of ideology, and let me add, in an ideology of what seems to have 'founded' this conception since the emergence of the sciences, i. e. what the practicians of the sciences represent to themselves in their spontaneous ideology as 'ideas,' true or false. Of course, presented in affirmative form, this thesis is unproven. I simply ask that the reader be favourably disposed towards it, say, in the name of materialism. A long series of arguments would be necessary to prove it.

This hypothetical thesis of the not spiritual but material existence of 'ideas' or other 'representations' is indeed necessary if we are to advance in our analysis of the nature of ideology. Or rather, it is merely useful to us in order the better to reveal what every at all serious analysis of any ideology will immediately and empirically show to every observer, however critical.

While discussing the ideological State apparatuses and their practices, I said that each of them was the realization of an ideology (the unity of these different regional ideologies—religious, ethical, legal, political, aesthetic, etc.—being assured by their subjection to the ruling ideology). I now return to this thesis: an ideology always exists in an apparatus, and its practice, or practices. This existence is material.

Of course, the material existence of the ideology in an apparatus and its practices does not have the same modality as the material existence of a paving-stone or a rifle. But, at the risk of being taken for a Neo-Aristotelian (NB Marx had a very high regard for Aristotle), I shall say that 'matter is discussed in many senses,' or rather that it exists in different modalities, all rooted in the last instance in 'physical' matter.

Having said this, let me move straight on and see what happens to the 'individuals' who live in ideology, i. e. in a determinate (religious, ethical, etc.) representation of the world whose imaginary distortion depends on their imaginary relation to their conditions of existence, in other words, in the last instance, to the relations of production and to class relations (ideology = an imaginary relation to real relations). I shall say that this imaginary relation is itself endowed with a material existence.

Now I observe the following.

An individual believes in God, or Duty, or Justice, etc. This belief derives (for everyone, i. e. for all those who live in an ideological representation of ideology, which reduces ideology to ideas endowed by definition with a spiritual existence) from the ideas of the individual concerned, i. e. from him as a subject with a consciousness which contains the ideas of his belief. In this way, i. e. by means of the absolutely ideological 'conceptual' device (*dispositif*) thus set up (a subject endowed with a consciousness in which he freely forms or freely recognizes ideas in which he believes), the (material) attitude of the subject concerned naturally follows.

The individual in question behaves in such and such a way, adopts such and such a practical attitude, and, what is more, participates in certain regular practices which are those of the ideological apparatus on which 'depend' the ideas which he has in all consciousness freely chosen as a subject. If he believes in God, he goes to Church to attend Mass, kneels, prays, confesses, does penance (once it was material in the ordinary sense of the term) and naturally repents and so on. If he believes in Duty, he will have the corresponding attitudes, inscribed in ritual practices 'according to the correct principles.' If he believes in Justice, he will submit unconditionally to the rules of the Law, and may even protest when they are violated, sign petitions, take part in a demonstration, etc.

Throughout this schema we observe that the ideological representation of ideology is itself forced to recognize that every 'subject' endowed with a 'consciousness' and believing in the 'ideas' that his 'consciousness' inspires in him and freely accepts, must 'act according to his ideas,' must therefore inscribe his own ideas as a free subject in the actions of his material practice. If he does not do so, 'that is wicked.'

Indeed, if he does not do what he ought to do as a function of what he believes, it is because he does something else, which, still as a function of the same idealist scheme, implies that he has other ideas in his head as well as those he proclaims, and that he acts according to these other ideas, as a man who is either 'inconsistent' ('no one is willingly evil') or cynical, or perverse.

In every case, the ideology of ideology thus recognizes, despite its imaginary distortion, that the 'ideas' of a human subject exist in his actions, or ought to exist in his actions, and if that is not the case, it lends him other ideas corresponding to the actions (however perverse) that he does perform. This ideology talks of actions: I shall talk of actions inserted into *practices*. And I shall point out that these practices are governed by the *rituals* in which these practices are inscribed, within the *material existence of an ideological apparatus*, be it only a small part of that apparatus: a small mass in a small church, a funeral, a minor match at a sports' club, a school day, a political party meeting, etc.

Besides, we are indebted to Pascal's[5] defensive 'dialectic' for the wonderful formula which will enable us to invert the order of the notional schema of ideology. Pascal says more or less: 'Kneel down, move your lips in prayer, and you will believe.' He thus scandalously inverts the order of things, bringing, like Christ, not peace but strife, and in addition something hardly Christian (for woe to him who brings scandal into the world!)—scandal itself. A fortunate scandal which makes him stick with Jansenist[6] defiance to a language that directly names the reality.

I will be allowed to leave Pascal to the arguments of his ideological struggle with the religious ideological State apparatus of his day. And I shall be expected to use a more directly Marxist vocabulary, if that is possible, for we are advancing in still poorly explored domains.

I shall therefore say that, where only a single subject (such and such an individual) is concerned, the existence of the ideas of his belief is material in that *his ideas are his material actions inserted into material practices governed by material rituals which are themselves defined by the material ideological apparatus from which derive the ideas of that subject*. Naturally, the four inscriptions of the adjective 'material' in my proposition must be affected by different modalities: the materialities of a displacement for going to mass, of kneeling down, of the gesture of the sign of the cross, or of the *mea culpa*, of a sentence, of a prayer, of an act of contrition, of a penitence, of a gaze, of a hand-shake, of an external verbal discourse or an 'internal' verbal discourse (consciousness), are not one and the same materiality. I shall leave on one side the problem of a theory of the differences between the modalities of materiality.

It remains that in this inverted presentation of things, we are not dealing with an 'inversion' at all, since it is clear that certain notions have purely and simply disappeared from our presentation, whereas others on the contrary survive, and new terms appear.

Disappeared: the term *ideas*.

Survive: the terms *subject*, *consciousness*, *belief*, *actions*.

Appear: the terms *practices*, *rituals*, *ideological apparatus*.

It is therefore not an inversion or overturning (except in the sense in which one might say a government or a glass is overturned), but a reshuffle (of a non-ministerial type), a rather strange reshuffle, since we obtain the following result.

Ideas have disappeared as such (insofar as they are endowed with an ideal or spiritual existence), to the precise extent that it has emerged that their existence is inscribed in the actions of practices governed by rituals defined in the last instance by an ideological apparatus. It therefore appears that the subject acts insofar as he is acted by the following system (set out in the order of its real determination): ideology existing in a material ideological apparatus, prescribing material practices governed by a material ritual, which practices exist in the material actions of a subject acting in all consciousness according to his belief.

But this very presentation reveals that we have retained the following notions: subject, consciousness, belief, actions. From this series I shall immediately extract the decisive central term on which everything else depends: the notion of the *subject*.

And I shall immediately set down these two conjoint theses:

1. there is no practice except by and in an ideology;
2. there is no ideology except by the subject and for subjects.

I can now come to my central thesis.

注释：

1. 乔治・卡巴尼斯（1757—1808），法国生理心理学家，著有《人的肉体与道德方面之间的关系》。

2. 德斯蒂・德・特拉西（1754—1836），法国哲学家，意识形态学派创始人。

3. 路德维希・安德列斯・费尔巴哈（1804—1872），后黑格尔德国哲学家，唯物主义代表人物，对马克思影响很大。

4. 约翰・巴思（1930— ），美国著名的后现代主义和元小说作家。

5. 布莱士・帕斯卡（1623—1662），法国数学家、物理学家、哲学家、作家和天主教神学家。

6. 詹森主义者。詹森主义是主要发生在法国的一个神学运动，强调原罪、人类堕落、神圣恩典和宿命。这场运动得名于1638年去世的荷兰神学家康内留斯・詹森（1585—1638），他的遗作《奥古斯丁传》成为詹森派主要的神学著作。詹森被称为詹森主义的神学运动之父。

Terry Eagleton

特里・伊格尔顿(1943—),生于一个工人阶级的爱尔兰天主教的家庭,是当代著名的西方马克思主义文学理论家、文化批评家、文学批评家和公共知识分子。曾求学于剑桥大学,师从威廉斯,后在牛津大学任教,现为曼彻斯特大学英文客座教授。曾在康奈尔大学、杜克大学、艾奥瓦大学、墨尔本大学、都柏林三一学院、耶鲁大学等世界名校进行访问。他一直以正统的马克思主义者或马克思主义"左派"自居,他对马克思主义的坚守和发展使其理论独树一帜,备受当今国际学术界的关注。主要著作有《批评与意识形态》(1976)、《马克思主义与文学批评》(1976)、《文学理论导论》(1983)、《意识形态导论》(1991)、《后现代主义的幻象》(1996)等。

Ideology and Literary Form

(Eagleton, Terry. Ideology and Literary Form. *New Left Review I*/90, March/April, 1975, pp. 81-109.)

在《意识形态和文学形式》中,伊格尔顿从意识形态概念出发,对形式的意识形态性及其马克思主义文学批评在审美形式方面的理论拓展与审美表达机制等问题进行了深入的探究,并对形式主义文学批评的陌生化问题、本体论倾向及其反历史主义色彩进行了反思与批判。伊格尔顿强调文学与意识形态的关系,试图揭示文学中隐藏的、自身不能表达的社会现实和社会矛盾。他提出了马克思主义文学批评应从政治出发,而不是探索任何空洞哲学的观点;批评的任务是打破现有的文学观念,揭示其意识形态角色,创造读者的主体性。

Bourgeois ideology in nineteenth-century England confronted a severe problem.[1] Its withered roots in the sparse soil of utilitarianism seriously limited its ability to produce a richly symbolic, potently affective set of mythologies capable of permeating the texture of lived experience and so of performing the functions of an ideology in the fullest sense. Permanently crippled in phenomenological capacity, it needed to have constant resort to the Romantic humanist heritage—to that nebulous, elusive amalgam of Burkean conservatism[1] and German idealism, forged by the later Coleridge[2] and transmitted to Carlyle, Disraeli[3], Arnold[4] and Ruskin[5], which offered an idealist critique of bourgeois social relations coupled with a consecration of the rights of capital. Part of the specific complexity of English nineteenth-century bourgeois ideology, founded on a complex conjuncture of bourgeois and aristocratic classes within the hegemonic bloc, lies in this contradictory unity of 'organic' and 'traditional' elements, whereby an impoverished empiricist liberalism exploits the symbolically fertile, metaphysically coercive resources of Romantic humanism, with its nostalgic, reactionary, quasi-feudal social models, to stabilize and ratify bourgeois property relations. The 'Culture and Society' tradition is the literary record of this ideological conjuncture; John Stuart Mill[6], mechanistically harnessing Coleridge to Bentham[7] in the late eighteen thirties, provides one of its more palpable instances.

Antonio Gramsci[8] has commented on this ideological formation in nineteenth-century England. 'There is a very extensive category of organic intellectuals—those, that is, who come into existence on the same industrial terrain as the economic group—but in the higher sphere we find that the old land-owning class preserves its position of virtual monopoly. It loses its economic supremacy but maintains for a long time a politico-intellectual supremacy and is assimilated as "traditional intellectuals" and as directive (*dirigente*) group by the new group in power. The old land-owning aristocracy is joined to the industrialists by a kind of suture which is precisely that which in other countries unites the traditional intellectuals with the new dominant classes.'

Hegemonic Aspirations

That assimilation of 'traditional' and 'organic' intellectuals is the key to the historic significance in Victorian England of Matthew Arnold. The thrust of Arnold's social criticism, partly concealed by his best-known work *Culture and Anarchy*, is to convert a sectarian, internally divided and visionless industrial bourgeoisie pragmatically sunk in its own material interests into a cohesive, truly *hegemonic* class, capable of elaborating in the ideological sphere the predominance it has come to hold in history. To achieve this goal the bourgeoisie must be inserted into the organic totality of 'Culture', that spiritual Absolute which subsumes one-sided class interests into transcendental unity. More specifically, it must appropriate the civilized aesthetic heritage of the aristocracy in order to equip itself with a world view capable of incorporating the proletariat. 'The middle classes, remaining as they are now, with their narrow, harsh, unintelligent and unattractive spirit and culture, will almost certainly fail to mould or assimilate the masses below them.' For Arnold, the aristocracy is losing political hegemony but its historical successor, the bourgeoisie, is disastrously unprepared ideologically to assume it; as a Government Inspector of Schools and the son of Thomas Arnold[9] of Rugby, his insistence is accordingly on the historical necessity for the bourgeoisie to attain to 'higher', more unified forms by enshrining itself in national culture and educational institutions.

Idealist and historicist though Arnold's conception of ideological hegemony is, his relation of 'organic' cultural modes to the drive to consolidate a corporate social formation in which the bourgeoisie can install itself as a 'national' class has a significance for Victorian and modern literature which it is the purpose of this article to examine. Arnold's work belongs to a significant mutation in nineteenth-century liberalism: as Victorian capitalism is driven to transcend its earlier, nakedly competitive phase of primitive accumulation and organize itself into more corporate forms, a transformation of the classical liberalism which finds a late formulation in Mill's *On Liberty* (1859) proves increasingly essential. In this process, 'organic' bourgeois ideology (in Gramsci's sense) has more intensive resort to the social and aesthetic organicism of the Romantic humanist tradition, finding in aesthetic production models of totality and affectivity relevant to its ideological demands. During the period of Arnold's social criticism, the initially poetic notion of 'organic form' becomes increasingly extended to the dominant literary mode of the time, fiction. A serious aesthetics of fiction consequently develops, to discover its major ideologue at the end of the century in Henry James. This article will survey in skeletal and schematic form some relations between a sector of the major literature of the last century and the ideological formations in which it is set, taking the concepts of 'organic form' and 'organicism' as one crucial nexus between history and literary production.

George Eliot

George Eliot[10]'s literary career from her translation of Strauss's *Das Leben Jesu* (1846) to *Daniel Deronda* (1876) is almost exactly coterminous with the period of Victorian prosperity which follows the severe depression and fierce class struggles of the eighteen thirties and forties. During this period productive output increased spectacularly, Britain's volume of world trade grew rapidly, and money-wages probably rose by at least a third between 1850 and 1870. A familiar political consequence of this prosperity was a partial though marked incorporation of the working class. From the mid-century onwards, until the resurgence of proletarian militancy in the depressed eighties, corporatism becomes a prominent characteristic of wide areas of the working-class movement. Having defeated the first wave of working-class militancy, the industrial bourgeoisie had begun by 1850 to consolidate its victory. Sections of the working class advanced economically, only to become at each stage politically incorporated. On the eve of the second Reform Bill, R. H. Hutton argued in *Essays in Reform* (1867) that the trade unions had taught the workers the value of co-operation, sacrifice and solidarity, and that this principle might be usefully integrated into society as a whole. Through the unions, the working class had come to appreciate the value of true government and a 'distrust of mere scattered energies'. This 'class-patriotism' must at all costs be channelled to national account; the spirit of trade unionism must be grafted 'into the richer growth of our national politics'.

The ideological matrix of George Eliot's fiction is determined by the increasingly corporate character of Victorian capitalism and its political apparatus. Eliot's work attempts to resolve a structural conflict between two forms of mid-Victorian bourgeois ideology—between a still buoyant though progressively muted Romantic individualism preoccupied with the untrammelled evolution of the 'free spirit', and certain 'higher' corporate ideological modes whose object is to isolate the immutable social laws to which that individualism, if it is to avoid social disruption and ethical anarchy, must self-sacrificially conform. Those 'higher' ideological forms are for Eliot Feuerbachian humanism and scientific rationalism—a conjuncture which in principle complements the imperatives of Romantic individualism, since both disclose historically progressive laws with which the exploratory individual may imaginatively unite. Scientific rationalism, in judiciously curbing the disruptively egoistic tendencies of Benthamite hedonism, also obstructs Romantic self-expression. Yet conversely Feuerbachian humanism protects those Romantic values against an aggressively un-diluted rationalism, and by rooting them in the human collectivity defends them equally from an unbridled individualism. The Religion of Humanity, more effectively than the laboriously abstract, obsessively systemic symbology of Comtism, imbues scientific law with Romantic humanist spirit, discovering that law inscribed in the passions and pieties of men; it can thus offer itself as a totalizing doctrine without detriment to an imaginative empathy with empirical experience. By virtue of this ideological conjuncture, the Romantic individualist may submit to the social totality without sacrificing personal self-fulfilment.

In principle, that is; in practice, a potentially tragic collision between 'corporate' and 'individualist' ideologies is consistently defused and repressed by the forms of Eliot's fiction. As the daughter of a farm-agent, the social locus of corporate value for Eliot is rural society; it is here, most obviously in *Adam Bede* and *Silas Marner*, that the cluster of traditionalist practices and organic affiliations imputed to the English provincial countryside is 'selected' by the national ideology as socially paradigmatic, at a point where that ideology demands precisely such images of social incorporation. Rural society in *Adam Bede*, as John Goode has commented, is chosen as a literary subject not for its remote idiosyncratic charm but as a simplificatory model of the whole social formation, whose uniformly determining laws may be focused there in purer, more diagrammatic form. But if the framing, externalizing literary forms of *Adam Bede* and *Silas Marner* (pastoral, myth, moral fable) permit such transparency, they also mystify the historical contradictions at the core of Eliot's fiction by projecting them into ideologically resolvable form. The social organicism of Adam Bede, with his stiff-necked moralism and pragmatic petty-bourgeois politics, is forbidden from entering into significant deadlock with any 'authentic' liberal individualism, since that individualism figures in the novel only in the debased, trivialized form of a hedonist egoism (the anarchic sexual appetite of Arthur Donnithorne and Hetty Sorrel) which the stable moulds of rural life can displace without notable self-disruption. The class violence of Arthur's seduction of Hetty is reduced to an ethical issue; and the upshot of that ethical drama is to liberalize Adam's moral intransigence to the point where he can advance into more flexibly individualized consciousness without damage to his mythological status as organic type, an admirable amalgam of naturalized culture and cultivated nature.

Ambiguous Stance

In selecting rural petty-bourgeois life as a paradigmatic region, Eliot betrays an ambiguous attitude towards it which is a function of her problematical authorial relationship to her readership. In endorsing an extension of conventional literary realism to a sensitive treatment of socially obscure destinies, she both insists on the potentially world-historical significance of the apparently peripheral lives she delineates and apologizes, with a blend of genial patronage and tentative irony, for choosing such an unenlightened enclave as the subject-matter of serious fiction. These tonal hesitancies focus an ideological conflict. A rationalist critique of rural philistinism, coupled with a Romantic individualist striving beyond its spiritually constrictive confines, enters into contradiction with a deep-seated ideological imperative to celebrate the value of inert and bigoted traditionalism, as the humble but organically nourishing soil which feeds the flower of higher individual achievement. *Adam Bede* attempts a partial solution of this dilemma by romantically idealizing the common life in the figures of Adam and Dinah Morris; in *The Mill on the Floss*, however, such a synthesis demands a considerably more obtrusive manipulation of literary devices.

The rural society of the *Mill* — one of struggling tenant farmers becoming enmortgaged and forced to ruin by the pressures of urban banking and agricultural industry — is less easily idealized than in *Adam Bede*; as urban capital penetrates into the countryside, those conflicts in the rural social structure suggested but suppressed in the latter novel erupt to provide one of the *Mill* 's central images, the financial collapse of the mill itself. Moreover, if Hetty Sorrel can be effectively externalized as socially disruptive egoist, Maggie Tulliver of the *Mill* is a bearer of authentic liberal values who is by no means so easily dislodged. Allured by a liberal individualism which decisively ruptures with the stagnant moral oppressiveness of the rural petty bourgeoisie, Maggie must nonetheless refuse that ethic in the name of a commitment to the settled, traditionalist social milieu of her childhood. Nostalgia for an idealized upbringing at the mill is translated into an idealist defence of clannish, claustrophobic rural *mores* against the Romantic spontaneity of the self, treacherously entwined as it is with appetitive egoism. Yet the novel's transparently engineered conclusion — Maggie's self-sacrificial drowning with her brother — suppresses that ideological conflict by the magical strategem of a literary device. Maggie's death is at once guiltily submissive expiation and affirmative self-achievement; in uniting with her brother, at once object of romantic love and bigoted type of organic community, she achieves and abnegates herself in the same act, endorsing the imperatives of 'organic' morality while attaining a fulfilling individual transcendence of them.

That the nostalgic organicism of Eliot's historically backdated rural fiction is determined in the last instance by the exigencies of the present is evident enough in *Felix Holt, The Radical*, written about the first Reform Bill on the eve of the second. Felix is essentially an urban version of *Adam Bede*, a petty-bourgeois craftsman no more representative of the proletariat in whose name he speaks than his pre-industrial predecessor. His 'radicalism', accordingly, consists in a reformist trust in education and a positivist suspicion of political change, heroically opposed to an unsavoury alliance of unscrupulously opportunist Radical politics and the insensate irrationality of the masses. His 'Address to Working Men', with its call for a conversion of class interests into class duties, apologia for cultural privilege and fear of mass action, merely projects the novel's sustaining ideology of organic evolutionary change into more crudely explicit terms. Yet *Felix Holt* betrays in its formal structure a self-division which fails to achieve thematic articulation. This lies in the notable disjunction of the political region of the novel, focused on Felix, from those episodes centred on Mrs Transome, the suffering, spiritually broken mother of the novel's callous careerist Radical. The aesthetic potency of these scenes suggests the residual, ineradicable presence of a 'personal' disillusionment which refuses to be totalized and absorbed by the novel's official ideology of organic historical progress. Empiricist liberalism, sublated on the one hand to more corporate and 'scientific' forms, in the same act critically disengages from those potentially tyrannic totalities to defend the 'personal' values they threaten. The structural dislocations of *Felix Holt* embody that ideological dissonance: it is in the hiatus between its 'Felix' and 'Mrs Transome' episodes that the contradictions which found the novel are most visibly revealed.

Liberal Impasse

Eliot's fiction, indeed, displays from the outset a conflict between the urge to dramatize ideological totalities which transcend the limits of classical liberalism, and a fear of the disruptive effect of such formations on a range of 'personal' values bred precisely by that liberal lineage. (It is a conflict revealed in her ambiguous fellow-travelling relations with the English positivists, whom she supported but could not bring herself to join.) Fiction is organic totality, but *phenomenological* totality; its intensive incorporation of life into seamless, symmetrical wholes must be achieved without damage to the empirical specificity of experience. That problem is thematically evident in *Romola*, where Savonarola's 'passionate sense of the infinite', his seductively corporate vision, is entwined with a moral despotism which violates liberal sanctities. Yet those sanctities are in themselves insufficient: 'tender fellow-feeling for the nearest has its danger too, and is apt to be timid and sceptical towards the larger aims without which life cannot rise to religion'. In Arnold's terms, it is a conflict between a many-sided Hellenism which dangerously displaces a cohering absolute, and a morally absolutist Hebraism which proves damagingly sectarian.

The novel which explores these contradictions most fully is *Middlemarch*. The irony of *Middlemarch* is that it is a triumph of aesthetic totalization deeply suspicious of ideological totalities. Each of the novel's four central characters represents such an historically typical totalization: Casaubon idealism, Lydgate scientific rationalism, Bulstrode evangelical Christianity, Dorothea Brooke Romantic self-achievement through a unifying principle of action. Each of these totalities crumbles, ensnared and dissolved in the quotidian; and that dissolution is in part a salutary empiricist check to the tyranny of theoreticism, in part a victory of entrenched petty-bourgeois provincial consciousness over rationalist or Romantic drives to transcend it. That stalemate, the novel's title suggests, springs from a transitional phase of rural society at the time of the first Reform Bill; yet there is no doubt that the novel's judiciously muted disillusion, its 'end-of-ideologies' ambience, belongs to its post-second Reform Bill present. The question which *Middlemarch* objectively poses and fails to resolve is how ideology is to be conceptually elaborate yet emotionally affective, nurturing 'irrational' personal pieties while cohering them into a structural whole which sublates empiricism and Romantic spontaneity. Confronted with the aggressive modes of working-class consciousness caricatured in *Felix Holt*, the cautious empiricism of classical liberalism must be reaffirmed; yet that empiricism is in itself an ideologically inadequate response to the historical conjuncture of post-Reform Bill England, with its demand for a more elaborately structured ideological formation capable of more intensive political incorporation.

This dilemma is figured in *Middlemarch* in one of its key images: that of the *web* as image of the social totality. The web is a *derivative* organic image, a mid-point between the animal imagery of *Adam Bede* and some more developed theoretical concept of *structure*. The complexity of the web, its subtle interlacing of relatively autonomous strands, its predatory overtones, the possibilities of empirical entanglement and local complication it permits, imaginatively accommodates forms of conflict excluded by the more fundamentally organicist imagery of *Adam Bede*. But at the same time the web's symmetry, its 'spatial' de-historicizing of the social process, its exclusion of levels of contradiction, maintains the essential unity of the organic mode. Its fragility and complexity impel a prudent political conservatism—the more delicately interlaced the web's strands, the more the disruptive, uncontrollable consequences of action can multiply, and so the more circumspect one must be in launching ambitiously totalizing projects. Yet conversely, if action at any point in the web will vibrate through its filaments to affect the whole formation, a semi-mystical relation to the totality is nonetheless maintained. Natural imagery, as in the novel's closing trope of the river which in diffusing its unified force to tributaries intensifies its total impact, is exploited to suggest how a fulfilling relation to the social totality can be achieved, not by ideological abstraction, but by pragmatic, apparently peripheral work. And if *Middlemarch*'s natural metaphors perform this function, so does its aesthetic imagery. The problem of totality in the novel is effectively displaced to the question of aesthetic form itself, which structures its materials without damage to their empirical richness. The novel, in other words, formally answers the problem it thematically poses. Only the novelist can be the centred subject of her own de-centred fictional structure, the privileged consciousness which at once supervenes on the whole as its unitary source and enters into phenomenological relation with each part.

Magical Solution

A purely aesthetic resolution, however, is ideologically insufficient. What is demanded is a totalizing vision which binds the individual to the laws of a social formation, preserves the 'personal' pieties violated by such visions in *Romola* and *Middlemarch*, and romantically liberates the self. The answer to this problem is *Daniel Deronda*. In that novel, Eliot finds a magical solution to her ideological dilemma in Deronda's Jewishness, which provides him with a fulfilling romantic identity while incorporating him into the complex totality of a corporate historical culture. The problem, in other words, can be 'solved' only by the invention of a *displaced* totality outside the sterile detotalization of post-Reform Bill England—a totality which is then instantly *exported*, as Deronda leaves to discover his destiny in the Middle East. The difficulty then is to bring this factitious totality into regenerative relation with bourgeois England—a difficulty 'solved' by Deronda's redemptive influence on the broken, dispirited victim of that society, Gwendolen Harleth. But in attempting this 'solution' the novel splits into self-contradiction—splits, indeed, down the middle. For Daniel can only fulfil his destiny by withdrawing from Gwendolen to the Middle East, abandoning her to a nebulous Arnoldian trust in some ideal goodness which, given her social conditions, is incapable of being socially articulated. The formal dislocations of *Daniel Deronda* enact the historical contradictions in which Eliot is trapped; it is in the silence between its 'Gwendolen' and 'Daniel' episodes that the truth of those contradictions speaks most eloquently.

Eliot's fiction, then, represents an imaginative attempt to integrate liberal ideology, in both its rationalist and Romantic modes, with certain pre-industrial, idealist or religious organicist models—an enterprise determined by the increasingly corporate economic, political and ideological character of nineteenth-century capitalism during the period of her literary production. As that capitalism moves into its imperialist stage, the historical basis of the 'idyllic' rural organicism of *Adam Bede* is progressively revealed; *Impressions of Theophrastus Such* (1879) places its plea for 'corporate existence' in the context of nationalist rhetoric and a warning of the dangers involved in undergoing 'a pre-mature fusion with immigrants of alien blood'. The voice of liberal humanism becomes the voice of jingoist reaction.

注释:

1. 伯克的保守主义。埃德蒙·伯克（1729—1797），爱尔兰政治家，他经常被视作英美保守主义的奠基者。

2. 塞缪尔·泰勒·柯勒律治（1772—1834），英国诗人、文学评论家、哲学家和神学家，英国浪漫主义文学的奠基人之一。

3. 本杰明·迪斯雷利（1804—1881），英国保守党的政治家，曾两次担任英国首相。

4. 马修·阿诺德（1822—1888），英国诗人和文化评论家，拉格比公学校长托马斯·阿诺德之子。

5. 约翰·拉斯金（1819—1900），维多利亚时代英国主要的艺术评论家，同时也是艺术赞助人、画家、社会思想家和慈善家。

6. 约翰·斯图尔特·密尔（1806—1873），英国哲学家、政治经济学家，古典自由主义史上最具影响力的思想家之一，对社会理论、政治理论和政治经济学有着广泛的贡献。

7. 杰里米·边沁（1748—1832），英国哲学家、法学家和社会改革家，功利主义哲学的创立者。

8. 安东尼奥·葛兰西（1891—1937），意大利马克思主义哲学家和共产主义政治家，著作涉及政治理论、社会学和语言学。

9. 托马斯·阿诺德（1795—1842），英国教育家和历史学家。

10. 乔治·艾略特（1819—1880），英国维多利亚时代著名作家、诗人、记者和翻译家，原名玛丽·安·埃文斯。

Chapter Eight Post-structuralism

后结构主义最初是由20世纪60年代继承却批判结构主义的法国知识分子和哲学家发起的先锋运动和政治思潮，后来迅速蔓延至全球。其代表人物大多是原来的结构主义者，后结构主义标志着结构主义的终结。到20世纪末，后结构主义已经成为后现代主义的前沿，经常被冠以"后现代理论"的称号。后结构主义很少有互相一致的理论，但每个理论都以对结构主义的批判为起点。米歇尔·福柯(Michel Foucault)、雅克·德里达(Jacques Derrida)、罗兰·巴特(Roland Barthes)和其他以"后结构主义"为名的学者都不承认他们有共同的信条和方法。然而，他们对现代性传统的怀疑和颠覆态度是一致的：福柯对权力和知识建构的探索，德里达对形而上学的批判，巴特对封闭结构的质疑，以及女性主义在其影响下对男性中心主义的批判都表现出反传统的姿态。后结构主义采用索绪尔提出的概念以及以其理论为主要基础的结构主义符号学的因果关系，旨在削弱索绪尔体系和结构主义本身的基础。后结构主义主要批判结构主义对形而上学传统的依附，反对传统结构主义把研究的重点放在客观性和理性问题上，企图恢复非理性倾向，追求从逻辑出发而得出非逻辑的结果，揭示语言的规律。

德里达在《论文字学》和《书写与差异》中倡导解构主义，首先将矛头指向索绪尔和施特劳斯的基本文本，颠覆了以符号系统为稳定建构的结构概念。在社会观念和科学的哲学领域，福柯将方法论从考古学发展到谱系学，从科学与认识论、戒律与惩罚、医学、伦理学、性行为和自我表达技巧等不同的领域来发掘知识主体的意义。巴特的作品追溯了从结构主义到后结构主义各个领域的理论转向，关注从作品到文本、从陈述到解释行动、从故事到话语、从结构到一系列有效的话语活动。巴特认为，如果一部作品是一个与自身一致的，并按照先验的叙事逻辑来组织的稳定而封闭的结构，那么这部作品的文本就是一个生产和扩散的地方，作者自己只是一个访客或者是一个写作的角色，他没有任何特殊的方式去了解意义。文本摆脱了作者的羁绊，成为突破单向意义结构的开放性文本，由单一走向多元，由封闭走向无限开放，不断地产生多重意义，但不能形成最终的大聚合或最终的结构。弗洛伊德的"无意识"理论也对后结构主义产生了重大影响。他通过在话语顺序中重新嵌入被压抑和被排斥的声音来动摇话语机制,这一策略为后结构主义者所借鉴。例如,福柯的《词与物》揭示了知识无意识,《精神病史》揭示了压抑和非理性的声音。这都打破了科学与理性话语的"主人"地位。拉康的三界(想象、符号、真实)理论指出真实是理论和主体无法接触的不存在的对象。在精神分析和解构主义的影响下,后结构主义的女性主义试图在哲学、批评和叙事等主流话语中还原被排斥的女性,在科学、哲学、文学、艺术和女性主义作品中寻找这种被排斥的声音。

Jacques Derrida

雅克·德里达(1930—2004),法国著名哲学家、符号学家、文艺理论家和美学家,解构主义代表人物。德里达生于阿尔及利亚,求学于巴黎高等师范学校,曾在美国哈佛大学进修,后一直在巴黎高师进行教学和研究。德里达以其"去中心"观念,反对西方哲学史上自柏拉图以来的"逻各斯中心主义"传统,批判的矛头直指结构主义语言学理论。他的思想在 20 世纪 60 年代以后掀起了巨大波澜,成为欧美知识界最有争议性的人物。德里达的理论动摇了整个传统人文科学的基础,也是整个后现代思潮最重要的理论源泉之一。代表作有《论文字学》(1967)、《声音与现象》(1967)、《书写与差异》(1967)、《立场》(1972)、《丧钟》(1974)、《人的目的》(1980)、《胡塞尔现象学中的起源问题》(1990)、《马克思的幽灵》(1993)等四十多部。

Structure, Sign, and Play in the Discourse of the Human Sciences

(Derrida, Jacques. Structure, Sign, and Play in the Discourse of the Human Sciences. *A Postmodern Reader*. Joseph Natoli and Linda Hutcheon eds. Albany: State University of New York Press, 1993, pp. 223-242.)

1966 年 10 月,德里达在美国霍布金斯大学召开的批判语言和人文科学国际座谈会上,发表了他划时代的著名演讲《人类科学话语中的结构、符号和游戏》。该演讲的矛头直指当时法国乃至国际学术界风头最盛的结构主义,德里达提出"解构"概念,以示拆解、消解传统的理解模式、习惯和结构。德里达这次著名的讲演被称为解构主义的宣言。此后,德里达全面推出反传统的解构主义理论,以"语音与文字"作为消解的对象,创立了"文字学",并以之为武器来批判西方的"语音中心主义",再逐步扩展到

"逻各斯中心主义",最终动摇形而上学的西方哲学传统。德里达对符号的批评开创了文本批评的新模式,重新审视了语言与真理、谬论、知识、权力、理性、欲望乃至整个人文学科话语对象的关系。

Perhaps something has occurred in the history of the concept of structure that could be called an "event," if this loaded word did not entail a meaning which it is precisely the function of structural—or structuralist—thought to reduce or to suspect. But let me use the term "event" anyway, employing it with caution and as if in quotation marks. In this sense, this event will have the exterior form of a *rupture* and a *redoubling*.

It would be easy enough to show that the concept of structure and even the word "structure" itself are as old as the *epistémé* —that is to say, as old as western science and western philosophy—and that their roots thrust deep into the soil of ordinary language, into whose deepest recesses the *epistémé* plunges to gather them together once more, making them part of itself in a metaphorical displacement. Nevertheless, up until the event which I wish to mark out and define, structure—or rather the structurality of structure—although it has always been involved, has always been neutralized or reduced, and this by a process of giving it a center or referring it to a point of presence, a fixed origin. The function of this center was not only to orient, balance, and organize the structure—one cannot in fact conceive of an unorganized structure—but above all to make sure that the organizing principle of the structure would limit what we might call the *freeplay* of the structure. No doubt that by orienting and organizing the coherence of the system, the center of a structure permits the freeplay of its elements inside the total form. And even today the notion of a structure lacking any center represents the unthinkable itself.

Nevertheless, the center also closes off the freeplay it opens up and makes possible. *Qua* center, it is the point at which the substitution of contents, elements, or terms is no longer possible. At the center, the permutation or the transformation of elements (which may of course be structures enclosed within a structure) is forbidden. At least this permutation has always remained i *nterdicted* (I use this word deliberately). Thus it has always been thought that the center, which is by definition unique, constituted that very thing within a structure which governs the structure, while escaping structurality. This is why classical thought concerning structure could say that the center is, paradoxically, *within* the structure and *outside* it. The center is at the center of the totality, and yet, since the center does not belong to the totality (is not part of the totality), the totality *has its center elsewhere*. The center is not the center. The concept of centered structure—although it represents coherence itself, the condition of the *epistémé* as philosophy or science—is contradictorily coherent. And, as always, coherence in contradiction expresses the force of a desire. The concept of centered structure is in fact the concept of a freeplay based on a fundamental ground, a freeplay which is constituted upon a fundamental immobility and a reassuring certitude, which is itself beyond the reach of the freeplay. With this certitude anxiety can be mastered, for anxiety is invariably the result of a certain mode of being implicated in the game, of being caught by the game, of being as it were from the very beginning at stake in the game. From the basis of what we therefore call the center (and which, because it can be either inside or outside, is as readily called the origin as the end, as readily *arché* as *telos*), the repetitions, the substitutions, the transformations, and the permutations are always *taken* from a history of meaning [*sens*]—that is, a history, period—whose origin may always be revealed or whose end may always be anticipated in the form of presence. This is why one could perhaps say that the movement of any archeology, like that of any eschatology, is an accomplice of this reduction of the structurality of structure and always attempts to conceive of structure from the basis of a full presence which is out of play.

If this is so, the whole history of the concept of structure, before the rupture I spoke of, must be thought of as a series of substitutions of center for center, as a linked chain of determinations of the center. Successively, and in a regulated fashion, the center receives different forms or names. The history of metaphysics, like the history of the West, is the history of these metaphors and metonymies. Its matrix—if you will pardon me for demonstrating so little and for being so elliptical in order to bring me more quickly to my principal theme—is the determination of being as *presence* in all the senses of this word. It would be possible to show that all the names related to fundamentals, to principles, or to the center have always designated the constant of a presence— *eidos*, *arché*, *telos*, *energeia*, *ousia* (essence, existence, substance, subject) *aletheia*, transcendentality, consciousness, or conscience, God, man, and so forth.

The event I called a rupture, the disruption I alluded to at the beginning of this paper, would presumably have come about when the structurality of structure had to begin to be thought, that is to say, repeated, and this is why I said that this disruption was repetition in all of the senses of this word. From then on it became necessary to think the law which governed, as it were, the desire for the center in the constitution of structure and the process of signification prescribing its displacements and its substitutions for this law of the central presence—but a central presence which was never itself, which has always already been transported outside itself in its surrogate. The surrogate does not substitute itself for anything which has somehow pre-existed it. From then on it was probably necessary to begin to think that there was no center, that the center would not be thought in the form of a being-present, that the center had no natural locus, that it was not a fixed locus but a function, a sort of non-locus in which an infinite number of sign-substitutions came into play. This moment was that in which language invaded the universal problematic; that in which, in the absence of a center or origin, everything became discourse-provided we can agree on this word—that is to say, when everything became a system where the central signified, the original or transcendental signified, is never absolutely present outside a system of differences. The absence of the transcendental signified extends the domain and the interplay of signification *ad infinitum*.

Where and how does this decentering, this notion of the structurality of structure, occur? It would be somewhat naive to refer to an event, a doctrine, or an author in order to designate this occurrence. It is no doubt part of the totality of an era, our own, but still it has already begun to proclaim itself and begun to *work*. Nevertheless, if I wished to give some sort of indication by choosing one or two "names," and by recalling those authors in whose discourses this occurrence has most nearly maintained its most radical formulation, I would probably cite the Nietzschean critique of metaphysics, the critique of the concepts of being and truth, for which were substituted the concepts of play, interpretation, and sign (sign without truth present); the Freudian critique or self-presence, that is, the critique of consciousness, of the subject, of self-identity and of self-proximity or self-possession; and, more radically, the Heideggerean destruction of metaphysics, of onto-theology, of the determination of being as presence. But all these destructive discourses and all their analogues are trapped in a sort of circle. This circle is unique. It describes the form of the relationship between the history of metaphysics and the destruction of the history of metaphysics. *There is no sense* in doing without the concepts of metaphysics in order to attack metaphysics. We have no language—no syntax and no lexicon—which is alien to this history; we cannot utter a single destructive proposition which has not already slipped into the form, the logic, and the implicit postulations of precisely what it seeks to contest. To pick out one example from many: the metaphysics of presence is attacked with the help of the concept of the *sign*. But from the moment anyone wishes this to show, as I suggested a moment ago, that there is no transcendental or privileged signified and that the domain or the interplay of signification has, henceforth, no limit, he ought to extend his refusal to the concept and to the word sign itself—which is precisely what cannot be done. For the signification "sign" has always been comprehended and determined, in its sense, as sign-of, signifier referring to a signified, signifier different from its signified. If one erases the radical difference between signifier and signified, it is the word signifier itself which ought to be abandoned as a metaphysical concept. When Lévi-Strauss[1] says in the preface to *The Raw and the Cooked* that he has "sought to transcend the opposition between the sensible and the intelligible by placing [himself] from the very beginning at the level of signs," the necessity, the force, and the legitimacy of his act cannot make us forget that the concept of the sign cannot in itself surpass or bypass this opposition between the sensible and the intelligible. The concept of the sign is determined by this opposition: through and throughout the totality of its history and by its system. But we cannot do without the concept of the sign, we cannot give up this metaphysical complicity without also giving up the critique we are directing against this complicity, without the risk of erasing difference [altogether] in the self-identity of a signified reducing into itself its signifier, or, what amounts to the same thing, simply expelling it outside itself. For there are two heterogenous ways of erasing the difference between the signifier and the signified: one, the classic way, consists in reducing or deriving the signifier, that is to say, ultimately in *submitting* the sign to thought; the other, the one we are using here against the first one, consists in putting into question the system in which the preceding reduction functioned: first and foremost, the opposition between the sensible and the intelligible. The *paradox* is that the metaphysical reduction of the sign needed the opposition it was reducing. The opposition is part of the system, along with the reduction. And what I am saying here about the sign can be extended to all the concepts and all the sentences of metaphysics, in particular to the discourse on "structure." But there are many ways of being caught in this circle. They are all more or less naive, more or less empirical, more or less systematic, more or less close to the formulation or even to the formalization of this circle. It is these differences which explain the multiplicity of destructive discourses and the disagreement between those who make them. It was within concepts inherited from metaphysics that Nietzsche[2], Freud, and Heidegger[3] worked, for example. Since these concepts are not elements or atoms and since they are taken from a syntax and a system, every particular borrowing drags along with it the whole of metaphysics. This is what allows these destroyers to destroy each other reciprocally—for example, Heidegger considering Nietzsche, with as much lucidity and rigor as bad faith and misconstruction, as the last metaphysician, the last "Platonist." One could do the same for Heidegger himself, for Freud, or for a number of others. And today no exercise is more widespread.

What is the relevance of this formal schema when we turn to what are called the "human sciences"? One of them perhaps occupies a privileged place—ethnology. One can in fact assume that ethnology could have been born as a science only at the moment when a de-centering had come about: at the moment when European culture—and, in consequence, the history of metaphysics and of its concepts—had been *dislocated*, driven from its locus, and forced to stop considering itself as the culture of reference. This moment is not first and foremost a moment of philosophical or scientific discourse, it is also a moment which is political, economic, technical, and so forth. One can say in total assurance that there is nothing fortuitous about the fact that the critique of ethnocentrism—the very condition of ethnology—should be systematically and historically contemporaneous with the destruction of the history of metaphysics. Both belong to a single and same era.

Ethnology—like any science—comes about within the element of discourse. And it is primarily a European science employing traditional concepts, however much it may struggle against them. Consequently, whether he wants to or not—and this does not depend on a decision on his part—the ethnologist accepts into his discourse the premises of ethnocentrism at the very moment when he is employed in denouncing them. This necessity is irreducible; it is not a historical contingency. We ought to consider very carefully all its implications. But if nobody can escape this necessity, and if no one is therefore responsible for giving in to it, however little, this does not mean that all the ways of giving in to it are of an equal pertinence. The quality and the fecundity of a discourse are perhaps measured by the critical rigor with which this relationship to the history of metaphysics and to inherited concepts is thought. Here it is a question of a critical relationship to the language of the human sciences and a question of a critical responsibility of the discourse. It is a question of putting expressly and systematically the problem of a discourse which borrows from a heritage the resources necessary of that heritage itself. A problem of *economy* and *strategy*.

If I now go on to employ an examination of the texts of Lévi-Strauss as an example, it is not only because of the privilege accorded to ethnology among the human sciences, nor yet because the thought of Lévi-Strauss weighs heavily on the contemporary theoretical situation. It is above all because a certain choice has made itself evident in the work of Lévi-Strauss and because a certain doctrine has been elaborated there, and precisely in a *more or less explicit manner*, in relation to this critique of language and to this critical language in the human sciences.

In order to follow this movement in the text of Lévi-Strauss, let me choose as one guiding thread among others the opposition between nature and culture. In spite of all its rejuvenations and its disguises, this opposition is congenital to philosophy. It is even older than Plato. It is at least as old as the Sophists. Since the statement of the opposition— *physis/nomos*, *physis/techné* [nature/culture, nature/art or making]—it has been passed on to us by a whole historical chain which opposes "nature" to the law, to education, to art, to technics—and also to liberty, to the arbitrary, to history, to society, to the mind, and so on. From the beginnings of his quest and from his first book, *The Elementary Structures of Kinship*, Lévi-Strauss has felt at one and the same time the necessity of utilizing this opposition and the impossibility of making it acceptable. In the *Elementary Structures*, he begins from this axiom or definition: that belongs to nature which is *universal* and spontaneous, not depending on any particular culture or on any determinate norm. That belongs to culture, on the other hand, which depends on a system of *norms* regulating society and is therefore capable of *varying* from one social structure to another. These two definitions are of the traditional type. But, in the very first pages of the *Elementary Structures*, Lévi-Strauss, who has begun to give these concepts an acceptable standing, encounters what he calls a *scandal*, that is to say, something which no longer tolerates the nature/culture opposition he has accepted and which seems to require at *one and the same time* the predicates of nature and those of culture. This scandal is the *incest-prohibition*. The incest-prohibition is universal; in this sense one could call it natural. But it is also a prohibition, a system of norms and interdicts; in this sense one could call it cultural.

> Let us assume therefore that everything universal in man derives from the order of nature and is characterized by spontaneity, that everything which is subject to a norm belongs to culture and presents the attributes of the relative and the particular. We then find ourselves confronted by a fact, or rather an ensemble of facts, which, in the light of the preceding definitions, is not far from appearing as a scandal: the prohibition of incest presents without the least equivocation, and indissolubly linked together, the two characteristics in which we recognized the contradictory attributes of two exclusive orders. The prohibition of incest constitutes a rule, but a rule, alone of all the social rules, which possesses at the same time a universal character.

Obviously there is no scandal except in the *interior* of a system of concepts sanctioning the difference between nature and culture. In beginning his work with the *factum* of the incest-prohibition, Lévi-Strauss thus puts himself in a position entailing that this difference, which has always been assumed to be self-evident, becomes obliterated or disputed. For, from the moment that the incest-prohibition can no longer be conceived within the nature/culture opposition, it can no longer be said that it is a scandalous fact, a nucleus of opacity within a network of transparent significations. The incest-prohibition is no longer scandal one meets with or comes up against in the domain of traditional concepts; it is something which escapes these concepts and certainly precedes them—probably as the condition of their possibility. It could perhaps be said that the whole of philosophical conceptualization, systematically relating itself to the nature/culture opposition, is designed to leave in the domain of the unthinkable the very thing that makes this conceptualization possible: the origin of the prohibition of incest.

I have dealt too cursorily with this example, only one among so many others, but the example nevertheless reveals that language bears within itself the necessity of its own critique. This critique may be undertaken along two tracks, in two "manners." Once the limit of nature/culture opposition makes itself felt, one might want to question systematically and rigorously the history of these concepts. This is a first action. Such a systematic and historic questioning would be neither a philological nor a philosophical action in the classic sense of these words. Concerning oneself with the founding concepts of the whole history of philosophy, de-constituting them, is not to undertake the task of the philologist or of the classic historian of philosophy. In spite of appearances, it is probably the most daring way of making the beginnings of a step outside of philosophy. The step "outside philosophy" is much more difficult to conceive than is generally imagined by those who think they made it long ago with cavalier ease, and who are in general swallowed up in metaphysics by the whole body of the discourse that they claim to have disengaged from it.

In order to avoid the possibly sterilizing effect of the first way, the other choice—which I feel corresponds more nearly to the way chosen by Lévi-Strauss—consists in conserving in the field of empirical discovery all these old concepts, while at the same time exposing here and there their limits, treating them as tools which can still be of use. No longer is any truth-value attributed to them; there is a readiness to abandon them if necessary if other instruments should appear more useful. In the meantime, their relative efficacy is exploited, and they are employed to destroy the old machinery to which they belong and of which they themselves are pieces. Thus it is that the language of the human sciences criticizes *itself*. Lévi-Strauss thinks that in this way he can separate *method* from *truth*, the instruments of the method and the objective significations aimed at by it. One could almost say that this is the primary affirmation of Lévi-Strauss; in any event, the first words of the *Elementary Structures* are: "One begins to understand that the distinction between state of nature and state of society (we would be more apt to say today: state of nature and state of culture), while lacking any acceptable historical signification, presents a value which fully justifies its use by modern sociology: its value as a methodological instrument."

Lévi-Strauss will always remain faithful to this double intention: to preserve as an instrument that whose truth-value he criticizes.

On the one hand, he will continue in effect to contest the value of the nature/culture opposition. More than thirteen years after the *Elementary Structures*, *The Savage Mind* s faithfully echoes the text I have just quoted: "The opposition between nature and culture which I have previously insisted on seems today to offer a value which is above all methodological." And this methodological value is not affected by its "ontological" non-value (as could be said, if this notion were not suspect here): "It would not be enough to have absorbed particular humanities into a general humanity; this first enterprise prepares the way for others... which belong to the natural and exact sciences: to reintegrate culture into nature, and finally, to reintegrate life into the totality of its physiochemical conditions".

On the other hand, still in *The Savage Mind*, he presents as what he calls *bricolage* which might be called the discourse of this method. The *bricoleur*, says Lévi-Strauss, is someone who uses "the means at hand," that is, the instruments he finds at his disposition around him, those which are already there, which had not been especially conceived with an eye to the operation for which they are to be used and to which one tries by trial and error to adapt them, not hesitating to change them whenever it appears necessary, or to try several of them at once, even if their form and their origin are heterogenous—and so forth. There is therefore a critique of language in the form of *bricolage*, and it has even been possible to say that *bricolage* is the critical language itself. I am thinking in particular of the article by G. Genette[4], "Structuralisme et Critique litteraire," published in homage to Lévi-Strauss in a special issue of *L'Arc* (no. 26, 1965), where it is stated that the analysis of *bricolage* could "be applied almost word for word" to criticism, and especially to "literary criticism."

注释:

1. 克洛德·列维-斯特劳斯（1908—2009），出生于比利时的法国人类学家和民族学家，是结构主义和结构人类学的代表人物。

2. 尼采（1844—1900），德国哲学家、文化批评家、作曲家、诗人、语言学家、拉丁和希腊学者，其作品对现代思想史产生了深远的影响。

3. 马丁·海德格尔（1889—1976），德国哲学家，是大陆哲学传统中具有开创性的思想家。他对现象学、诠释学和存在主义的贡献最为著名。

4. 杰拉德·热奈特（1930—2018），法国文学理论家。

Roland Barthes

罗兰·巴特(1915—1980),法国文学理论家、哲学家、语言学家、批评家和符号学家,推动了结构主义、符号学、社会理论、人类学和后结构主义等理论流派的发展。巴特早期关注语言结构的随意性和大众文化现象,借助索绪尔的语言学理论深入研究文学符号学,为结构主义符号学的研究奠定了基础,后期将研究视角转向了读者,逐渐突破了结构主义符号学的封闭文本结构理论,转向后结构主义批评,影响了人们对文学和文化的看法。他出版了许多别具一格的著作，展示了个人非凡的想象力，主要有《写作的零度》(1953)、《神话》(1957)、《符号学基础》(1965)、《批评与真理》(1966)、《S/Z》(1970)、《文本的快乐》(1973)等二十余部。

The Death of the Author

(Barthes, Roland. The Death of the Author. Richard Howard trans. *Literary Theory: An Anthology* (Third Edition). Julie Rivkin and Michael Ryan eds. Hoboken: Wiley Blackwell, 2017, pp. 518-521.)

受德里达解构主义理论影响，巴特于1967年发表了他最著名的论文《作者之死》，改变了文学批评的方向，这篇论文也成为他向结构主义思想告别的转折。在该文中，巴特指出，一部作品一旦完成，作者的使命就已经终结，文本中的语言符号开始起作用，而文本的意义则取决于读者的阐释。任何文学文本都有多重含义，作者并不是作品意义的主要来源；"作者之死"是"读者之诞生"，读者的诞生必须以作者的死亡为代价，文学使得读者独具创造性。他颠覆了作者在文学活动中的权威身份和支配地位，文学的独创性被互文性所代替，文本解读不再是自上而下，而是自下而上，使得文本摆脱作者单一意义的束缚，强调了读者的主体性。巴特的"作者之死"实际上是对"作者"概念背后隐藏的诸如上帝、创造者、主体性和中心论等形而上学观念的批判。

In his story Sarrasine, Balzac[1], speaking of a castrato disguised as a woman, writes this sentence: "It was Woman, with her sudden fears, her irrational whims, her instinctive fears, her unprovoked bravado, her daring and her delicious delicacy of feeling." Who is speaking in this way? Is it the story's hero, concerned to ignore the castrato concealed beneath the woman? Is it the man Balzac, endowed by his personal experience with a philosophy of Woman? Is it the author Balzac, professing certain "literary" ideas of femininity? Is it universal wisdom? or romantic psychology? It will always be impossible to know, for the good reason that all writing is itself this special voice, consisting of several indiscernible voices, and that literature is precisely the invention of this voice, to which we cannot assign a specific origin: literature is that neuter, that composite, that oblique into which every subject escapes, the trap where all identity is lost, beginning with the very identity of the body that writes.

Probably this has always been the case: once an action is recounted, for intransitive ends, and no longer in order to act directly upon reality—that is, finally external to any function but the very exercise of the symbol—this disjunction occurs, the voice loses its origin, the author enters his own death, writing begins. Nevertheless, the feeling about this phenomenon has been variable; in primitive societies, narrative is never undertaken by a person, but by a mediator, shaman or speaker, whose "performance" may be admired (that is, his mastery of the narrative code), but not his "genius." The author is a modern figure, produced no doubt by our society insofar as, at the end of the middle ages, with English empiricism, French rationalism and the personal faith of the Reformation, it discovered the prestige of the individual, or, to put it more nobly, of the "human person." Hence it is logical that with regard to literature it should be positivism, resume and the result of capitalist ideology, which has accorded the greatest importance to the author's "person." The author still rules in manuals of literary history, in biographies of writers, in magazine interviews, and even in the awareness of literary men, anxious to unite, by their private journals, their person and their work; the image of literature to be found in contemporary culture is tyrannically centered on the author, his person, his history, his tastes, his passions; criticism still consists, most of the time, in saying that Baudelaire's work is the failure of the man Baudelaire[2], Van Gogh's[3] work his madness, Tchaikovsky's[4] his vice: the explanation of the work is always sought in the man who has produced it, as if, through the more or less transparent allegory of fiction, it was always finally the voice of one and the same person, the author, which delivered his "confidence."

Though the Author's empire is still very powerful (recent criticism has often merely consolidated it), it is evident that for a long time now certain writers have attempted to topple it. In France, Mallarmé was doubtless the first to see and foresee in its full extent the necessity of substituting language itself for the man who hitherto was supposed to own it; for Mallarmé, as for us, it is language which speaks, not the author: to write is to reach, through a preexisting impersonality—never to be confused with the castrating objectivity of the realistic novelist—that point where language alone acts, "performs," and not "oneself": Mallarmé's entire poetics consists in suppressing the author for the sake of the writing (which is, as we shall see, to restore the status of the reader.) Valery[5], encumbered with a psychology of the Self, greatly edulcorated Mallarmé's theory, but, turning in a preference for classicism to the lessons of rhetoric, he unceasingly questioned and mocked the Author, emphasized the linguistic and almost "chance" nature of his activity, and throughout his prose works championed the essentially verbal condition of literature, in the face of which any recourse to the writer's inferiority seemed to him pure superstition. It is clear that Proust[6] himself, despite the apparent psychological character of what is called his analyses, undertook the responsibility of inexorably blurring, by an extreme subtilization, the relation of the writer and his characters: by making the narrator not the person who has seen or felt, nor even the person who writes, but the person who will write (the young man of the novel—but, in fact, how old is he, and who is he? — wants to write but cannot, and the novel ends when at last the writing becomes possible), Proust has given modern writing its epic: by a radical reversal, instead of putting his life into his novel, as we say so often, he makes his very life into a work for which his own book was in a sense the model, so that it is quite obvious to us that it is not Charlus who imitates Montesquiou[7], but that Montesquiou in his anecdotal, historical reality is merely a secondary fragment, derived from Charlus. Surrealism lastly—to remain on the level of this prehistory of modernity—surrealism doubtless could not accord language a sovereign place, since language is a system and since what the movement sought was, romantically, a direct subversion of all codes—an illusory subversion, moreover, for a code cannot be destroyed, it can only be "played with"; but by abruptly violating expected meanings (this was the famous surrealist "jolt"), by entrusting to the hand the responsibility of writing as fast as possible what the head itself ignores (this was automatic writing), by accepting the principle and the experience of a collective writing, surrealism helped secularize the image of the Author. Finally, outside of literature itself (actually, these distinctions are being superseded), linguistics has just furnished the destruction of the Author with a precious analytic instrument by showing that utterance in its entirety is a void process, which functions perfectly without requiring to be filled by the person of the interlocutors: linguistically, the author is never anything more than the man who writes, just as I is no more than the man who says I: language knows a "subject," not a "person," end this subject, void outside of the very utterance which defines it, suffices to make language "work," that is, to exhaust it.

The absence of the Author (with Brecht, we might speak here of a real "alienation:" the Author diminishing like a tiny figure at the far end of the literary stage) is not only a historical fact or an act of writing: it utterly transforms the modern text (or—what is the same thing—the text is henceforth written and read so that in it, on every level, the Author absents himself). Time, first of all, is no longer the same. The Author, when we believe in him, is always conceived as the past of his own book: the book and the author take their places of their own accord on the same line, cast as a before and an after: the Author is supposed to feed the book—that is, he pre-exists it, thinks, suffers, lives for it; he maintains with his work the same relation of antecedence a father maintains with his child. Quite the contrary, the modern writer (scriptor) is born simultaneously with his text; he is in no way supplied with a being which precedes or transcends his writing, he is in no way the subject of which his book is the predicate; there is no other time than that of the utterance, and every text is eternally written here and now. This is because (or: it follows that) to write can no longer designate an operation of recording, of observing, of representing, of "painting" (as the Classic writers put it), but rather what the linguisticians, following the vocabulary of the Oxford school, call a performative, a rare verbal form (exclusively given to the first person and to the present), in which utterance has no other content than the act by which it is uttered: something like the / Command of kings or the I Sing of the early bards; the modern writer, having buried the Author, can therefore no longer believe, according to the "pathos" of his predecessors, that his hand is too slow for his thought or his passion, and that in consequence, making a law out of necessity, he must accentuate this gap and endlessly "elaborate" his form; for him, on the contrary, his hand, detached from any voice, borne by a pure gesture of inscription (and not of expression), traces a field without origin—or which, at least, has no other origin than language itself, that is, the very thing which ceaselessly questions any origin.

We know that a text does not consist of a line of words, releasing a single "theological" meaning (the "message" of the Author-God), but is a space of many dimensions, in which are wedded and contested various kinds of writing, no one of which is original: the text is a tissue of citations, resulting from the thousand sources of culture. Like Bouvard and Pecuchet, those eternal copyists, both sublime and comical and whose profound absurdity precisely designates the truth of writing, the writer can only imitate a gesture forever anterior, never original; his only power is to combine the different kinds of writing, to oppose some by others, so as never to sustain himself by just one of them; if he wants to express himself, at least he should know that the internal "thing" he claims to "translate" is itself only a readymade dictionary whose words can be explained (defined) only by other words, and so on ad infinitum: an experience which occurred in an exemplary fashion to the young De

Quincey[8], so gifted in Greek that in order to translate into that dead language certain absolutely modern ideas and images, Baudelaire tells us, "he created for it a standing dictionary much more complex and extensive than the one which results from the vulgar patience of purely literary themes" (Paradis Artificiels). Succeeding the Author, the writer no longer contains within himself passions, humors, sentiments, impressions, but that enormous dictionary, from which he derives a writing which can know no end or halt: life can only imitate the book, and the book itself is only a tissue of signs, a lost, infinitely remote imitation.

Once the Author is gone, the claim to "decipher" a text becomes quite useless. To give an Author to a text is to impose upon that text a stop clause, to furnish it with a final signification, to close the writing. This conception perfectly suits criticism, which can then take as its major task the discovery of the Author (or his hypostases: society, history, the psyche, freedom) beneath the work: once the Author is discovered, the text is "explained:" the critic has conquered; hence it is scarcely surprising not only that, historically, the reign of the Author should also have been that of the Critic, but that criticism (even "new criticism") should be overthrown along with the Author. In a multiple writing, indeed, everything is to be distinguished, but nothing deciphered; structure can be followed, "threaded" (like a stocking that has run) in all its recurrences and all its stages, but there is no underlying ground; the space of the writing is to be traversed, not penetrated: writing ceaselessly posits meaning but always in order to evaporate it: it proceeds to a systematic exemption of meaning. Thus literature (it would be better, henceforth, to say writing), by refusing to assign to the text (and to the world as text) a "secret:" that is, an ultimate meaning, liberates an activity which we might call counter-theological, properly revolutionary, for to refuse to arrest meaning is finally to refuse God and his hypostases, reason, science, the law.

Let us return to Balzac's sentence: no one (that is, no "person") utters it: its source, its voice is not to be located; and yet it is perfectly read; this is because the true locus of writing is reading. Another very specific example can make this understood: recent investigations (J. P. Vernant[9]) have shed light upon the constitutively ambiguous nature of Greek tragedy, the text of which is woven with words that have double meanings, each character understanding them unilaterally (this perpetual misunderstanding is precisely what is meant by "the tragic"); yet there is someone who understands each word in its duplicity, and understands further, one might say, the very deafness of the characters speaking in front of him: this someone is precisely the reader (or here the spectator). In this way is revealed the whole being of writing: a text consists of multiple writings, issuing from several cultures and entering into dialogue with each other, into parody, into contestation; but there is one place where this multiplicity is collected, united, and this place is not the author, as we have hitherto said it was, but the reader: the reader is the very space in which are inscribed, without any being lost, all the citations a writing consists of; the unity of a text is not in its origin, it is in its destination; but this destination can no longer be personal: the reader is a man without history, without biography, without psychology; he is only that someone who holds gathered into a single field all the paths of which the text is constituted. This is why it is absurd to hear the new writing condemned in the name of a humanism which hypocritically appoints itself the champion of the reader's rights. The reader has never been the concern of classical criticism; for it, there is no other man in literature but the one who writes. We are now beginning to be the dupes no longer of such antiphrases, by which our society proudly champions precisely what it dismisses, ignores, smothers or destroys; we know that to restore to writing its future, we must reverse its myth: the birth of the reader must be ransomed by the death of the Author.

注释:

1. 巴尔扎克(1799—1850),法国小说家和剧作家。
2. 夏尔·皮埃尔·波德莱尔(1821—1867),法国19世纪最著名的现代派诗人,象征派诗歌先驱。
3. 凡·高(1853—1890),荷兰后印象派画家,西方艺术史上最著名、最有影响力的人物之一。
4. 柴可夫斯基(1840—1893),俄罗斯浪漫主义时期的作曲家。
5. 瓦莱里(1871—1945),法国著名诗人和文艺理论家。
6. 马塞尔·普鲁斯特(1871—1922),法国著名小说家、评论家和散文家。
7. 孟德斯鸠 (1689—1755),法国伟大的启蒙思想家、作家、法学家,西方国家学说以及法学理论的奠基人。
8. 托马斯·德·昆西(1785—1859),英国著名的浪漫主义散文作家、文学批评家,著有《一个鸦片服用者的自白》。
9. 让-皮埃尔·韦尔南(1914—2007),法国历史学家和人类学家、古希腊专家。

Chapter Nine **Postmoderninsm**

在当今的批判理论中,后现代主义无疑是人们谈论最多的一个术语。后现代主义,是指 20 世纪 60 年代以来整个西方以反传统哲学为特征的社会和文化思潮,也是对现代文化哲学和精神价值取向进行批判和解构的一种哲学思维方式和态度。后现代主义几乎涵盖哲学、社会学、建筑、绘画、音乐、历史、文学、文化等人文社会科学的所有领域。

“后现代”(postmodern)、“后现代性”(postmodernity)与“后现代主义”(postmodernism)这三个术语经常被混为一谈。简单地说,“后现代”是一个时间概念,指的是晚期资本主义,又称后工业社会、信息社会、跨国资本时期或现代化后的时代。后现代性是一个社会学概念,反映了后现代时期的社会特征,涉及生产方式、生产关系、社会结构、意识形态等多个方面,具有明显的历史和哲学意义。后现代主义是一个风格概念,指的是后现代时期文化艺术表现形式的特征,包括建筑、文学、音乐、绘画、电影、电视等范畴。

在这三个概念中,更重要的是区分后现代性与后现代主义。后现代性是一个涉及面广,富有社会、历史、哲学内涵的概念;后现代主义是一个相对狭隘的概念,强调文化和审美特征。后现代性反对真理、理性、科学、进步、普遍解放等宏大叙事,意味着现代性的终结,认为真理是解释的产物,事实是话语的形成,客观性只是已经获得权力的有争议的解释,而人作为主体是一种与他所思考的现实完全一致的虚构,或是一个没有任何固定品质和性质的自我分裂的实体。后现代主义可以说是一种适应后现代性的文化形态。典型的后现代主义艺术作品具有随意性、折中性、混合性、无中心性、不确定性、不连贯性、拼凑性、模仿性等特点。他们忠于后现代性原则,摒弃形而上学的深度,追求一种人为的深度,因而具有丰富的游戏性和享乐性,但缺乏情感,只有表面的或暂时的强化。后现代主义是对现代化过程中出现的剥夺人的主体性和感觉丰富性的整体性、中心性、同一性等思维方式的批判与解构,也是对西方传统哲学的本质主义、基础主义、“形而上学的在场”、“逻各斯中心主义”等的批判与解构。在后现代主义者看来,文本、表征和符号的解释有无限可能性。

后现代性和后现代主义的争论一直存在,其形式多种多样。根据大卫·哈维(David Harvey)1989 年在《后现代状况》一书中的论述,后现代主义是对资本主义过度积累危机的历史回应。这场危机的标志包括:中心主体的分裂;指称对象的丧失;道德判断与科学判断关系的瓦解;具有叙述优势的意象;具有伦理优势的美学;超越永恒真理和统一政治的暂时性和分裂性。哈维指出,里根的经济学和巫术式的形象生产可以说是后现代主义观点的缩影。

利奥塔(Jean-Francois Lyotard)反对哈贝马斯(Jürgen Habermas)对后现代主义的批判,反对后现代主义背叛启蒙运动的理想,如客观科学、普遍的道德和法律、独立的艺术等,否定黑格尔的整体性的世界观,指出这一世界观导致了国家暴力所造成的有机的、全面的、超然的幻觉。对他来说,个人的现代性等同于恐怖主义。因此,他坚持消解自我认识主体的概念,消解单一的历史目的,代之以尼采式的虚无主义或概念主义。更确切地说,他提倡以一种新康德的崇高美学来再现那些无法再现的事物。

弗雷德里克·詹明信(Fredric Jameson)认为,后现代主义是晚期资本主义文化的内在逻辑,是商业形式对文化本身的渗透,简言之是"文化的商业化和商业的文化化"。对詹明信来说,后现代主义表达了一种全新的艺术的社会定位。后现代主义不是主题问题,也不是主体问题,而是艺术进入商品生产世界的问题。詹明信的解释与马克思主义有关,他认为全球和跨国资本主义时期标志着资本主义发展的新时期。因此,后现代主义是当代晚期资本主义的一种文化形态,与之相似,现实主义是与资本主义工业发展阶段相对应的艺术形态,现代主义是帝国主义和垄断资本主义时期相对应的艺术形态。

Jonathan Arac

乔纳森·阿拉克,美国文学学者、评论家、历史学家、新美国主义者,被称为 21 世纪美国的巴赫金,是匹兹堡大学的安德鲁·梅隆英语教授兼人文中心主任,1989 年加入英语系任教至今。他主要教授 1820 年以来的美国文学和文化、1740—1940 年的英国文学和文化、文学批评和理论。他一直在国际学术期刊《边界 2》编辑组工作。《边界 2》创刊于 1979 年,致力于后现代理论、文学和文化研究,涉及建筑、视觉艺术、音乐、文学、历史、社会和自然科学等领域,是具有国际性和跨学科性的学术期刊。阿拉克眼光卓越,视野开阔,对现代主义经典文本进行创新性的后现代解读,试图打破文学的界限,探索文学批评在国家政治话语中的作用,也对美国文学研究的前提、方法和实践提出质疑。

An Introduction: Postmodernism

(Arac, Jonathan. An Introduction: Postmodernism. *Postmodernism and Politics*. Jonathan Arac ed. Minneapolis: University of Minnesota Press, 1986, pp. ix-xiii.)

《后现代主义和政治》是一本选自《边界 2》的散文集，包括八篇关于后现代主义的文章，重点关注知识、艺术和社会问题。后现代主义与政治的联系很难定义，但该书使人们重新思考许多人文主义研究的特权对象：批评的纪律、书籍的读者或电影的观众、艺术家、"主要知识分子"，甚至是体验本身的概念，由此引发对后现代主义和政治的反省。《后现代导论》是《后现代主义和政治》一书的序言，下面的选读文章是《后现代主义和政治》序言的部分节选。

In the two decades since it first consciously began to define itself, postmodern criticism has chosen to be worldly. Not that it is urbane; this is not a world in which one can or should too easily be at home. Yet the struggle against received forms of reading, writing, and public discourse has not been mundane either. Philosophy, and its difficulties, served a necessary function in countering the technicist emphases of New Criticism and structuralism alike, as well as in marking the difference between a simple quest for relevance and a movement that was willing to wield the weapons of criticism in all their cultural elaboration. Then, in the seventies, postmodernism experienced an exhilarating but unsettling confluence with poststructuralism, the critique of method, the philosophic cure, that sprung up athwart structuralism.

Now that the sixties have faded emphatically into a past, the radical social and political activities, the urgency of questioning that formed the atmosphere from which postmodernism condensed, no longer define our immediate world. They must not be repressed, however; we must solicit the uncanny without becoming somnambulists. This need locates the dialogue between postmodern criticism and the Anglo-American renewal of Marxism that is itself a product of the sixties. The problems of "Western Marxism" are well known from discussions by Perry Anderson[1] and Russell Jacoby[2], and Edward Said[3] has pertinently exposed the dangers of "traveling theory." Nonetheless, this new Marxism and postmodernism share the conviction that literature and theory and criticism are not only contemplative, not mere superstructure, but active; they share commitments to human life in history. In short, they share the world.

It would be foolish, however, to suggest that this beginning heralds the dawn of a new day. Irving Howe recently looked back to the founding of *Dissent* in 1954 and ruefully explained its premise: "We were saying... that socialism in America had to be seen mostly as an intellectual problem before it could even hope to become a viable movement" (*Margin of Hope* 236). At about the same time as Howe's explanation, *Diacritics* published an interview with Fredric Jameson, in which his own current theoretical concerns and the project of *Social Text* are similarily summarized: "No real systemic change in this country will be possible without the minimal first step of the achievement of a social democratic movement [but] that first step will not be possible without two other preconditions... the creation of a Marxist intelligentsia, and that of a Marxist culture" (73). The congruence of analysis is striking, and the endurance of the problem is dismaying.

The bar between culture and politics in the United States that seems to be marked here has stood at least since the first great American novel appeared. Hawthorne set "The Prison Door" as the title of his first chapter. It stands between the "official," political life of "The Custom House" and the passionate, artistic representation of "The Scarlet Letter," and it blocks the passage from one to the other. Of these two unequal parts that together make up *The Scarlet Letter*, each may be read as the source of the other, yet each is unconscious of the other. The marks that trace their relations remain to be produced through our reading, beyond which lies a task of historical interpretation to revise our sense of politics in the American life of letters.

Postmodernism. *boundary* 2 and the Wider Debate

The preceding remarks introduced a special issue of *boundary* 2: *a journal of postmodern literature*, from which the essays in this volume have been selected. The history of *boundary* 2 therefore forms a first context for understanding them. When it was founded in the early 1970s, *boundary* 2 projected a clear sense of the "postmodern"; as a university-based intervention in the world of literature, it stood against the classics of modernism as they had been interpreted and institutionalized by the New Criticism. A Sartrean, existential concern for the engagements of worldly life opposed New Critical emphasis on "impersonality" in its many forms, whether distance through myth, hardness through image, or lucidity through point of view. The journal's roots in phenomenology reached back from Sartre[4] to Heidegger, toward a sense of temporality against New Critical modernist spatialization; and beyond Heidegger to Kierkegaard[5], who offered an understanding of irony quite different from that which was popularized by Robert Penn Warren[6] and Cleanth Brooks[7]. This renewed sense of irony enabled *boundary* 2 critics to elaborate postmodern interpretations of Eliot, Joyce, Yeats, Conrad, and other modernist classics. The "postmodern" thus proved not straightforwardly chronological. It partook of a more complex hermeneutical temporality, which proved confusing to some observers(Berman 351, n. 24 and Jameson, "Politics of Theory." 55-56. n. 1) as the journal uncovered an ever-receding history of postmodernism through unsettling received New-Critical interpretations over the whole of Western literature. The best current statement of the journal's point of view is W. V. Spanos[8], "Postmodern Literature and Its Occasion."

A further complication in the position of *boundary* 2 emerged over time in its relation to issues of political and social life. Although conceived from the beginning as oppositional, its concerns might at first have seemed those of a "personal" individualism, which, however full-bodied in comparison to New Criticism, would remain no more than an alternative aestheticism. Already by the middle of the 1940s, however, Sartre had visibly begun his own turn to politics, and Lucien Goldmann[9] had offered the suggestion that Heidegger's existential phenomenology took its point of departure from the critique of "reification" by Georg Lukács[10] in *History and Class Consciousness* (1923), to which *Being and Time* (1927) offered an ontological rather than historical analysis. Since, moreover, *boundary* 2 had been founded in part as an attempt to prolong the energies of the 1960s, both its situation and its intellectual genealogy pointed toward what in fact occurred: postmodernism and politics came together in the journal's agenda. Yet Lukács's insistence on "totality" seemed suspiciously like that of the New Critics on the "tradition" or on the work as "icon." In confluence with contemporary revisions of Heidegger in France, the politics of *boundary* 2 proved "deconstructive" like Derrida; like Foucault more concerned with the fields of "micro-politics." This acknowledgment of the micro-political has allowed *boundary* 2 to take seriously its location as an academic journal, rather than yearning nostalgically for the days of the independent man of letters and looking only with disabling self-contempt at the current place of literary intellectuals.

The postmodernism of *boundary* 2 is only one of many varieties; these essays are part of a larger debate that has been going on around the notion. The discussion has been most notable for its international and interdisciplinary extent, running from architecture through the visual arts and music, through literature and history, to the social and natural sciences, while bringing in contributions from several European cultures beyond the anglophone world(see Hassan, "Postface 1982"). Yet almost no women have figured in the debate, even though many analysts include current feminism among the features of postmodernity. Nancy Fraser's[11] important feminist critique of Habermas[12] ("What's Critical") stands nearly alone(see also Kristeva), although Craig Owens and Andrew Ross[13] have effectively situated feminist work by women in relation to postmodernism. A sampling of significant positions in the overall debate would include those of the English historian Perry Anderson, who was long editor of *New Left Review*; the Harvard sociologist Daniel Bell[14], whose collaboration with Irving Kristol[15] on *The Public Interest* led to his characterization as a "neoconservative"; the German social philosopher Jürgen Habermas, who is often treated as the heir of Frankfurt-school critical theory; Fredric Jameson, who revitalized American Marxist cultural studies while Professor of French at Yale amid the controversy over deconstruction; Jean-Francois Lyotard, a French philosopher and former independent socialist activist, long involved with the critique of Stalinism; Richard Rorty[16], whose renewal of American pragmatism led him out of Princeton's philosophy department and into the pages of general literary and cultural journals.

Using even this limited group as a field for comparison, it becomes obvious how little the debate has reached clarity. To begin with, the debate is motivated by evaluative differences. The first significant literary discussions of the "postmodern" some quarter-century ago by Irving Howe and Harry Levin established a clear negative stance: the postmodern was a weak successor to the vigorous glory of literary modernism, brought about because mass society had eroded the artist's vital distance. During the sixties, a more complex attention to new modes of mass media in work by Leslie Fiedler[17], Susan Sontag[18], Richard Poirier[19], and above all Ihab Hassan[20](see "POST modern ISM") helped to establish the context within which *boundary* 2 appeared. In recent years, however, the initial hostility, exacerbated by a sense of beleaguerment, has fueled new antipostmodern projects like that of Hilton Kramer's[21] *New Criterion*. So it remains even now typically the case that to "have a position" on postmodernism means not just to offer an analysis of its genesis and contours but to let the world know whether you are for it or against it, and in fairly bald terms. Thus Anderson, Bell, and Habermas all treat postmodernism as something that we could be spared if only people would trade excessive rhetoric for sensible analysis (at just these moments, however, their own rhetoric swells); Lyotard and Rorty, on the other hand, urge us to adopt postmodern positions. Jameson argues that postmodernism necessarily includes both positive and negative aspects, but that the notion helps us to make sense of our times and therefore should be used; to all who oppose the postmodern, however, this can seem no more than disguised advocacy.

It remains wholly unsettled whether the relation of the "postmodern" to the "modern" is more a break or a continuity. Anderson finds "modern" and "postmodern" alike terms that mask more important facts about the times they purport to describe; Bell finds the postmodern acting out principles that were already dangerous within modernism; and Lyotard finds in the postmodern a sublime potentiality that is realized in the modern, unsettling our usual conception of sequence. Habermas, Jameson, and Rorty agree in finding a significant break between the modern and the postmodern, but there is no consensus as to where the break falls. Jameson, perhaps because he is a professional student of literature, roughly identifies the modern with the first half of the twentieth century and the postmodern with what has come later. Habermas, perhaps because professionally a student of social philosophy, identifies the modern with the still-unfulfilled project of the eighteenth-century Enlightenment, while the postmodern remains a threatening shadow rather than something that has quite occurred. Rorty, perhaps because his defining professional engagement was with the analytic epistemological tradition, locates the modern with Descartes[22] and finds the major contours of the postmodern already visible in Hegel.

In their methods of analysis, these figures fall into yet further combinations. Habermas, Lyotard, and Rorty all employ versions of "thin" or "philosophical" history to establish their points; in contrast, Anderson, Bell, and Jameson, even though also writing relatively brief treatments, draw upon a much wider range of empirical materials. On the other hand, Bell joins Lyotard and Rorty in de-emphasizing "totalizing" modes of description and explanation. Among these three, however, further splits appear.

Against attempts to ground Value in Humanity, Nature, or Reason, Rorty insists on the local contingencies of values, approaching a position like that of current literary theory on "interpretive communities." Yet Rorty still relies on the integrity of his local units. He therefore warns "the intellectual" not to become separated from "the social needs of his community"("Habermas and Lyotard" 175), learning from American intellectuals' response to the Vietnam War, which acted "to separate the intellectuals from the moral consensus of the nation" ("Postmodernist Bourgeois Liberalism" 588). Lyotard's overall position seems to agree with Rorty's; Lyotard contrasts the "*grands récits*" (perhaps best translated "tall tales") that unify human history in the name of Emancipation (the French Revolution) or Speculation (the German university) or both (Marxism) with the language games of "*petits récits*" ("white lies") that operate over smaller units both conceptually and demographically. Yet in exploring "the differend" (dispute, conflict, difference), Lyotard looks to situations where power and language intersect to victimize minorities wrongly treated as if they were members of a community from which they actually differ in ways that are "not presentable under the rules of knowledge". As against Rorty, Lyotard does not trust the integrity of "communities" any more than of "totality."

In a mode that he might blush to find Lyotard characterizing as postmodern, Daniel Bell insists against both functionalists and Marxists that there is no integral entity called "society"; between the separate realms of the polity, the economy, and the culture "disjunction" prevails. Bell can therefore assert, in a statement that would seem to be so scandalous that his critics in the debate do not even comment on it, that he is "a socialist in economics, a liberal in politics, and a conservative in culture"("Modernism and Capitalism" 206). This takes to an extreme a notion like that of the "relative autonomy" with which Althusser made possible fresh Marxist thought regarding questions of the state and of culture, and which remains crucial in the attempts by Anderson and Jameson at a "totalizing" frame of argument. Habermas, while insisting on Weber's neo-Kantian separation of rationality into separate spheres of knowledge, morality, and taste (corresponding to science, social organization, and art), tries to establish a new, if reduced, totality of "everyday life," which in order to flourish must be kept in contact with the results of all three spheres.

It might be thought that the question of art's autonomy would only be a special case of "totality," but in fact yet-different alignments emerge on this issue, which has been crucial, as we have already noted, since the beginning of the postmodernism debate. In Anderson's argument, surprisingly close to traditional Marxist "reflection" theory, the possibilities of art are determined by social conditions but art does not have the power to alter those conditions; for Lyotard, art's value depends on its maintaining itself as a separate "language game," distinct from the discourses of power. On the other side, Rorty's pragmatic anti-Kantianism grants, and encourages, that art and criticism may intervene in speculation and debate on issues that would traditionally have been reserved for natural or moral philosophy; Bell, however, is distressed at the incursion achieved by cultural values into the separate realms of politics and, especially, economics. Habermas and Jameson stand as if explicitly opposed to each other. For Habermas, the postmodern is the threat, carried on from surrealism, to deautonomize art, freeing its energies for use in all of life, but he claims that this is based on a misunderstanding, for: "When the containers of an autonomously developed cultural space are shattered, the contents get dispersed. Nothing remains from a desublimated meaning or a destructured form" ("Modernity" 11). Jameson argues that capitalist reification has already destroyed any cultural autonomy, but that cultural modes and practices are now spread throughout the fabric of social life by a process of "acculturation" ("Periodizing the 60s" 201). What remains, therefore, are opportunities for cultural production and criticism much more significant than those that had existed under earlier conditions. The struggle over what Gramsci called "hegemony" (see Williams, "Base and Superstructure" and Buttigieg) in everyday life becomes a significantly political activity once there is no longer a decisive separation of the cultural sphere. The example of Latin American liberation theology powerfully exemplifies the political potential of cultural issues.

I shall return to this question whether a change in the place of art has occurred and if so with what consequences for the power of culture, but first it is necessary to address an embarrassing fact that this survey of some exemplary positions in the postmodernism debate has rendered painfully plain. A great deal of the controversy in this debate depends on misunderstandings, not at all surprising across so wide a range of disciplinary and national traditions, which obstruct significant direct engagement with the arguments, motives, and implications of the various positions. (In "Mapping the Postmodern," Huyssen offers the most specific discriminations of American, French, and German emphases.) I shall first examine several such misunderstandings in one of the most important essays in the debate, and I shall then turn to one of the most important issues associated with the debate as it has been conducted within the profession of literary study in the United States.

注释:

1. 佩里·安德森（1938—　），英国当代著名的马克思主义史学家、思想家和活动家。他的作品涉及历史社会学、思想史和文化分析。

2. 拉塞尔·雅各比（1945—　），作家和学术文化评论家，加州大学洛杉矶分校的历史学教授。

3. 爱德华·沃第尔·萨义德（1935—2003），巴勒斯坦裔美国人，哥伦比亚大学文学教授，著名文学理论家与批评家，后殖民研究学术领域的奠基人。

4. 萨特（1905—1980），20 世纪法国著名的文学家、哲学家和政治评论家，法国无神论存在主义的主要代表人物，同时也是优秀的剧作家、小说家、编剧、传记作家和社会活动家。其作品对社会学、批判理论、后殖民理论和文学研究产生重大影响。

5. 索伦·克尔凯郭尔（1813—1855），丹麦哲学家、神学家、诗人、社会批评家和宗教作家。

6. 罗伯特·佩恩·沃伦（1905—1989），美国诗人、小说家和文学评论家，新批评的创始人之一。

7. 克林斯·布鲁克斯（1906—1994），美国文学评论家和教授，英美新批评重要成员之一。

8. 威廉·维奥斯·斯帕诺斯（1924—2017），海德格尔文学评论家。

9. 吕西安·戈德曼（1913—1970），法国哲学家、社会学家和马克思主义理论家。

10. 格奥尔格·卢卡奇（1885—1971），匈牙利马克思主义哲学家、文学史学家和批评家，是西方马克思主义的奠基人之一。

11. 南希·弗雷泽（1947—　），美国批判理论家，女权主义者。弗雷泽以其对身份政治的批判和对正义概念的哲学研究而闻名。

12. 尤尔根·哈贝马斯（1929—　），德国哲学家、社会学家，法兰克福学派的第二代旗手。

13. 安德鲁·罗斯（1956—　），纽约大学社会和文化分析教授，也是一位社会活动家和分析家。

14. 丹尼尔·贝尔（1919—2011），美国社会学家、作家、编辑，哈佛大学教授，因后工业主义研究而闻名。

15. 欧文·克里斯托（1920—2009），一位被称为“新保守主义教父”的美国记者。作为各种杂志的创办人、编辑和撰稿人，他在 20 世纪后半叶美国的知识和政治文化领域发挥了重要作用。

16. 理查德·麦凯·罗蒂（1931—2007），美国哲学家。

17. 莱斯利·亚伦·费德勒（1917—2003），美国文学评论家，美国大众文化批评的先驱。

18. 苏珊·桑塔格（1933—2004），美国作家、艺术评论家。

19. 理查德·波里尔（1925—2009），美国文学评论家。

20. 哈比卜·哈桑（1925—2015），出生于埃及的阿拉伯裔美国文学理论家和作家。

21. 希尔顿·克莱默（1928—2012），美国艺术评论家和散文家。
22. 勒内·笛卡尔（1596—1650），法国哲学家、数学家和物理学家。

Fredric Jameson

弗雷德里克·詹明信(1934—)，美国当代著名的马克思主义批评家、文学理论家和文化批评家。詹明信出生于俄亥俄州的克里夫兰，25岁获耶鲁大学文学博士学位，曾任哈佛大学、加州大学圣迭戈分校、耶鲁大学的教授，现任教于杜克大学。他研究兴趣广泛，包括历史理论、解释学、文学批评、文化政治、通俗小说、电影、视像艺术、音乐和建筑学等，关注世界范围内的后现代主义文化现象，并将其纳入历史化的语境中条分缕析。其著作《马克思主义与形式》(1971)、《语言的牢笼》(1972)、《政治无意识》(1981)获得了极高的声誉，被称为“马克思主义的三部曲”。其他著作还包括《可见的签名》(1990)、《后现代主义，或晚期资本主义的文化逻辑》(1991)、《地缘政治美学》(1992)、《时间的种子》(1994)、《文化转向》(1998)等等。

The Adventures of the Sign

(Jameson, Fredric. Periodizing the 60s. *Social Text*, No. 9/10, The 60's without Apology (Spring-Summer, 1984), pp. 178-209)

《符号的探险》出自詹明信的《60年代：从历史阶段论的角度看》一文的第五小节。《符号的探险》从主体的“死亡”，到深度和历史性的销蚀，再到现在经典的符号从意义和指涉物中“解放”，对整个后现代主义做了明确描述和广泛讨论。他认为，后现代主义与高现代主义在“文化的社会功能”方面有所不同，因为高现代主义“无论其公开的政治内容是什么，它还是处于对立和边缘的位置”，而后现代主义已经达到了“文化主导，具有精确的社会经济功能”的地位。

Postmodernism is one significant framework in which to describe what happened to culture in the 60s, but a full discussion of this hotly contested concept is not possible here. Such a discussion would want to cover, among other things, the following features: that well-known post-structuralist theme, the “death” of the subject (including the creative subject, the *auteur* or the “genius”); the nature and function of *a culture of the simulacrum* (an idea developed out of Plato by Deleuze[1] and Baudrillard[2] to convey some specificity of a reproducible object world, not of copies or reproductions marked as such, but of a proliferation of trompe-l'oeil copies *without originals*); the relation of this last to media culture or the "society of the speatacle" (Debord[3]), under two heads: 1/ the peculiar new status of the image, the "material" or what might better be called the "literal," signifier: a materiality or literality from which the older sensory richness of the medium has been abstracted (just as on the other side of the dialectical relationship, the old individuality of the subject and his/her "brushstrokes" have equally been effaced); and 2/ the emergence, in the work's temporality, of an aesthetic of *textuality* or what if often described as schizophrenic time; the eclipse, finally, of all depth, especially *historicity* itself, with the subsequent appearance of pastiche and nostalgia art (what the French call *la mode rétro*) and including the supercession of accompanying models of depth-interpretation in philosophy (the various forms of hermeneutics, as well as the Freudian conception of "repression," of manifest and latent levels).

What is generally objected to in characterizations of this kind is the empirical observation that all of these features can be abundantly located in this or that variety of high modernism; indeed, one of the difficulties in specifying postmodernism lies in its symbiotic or parasitical relationship to the latter. In effect, with the canonization of a hitherto scandalous, ugly, dissonant, amoral, anti-social, bohemian high modernism offensive to the middle classes, its promotion to the very figure of high culture generally, and perhaps most important, its enshrinement in the academic institution, postmodernism emerges as a way of making creative space for artists now oppressed by those henceforth hegemonic modernist categories of irony, complexity, ambiguity, dense temporality, and particularly, aesthetic and utopian monumentality. In some analogous way, it will be side, high modernism itself won its autonomy from the preceding hegemonic realism (the symbolic language or mode of representation of classical or market capitalism). But there is a difference in that realism itself underwent a significant mutation: it become *naturalism* and at once generated the representational forms of mass culture (the narrative apparatus of the contemporary bestsèller is an invention of naturalism and one of the most stunningly successful French cultural exports). High modernism and mass culture then develop in dialectical opposition and interrelationship with one another. It is precisely the waning of their opposition, and some new conflation of the forms of high and mass culture, which characterizes postmodernism itself.

The historical specificity of postmodernism must therefore finally be argued in terms of the social functionality of culture itself. As stated above, high modernism, whatever its overt political content, was oppositional and marginal within a middle-class Victorian or philistine or gilded age culture. Although postmodernism is equally offensive in all the respects enumerated (think of punk rock or pornography), it is no longer at all "oppositional" in that sense; indeed, it constitutes the very dominant or hegemonic aesthetic of consumer society itself and significantly serves the latter's commodity production as a virtual laboratory of new forms and fashions. The argument for a conception of postmodernism as a periodizing category is thus based on the presupposition that, even if *all* the forms features enumerated above were already present in the order high modernism, the very significance of those features changes when they become a cultural *dominant*, with a precise socioeconomic functionality.

At this point it may be well to shift the terms (or the "code") of our description to the seemingly more traditional one of a cultural "sphere", a conception developed by Herbert Marcuse[4] in what is to my mind his single most important text, the great essay on "The Affirmative Character of Culture." (It should be added that the conception of a "public sphere" generally is a very contemporary one in Germany in the works of Habermas and of Negt[5] and Kluge[6], where such a system of categories stands in interesting contrast to the code of "levels" or "instances" in French poststructuralism.) Marcuse there rehearse the paradoxical dialectic of the classical (German) aesthetic, which projects as play and "purposefulness without purpose" a utopian realm of beauty and culture beyond the fallen empirical word of money and business activity, thereby winning a powerful critical and negative value through its capacity to condemn, by its own very existence, the totality of *what is*, by virtue of its constitutive disjunction or autonomy from society and history.

The accountant therefore begins to coincide in a suggestive way with the problematic of autonomous or semi-autonomous levels developed in the preceding sections. To historicize Marcuse's dialectic, however, would demand that we take into account the possibility that in our time this very autonomy of the cultural sphere (or level or instance) may be in the process of modification; and also, that we develop the means to furnish a description of the process whereby such modification might take place, as well as the prior process whereby culture become "autonomous" or "semi-autonomous" in the first place.

This requires recourse to yet another (unrelated) analytic code, one more generally familiar to us today, since it involves the now classical structural concept of the *sign*, with its two components, the signifier (the material vehicle or image—sound or printed world) and the signified (the mental image, meaning or "conceptual" content), and a third component—the external object of the sign, its reference or "referent"—henceforth expelled from the unity and yet haunting it as a ghostly residual aftereffect (illusion or ideology). The scientific value of this conception of the sign will be bracketed here since we are concerned, on the one hand, to historicize it, to interpret it as a conceptual symptom of developments in the period, and on the other, to "set it in motion," to see whether changes in its inner structure can offer some adequate small-scale emblem or electrocardiogram of changes and permutations in the cultural sphere generally throughout this period.

Such changes are already suggested by the fate of the "referent" in the "conditions of the possibility" of the new structural concept of the sign (a significant ambiguity must however be noted: theorists of the sign notoriously glide from a conception of reference as designating a "real" object outside the unity of Signifier and Signified to a position in which the Signified itself—or meaning or the idea or the concept of a thing—becomes somehow identified with the referent and stigmatized along with it; we will return to this below). Saussure, at the dawn of the semiotic revolution, liked to describe the relationship of Signifier to Signified as that of the two sides, the recto and verso, of a sheet of paper. In what is then a logical sequel, and a text which naturally enough becomes equally canonical, Borges[7] will push "representation" to the point of imaging a map so rigorous and referential that it becomes coterminous with its object. The stage is then set for the structuralist emblem par excellence , the Moebius Strip, which succeeds in peeling itself of its referent altogether and thus achieves a free-floating closure in the void, a kind if absolute self-referentiality and autocircularity from which all remaining traces of reference, or of any externality, have triumphantly been effaced.

To be even more eclectic about it, I will suggest that this process, seemingly internal to the Sign itself, requires a supplementary explanatory code, that of the more universal process of reification and fragmentation at one with the logic of capital itself. Nonetheless, taken on its own terms, the inner convulsions of the Sign is a useful initial figure of the process of transformation of culture generally, which must in some first moment (that described by Marcuse) separate itself from the "referent" the existing social and historical world itself, only in a subsequent stage of the 60s, in what is here termed "postmodernism," to develop further into some new and heightened, free-floating, self-referential "autonomy."

The problem now turns around this very term, "autonomy," with its paradoxical Althusserian modification, the concept of "semi-autonomy." The paradox is that the Sign, as an "autonomous" unity in its own right, as a realm divorced from the referent, can preserve that initial autonomy, and the unity and coherence demanded by it, only at the price of keeping a phantom of reference alive, as the ghostly reminder of its own outside or exterior, since this allows it closure, self-definition and an essential boundary line. Marcuse's own tormented dialectic expresses this dramatically in the curious oscillation whereby his autonomous realm of beauty and culture both returns upon some "real world" to judge and negate it, at the same time that it separates itself so radically from that real world as to become a place of mere illusion and impotent "ideals," the "infinite," etc.

The first moment in the adventures of the Sign is perplexing enough as to demand more concrete, if schematic, illustration in the most characteristic cultural productions themselves. It might well be demonstrated in the classical French *nouveau roman* (in particular, the novels of Robbe-Grillet[8] himself), which established its new language in the early 1960s, using systematic variations of narrative segments to "undermine" representation, yet in some sense confirming this last by teasing and stimulating an appetite for it.

As an American illustration seems more appropriate, however, something similar may be seen in connection with the final and canonical form of high modernism in American poetry, namely the work of Wallace Stevens[9], which becomes, in the years following the poet's death in 1956, institutionalized in the university as a purer and more quintessential fulfillment of poetic language than the still impure (read: ideological and political) works of an Eliot or a Pound, and can therefore be numbered among the literary "events" of the early 60s. As Frank Lentricchia[10] has shown, in *Beyond the New Criticism*, the serviceability of Stevens' poetic production for this normative and hegemonic role depends in large measure on the increasing conflation, in that work, of poetic practice and poetic theory:

This endlessly elaborating poem
Displays the theory of poetry
As the life of poetry...

"Stevens" is therefore a locus and fulfillment of aesthetics and aesthetic theory fully as much as the latter's exemplar and privileged exegetical object; the theory or aesthetic ideology in question being very much an affirmation of the "autonomy" of the cultural sphere in the sense developed above, a valorization of the supreme power of the poetic imagination over the "reality" it produces. Stevens' work, therefore, offers an extraordinary laboratory situation in which to observe the autonomization of culture as a process: a detailed examination of his development (something for which we have no space here) would show how some initial "set towards" or "attention to" a kind of poetic *pensée sauvage*, the operation of great preconscious *stereotypes*, opens up a vast inner world in which little by little the images of things and their "ideas" begin to be substituted for the things themselves. Yet what distinguishes this experience in Stevens is the sense of a vast systematicity in all this, the operation of a whole set of cosmic oppositions far too complex to be reduced to the schemata of "structuralist" binary oppositions, yet akin to those in spirit, and somehow pregiven in the Symbolic Order of the mind, discoverable to the passive exploration of the "poetic imagination," that is, of some heightened and impersonal power of free association in the realm of "objective spirit" or "objective culture." The examination would further show the strategic limitation of this process to landscape, the reduction of the ideas and images of things to the names for things, and finally to those irreducibles which are place names, among which the exotic has a privileged function (Key West, Oklahoma, Yucatan, Java). Here the poetic "totality" begins to trace a ghostly mimesis or *analogon* of the totality of the imperialist world system itself, with third world materials in a similarly strategic, marginal yet essential place (much as Adorno showed how Schoenberg's[11] twelve-tone system unconsciously produced a formal imitation of the "total system" of capital). This very unconscious replication of the "real" totality of the world system in the mind is then what allows culture to separate itself as a closed and self-sufficient "system" in its own right: reduplication, and at the same time, floating above the real. It is because of this essential lack of content in Stevens' verse that his poetry ultimately comes to be auto-referential with a vengeance, taking as its primal subject matter the very operation of poetic production itself. This is an impulse shared by most of the great high modernisms, as has been shown most dramatically in the recent critiques of architectural modernism, in particular of the International style, whose great monumental objects constitute themselves, by projecting a protopolitical and utopian spirit of transformation, *against* a fallen city fabric all around them and, as Venturi[12] has demonstrated, end up necessarily displaying and speaking of themselves alone. Now, this also accounts for what must puzzle any serious reader of Stevens' verse, namely the extraordinary combination of verbal richness and experimental hollowness or impoverishment in it (the latter being attributable as well to the impersonality of the poetic imagination in Stevens, and to the essentially contemplative and epistemological stance of the subject in it, over and against the static object world of his landscapes).

The essential point here, however, is that this characteristic movement of the high modernist impulse needs to justify itself by way of an ideology, an ideological supplement which can generally be described as that of "existentialism" (the supreme fiction, the meaninglessness of a contingent object-world unredeemed by the imagination, etc.). This is the most uninteresting and banal dimension of Stevens' work, yet it betrays along with other existentialisms (e. g., Sartre's tree root in *Nausea*) that fatal seam or link which must be retained in order for the contingent, the "outside world," the meaningless referent, to be just present enough dramatically to be overcome within the language: nowhere is this ultimate point so clearly deduced, over and over again, as in Stevens, in the eye of the blackbird, the angels or the Sun itself—that last residual vanishing point of reference as distant as a dwarf star upon the horizon, yet which cannot disappear altogether without the whole vocation of poetry and the poetic imagination being called back into question. Stevens thus exemplifies for us the fundamental paradox of the "autonomy" of the cultural sphere: the sign can only become autonomous by remaining semi-autonomous and the realm of culture can absolutize itself over against the real world only at the price of retaining a final tenuous sense of that exterior or external world of which it is the replication and the imaginary double.

All of which can also be demonstrated by showing what happens when, in a second moment, the perfectly logical conclusion is drawn that the referent is itself a myth and does not exist, a second moment hitherto described as postmodernism. Its trajectory can be seen as a movement from the older *nouveau roman* to that of Sollers or of properly "schizophrenic" writing, or from the primacy of Stevens to that of John

Ashbery[13]. This new moment is a radical break (which can be localized around 1967 for reasons to be given later on), but it is important to grasp it as dialectical, that is, as a passage from quantity to quality in which the *same* force, reaching a certain threshold of excess, in its prolongation now produces qualitatively distinct effects and seems to generate a whole new system.

That force has been described as reification, but we can now also begin to make some connections with another figural language used earlier: in a first moment, reification "liberated" the Sign from its referent, but this is not a force to be released with impunity. Now, in a second moment, it continues its work of dissolution, penetrating the interior of the Sign itself and liberating the Signifier from the Signified, or from meaning proper. This play, no longer of a realm of signs, but of pure or literal signifiers freed from the ballast of their signifieds, their former meanings, now generates a new kind of textuality in all the arts (and in philosophy as well, as we have seen above), and begins to project the mirage of some ultimate language of pure signifiers which is also frequently associated with schizophrenic discourse. (Indeed, the Lacanian theory of schizophrenia—a language disorder in which syntactical time breaks down, and leaves a succession of empty Signifiers, absolute moments of a perpetual present, behind itself—has offered one of the more influential explanations and ideological justifications for postmodernist textual practice.)

All of which would have to be demonstrated in some detail by way of a concrete analysis of the postmodernist experience in all the arts today: but the present argument can be concluded by drawing the consequences of this second moment—the culture of the Signifier or of the Simulacrum—for the whole problematic of some "autonomy" of the cultural sphere which has concerned us here. For that autonomous realm is not itself spared by the intensified process by which the classical Sign is dissolved: if its autonomy depended paradoxically on its possibility of remaining "semi-autonomous" (in an Althusserian sense) and of preserving the last tenuous link with some ultimate referent (or, in Althusserian language, of preserving the ultimate unity of a properly "structural totality"), then evidently in the new cultural moment culture will have ceased to be autonomous, and the realm of an autonomous play of signs becomes impossible, when that ultimate final referent to which the balloon of the mind was moored is now definitively cut. The break-up of the Sign in mid-air determines a fall back into a now absolutely fragmented and anarchic social reality;

the broken pieces of language (the pure Signifiers) now falling again into the world, as so many more pieces of material junk among all the other rusting and superannuated apparatuses and buildings that litter the commodity landscape and that strew the "collage city," the "delirious New York" of a postmodernist late capitalism in full crisis.

But, returning to a Marcusean terminology, all of this can also be said in a different way: with the eclipse of culture as an autonomous space or sphere, culture itself falls into the world, and the result is not its disappearance but its prodigious expansion, to the point where culture becomes coterminous with social life in general: now all the levels become "acculturated," and in the society of the spectacle, the image, or the simulacrum, everything has at length become cultural, from the superstructures down into the mechanisms of the infrastructure itself. If this development then places acutely on the agenda the neo Gramscian problem of a new cultural politics today—in a social system in which the very status of both culture and politics have been profoundly, functionally and structurally modified—it also renders problematic any further discussion of what used to be called "culture" proper, whose artifacts have become the random experiences of daily life itself.

注释：

1. 吉尔·德勒兹（1925—1995），法国哲学家，从事哲学、文学、电影和美术创作。
2. 让·鲍德里亚（1929—2007），法国社会学家、哲学家和文化理论家，以对媒体、当代文化和技术传播的分析，对模拟和超现实等概念的表述而闻名。
3. 居伊·德波（1931—1994），法国马克思主义理论家、哲学家和电影导演。
4. 赫伯特·马尔库塞（1898—1979），德裔美籍哲学家、社会学家和政治理论家，法兰克福学派代表人物。
5. 奥斯卡·内格特（1934— ），德国社会学家、哲学家。
6. 亚历山大·克鲁格（1932— ），德国作家、哲学家和电影导演。
7. 豪尔赫·路易斯·博尔赫斯（1899—1986），阿根廷短篇小说作家、散文家、诗人和翻译家。
8. 阿兰·罗伯-格里耶（1922—2008），法国作家和电影制片人，“新小说”派作家代表人物。
9. 华莱士·史蒂文斯（1879—1955），美国著名现代诗人。
10. 弗兰克·伦特里奇亚（1940— ），美国文学评论家、小说家和电影研究教授。
11. 阿诺德·勋伯格（1874—1951），奥地利裔美籍作曲家、音乐教育家和音乐理论家，西方现代主义音乐的代表人物。
12. 罗伯特·文丘里（1925—2018），美国建筑师。
13. 约翰·阿什贝利（1927—2017），美国诗人和艺术评论家。

Volume 2

陈世丹 王小会 黄贺 编

Chapter Ten **Feminism**

女性主义批评理论，又称女权主义，其源于西方女性解放运动，是其高涨并深入文化、文学领域的成果，具有较为鲜明的政治倾向。相对于西方蓬勃发展的女性解放运动，女性主义批评理论诞生于20世纪60年代末70年代初的欧美，至今仍极富活力地在西方思想界发展。女性主义理论以妇女为中心，研究内容包括文学作品中的女性形象、女性创作环境以及女性阅读等女性特有的经历。女性主义批评理论包括英美流派、法国派、黑人女性主义（妇女主义）等。不仅如此，女性主义批评在发展过程中广泛吸收了当代西方新马克思主义、精神分析、解构主义和新历史主义等流派的营养，其丰富的内容使女性批评在文学理论领域占有重要的地位。

女性主义批评理论大致经历了三个主要发展阶段。第一阶段主要是以妇女形象批评为主，揭露男性文化对女性形象的扭曲，批评文学中对女性形象的非客观化书写，充分表现了菲勒斯批评中性别类推的思维习惯，揭示了女性形象不真实的深层原因，代表作有凯特·米勒特的《性政治》等。女性主义批评理论的第二阶段是从20世纪70年代中期到80年代中期，这一阶段重在分析文学史上女作家自己的文学传统，重新挖掘各时期妇女文学，倾心于语言文学的批判，代表作有伊莱恩·肖瓦尔特的《她们自己的文学》、桑德拉·吉尔伯特和苏珊·古芭的合著《阁楼上的疯女人》等。第三阶段自20世纪80年代中期以后，这一阶段女性主义重在反思，重新思考文学研究的基本概念，不再拘泥于文学本身，兴起了对性别差异研究的“性别诗学”。也就是在这一阶段，女性主义批评开始走向一种多元化、跨学科的发展态势，代表作有茱莉亚·克里斯蒂娃的《女性的时间》等。

女性主义批评理论最初主张的是男女平等思想，后开始诉求政治平等权，逐渐地女性主义批评理论的视野转向更广阔的社会文化领域，其矛头指向西方男女二元对立的思想禁锢，批判父权制文化对女性的压迫、男权制意识形态，指出女性是反对男性在一个精神压迫的行为中对女性自己进行定义的他者。法国后现代女性主义哲学家更强调女性特质、女性气质，美国黑人女性批评家爱丽丝·沃克注意到，女性主义仅仅维护的是白人女性，是将黑人女性排除在外的。她创造了妇女主义（womanism）一词，将女性主义批评理论推向了一个新的高潮。

Elaine Showalter

伊莱恩·肖瓦尔特（1941— ），生于美国马萨诸塞州，于布林莫尔学院获得学士学位，于布兰迪斯大学获得硕士学位，加利福尼亚大学获得哲学博士学位，此后在美国罗格斯大学道格拉斯学院担任副教授。1984 年起，在普林斯顿大学任教授。主要理论著作有《她的同性陪审团：从安妮·布雷兹特利特至安妮·普鲁克斯的美国女性作家》《她们自己的文学：从勃朗特到莱辛的英国妇女小说家》《女性之病：妇女、疯狂与英国文化，1830—1980》等，她的每部专著对于女性主义批评理论的发展都具有重要的意义。

Toward a Feminist Poetics

（Showalter, Elaine. Toward a Feminist Poetics. *The New Feminist Criticism: Essays on Women, Literature, and Theory*. Elaine Showalter ed. New York: Pantheon Books, 1985, pp. 131-139.）

肖瓦尔特的这篇论文收集在她编辑的《新女性主义批评：女性、文学和理论》中。论文认为，陈旧的文学批判理论是社会上父权制度的根本体现，是男性意志的表征，女性是被男性理论话语边缘化的。但她并没有完全否定传统的文学理论，而是竭力主张建构女性经验的批判方式，颠覆、解构传统男性话语标准，建构从女性读者视角出发的独特理论观点。她强调女性经验的独特性、重要性，呼吁以全新的理念进行文学阅读。相对于男性话语控制下的女权主义批评，女性主义诗学更能反映女性的生活、追求以及心理，更能够提升学术界女性存在的地位。

Gynocritics and Famale Culture

In contrast to this angry or loving fixation on male literature, the program of gynocritics is to construct a female framework for the analysis of women's literature, to develop new models based on the study of female experience, rather than to adapt male models and theories. Gynocritics begins at the point when we free ourselves from the linear absolutes of male literary history, stop trying to fit women between the lines of the male tradition, and focus instead on the newly visible world of female culture. This is comparable to the ethnographer's effort to render the experience of the "muted" female half of a society, which is described in Shirley Ardener's collection *Perceiving Women*.[1] Gynocritics is related to feminist research in history, anthropology, psychology, and sociology, all of which have developed hypotheses of a female subculture including not only the ascribed status, and the internalized constructs of feminity, but also the occupations, interactions, and consciousness of women. Anthropologists study the female subculture in the relationships between women, as mothers, daughters, sisters, and friends; in sexuality, reproduction, and ideas about the body; and in rites of initiation and passage, purification ceremonies, myths, and taboos. Michelle Rosaldo writes in *Woman, Culture, and Society*:

> The very symbolic and social conceptions that appear to set women apart and to circumscribe their activities may be used by women as a basis for female solidarity and worth. When men live apart from women, they in fact cannot control them, and unwittingly they may provide them with the symbols and social resources on which to build a society of their own.[2]

Thus in some women's literature, feminine values penetrate and undermine the masculine systems that contain them; and women have imaginatively engaged the myths of the Amazons, and the fantasies of a separate female society, in genres from Victorian poetry to contemporary science fiction.

In recent years, pioneering work by four young American feminist scholars has given us some new ways to interpret the culture of nineteenth-century American women and the literature that was its primary expressive form. Carroll Smith-Rosenberg's essay "The Female World of Love and Ritual" examines several archives of letters between women, and outlines the homosocial emotional world of the nineteenth century. Nancy Cott's *The Bonds of Womanhood: Woman's Sphere in New England, 1780-1835* explores the paradox of a cultural bondage, a legacy of pain and submission, which nonetheless generates a sisterly solidarity, a bond of shared experience, loyalty, and compassion. Ann Douglas's ambitious book, *The Feminization of American Culture*, boldly locates the genesis of American mass culture in the sentimental literature of women and clergymen, two allied and "disestablished" postindustrial groups. These three are social historians; but Nina Auerbach's *Communities of Women: An Idea in Fiction* seeks the bonds of womanhood in women's literature, ranging from the matriarchal households of Louisa May Alcott and Mrs. Gaskell to the women's schools and colleges of Dorothy Sayers, Sylvia Plath, and Muriel Spark. Historical and literary studies like these, based on English women, are badly needed; and the manuscript and archival sources for them are both abundant and untouched.[3]

Gynocritics: Elizabeth Barrett Browning and Muriel Spark

Gynocritics must also take into account the different velocities and curves of political, social, and personal histories in determining women's literary choices and careers. "In dealing with women as writers," Virginia Woolf wrote in her 1929 essay, "Women and Fiction," "as much elasticity as possible is desirable; it is necessary to leave oneself room to deal with other things besides their work, so much has that work been influenced by conditions that have nothing whatever to do with art."[4] We might illustrate the need for this completeness by looking at Elizabeth Barrett Browning, whose verse novel *Aurora Leigh* (1856) has recently been handsomely reprinted by the Women's Press. In her excellent introduction Cora Kaplan defines Barrett Browning's feminism as romantic and bourgeois, placing its faith in the transforming powers of love, art, and Christian charity. Kaplan reviews Barrett Browning's dialogue with the artists and radicals of her time; with Tennyson and Clough, who had also written poems on the "woman question"; with the Christian Socialism of Fourier, Owen, Kingsley, and Maurice; and with such female predecessors as Madame de Stäel and George Sand. But in this exploration of Barrett Browning's intellectual milieu, Kaplan omits discussion of the male poet whose influence on her work in the 1850s would have been most pervasive: Robert Browning. When we understand how susceptible women writers have always been to the aesthetic standards and values of the male tradition, and to male approval and validation, we can appreciate the complexity of a marriage between artists. Such a union has almost invariably meant internal conflicts, self-effacement, and finally obliteration for the woman, except in the rare cases—Eliot and Lewes, the Woolf's—where the husband accepted a managerial rather than a competitive role. We can see in Barrett Browning's letters of the 1850s the painful, halting, familiar struggle between her womanly love and ambition for her husband and her conflicting commitment to her own work. There is a sense in which she *wants* him to be the better artist. At the beginning of the decade she was more famous than he; then she notes with pride a review in France which praises him more; his work on *Men and Women* goes well; her work on *Aurora Leigh* goes badly (she had a young child and was recovering from the most serious of her four miscarriages). In 1854 she writes to a woman friend:

> I am behind hand with my poem... Robert swears he shall have his book ready in spite of everything for print when we shall be in London for the purpose, but, as for mine, it must wait for the next spring I begin to see clearly. Also it may be better not to bring out the two works together.

And she adds wryly, "If mine were ready I might not say so perhaps."[5]

Without an understanding of the framework of the female subculture, we can miss or misinterpret the themes and structures of women's literature, fail to make necessary connections within a tradition. In 1852, in an eloquent passage from her autobiographical essay "Cassandra," Florence Nightingale identified the pain of feminist awakening as its essence, as the guarantee of progress and free will. Protesting against the protected unconscious lives of middle-class Victorian women, Nightingale demanded the restoration of their suffering:

> Give us back our suffering, we cry to Heaven in our hearts—suffering rather than indifferentism—for out of suffering may come the cure. Better to have pain than paralysis: A hundred struggle and drown in the breakers. One discovers a new world.[6]

It is fascinating to see how Nightingale's metaphors anticipate not only her own medical career but also the fate of the heroines of women's novels in the nineteenth and twentieth centuries. To waken from the drugged, pleasant sleep of Victorian womanhood was agonizing; in fiction it is much more likely to end in drowning than in discovery. It is usually associated with what George Eliot in *Middlemarch* calls "the chill hours of a morning twilight," and the sudden appalled confrontation with the contingencies of adulthood. Eliot's Maggie Tulliver, Edith Wharton's Lily Bart, Olive Schreiner's Lyndall, Kate Chopin's Edna Pontellier wake to worlds which offer no places for the women they wish to become; and rather than struggling they die. Female suffering thus becomes a kind of literary commodity which both men and women consume. Even in these important women's novels—*The Mill on the Floss*, The *Story of an African Farm*, *The House of Mirth*—the fulfillment of the plot is a visit to the heroine's grave by a male mourner.

According to Dame Rebecca West, unhappiness is still the keynote of contemporary fiction by English women. Certainly the literary landscape is strewn with dead female bodies. In Fay Weldon's *Down Among the Women and Female Friends*, suicide has come to be a kind of domestic accomplishment, carried out after the shopping and the washing-up. When Weldon's heroine turns on the gas, "she feels that she has been half-dead for so long that the difference in state will not be very great." In Muriel Spark's stunning short novel of 1970, *The Driver's Seat*, another half-dead and desperate heroine gathers all her force to hunt down a woman-hating psychopath and persuade him to murder her. Garishly dressed in a purposely bought outfit of clashing purple, green, and white—the colors of the suffragettes (and the colors of the school uniform in *The Prime of Miss Jean Brodie*)—Lise goes in search of her killer, lures him to a park, gives him the knife. But in Lise's careful selection of her death-dress, her patient pursuit of her assassin, Spark has given us the devastated postulates of feminine wisdom: that a woman creates her identity by choosing her clothes, that she creates her history by choosing her man. That, in the 1970s, Mr. Right turns out to be Mr. Goodbar is not the sudden product of urban violence but a latent truth fiction exposes. Spark asks whether men or women are in the driver's seat and whether the power to choose one's destroyer is women's only form of self-assertion. To label the violence or self-destructiveness of these painful novels as neurotic expressions of a personal pathology, as many reviewers have done, is to ignore, Annette Kolodny suggests,

> the possibility that the worlds they inhabit may in fact be real, or true, and for them the only worlds available, and further, to deny the possibility that their apparently "odd" or unusual responses may in fact be justifiable or even necessary.[7]

But women's literature must go beyond these scenarios of compromise, madness, and death. Although the reclamation of suffering is the beginning, its purpose is to discover the new world. Happily, some recent women's literature, especially in the United States, where novelists and poets have become vigorously involved in the women's liberation movement, has gone beyond reclaiming suffering to its reinvestment. This newer writing relates the pain of transformation to history. "If I'm lonely," writes Adrienne Rich in "Song,"

it must be the loneliness
of waking first, of breathing
dawn's first cold breath on the city
of being the one awake
in a house wrapped in sleep [8]

Rich is one of the spokeswomen for a new women's writing which explores the will to change. In her recent book, *Of Woman Born: Motherhood as Experience and Institution*, Rich challenges the alienation from and rejection of the mother that daughters have learned under patriarchy. Much women's literature in the past has dealt with "matrophobia" or the fear of becoming one's mother. In Sylvia Plath's *The Bell Jar*, for example, the heroine's mother is the target for the novel's most punishing contempt. When Esther announces to her therapist that she hates her mother, she is on the road to recovery. Hating one's mother was the feminist enlightenment of the fifties and sixties; but it is only a metaphor for hating oneself. Female literature of the 1970s goes beyond matrophobia to a courageously sustained quest for the mother, in such books at Margaret Atwood's *Surfacing*, and Lisa Alther's recent *Kinflicks*. As the death of the father has always been an archetypal rite of passage for the Western hero, now the death of the mother as witnessed and transcended by the daughter has become one of the most profound occasions of female literature. In analyzing these purposeful awakenings, these reinvigorated mythologies of female culture, feminist criticism finds its most challenging, inspiriting, and appropriate task.

Women and the Novel: The "Precious Specialty"

The most consistent assumption of feminist reading has been the belief that women's special experience would assume and determine distinctive forms in art. In the nineteenth century, such a contribution was ambivalently valued. When Victorian reviewers like G. H. Lewes, Richard Hutton, and Richard Simpson began to ask what the literature of women might mean and what it might become, they focused on the educational, experiential, and biological handicaps of the woman novelist, and this was also how most women conceptualized their situation. Some reviewers, granting women's sympathy, sentiment, and powers of observation, thought that the novel would provide an appropriate, even a happy, outlet for female emotion and fantasy. In the United States, the popular novelist Fanny Fern understood that women had been granted access to the novel as a sort of repressive desublimation, a harmless channel for frustrations and drives that might otherwise threaten the family, the church, and the state. Fern recommended that women write as therapy, as a release from the stifling silence of the drawing room, and as a rebellion against the indifference and insensitivity of the men closest to them:

> Look around, and see innumerable women, to whose barren and loveless lives this would be improvement and solace, and I say to them, write! write! It will be a safe outlet for thoughts and feelings that maybe the nearest friend you have has never dreamed had place in your heart and brain. … It is not *safe* for the women of 1867 to shut down so much that cries out for sympathy and expression, because life is such a maelstrom of business or folly or both that those to whom they have bound themselves, body and soul, recognize only the needs of the former.... One of these days, when that diary is found, when the hand that penned it shall be dust, with what amazement and remorse will many a husband or father exclaim, I never knew my wife or my child until this moment.[9]

Fern's scribbling woman spoke with fierce indirectness to the male audience, to the imagined husband or father; her purpose was to shock rather than to please, but the need to provoke masculine response was the controlling factor in her writing. At the turn of the century, members of the Women Writers Suffrage League[10], an important organization of English novelists and journalists, began to explore the psychological bondage of women's literature and its relationships to a male-dominated publishing industry. Elizabeth Robins, the first president of the league, a novelist and actress who had starred in early English productions of Ibsen, argued in 1908 that no woman writer had ever been free to explore female consciousness:

> The realization that she had access to a rich and as yet unrifled storehouse may have crossed her mind, but there were cogent reasons for concealing her knowledge. With that wariness of ages which has come to be instinct, she contented herself with echoing the old fables, presenting to a man-governed world puppets as nearly as possible like those that had from the beginning found such favour in men's sight.
>
> Contrary to the popular impression, to say in print what she thinks is the last thing the woman-novelist or journalist is so rash as to attempt. There even more than elsewhere (unless she is reckless) she must wear the aspect that shall have the best chance of pleasing her brothers. Her publishers are not women.[11]

It was to combat this inhibiting commercial monopoly that nineteenth-century women began to organize their own publishing houses, beginning with Emily Faithfull's Victoria Press in the 1870s, and reaching a peak with the flourishing suffrage presses at the beginning of this century. One of the most fervent beliefs of the Women Writers Suffrage League was that the *terra incognita* of the female psyche would find unique literary expression once women had overthrown male domination. In *A Room of One's Own*, Virginia Woolf argued that economic independence was the essential precondition of an autonomous women's art. Like George Eliot before her, Woolf also believed that women's literature held the promise of a "precious speciality," a distinctly female vision.

Feminine, Feminist, Female

All of these themes have been important to feminist literary criticism in the 1960s and 1970s, but we have approached them with more historical awareness. Before we can even begin to ask how the literature of women would be different and special, we need to reconstruct its past, to rediscover the scores of women novelists, poets, and dramatists whose work has been obscured by time, and to establish the continuity of the female tradition from decade to decade, rather than from Great Woman to Great Woman. As we re-create the chain of writers in this tradition, the patterns of influence and response from one generation to the next, we can also begin to challenge the periodicity of orthodox literary history and its enshrined canons of achievement. It is because we have studied women writers in isolation that we have never grasped the connections between them. When we go beyond Austen, the Brontës, and Eliot, say, to look at a hundred and fifty or more of their sister novelists, we can see patterns and phases in the evolution of a female tradition which correspond to the developmental phases of any subcultural art. In my book on English women writers, *A Literature of Their Own*, I have called these the Feminine, Feminist, and Female stages[12]. During the Feminine phase, dating from about 1840 to 1880, women wrote in an effort to equal the intellectual achievements of the male culture, and internalized its assumptions about female nature. The distinguishing sign of this period is the male pseudonym, introduced in England in the 1840s, and a national characteristic of English women writers. In addition to the famous names we all know—George Eliot, Currer, Ellis, and Acton Bell—dozens of other women chose male pseudonyms as a way of coping with a double literary standard. This masculine disguise goes well beyond the title page; it exerts an irregular pressure on the narrative, affecting tone, diction, structure, and characterization. In contrast to the English male pseudonym, which-signals such clear self-awareness of the liabilities of female authorship, American women during the same period adopted superfeminine, little-me pseudonyms (Fanny Fern, Grace Greenwood, Fanny Forester), disguising behind these nominal bouquets their boundless energy, powerful economic motives, and keen professional skills. It is pleasing to discover the occasional Englishwoman who combines both these techniques, and creates the illusion of male authorship with a name that contains the encoded domestic message of femininity—such as Harriet Parr who wrote under the pen name "Holme Lee." The feminist content of feminine art is typically oblique, displaced, ironic, and subversive; one has to read it between the lines, in the missed possibilities of the text.

In the Feminist phase, from about 1880 to 1920, or the winning of the vote, women are historically enabled to reject the accommodating postures of femininity and to use literature to dramatize the ordeals of wronged womanhood. The personal sense of injustice which feminine novelists such as Elizabeth Gaskell and Frances Trollope expressed in their novels of class struggle and factory life become increasingly and explicitly feminist in the 1880s, when a generation of New Women redefined the woman artist's role in terms of responsibility to suffering sisters. The purest examples of this phase are the Amazon utopias of the 1890s, fantasies of perfected female societies set in an England or an America of the future, which were also protests against male government, male laws, and male medicine. One author of Amazon utopias, the American Charlotte Perkins Gilman, also analyzed the preoccupations of masculine literature with sex and war, and the alternative possibilities of an emancipated feminist literature. Gilman's utopian feminism carried George Eliot's idea of the "precious speciality" to its matriarchal extremes. Comparing her view of sisterly collectivity to the beehive, she writes that

> the bee's fiction would be rich and broad, full of the complex tasks of comb-building and filling, the care and feeding of the young… It would treat of the vast fecundity of motherhood, the educative and selective processes of the group-mothers, and the passion of loyalty, of social service, which holds the hives together.[13]

This is Feminist Socialist Realism with a vengeance, but women novelists of the period—even Gilman, in her short stories—could not be limited to such didactic formulas, or such maternal topics.

In the Female phase, ongoing since 1920, women reject both imitation and protest—two forms of dependency—and turn instead to female experience as the source of an autonomous art, extending the feminist analysis of culture to the forms and techniques of literature. Representatives of the formal Female Aesthetic, such as Dorothy Richardson and Virginia Woolf, begin to think in terms of male and female sentences, and divide their work into "masculine" journalism and "feminine" fictions, redefining and sexualizing external and internal experience. Their experiments were both enriching and imprisoning retreats into the celebration of consciousness; even in Woolf's famous definition of life: "a luminous halo, a semi-transparent envelope surrounding us from the beginning of consciousness to the end,"[14] there is a submerged metaphor of uterine withdrawal and containment. In this sense, the Room of One's Own becomes a kind of Amazon utopia, population.

注释：

1. 这里指 Shirley Ardener, ed, *Perceiving Women* (New York: Halsted Press, 1975)。

2. 这里指 Michelle Z. Rosaldo, "Women, Culture, and Society: A Theoretical Overview," in *Women, Culture, and Society*, ed. Michelle Z. Rosaldo and Louise Lamphere (Stanford, Calif.: Stanford University Press, 1974), p. 39。

3. Carroll Smith-Rosenberg, "The Female World of Love and Ritual: Relations Between Women in Nineteenth-Century America," *Signs* 1 (Fall 1975): 1-30; Nancy F. Cott, *The Bonds of Womanhood: "Woman's Sphere" in New England*, 1780—1835 (New Haven, Conn.: Yale University Press, 1977); Ann Douglas, *The Feminization of American Culture* (New York: Alfred A. Knopf, 1977); Nina Auerbach, *Communities of Women: An Idea in Fiction* (Cambridge, Mass.: Harvard University Press, 1978).

4. 参见 Virginia Woolf, "Women and Fiction," *Collected Essays*, vol. 2 (London: Chatto & Windus, 1967), p. 141。

5. 这一观点参见原文。Peter N. Heydon and Philip Kelley, eds, *Elizabeth Barrett Browning's Letters to Mrs. David Ogilvy* (New York: Quadrangle Books, 1973), p. 115.

6. 引自: Florence Nightingale, "Cassandra," in *The Cause: A History of the Women's Movement in Great Britain*, ed, Ray Strachey (1928; reprint ed., Port Washington, N. Y.: Kennikat Press, 1969), p. 398。

7. Annette Kolodny, "Some Notes on Defining a 'Feminist Literary Criticism,'" *Critical Inquiry* 2 (Fall 1975): 84. For an illuminating discussion of *The Driver's Seat* see Auerbach, *Communities of Women*, p. 181.

8. Adrienne Rich, *Diving into the Wreck* (New York: W. W. Norton, 1973), p. 20.

9. Quoted in Ann Douglas Wood, "The 'Scribbling Women' and Fanny Fern: Why Women Wrote," *American Quarterly* 23 (Spring 1971), pp. 3-24.

10. 英国女性主义作家代表人物伊丽莎白·罗宾斯(Elizabeth Robins, 1862—1952)和茜茜莉·汉密尔顿(Cicely Hamilton, 1872—1952)于1908年共同创建的"女作家权力联合会",通过这一民间组织,女性作家有机会讨论妇女切身利益相关议题。

11. Rebecca West, "And They All Lived Unhappily Ever After," *Times Literary Supplement*, July 26, 1974, p. 779.

12. Elaine Showalter, *A Literature of Their Own: British Women Novelists from Brontë to Lessing* (Princeton, N.J.: Princeton University Press, 1977).

13. Charlotte Perkins Gilman, *The Man-made World: or, Our Androcentric Culture* (1911; reprinted., New York: Johnson Reprints, 1971), pp. 101-2.

14. 生活并非是一串对称排放的马车灯,生活是一圈明亮的光环,是一个伴随我们意识始终、将我们包裹在内的半透明封套。见伍尔夫"论现代小说", Virginia Woolf, "Modern Fiction," *Collected Essays*, vol. 2, p. 106.

Sandra M. Gilbert

桑德拉·吉尔伯特(1936—),于康奈尔大学获得学士学位,于纽约大学获得硕士学位，于哥伦比亚大学获英国文学方向博士学位，美国加州大学戴维斯分校杰出英语教授，西方女性主义批评理论代表人物，著名作家、诗人及批评家。她曾担任康奈尔大学客座教授，获得众多奖项，出版八部诗歌集、一部回忆录以及其他重要作品，其中较为出名的是《非正常死亡：一场医学悲剧》和诗歌集《创伤：诗歌》。与苏珊·古芭合著《阁楼上的疯女人》，获得1979年"美国文学书评奖"提名，获得1980年普利策奖非小说领域第二名，成为女性主义经典名作。此外，她们还继续合著了三部作品，包括《无人地带：二十世纪女作家的地位》和《前线来信》。

What Do Feminist Critics Want? *A Postcard from the Volcano*

（Gilbert，Sandra M. What Do Feminist Critics Want? *A Postcard from the Volcano*. *The New Feminist Criticism：Essays on Women，Literature，and Theory*. Elaine Showalter ed. New York：Pantheon Books，1985，pp. 29-45.）

《女性批评家想干什么？来自火山的明信片》是吉尔伯特对女性主义批评理论的重要贡献。她探讨了女性主义评论家在西方文化中，尤其是在文学领域的探索任务以及所面临的困难。她从女性主义视角出发，对当今学术研究中的女性批评理论研究现状进行了审视，认为男性研究导向依旧占主导地位，要摆脱这种研究范式很困难，因此，从女性主义视角对西方文学进行研究十分必要，也具有迫切性。

At the risk of revealing something that will be bad for all feminist critics everywhere，I must confess that I have hardly been able to make up my mind what aspect of feminist criticism to discuss here. I have therefore decided to offer，not a single，unified essay，but what may well seem to be three mini-essays，complete with three different（and I think rather impressive）titles：（1）"The Revisionary Imperative：Feminist Criticism and Western Culture"；（2）"Redundant Women：The Economics of Feminist Criticism"；and（3）"Feminist Mysteries：Male Critics and Feminist Criticism."

Before I launch into the first of these "essays，" however，let me take a moment to explain my odd self-division，for so bizarre a rhetorical strategy does require some justification. To begin with，I should note that when I was first asked to participate in this seminar，I felt not only honored but extraordinary pleased and excited. I knew that as a feminist critic I was going to have an exceptional opportunity，an opportunity to tell an important audience（which would consist largely of chair *man* rather than of chair *persons*) about the work I do and the field I represent. Few feminist critics have such chances. Indeed, we seem lately to have been left to speak more and more to one another rather than to those "out there" whose minds we passionately wish to reach. Thus, flushed with comfortable anticipation, I accepted this opportunity in the most optimistic mood.

However, my mood soon darkened. For when I began thinking about what I ought to say, discussing the matter with friends, organizing priorities, considering possible titles, my confusion grew. As a representative feminist critic, I must make this count and therefore—so my feminist friends told me and so I heartily agreed—I must not only outline a theory of literary criticism but also summarize a number of crucial moral and political points. Here, in brief and in no special order, are some of the suggestions that were urged on me:

Tell them what we can do for them.

Tell them what they can do for us.

Tell them to hire feminists.

Tell them not to fire feminists.

Tell them about the cases of X or the fate of Y (feminists who were fired or feminists who weren't).

Tell them to come to our talks.

Tell them to read our books.

Tell them what we do.

Tell them we don't do what they think we do.

Tell them why they think we do what we don't really do.

Tell them why they think we are what we really aren't.

Tell them who we really are and what we really do.

Such a bewildering proliferation of points made three distinct essays almost inevitable. Each would deal in some sense with a pair of central questions—namely, What do feminist critics want? and, How can English departments give it to them?—or with the converse of those questions—namely, What do English department want? and, How can feminist critics give it to them? But one of these presentations, the most important in the long run, would have to outline a theory of what feminist critics want philosophically, as a way of thinking about literary texts. A second, perhaps more immediately pressing discussion would have to analyze the politics of what feminist criticism wants from the structural realities of English departments—that is, what jobs and courses it imagines for its proponents. And a third, the most interesting to a social and literary historian like me, would try to bridge the gulf between the first two. This last little essay would have to present, in other words, a kind of sociology or psychohistory of feminist criticism as it has functioned in today's academy, explaining why and how the philosophy underlying this particular critical "ism" has so far had comparatively little effect on such political realities of English departments as hiring, promotion, and curriculum development.

Of course, all these potential discussions had even more in common than their concern with different aspects of feminist criticism. It is an axiom of the women's movement that the personal *is* the political: the very title of Kate Millett's influential analysis of feminism and masculinism today— *Sexual Politics* —insists on an inescapable connection between private relationships (bedroom or parlor politics, as it were) and public ones. For feminist critics, however, the axiom can be modified and expanded: not only is the personal the political; the aesthetic is the political, the literary is the political, the rhetorical is the political. In other words, even what appears to be the theoretical cannot easily be disengaged or abstracted from the practical, for every text can be seen as in some sense a political gesture and more specifically as a gesture determined by a complex of assumptions about male-female relations, assumptions we might call sexual poetics.

Perhaps this can most readily be seen if we look back and notice the form in which both I and my feminist colleagues conceived of the points my presentation should make: "Tell *them* what we can do for them…. Tell *them* what we do.... Tell *them* who we really are." On reflection, my constant reiteration of the word "them" seems odd. Wouldn't it have been more natural *not* to dwell so obsessively on the otherness of my audience? Couldn't my friends and I have devised a list that would read, for example, "describe what we do, explain who we are, analyze our assumptions, defend our poetics," and so forth? Yet I think that we all felt it inevitable to list things in terms of what *I*, representing *us*, should say to *them*. For women's alienation from the sources of power is profound, and I want to argue here that it is not just a personal or a political alienation but that—at least until quite recently—it has also been a philosophical alienation, an aesthetic alienation, a literary alienation.

Ultimately, in fact, it is women's ubiquitous cultural alienation that necessitates what I have called a "revisionary imperative." Thus, as both a problem and a perception, women's otherness is the intellectual center around which my first discussion revolves. For of course women—especially educated women like me, a representative feminist critic—do not seem *obviously* alienated. On the contrary, in our use of academic tools—texts, techniques, terminology—I imagine we must appear as deeply implicated in cultural intellectual styles and subjects as our male colleagues are. What, then, do I mean when I speak of the cultural alienation of women and what is this revisionary imperative that I insist on as a solution to the problem? I can best begin to answer these questions by telling one of many stories about my own feminist "conversion."

In 1970 I had a job interview with an English department chairman who quite unexpectedly confided in the middle of an otherwise ordinary conversation that he was alarmed by the demands of some female graduate students. These radical young women believed that classes ought to be devoted to the study of women—women in literature, literature by women!

"They want to throw out a thousand years of Western culture," he suddenly said. He spoke bitterly, with a soft, regretful Southern accent. "A thousand yeahs of Westuhn culchuh!"

I was shocked. "Surely not!" I exclaimed.

Looking something like majestic procession that passes through the third act of *Die Meistersinger*, a thousand years of Western culture paraded across my mind: grave monkish scholars, impassioned poets, through-worn philosophers, and beautiful stately ladies, all dimly glowing, all holding out faintly imploring hands to me, their heir and guardian. *Remember us*, they seemed to signal as their noble robes swept by. *Don't throw us out*!

"Surely," I added (a bit priggishly, I now realize), "we're all equally committed to the preservation of Western culture."

But of course I was wrong. For what feminist criticism and scholarship have taught me in the last twelve years is that, although we obviously can't "throw out a thousand years of Western culture," we can and must redo our history of those years. Nothing may have been thrown out of that record, but something has been left out: "merely," in Carolyn Kizer's ironic understatement, "the private lives of one-half of humanity"—the private lives of women and sometimes their public lives, too.[1] When I say we must redo our history, therefore, I mean we must review, reimagine, rethink, rewrite, revise, and reinterpret the events and documents that constitute it.

I should note here, incidentally, that words beginning with the prefix *re-* have lately become prominent in the language of feminist humanists, all of whom feel that, if feminism and humanism are not to be mutually contradictory terms, we must return to the history of what is called Western culture and reinterpret its central texts. Virginia Woolf speaks of "rewriting history"; Adrienne Rich notes that women's writing must begin with a "re-vision" of the past; Carolyn Heilbrun observes that we must "reinvent" womanhood; and Joan Kelly declares that we must "restore women to history and... restore our history to women."[2] All, I would argue, are articulating the revisionary imperative that has involved feminist critics in a massive attempt to reform "a thousand years of Western culture."

I myself began to experience this revisionary imperative a few years after my interview with that harassed chairman, and at first my revisionary activities seemed minor enough. My nine-year-old daughter was reading *Litter Women* and loving it so much that I reread it along with her, a few months later we read/reread *Jane Eyre* and *Wuthering Heights*. Rereading led to reinterpretations, and my revisionary impulse became so strong that I was delighted when Susan Gubar, a colleague who was also revising her ideas about these books, suggested that we team-teach a course in literature by women.

Revisionary as we felt—and we were both by now reading and rereading key feminist texts—my colleague and I were not entirely prepared for the new view of literaryhistory that our classroom reinterpretations revealed. We had believed, I guess, that women and men participate equally in a noble republic of the spirit and that both sexes are equal inheritors of "a thousand years of Western culture." Rereading literature by both women *and* man, however, we learned that, though the pressures and oppressions of gender may be as invisible as air, they are also as inescapable as air, and, like the weight of air, they imperceptibly shape the forms and motions of our lives. Assumptions about the sexes, we saw, are entangled with some of the most fundamental assumptions Western culture makes about the very nature of culture—that "culture" is male, for example, and "nature" female—and we decided that, at least until the nineteenth century, even apparently abstract definitions of literary genres were deeply influenced by psychosocial notions about gender.[3] Again and again, as we explored such sexual poetics, we encountered definitions based on the notion that (in the words of Gerard Manley Hopkins) "the male quality *is* the creative gift."[4] The treasures of Western culture, it began to seem, were the patrimony of male writers, or to put it another way, Western culture itself was a grand ancestral property that educated men had inherited from their intellectual forefathers, while their female relatives, like characters in a Jane Austen novel, were relegated to modest dower houses on the edge of the estate.

This distinction between male patrimony, on the one hand, and female penury, on the other, can be seen in countless self-defining texts by male and female writers. But perhaps quotations from two volcano poems, besides being particularly pertinent here, will begin to illustrate both my meaning and my subtitle. Wallace Stevens's "A Postcard from the Volcano" employs very much the same metaphor of the world as ancestral property that I have just used. Imagining his own and his generation's extinction by the symbolic Mount Saint Helens that annihilates every generation, Stevens prophesies also the imaginings of hisheirs, "children picking up [his] bones" who will never entirely comprehend his passions. But these uncomprehending children *will* inherit a cosmic mansion that has been in some deep way transformed by his language, his literary authority, his power: "We knew for a long the mansion's look," he notes. "And what we said of it became / A part of what it is...," adding that when he is gone "Children... will say of the mansion that it seems / As if he that lived there left behind / A spirit storming in blank walls."[5]

Emily Dickinson, who wrote many more volcano poems than Stevens did, had quite a different attitude toward both the mansion of the cosmos and her own Vesuvian presence:

On my volcano grows the Grass
A meditative spot—
An acre for a Bird to choose
Would be the General thought—

How red the Fire rocks below—
How insecure the sod
Did I disclose
Would populate with awe my solitude.[6]

For Dickinson, the gulf between appearance and reality is bleaker, blacker, and more unbridgeable than the one Stevens records. Trained and defined as a lady, she is conscious thatshe herself seems to be a sort of decorous (and marginal) landscape, "a meditative spot" on the edge of the patriarchal estate, a quiet "acre for a Bird to choose." What is unimaginable is her volcanic (and powerful) interiority: the fierce fire, the insecure sod, and the awesomely quaking rock that not only enforce but create her "solitude." Moreover, it is that solitude, so different from Stevens's authoritative wistfulness, which in turn both determines and defines her alienation. Alone, unknown, and unimaginable, she is *other* and possibly awful to everyone, even to herself.

Reading many texts like these two volcano poems and trying to understand their implications for a sexual poetics, I began to have a different vision—literally a re-vision—of "a thousand years of Western culture," that grand procession from *Die Meistersinger*. Those grave scholars, impassioned poets, and thought-worn philosophers were all male; the cosmos was their hereditary home, their ancestral mansion, as it was Stevens', and thus they were the apprentices as well as the lords and masters who marched across Wagner's glittering stage, while the beautiful stately ladies of my vision, like Wagner's Eva, were quite conscious of being their goals, their prizes, the objects of their desire. And if, like the voice that was great within Wallace Stevens or like Wagner's master singers, the men had the power of speech, the women, like Emily Dickinson, knew that they had, or were supposed to have, the graceful obligation of silence.

But what of the women who refused to be silent or who (again like Dickinson) could not manage an enduring silence? My colleague and I realized that, more than most other participants in a thousand years of Western culture, these women had been forgotten, misunderstood, or misinterpreted. Yet it was they who inspired Virginia Woolf's remark that "towards the end of the eighteenth century a change came about which, if I were rewriting history, I should describe more fully, and think of greater importance than the Crusades or the Wars of the Roses. The middle-class woman began to write."[7]

Significantly, as my colleague and I reread the literature of these women, we saw that what they wrote may have seemed docile enough—may have seemed, indeed, "A meditative spot / An acre for a Bird to choose"—but that, like Dickinson's work, it was often covertly subversive, even volcanic, and almost always profoundly revisionary. In fact, we came to understand that the revisionary imperative we had experienced was itself both an essential part of the female literary tradition we were attempting to recover and a crucial antidote to the female cultural alienation we were trying to overcome. Thus, as we have argued elsewhere, women writers have frequently responded to sociocultural constraints by creating symbolic narratives that express their common feelings of constriction, exclusion, dispossession.[8] In these narratives madwomen like Bertha Mason Rochester function as doubles through whom sane ladies like Jane Eyre (and Charlotte Brontë) can act out fantastic dreams of escape, or volcanic landscapes serve as metaphors through which apparently decorous spinsters like Emily Dickinson can image the eruption of anger into language. But in creating such symbolic narratives these literary women were revising the world view they had inherited from a society that said women mattered less than man did, a society that thought women barely belonged in the great parade of culture, that defined women as at best marginal and silent tenants of the cosmic mansion and at worst guilty interlopers in that house.

Replacing heroes with heroines, these writers insisted, like Jane Eyre, that "women feel just as men feel... they suffer from too rigid a constraint... precisely as men would suffer." Revising the story of Western culture, they looked at an ordinary woman—a shopgirl, for instance—and declared, with Virginia Woolf, "I would as soon have her true history as the hundred and fiftieth life of Napoleon or seventieth study of Keats which old Professor Z and his like are now inditing."[9] Creating new accounts of the Creation, they asked, with the eighteenth-century port Anne Finch, Countess of Winchilsea, "How are you fall'n? by mistaken rules? / And Education's, more than Nature's fools... ?"[10] In other words, over and over again these women writers asked, as we feminist critics did and do, what has caused the cultural alienation—the silence, the marginality, the secondary status—of women.

But of course, to ask and to try to give revisionary answers to such questions about literary women is also to ask and answer questions about literary man, about the dynamics of male-female relations in the world of letters, about the nexus of genre and gender, about the secret intersections of sexuality and textuality. That these questions address long-standing problems and long-established texts is undeniable, and it is equally undeniable that literary women have asked and answered them for centuries. I would also argue, though, that until quite recently such literary questions and answers have been as prudently disguised, as decorously encoded, as all the symbolic and revisionary narratives the female imagination has produced.

What may most distinguish the new literary movement called feminist criticism is precisely its effort to bring to consciousness such ancient, half-conscious questions about textuality and sexuality. Indeed, if I were to try to articulate very succinctly what feminist criticism, as a way of thinking about literary texts, wants philosophically, I would say that at its most ambitious it wants to decode and demystify all the disguised questions and answers that have always shadowed the connections between textuality and sexuality, genre and gender, psychosexual identify and cultural authority.

Such an enterprise is profoundly exciting. The impulse to revise our understanding of Western literary history and culture is, after all, energizing (and here I understate the case); as a well-known (male) medievalist remarked to me not long ago, "Everything has to be done again," and at the very least our awareness of such a revisionary imperative makes us feminist critics feel *needed*. Moreover, the questions about sexuality and textuality that we have lately decoded or brought to consciousness seem equally invigorating, for all touch on issues that are almost bracingly ontological. What, for instance, could be more fundamental, more a matter of ultimate realities, than an exploration of the relationships between sexual self-definition and literary authority, or an examination of the hidden psychosexual meanings of writing itself, the quintessentially cultural activity that distinguishes us not only from animals but also from one another?

Sadly, however—and here I move into my second essay—many of our male colleagues and students (and a few of our female ones) seem indifferent to the crucial questions that concern us feminist critics; worse, some even seem rather scornful of the excitement our enterprise has generated. Of course, I don't want to generalize too drastically; like every feminist critic, I must confess that some of my best friends are men, for I have a number of male colleagues who not only support and encourage my work (like the medievalist I quoted before) but engage in what I would call feminist criticism themselves. Yet it is nevertheless true—and I imagine I hardly need to document this assertion—that even the word "feminist" often evokes masculinist snickers or worse. Even if we are not seen as wanting to "throw out a thousand yeahs of Westuhn culchuh," we are perceived as self-indulgent, trendy, frivolous, polemical, or marginal. Indeed, where Bloomians, Derrideans, Marxists, or Freudians sometimes encounter the rage with which people respond to ideas that seem genuinely threatening (because truly important), we often meet with the kind of scorn that people reserve for notions they find boring or irritating (because merely trivial).

注释:

1. 参见 Carolyn Kizer, "Three," from "Pro Femina," in *No More Masks! An Anthology of poems by Women*, ed. Florence Howe and Ellen Bass (Garden City, N. Y.: Doubleday, 1973), p. 175.

2. 参见弗吉尼亚·伍尔夫《一间自己的屋子》、艾德里安娜·里奇《艾德里安娜·里奇诗选》、科洛林克·海尔布鲁恩《重建女性》。Virginia Woolf, *A Room of One's Own* (New York: Harcourt, Brace & World, 1928); Adrienne Rich, "When We Dead Awaken: Writing as Re-Vision," *Adrienne Rich's Poetry*, ed, Barbara Charlesworth Gelpi and Albert Gelpi (New York: W. W. Norton, 1975); Carolyn G. Heilbrun, *Reinventing Womanhood* (New York: W. W. Norton, 1979); Joan Kelly-Gadol, "The Social Relations of the Sexes: Methodological Implications of Women's History," *Signs* 1 (Summer 1976), pp 809-23.

3. 见《阁楼上的疯女人》。Sandra M. Gilbert and Susan Gubar, *The Madwoman in the Attic: The Woman Writer and the Nineteenth-Century Literary imagination* (New Haven: Yale University Press, 1979), esp. pt. 1, "Toward a Feminist Poetics." See also Sherry Ortner, "Is Female to Male as Nature Is to Culture?" in *Women, Culture, and Society*, ed, Michelle Zimbalist Rosaldo and Louise Lamphere (Stanford, Calif.: Stanford University Press, 1974), pp. 67-88.

4. Hopkins, *The Correspondence of Gerard Manley Hopkins and Richard Watson Dixon*, ed, C. C. Abbott (London: Oxford University Press, 1935), p. 133.

5. Wallace Stevens, "A Postcard from the Volcano," *The Collected Poems* (New York: Alfred A. Knopf, 1954), pp. 158-59.

6. Emily Dickinson, *The Complete Poems*, ed, Thomas H. Johnson (Boston: Little, Brown, 1960), no. 1677.

7. Woolf, *A Room of One's Own*, p. 64.

8. 见吉尔伯特与古芭合著《阁楼上的疯女人》。Gilbert and Gubar, *Madwoman in the Attic*, esp. chap. 2, "Infection in the Sentence."

9. Woolf, *A Room of One's Own*, p. 94.

10. "The Introduction," in *The Poems of Anne Countess of Winchilsea*. ed, Myra Reynolds (Chicago: University of Chicago Press, 1903), pp. 4-5.

Chapter Eleven **New Historicism**

新历史主义是研究文学与历史之间关系的一种新的批评范式，它不同于旧历史主义，也不同于形式主义、结构主义等强调文学本体论的批评思潮，相反是对前者的一种批判与反拨。美国加州大学伯克利分校的教授斯蒂芬·格林布拉特第一个使用"新历史主义"这个术语。作为一种文化批评，新历史主义受克利福德·格尔茨的文化人类学、福柯的不连续史观和话语霸权理论以及英国的"文化唯物主义"的影响。它始于 20 世纪 80 年代，在文艺复兴研究领域中初见端倪，随后这种阐释文学文本历史内涵的独特方法得到英美学界认可，迅速传播到世界各国。新历史主义的主要代表人物为美国著名学者斯蒂芬·格林布拉特（Stephen Greenblatt）、海登·怀特（Hayden White）和罗伊丝·泰森（Lois Tyson），他们为新历史主义批评的形成和发展做出了重要的贡献。

新历史主义在批评实践上具有明显的跨学科特征，是一种阐释文学文本的历史与文化内涵的批评方法，又称"文化诗学"，主要目的是重新描述文本与产生文本的文化体系之间的关系。首先，新历史主义消解了一直以来文学与历史之间的二元对立关系，认为历史与文学并未泾渭分明，不能孤立地看待历史和文学的关系。相反，它们都属于一种叙述。不仅如此，历史与文学之间存在一种互动关系：一方面，文学并非消极地反映历史事实，而是积极地参与创造历史意义的过程历史，甚至参与对政治话语、权力操纵和等级秩序的重新检视。另一方面，历史是文学素材的重要来源，历史通过文学表征重新获得新的意义，引发人们对历史问题的思考及对当下现实的深思。"历史的文本性"与"文本的历史性"也恰恰说明了文学与历史之间千丝万缕的复杂联系特质。其次，新历史主义认为历史是一种"情节编织"的运作，不仅是关于过去时间和程序的模式，也是隐喻的叙述。再次，新历史主义不再只关注文本的语言层面意义。相反，它更多地关注的是文化内涵，即语言背后的历史、文化、社会、政治背景。新历史主义使得文学研究从狭隘的文本世界转向了广大的社会和文化空间，从而打破了文本批评原有的思维模式，为文本研究开启了一方由语言学研究向文化研究转向的新的领域。

Hayden White

海登·怀特(1928—2018),美国著名的思想史家、历史哲学家和文学批评家,当代西方最著名的新历史主义批评家。他于密歇根大学获得哲学博士学位,后任教于美国加州大学圣塔克鲁兹分校,早年研究中世纪史和文化史,后开始涉足历史哲学领域,怀特主导了20世纪70年代以后历史哲学领域中的语言学转向,并将历史主义思想融入文学批评领域。他创造性地将解构主义和后结构主义理论引入史学领域,不对历史进行编纂,而是对各种历史的编纂进行理论的考察。对他来讲,历史首先是一种写作、一种修辞的灵活运用、一种语言结构的叙事构型。他的代表作《元史学:十九世纪欧洲的历史想象》被誉为20世纪后半叶最重要的历史哲学名著。此外,他还出版了《形式之内容》《历史的负担》等重要专著。

The Historical Text as Literary Artifact

(White, Hayden. The Historical Text as Literary Artifact. *The History and Narrative Reader*. Geoffrey Roberts ed. New York: Routledge, 2001, pp. 221-236.)

海登·怀特的《作为文学虚构的历史文本》重点探讨了历史叙事的虚构性,历史叙述中体现了大量的文学特征。历史与文学作品之间有许多共同特征,即历史的文学性,历史叙事中也带有明显的情节结构、象征意义、主观建构,历史叙事与文学叙事之间不可逾越的鸿沟被彻底逾越。怀特借鉴了弗莱和柯林伍德的观点,认为历史事件的叙写是一种"情节编织"的过程。他又从修辞手法入手,认为历史叙事具有隐喻性。最后,他谈到了历史真实到历史叙事的解构与重构,是一种以后现代历史观来解构和颠覆旧历史观,以一种文化观来理解历史的观点。这篇论文在新历史主义批评的形成过程中具有重要的意义。

One of the ways that a scholarly field takes stock of itself is by considering its history. Yet it is difficult to get an objective history of a scholarly discipline, because if the historian is himself a practitioner of it, he is likely to be a devotee of one or another of its sects and hence biased; and if he is not a practitioner, he is unlikely to have the expertise necessary to distinguish between the significant and the insignificant events of the field's development. One might think that these difficulties would not arise in the field of history itself, but they do and not only for the reasons mentioned above. In order to write the history of any given scholarly discipline or even of a science, one must be prepared to ask questions *about* it of a sort that do not have to be asked in the practice *of it*. One must try to get behind or beneath the presuppositions which sustain a given type of inquiry and ask the questions that can be begged in its practice in the interest of determining why this type of inquiry has been designed to solve the problems it characteristically tries to solve. This is what metahistory[1] seeks to do. It addresses itself to such questions as, What is the structure of a peculiarly *historical* Consciousness? What is the epistemological status of historical *explanations*, as compared with other kinds of explanations that might be offered to account for the materials with which historians ordinarily deal? What are the possible *forms* of historical representation and what are their bases? What authority can historical accounts claim as contributions to a secured knowledge of reality in general and to the human sciences in particular?

Now, many of these questions have been dealt with quite competently over the last quarter-century by philosophers concerned to define history's relationships to other disciplines, especially the physical and social sciences, and by historians interested in assessing the success of their discipline in mapping the past and determining the relationship of that past to the present. But there is one problem that neither philosophers nor historians have looked at very seriously and to which literary theorists have given only passing attention. This question has to do with the status of the historical narrative, considered purely as a verbal artifact purporting to be a model of structures and processes long past and therefore not subject to either experimental or observational controls. This is not to say that historians and philosophers of history have failed to take notice of the essentially provisional and contingent nature of historical representations and of their susceptibility to infinite revision in the light of new evidence or more sophisticated conceptualization of problems. One of the marks of a good professional historian is the consistency with which he reminds his readers of the purely provisional nature of his characterizations of events, agents, and agencies found in the always incomplete historical record. Nor is it to say that literary theorists have *never* studied the structure of historical narratives. But in general there has been a reluctance to consider historical narratives as what they most manifestly are: verbal fictions, the contents of which are as much *invented* as *found* and the forms of which have more in common with their counterparts in literature than they have with those in the sciences.

Now, it is obvious that this conflation of mythic and historical consciousness will offend some historians and disturb those literary theorists whose conception of literature presupposes a radical opposition of history to fiction or of fact to fancy. As Northrop Frye[2] has remarked, "In a sense the historical is the opposite of the mythical, and to tell the historian that what gives shape to his book is a myth would sound to him vaguely insulting." Yet Frye himself grants that "when a historian's scheme gets to a certain point of comprehensiveness it becomes mythical in shape, and so approaches the poetic in its structure." He even speaks of different kinds of historical myths: Romantic myths "based on a quest or pilgrimage to a City of God or classless society"; Comic "myths of progress through evolution or revolution"; Tragic myths of "decline and fall, like the works of Gibbon and Spengler"; and Ironic "myths of recurrence or casual catastrophe." But Frye appears to believe that these myths are operative only in such victims of what might be called the "poetic fallacy" as Hegel, Marx, Nietzsche, Spengler, Toynbee, and Sartre—historians whose fascination with the "constructive" capacity of human thought has deadened their responsibility to the "found" data. "The historian works inductively," he says, "collecting his facts and trying to avoid any informing patterns except those he sees, or is honestly convinced he sees, in the facts themselves." He does not work "from" a "unifying form," as the poet does, but "toward" it; and it therefore follows that the historian, like any writer of discursive prose, is to be judged "by the truth of what he says, or by the adequacy of his verbal reproduction of his external model," whether that external model be the actions of past men or the historian's own thought about such actions.

What Frye says is true enough as a statement of the *ideal* that has inspired historical writing since the time of the Greeks, but that ideal presupposes an opposition between myth and history that is as problematical as it is venerable. It serves Frye's purposes very well, since it permits him to locate the specifically "fictive" in the space between the two concepts of the "mythic" and the "historical." As readers of Frye's *Anatomy of Criticism*[3] will remember, Frye conceives fictions to consist in part of sublimates of archetypal myth-structures. These structures have been displaced to the interior of verbal artifacts in such a way as to serve as their latent meanings. The fundamental meanings of all fictions, their thematic content, consist, in Frye's view, of the "pre-generic plot-structures" or *mythoi* derived from the corpora of Classical and Judaeo-Christian religious literature[4]. According to this theory, we understand *why* a particular story has "turned out" as it has when we have identified the archetypal myth, or pregeneric plot structure, of which the story is an exemplification. And we see the "point" of a story when we have identified its theme (Frye's translation of *dianoia*), which makes of it a "parable or illustrative fable." "Every work of literature," Frye insists, "has both a fictional and a thematic aspect," but as we move from "fictional projection" toward the overt articulation of theme, the writing tends to take on the aspect of "direct address, or straight discursive writing and cease[s] to be literature." And in Frye's view, as we have seen, history (or at least "proper history") belongs to the category of "discursive writing," so that when the fictional element—or mythic plot structure—is *obviously* present in it, it ceases to be history altogether and becomes a bastard genre, product of an unholy, though not unnatural, union between history and poetry.

Yet, I would argue, histories gain part of their explanatory effect by their success in making stories out *otmere* chronicles; and stories in turn are made out of chronicles by an operation which I have elsewhere called "emplotment."[5] And by emplotment I mean simply the encodation of the facts contained in the chronicle as components of specific *kinds* of plot structures, in precisely the way that Frye has suggested is the case with "fictions" in general.

The late R. G. Collingwood[6] insisted that the historian was above all a story teller and suggested that historical sensibility was manifested in the capacity to make a plausible story out of a congeries of "facts" which, in their unprocessed form, made no sense at all. In their efforts to make sense of the historical record, which is fragmentary and always incomplete, historians have to make use of what Collingwood called "the constructive imagination," which told the historian—as it tells the competent detective— what "must have been the case" given the available evidence and the formal properties it displayed to the consciousness capable of putting the right question to it. This constructive imagination functions in much the same way that Kant supposed the *a priori* imagination functions when it tells us that even though we cannot perceive both sides of a tabletop simultaneously, we can be certain it has *two* sides if it has one, because the very concept of *one side* entails at least *one other*. Collingwood suggested that historians come to their evidence endowed with a sense of the *possible* forms that different kinds of recognizably human situations *can* take. He called this sense the nose for the "story" contained in the evidence or for the "true" story that was buried in or hidden behind the "apparent" story. And he concluded that historians provide plausible explanations for bodies of historical evidence when they succeed in discovering the story or complex of stories implicitly contained within them.

What Collingwood failed to see was that no given set of casually recorded historical events can in itself constitute a story; the most it might offer to the historian are story *elements*. The events are *made* into a story by the suppression or subordination of certain of them and the highlighting of others, by characterization, motific repetition, variation of tone and point of view, alternative descriptive strategies, and the like—in short, all of the techniques that we would normally expect to find in the emplotment of a novel or a play. For example, no historical event is *intrinsically tragic*; it can only be conceived as such from a particular point of view or from within the context of a structured set of events of which it is an element enjoying a privileged place. For in history what is tragic from one perspective is comic from another, just as in society what appears to be tragic from the standpoint of one class may be, as Marx purported to show of the 18th Brumaire of Louis Buonaparte[7], only a farce from that of another class. Considered as potential elements of a story, historical events are value-neutral. Whether they find their place finally in a story that is tragic, comic, romantic, or ironic—to use Frye's categories—depends upon the historian's decision to configure them according to the imperatives of one plot structure or mythos rather than another. The same set of events can serve as components of a story that is tragic or comic, as the case may be, depending on the historian's choice of the plot structure that he considers most appropriate for ordering events of that kind so as to make them into a comprehensible story.

This suggests that what the historian brings to his consideration of the historical record is a notion of the *types* of configurations of events that can be recognized as stories by the audience for which he is writing. True, he can misfire. I do not suppose that anyone would accept the emplotment of the life of President Kennedy as comedy, but whether it ought to be emplotted romantically, tragically, or satirically is an open question. The important point is that most historical sequences can be emplotted in a number of different ways, so as to provide different interpretations of those events and to endow them with different meanings. Thus, for example, what Michelet in his great history of the French Revolution construed as a drama of Romantic transcendence, his contemporary Tocqueville[8] emplotted as an ironic Tragedy. Neither can be said to have had more knowledge of the "facts" contained in the record; they simply had different notions of the kind of story that best fitted the facts they knew. Nor should it be thought that they told different stories of the Revolution because they had discovered different *kinds* of facts, political on the one hand, social on the other. They sought out different kinds of facts because they had different kinds of stories to tell. But why did these alternative, not to say mutually exclusive, representations of what was substantially the same set of events appear equally plausible to their respective audiences? Simply because the historians shared with their audiences certain preconceptions about how the Revolution might be emplotted, in response to imperatives that were generally extra historical, ideological, aesthetic, or mythical.

Collingwood once remarked that you could never explicate a tragedy to anyone who was not already acquainted with the kinds of situations that are regarded as "tragic" in our culture. Anyone who has taught or taken one of those omnibus courses usually entitled Western Civilization or Introduction to the Classics of Western Literature will know what Collingwood had in mind. Unless you have some idea of the generic attributes of tragic, comic, romantic, or ironic situations, you will be unable to recognize them as such when you come upon them in a literary text. But historical situations do not have built into them intrinsic meanings in the way that literary texts do. Historical situations are not *inherently* tragic, comic, or romantic. They may all be inherently ironic, but they need not be emplotted that way. All the historian needs to do to transform a tragic into a comic situation is to shift his point of view or change the scope of his perceptions. Anyway, we only think of situations as tragic or comic because these concepts are part of our generally cultural and specifically literary heritage. *How* a given historical situation is to be configured depends on the historian's subtlety in matching up a specific plot structure with the set of historical events that he wishes to endow with a meaning of a particular kind. This is essentially a literary, that is to say fiction-making, operation. And to call it that in no way detracts from the status of historical narratives as providing a kind of knowledge. For not only are the pregeneric plot structures by which sets of events can be constituted as stories of a particular kind limited in number, as Frye and other archetypal critics suggest; but the encodation of events in terms of such plot structures is one of the ways that a culture has of making sense of both personal and public pasts.

We can make sense of sets of events in a number of different ways. One of the ways is to subsume the events under the causal laws which may have governed their concatenation in order to produce the particular configuration that the events appear to assume when considered as "effects" of mechanical forces. This is the way of scientific explanation. Another way we make sense of a set of events which appears strange, enigmatic, or mysterious in its immediate manifestations is to encode the set in terms of culturally provided categories, such as metaphysical concepts, religious beliefs, or story forms. The effect of such encodations is to familiarize the unfamiliar; and in general this is the way of historiography, whose "data" are always immediately strange, not to say exotic, simply by virtue of their distance from us in time and their origin in a way of life different from our own.

The historian shares with his audience *general notions* of the *forms* that significant human situations *must* take by virtue of his participation in the specific processes of sense-making which identify him as a member of one cultural endowment rather than another. In the process of studying a given complex of events, he begins to perceive the *possible* story form that such events *may* figure. In his narrative account of how this set of events took on the shape which he perceives to inhere within it, he emplots his account as a story of a particular kind. The reader, in the process of following the historian's account of those events, gradually comes to realize that the story he is reading is of one kind rather than another: romance, tragedy, comedy, satire, epic, or what have you. And when he has perceived the class or type to which the story that he is reading belongs, he experiences the effect of having the events in the story explained to him. He has at this point not only successfully *followed* the story; he has grasped the point of it, *understood* it, as well. The original strangeness, mystery, or exoticism of the events is dispelled, and they take on a familiar aspect, not in their details, but in their functions as elements of a familiar kind of configuration. They are rendered comprehensible by being subsumed under the categories of the plot structure in which they are encoded as a story of a particular kind. They are familiarized, not only because the reader now has more *information* about the events, but also because he has been shown how the data conform to an *icon* of a comprehensible finished process, a plot structure with which he is familiar as a part of his cultural endowment.

This is not unlike what happens, or is supposed to happen, in psychotherapy. The sets of events in the patient's past which are the presumed cause of his distress, manifested in the neurotic syndrome, have been defamiliarized, rendered strange, mysterious, and threatening and have assumed a meaning that he can neither accept nor effectively reject. It is not that the patient does not *know* what those events were, does not know the facts; for if he did not in some sense know the facts, he would be unable to recognize them and repress them whenever they arise in his consciousness. On the contrary, he knows them all too well. He knows them so well, in fact, that he lives with them constantly and in such a way as to make it impossible for him to see any other facts except through the coloration that the set of events in question gives to his perception of the world. We might say that, according to the theory of psychoanalysis, the patient has overemplotted these events, has charged them with a meaning so intense that, whether real or merely imagined, they continue to shape both his perceptions and his responses to the world long after they should have become "past history." The therapist's problem, then, is not to hold up before the patient the "real facts" of the matter, the "truth" as against the "fantasy" that obsesses him. Nor is it to give him a short course in psychoanalytical theory by which to enlighten him as to the true nature of his distress by cataloguing it as a manifestation of some "complex." This is what the analyst might do in relating the patient's case to a third party, and especially to another analyst. But psychoanalytic theory recognizes that the patient will resist both of these tactics in the same way that he resists the intrusion into consciousness of the traumatized memory traces in *the form* that he obsessively remembers them. The problem is to get the patient to "reemplot" his whole life history in such a way as to change the *meaning* of those events for him and their *significance* for the economy of the whole set of events that make up his life. As thus envisaged, the therapeutic process is an exercise in the refamiliarization of events that have been defamiliarized, rendered alienated from the patient's life-history, by virtue of their overdetermination as causal forces. And we might say that the events are detraumatized by being removed from the plot structure in which they have a dominant place and inserted in another in which they have a subordinate or simply ordinary function as elements of a life shared with all other men.

注释:

1. 元历史，关于历史本身问题的研究。怀特的结论是没有所谓的“真的历史”，一切历史都是历史的哲学，编史的方式与历史思辨哲学的方式是一致的，这些方式是诗人洞察的形式化。

2. 诺思洛普·弗莱（1912—1991），加拿大著名的思想理论批评家。他所开创的神话-原型批评理论曾一度与马克思主义和精神分析性在20世纪五六十年代的西方理论界形成“三足鼎立”的局面。

3. 弗莱的著作《批评的剖析》从文化和文学角度对“原型”做进一步阐释，揭示了文学对应于神话的内在节奏，试图给予文学批评以独立的地位，使文学批评具有方法论原则和自然科学的连贯性，同时多角度地研究了西方文学的原型图式结构。

4. 犹太和基督教传统中共有的宗教文学。

5. emplotment，翻译为情节编织。

6. R.G.柯林伍德（1889—1943），英国哲学家、历史学家和考古学家，生于英国兰开郡的柯尼斯顿，著有《历史的观念》，是他的历史哲学思想的首次全面阐释。

7. 马克思的著作《路易·波拿巴的雾月十八日》。

8. 托克维尔（1805—1859），法国著名历史学家和政治家。

Stephen Greenblatt

斯蒂芬·格林布拉特(1943—)，当代美国著名的文学批评家和文化理论家，哈佛大学人文学教授，美国艺术与科学学院成员，专门从事跨学科研究，新历史主义理论的主要代表人物之一，代表性著作包括《文艺复兴时期的自我塑造：从莫尔到莎士比亚》《新历史主义实践》《炼狱中的哈姆雷特》《权力的即兴创造》等。哈佛大学霍米·巴巴教授曾高度评价他的成绩：“他不仅创建新历史主义批评学派，而且刷新了文学批评的思维习惯。”

Towards a Poetics of Culture

(Greenbaltt, Stephen. Towards a Poetics of Culture. *The New Historicism*. H. Aram Veeser ed. New York: Routledge. 1989, pp. 1-14.)

《走向一种文化主义诗学》是斯蒂芬·格林布拉特教授在西澳大利亚大学的一篇演讲稿，后收录在《新历史主义批评》一书中。在这篇论文中，他正式将“新历史主义”

的笼统提法更名为“文化诗学”，详细地论述了其独特的艺术文化历史观和历史语境观，分析了各种话语形式，如小说、现实生活中的各种类型文本之间的个体差异性和边界整体性。他将这些不同文本之间的转换称为话语的流通，话语在流通中通过“商谈”机制确立审美性话语，由此，文学艺术与社会现实生活、历史文化、主流意识形态、政治权利等多种社会关系不断渗透和融合，从而持续产生了新的意义。

I feel in a somewhat false position, which is not a particularly promising way to begin, and I might as well explain why. My own work has always been done with a sense of just having to go about and do it, without establishing first exactly what my theoretical position is. A few years ago I was asked by *Genre* to edit a selection of Renaissance essays, and I said OK. I collected a bunch of essays and then, out of a kind of desperation to get the introduction done, I wrote that the essays represented something I called a "new historicism." I've never been very good at making up advertising phrases of this kind; for reasons that I would be quite interested in exploring at some point, the name stuck much more than other names I'd very carefully tried to invent over the years. In fact I have heard—in the last year or so—quite a lot of talk about the "new historicism" (which for some reason in Australia is called Neohistoricism); there are articles about it, attacks on it, references to it in dissertations: the whole thing makes me quite giddy with amazement. In any case, as part of this peculiar phenomenon I have been asked to say something of a theoretical kind about the work I'm doing. So I shall try if not to define the new historicism, at least to situate it as a practice—a practice rather than a doctrine, since as far as I can tell (and I should be the one to know) it's no doctrine at all.

One of the peculiar characteristics of the "new historicism" in literary studies is precisely how unresolved and in some ways disingenuous it has been—I have been—about the relation to literary theory. On the one hand it seems to me that an openness to the theoretical ferment of the last few years is precisely what distinguishes the new historicism from the positivist historical scholarship of the early twentieth century. Certainly, the presence of Michel Foucault on the Berkeley campus for extended visits during the last five or six years of his life, and more generally the influence in America of European (and especially French) anthropological and social theorists, has helped to shape my own literary critical practice. On the other hand the historicist critics have on the whole been unwilling to enroll themselves in one or the other of the dominant theoretical camps.

I want to speculate on why this should be so by trying to situate myself in relation to Marxism on the one hand, and poststructuralism on the other. In the 1970s I used to teach courses with names like "Marxist Aesthetics" on the Berkeley campus. This came to an inglorious end when I was giving such a course—it must have been the mid-1970s—and I remember a student getting very angry with me. Now it's true that I tended to like those Marxist figures who were troubled in relation to Marxism—Walter Benjamin, the early rather than the later Lukács, and so forth—and I remember someone finally got up and screamed out in class "You're either a Bolshevilk or a Menshevik—make up your fucking mind," and then slammed the door. It was a little unsettling, but I thought about it afterwards and realized that I wasn't sure whether I was a Menshevik, but I certainly wasn't a Bolshevik. After that I started to teach courses with names like "Cultural Poetics." It's true that I'm still more uneasy with a politics and a literary perspective that is untouched by Marxist thought, but that doesn't lead me to endorse propositions or embrace a particular philosophy, politics or rhetoric, *faute de mieux*.

Thus the crucial identifying gestures made by the most distinguised American Marxist aesthetic theorist, Fredric Jameson, seem to me highly problematic. Let us take, for example, the following eloquent passage from *The Political Unconscious*:

> the convenient working distinction between cultural texts that are social and political and those that are not becomes something worse than an error: namely, a symptom and a reinforcement of the reification and privatization of contemporary life. Such a distinction reconfirms that structural, experiential, and conceptual gap between the public and the private, between the social and the psychological, or the political and the poetic, between history or society and the "individual", which—the tendential law of social life under capitalism—maims our existence as individual subjects and paralyzes our thinking about time and change just as surely as it alienates us from our speech itself.[2]

A working distinction between cultural texts that are social and political and those that are not—that is, an aesthetic domain that is in some way marked off from the discursive institutions that are operative elsewhere in a culture—becomes for Jameson a malignant symptom of "privatization." Why should the "private" immediately enter into this distinction at all? Does the term refer to private property, that is, to the ownership of the means of production and the regulation of the mode of consumption? If so, what is the historical relation between this mode of economic organization and a working distinction between the political and the poetic? It would seem that in print, let alone in the electronic media, private ownership has led not "privatization" but to the drastic communalization of all discourse, the constitution of an ever larger mass audience, the organization of a commercial sphere unimagined and certainly unattained by the comparatively modest attempts in pre-capitalist societies to organize public discourse. Moreover, is it not possible to have a communal sphere of art that is distinct from other communal spheres? Is this communal differentiation, sanctioned by the laws of property, not the dominant practice in capitalist society, manifestly in the film and television industries, but also, since the invention of movable type, in the production of poems and novels as well? Would we really find it less alienating to have no distinction at all between the political and the poetic—the situation, let us say, during China's Cultural Revolution? Or, for that matter, do we find it notably liberating to have our own country governed by a film actor who is either cunningly or pathologically indifferent to the traditional differentiation between fantasy and reality?

For *The Political Unconscious* any demarcation of the aesthetic must be aligned with the private which is in turn aligned with the psychological, the poetic, and the individual, as distinct form the public, the social, and the political. All of these interlocking distinctions, none of which seems to me philosophically or even historically bound up with the original "working distinction," are then laid at the door of capitalism with its power to "maim" and "paralyse" us as "individual subjects." Though we may find a differentiation between cultural discourses that are artistic and cultural discourses that are social or political well before the European seventeenth century, and in cultures that seem far removed from the capitalist mode of production, Jameson insists that somehow the perpetrator and agent of the alleged maiming is capitalism. A shadowy opposition is assumed between the "individual" (bad) and the "individual subject" (good); indeed the maiming of the latter creates the former.

The whole passage has the resonance of an allegory of the fall of man: once we were whole, agile, integrated; we were individual subjects but not individuals, we had no psychology distinct from the shared life of the society; politics and poetry were one. Then capitalism arose and shattered this luminous, benign totality. The myth echoes throughout Jameson's book, though by the close it has been eschatologically reoriented so that the totality lies not in a past revealed to have always already fallen but in the classless future. A philosophical claim then appeals to an absent empirical event. And literature is invoked at once as the dark token of fallenness and the shimmering emblem of the absent transfiguration.

But, of course, poststructuralism has raised serious questions about such a vision, challenging both its underlying oppositions and the primal organic unity that it posits as either paradisal origin or utopian, eschatological end.[3] This challenge has already greatly modified, though by no means simply displaced, Marxist discourse. I could exemplify this complex interaction between Marxism and poststructuralism by discussing Jameson's own most recent work in which he finds himself, from the perspective of postmodernism, deploring the loss of those "working distinctions" that at least enabled the left to identify its enemies and articulate a radical programme.[4] But to avoid confusions, I want to focus instead on the work of Jean-François Lyotard. Here, as in *The Political Unconscious*, the distinction between discursive fields is once again at stake: for Lyotard the existence of proper names makes possible

> the co-existence of those worlds that Kant calls fields, territories, and domains—those worlds which of course present the same object, but which also make that object the stakes of heterogenous (or incommensurable) expectations in universes of phrases, none of which can be transformed into any other.[5]

Lyotard's model for these differentiated discourses is the existence of proper names. But now it is the role of capitalism not to demarcate discursive domains but, quite the opposite, to make such domains untenable. "Capital is that which wants a single language and a single network, and it never stops trying to present them" (p. 55). Lyotard's principle exhibit of this attempt by capital to institute a single language—what Bakhtin would call monologism—is Faurisson's denial of the Holocaust, and behind this denial, the Nazis' attempt to obliterate the existence of millions of Jews and other undesirables, an attempt Lyotard characterizes as the will "to strike from history and from the map entire worlds of names."

The problem with this account is that the Nazis did not seem particularly interested in exterminating names along with the persons who possessed those names; on the contrary, they kept, in so far as was compatible with a campaign of mass murder, remarkably full records, and they looked forward to a time in which they could share their accomplishment with a grateful world by establishing a museum dedicated to the culture of the wretches they had destroyed. The Faurisson affair is at bottom not an epistemological dilemma, as Lyotard claims, but an attempt to wish away evidence that is both substantial and verifiable. The issue is not an Epicurean paradox—"if death is there, you are not there; if you are there, death is not there; hence it is impossible for you to prove that death is there"—but a historical problem: what is the evidence of mass murder? How reliable is this evidence? Are there convincing grounds for denying or doubting the documented events? And if there are not such grounds, how may we interpret the motives of those who seek to cast doubt upon the historical record?

There is a further problem in Lyotard's use of the Faurisson affair as an instance of capitalist hostility to names: the conflation of Fascist apologetics and capitalism would seem to be itself an instance of monologism, since it suppresses all the aspects of capitalism that are wedded to the generation and inscription of individual identities and to the demarcation of boundaries separating those identities. We may argue, of course, that the capitalist insistence upon individuality is fraudulent, but it is difficult, I think, to keep the principle of endlessly proliferated, irreducible individuality separate from the market place version against which it is set. For it is capitalism, as Marx suggested, that mounts the West's most powerful and sustained assault upon collective, communal values and identities. And it is in the market place and in the state apparatus linked to the circulation and accumulation of capital that names themselves are forged. Proper names, as distinct from common names, seem less the victims than the products of property—they are bound up not only with the property one has in oneself, that is, with the theory of possessive individualism, but quite literally with the property one possesses, for proper names are insisted upon in the early modern period precisely in order to register them in the official documents that enable the state to calculate and tax personal property.[6]

The difference between Jameson's capitalism, the perpetrator of separate discursive domains, the agent of privacy, psychology, and the individual, and Lyotard's capitalism, the enemy of such domains and the destroyer of privacy, psychology, and the individual, may in part be traced to a difference between the Marxist and poststructralist projects. Jameson, seeking to expose the fallaciousness of a separate artistic sphere and to celebrate the materialist integration of all discourses, finds capitalism at the root of the false differentiation; Lyotard, seeking to celebrate the differentiation of all discourses and to expose the fallaciousness of monological unity, finds capitalism at the root of the false integration. History functions in both cases as a convenient anecdotal ornament upon a theoretical structure, and capitalism appears not as a complex social and economic development in the West but as malign philosophical principle.[7]

I propose that the general question addressed by Jameson and Lyotard—what is the historical relation between art and society or between one institutionally demarcated discursive practice and another? —does not lend itself to a single, theoretically satisfactory answer of the kind that Jameson and Lyotard are trying to provide. Or rather theoretical satisfaction here seems to depend upon a utopian vision that collapses the contradictions of history into a moral imperative. The problem is not simply the incompatibility of two theories—Marxist and poststructuralist—with one another, but the inability of either of the theories to come to terms with the apparently contradictory historical effects of capitalism. In principle, of course, both Marxism and poststructuralism seize upon contradictions: for the former they are signs of repressed class conflicts, for the latter they disclose hidden cracks in the spurious certainties of logocentrism. But in practice Jameson treats capitalism as the agent of repressive differentiation, while Lyotard treats it as the agent of monological tantalization. And this effacement of contradiction is not the consequence of an accidental lapse but rather the logical outcome of theory's search for the obstacle that blocks the realization of its eschatological vision.

If capitalism is invoked not as a unitary demonic principle, but as a complex historical movement in a world without paradisal origins or chiliastic expectations, then an inquiry into the relation between art and society in capitalist cultures must address both the formation of the working distinction upon which Jameson remarks and the totalizing impulse upon which Lyotard remarks. For capitalism has characteristically generated neither regimes in which all discourses seem coordinated, nor regimes in which they seem radically isolated or discontinuous, but regimes in which the drive towards differentiation and the drive towards monological organization operate simultaneously, or at least oscillate so rapidly as to create the impression of simultaneity.

In a brilliant paper that received unusual attention, elicited a response from a White House speech-writer, and most recently generated a segment on CBB's "Sixty Minutes," the political scientist and historian Michael Rogin recently observed the number of times President Reagan has, at critical moments in his career, quoted lines from his own or other popular films. The President is a man, Rogin remarks, "whose most spontaneous moments—('Where do we find such men?' about the American D-Day dead; 'I am paying for this microphone, Mr Green,' during the 1980 New Hampshire primary debate)—are not only preserved and projected on film, but also turn out to be lines from old movies."[8] To a remarkable extent, Ronald Reagan, who made his final Hollywood film, *The killers* in 1964, continues to live within movies; he has been shaped by them, draws much of his cold war rhetoric from them, and cannot or will not distinguish between them and an external reality. Indeed his political career has depended upon an ability to project himself and his mass audience into a realm in which there is no distinction between simulation and reality.

The response from Anthony Dolan, a White House speech-writer who was asked to comment on Rogin's paper, was highly revealing. "What he's really saying," Dolan suggested, "is that all of us are deeply affected by a uniquely American art form: the movies."[9] Rogin had in fact argued that the presidential character "was produced from the convergence of two sets of substitutions which generated Cold War countersubversion in the 1940s and underlie its 1980 revival—the political replacement of Nazism by Communism, from which the national security state was born; and the psychological shift from an embodied self to its simulacrum on film." Both the political and the psychological substitution were intimately bound up with Ronald Reagan's career in the movies. Dolan in response rewrites Rogin's thesis into a celebration of the power of "a uniquely American art form" to shape "all of us." Movies, Dolan told the *New York Times* reporter, "heighten reality rather than lessen it."

Such a statement appears to welcome the collapse of the working distinction between the aesthetic and the real; the aesthetic is not an alternative realm but a way of intensifying the single realm we all inhabit. But then the spokesman went on to assert that the President "usually credits the films whose lines he uses." That is, at the moment of appropriation, the President acknowledges that he is borrowing from the aesthetic and hence acknowledges the existence of a working distinction. In so doing he respects and even calls attention to the difference between his own presidential discourse and the fictions in which he himself at one time took part: they are differences upon which his own transition from actor to politician in part depends, and they are the signs of the legal and economic system that he represents. For the capitalist aesthetic demands acknowledgements—hence the various marks of property rights that are flashed on the screen or inscribed in a text—and the political arena insists that it is not a fiction. That without acknowledgement the President delivers speeches written by Anthony Dolan or others does not appear to concern anyone; this has long been the standard operating procedure of American politician. But it would concern people if the President recited speeches that were lifted without acknowledgement from old movies. He would then seem not to know the difference between fantasy and reality. And that might be alarming.

注释:

1. 此文是 1986 年 9 月 4 日斯蒂芬·格林布拉特在西澳大利亚大学所做的演讲。

2. 弗雷德里克·詹明信:《政治无意识: 作为社会象征行为的叙事》。 Fredric Jameson, *The Political Unconscious: Narrative as a Socially Symbolic Act* (Ithaca: Cornell Univ. Press, 1981), p. 20.

3. 参见 Mark Poster, "Foucault, Poststructuralism, and the Mode of Information," in *The Aims of Representation*。

4. 詹明信本人并没有对他思想中的突然反复直接做出解释。

5. 参见 J. F. Lyotard, "Judiciousness in Dispute or, Kant after Marx," in *The Aims of Representation*, p. 37。

6. 参见 William E. Tate, *The Parish Chest: A Study in the Records of Parochial Administration in England* (Cambridge: Cambridge Univ. Press, 1946)。

7. 当然, 我们反过来也可以争辩, 正如詹明信实际上所做的那样, 声称有两种资本主义, 老牌的工业化资本主义是有区别的媒介, 新近的后期资本主义则抹杀了区别。 可以用残留和浮现之间的区分来揭示从理论上不属于资本主义阶段的这一或那一倾向。 作者认为这种在学术上挽救理论的做法十分令人沮丧。

8. 参见 Michael Rogin, "'Ronald Reagan': The Movie" (unpublished manuscript)。

9. 记者 Michael Tolchin 在《纽约时报》(*New York Times*) 上转引罗金的文章时提到了这点。 "How Reagan Always Gets the Best Lines," New York Times, 9 Sept. 1985, p. 10.

Chapter Twelve **Post-Colonialist Studies**

后殖民主义，又称后殖民批判主义，兴起于20世纪后半叶，是研究欧洲殖民主义对殖民地和第三世界在政治、经济、文化和历史方面的影响，具有交叉学科性质的批评理论。后殖民主义之“后”，与其他后学一样，既有时间上之后的意思，也有价值取向和批评策略上的“反”之意。简言之，后殖民主义就是反思批判殖民主义之下的文化状态。后殖民主义批评是第二次世界大战之后由历史学家引入研究领域的，其受到米歇尔·福柯的“话语”与“权力”理论、后结构主义以及安东尼奥·葛兰西的霸权主义、路易·阿尔都塞的意识形态理论的影响。由此，文学批评家使用这个术语作为研究文本中的殖民表征、殖民策略以及反殖民思想。最著名的后殖民批评理论家是爱德华·赛义德(Edward Said)，其他后殖民理论家还有霍米·巴巴(Homi Bhabha)、佳亚特里·斯皮瓦克(Gayatri C. Spivak)、弗朗兹·法农(Frantz Fanon)。

后殖民主义批评理论具有鲜明的政治倾向，其理论与实践的重要基础是赛义德的“东方主义”，这一术语运用后结构主义思想解构了西方欧洲中心论的隐含策略。欧洲中心论认为西方范围内具有规范性与优越地位，相反，东方则被构造为未开化、愚昧、落后、野蛮、怪异、次等的他者形象，这就树立了西方的“自我”与东方的“他者”之间的二元对立思想，而“他者”的概念实际上隐含着西方中心主义的意识形态。此后，后殖民主义批评围绕身份认同问题、文化霸权主义等关键词展开论述，它否认一切主导叙述，认为叙事都是欧洲中心主义的霸权表征。因此，批判欧洲中心主义是后殖民主义的基本任务，与此相关联，对“现代性”为基础的发展观念的质疑和批判也是其重要特征之一。后殖民主义对全部的“基础的”历史书写予以否定，认为一种基础的视角总是通过一种“同一性”而压制了“异质性”，从而否定了当代资本主义的世界结构。此外，后殖民主义借用了福柯关于“话语”和“权力”关系的理论，认为世界上任何“知识”归根到底都是一种“话语/权力”的较量。此外，霍米·巴巴的杂交性身份理论也为后殖民主义理论注入了新的活力。

Edward Said

爱德华·赛义德(1939—2003),生于巴勒斯坦的耶路撒冷,早年在耶路撒冷和开罗求学,中学毕业后到美国继续深造,先后取得普林斯顿大学学士、哈佛大学硕士和博士学位,之后在哥伦比亚大学任教,是英语和比较文学学院教授。他一直致力于文学和文化批评研究,当选为现代语言学会1999年度主席,他的重要著作包括《东方学:西方对于东方的观念》《世界·文本·批评家》《文化与帝国主义》《知识分子论》等。赛义德富有挑战的专著为后殖民主义的形成与发展开辟了一个崭新的理论视野。

Culture and Imperialism: Introduction

(Said, Edward W. *Culture and Imperialism*. New York: Vintage, 1993, pp. xi.-xxviii.)

1993年,赛义德出版了他的专著《文化与帝国主义》。此书建立在一个更深入的问题意识上,即文化是如何参与建构帝国主义世界观的,由此开始深入研究文化与帝国主义之间的关系,并且将西方文化与帝国主义共谋关系的分析扩展到小说的形式和风格层面,即形式上构成叙述的权威,内容上包含了帝国主义复杂的思想构造。本文是对整部著作的简要介绍,在英国文学中选取狄更斯、康拉德的作品进行深度文本分析,阐释其中的帝国主义意识。

Australia was established as a penal colony in the late eighteenth century mainly so that England could transport an irredeemable, unwanted excess population of felons to a place, originally charted by Captain Cook, that would also function as a colony replacing those lost in America. The pursuit of profit, the building of empire, and what Hughes calls social *apartheid* together produced modern Australia, which by the time Dickens first took an interest in it during the 1840s (in *David Copperfield* Wilkins Micawber happily immigrates there) had progressed somewhat into profitability and a sort of "free system" where laborers could do well on their own if allowed to do so. Yet in Magwitch

> Dickens knotted several strands in the English perception of convicts in Australia at the end of transportation. They could succeed, but they could hardly, in the real sense, return. They could expiate their crimes in a technical, legal sense, but what they suffered there warped them into permanent outsiders. And yet they were capable of redemption—as long as they stayed in Australia. [1]

Carter's exploration of what he calls Australia's spatial history offers us another version of that same experience. Here explorers, convicts, ethnographers, profiteers, soldiers chart the vast and relatively empty continent each in a discourse that jostles, displaces, or incorporates the others. Botany Bay is therefore first of all an Enlightenment discourse of travel and discovery, then a set of travelling narrators (including Cook) whose words, charts, and intentions accumulate the strange territories and gradually turn them into "home." The adjacence between the Benthamite[2] organization of space (which produced the city of Melbourne) and the apparent disorder of the Australian bush is shown by Carter to have become an optimistic transformation of social space, which produced an Elysium for gentlemen, an Eden for laborers in the 1840s. [3] What Dickens envisions for Pip, being Magwitch's "London gentleman," is roughly equivalent to what was envisioned by English benevolence for Australia, one social space authorizing another.

But *Great Expectations* was not written with anything like the concern for native Australian accounts that Hughes or Carter has, nor did it presume or forecast a tradition of Australian writing, which in fact came later to include the literary works of David Malouf, Peter Carey, and Patrick White. The prohibition placed on Magwitch's return is not only penal but imperial: subjects can be taken to places like Australia, but they cannot be allowed a "return" to metropolitan space, which, as all Dickens's fiction testifies, is meticulously charted, spoken for, inhabited by a hierarchy of metropolitan personages. So on the one hand, interpreters like Hughes and Carter expand on the relatively attenuated presence of Australia in nineteenth-century British writing, expressing the fullness and earned integrity of an Australian history that became independent from Britain's in the twentieth century; yet, on the other, an accurate reading of *Great Expectations* must note that after Magwitch's delinquency is expiated, so to speak, after Pip redemptively acknowledges his debt to the old, bitterly energized, and vengeful convict, Pip himself collapses and is revived in two explicitly positive ways. A new Pip appears, less laden than the old Pip with the chains of the past—he is glimpsed in the form of a child, also called Pip; and the old Pip takes on a new career with his boyhood friend Herbert Pocket, this time not as an idle gentleman but as a hardworking trader in the East, where Britain's other colonies offer a sort of normality that Australia never could.

Thus even as Dickens settles the difficulty with Australia, another structure of attitude and reference emerges to suggest Britain's imperial intercourse through trade and travel with the Orient. In his new career as colonial businessman, Pip is hardly an exceptional figure, since nearly all of Dickens's businessmen, wayward relatives, and frightening outsiders have a fairly normal and secure connection with the empire. But it is only in recent years that these connections have taken on interpretative importance. A new generation of scholars and critics—the children of decolonization in some instances, the beneficiaries (like sexual, religious, and racial minorities) of advances in human freedom at home—have seen in such great texts of Western literature a standing interest in what was considered a lesser world, populated with lesser people of color, portrayed as open to the intervention of so many Robinson Crusoes.

By the end of the nineteenth century the empire is no longer merely a shadowy presence, or embodied merely in the unwelcome appearance of a fugitive convict but, in the works of writers like Conrad, Kipling, Gide, and Loti, a central area of concern. Conrad's *Nostromo* (1904)—my second example—is set in a Central American republic, independent (unlike the African and East Asian colonial settings of his earlier fictions), and dominated at the same time by outside interests because of its immense silver mine. For a contemporary American the most compelling aspect of the work is Conrad's prescience: he forecasts the unstoppable unrest and "misrule" of the Latin American republics (governing them, he says, quoting Bolivar, is like plowing the sea), and he singles out North America's particular way of influencing conditions in a decisive yet barely visible way. Holroyd, the San Francisco financier who backs Charles Gould, the British owner of the San Tomé mine, warns his protégé that "we won't be drawn into any large trouble" as investors. Nevertheless,

> We can sit and watch. Of course, some day we shall step in. We are bound to. But there's no hurry. Time itself has got to wait on the greatest country in the whole of God's universe. We shall be giving the word for

> everything—industry, trade, law, journalism, art, politics, and religion, from Cape Horn clear over to Surith's Sound, and beyond it, too, if anything worth taking hold of turns up at the North Pole. And then we shall have the leisure to take in hand the outlying islands and continents of the earth. We shall run the world's business whether the world likes it or not. The world can't help it—and neither can we, I guess.[4]

Much of the rhetoric of the "New World Order" promulgated by the American government since the end of the Cold War—with its redolent self-congratulation, its unconcealed triumphalism, its grave proclamations of responsibility—might have been scripted by Conrad's Holroyd: we are number one, we are bound to lead, we stand for freedom and order, and so on. No American has been immune from this structure of feeling, and yet the implicit warning contained in Conrad's portraits of Holroyd and Gould is rarely reflected on since the rhetoric of power all too easily produces an illusion of benevolence when deployed in an imperial setting. Yet it is a rhetoric whose most damning characteristic is that it has been used before, not just once (by Spain and Portugal) but with deafeningly repetitive frequency in the modern period; by the British, the French, the Belgians, the Japanese, the Russians, and now the Americans.

Yet it would be incomplete to read Conrad's great work simply as an early prediction of what we see happening in twentieth-century Latin America, with its string of United Fruit Companies, colonels, liberation forces, and American-financed mercenaries. Conrad is the precursor of the Western views of the Third World which one finds in the work of novelists as different as Graham Greene, V. S. Naipaul, and Robert Stone, of theoreticians of imperialism like Hannah Arendt, and of travel writers, filmmakers, and polemicists whose specialty is to deliver the non-European world either for analysis and judgment or for satisfying the exotic tastes of European and North American audiences. For if it is true that Conrad ironically sees the imperialism of the San Tomé silver mine's British and American owners as doomed by its own pretentious and impossible ambitions, it is also true that he writes as a man whose *Western* view of the non-Western world is so ingrained as to blind him to other histories, other cultures, other aspirations. All Conrad can see is a world totally dominated by the Atlantic West, in which every opposition to the West only confirms the West's wicked power. What Conrad cannot see is an alternative to this cruel tautology. He could neither understand that India, Africa, and South America also had lives and cultures with integrities not totally controlled by the gringo imperialists and reformers of this world, nor allow himself to believe that anti-imperialist independence movements were not all corrupt and in the pay of the puppet masters in London or Washington.

These crucial limitations in vision are as much a part of *Nostromo*[5] as its characters and plot. Conrad's novel embodies the same paternalistic arrogance of imperialism that it mocks in characters like Gould and Holroyd. Conrad seems to be saying, "We Westerners will decide who is a good native or a bad, because all natives have sufficient existence by virtue of our recognition. We created them, we taught them to speak and think, and when they rebel they simply confirm our views of them as silly children, duped by some of their Western masters." This is in effect what Americans have felt about their southern neighbors: that independence is to be wished for them so long as it is the kind of independence *we* approve of. Anything else is unacceptable and, worse, unthinkable.

It is no paradox, therefore, that Conrad was both anti-imperialist and imperialist, progressive when it came to rendering fearlessly and pessimistically the self-confirming, self-deluding corruption of overseas domination, deeply reactionary when it came to conceding that Africa or South America could ever have had an independent history or culture, which the imperialists violently disturbed but by which they were ultimately defeated. Yet lest we think patronizingly of Conrad as the creature of his own time, we had better note that recent attitudes in Washington and among most Western policymakers and intellectuals show little advance over his views. What Conrad discerned as the futility latent in imperialist philanthropy—whose intentions include such ideas as "making the world safe for democracy"[6] the United States government is still unable to perceive, as it tries to implement its wishes all over the globe, especially in the Middle East. At least Conrad had the courage to see that no such schemes ever succeed—because they trap the planners in more illusions of omnipotence and misleading self-satisfaction (as in Vietnam), and because by their very nature they falsify the evidence.

All this is worth bearing in mind if *Nostromo* is to be read with some attention to its massive strengths and inherent limitations. The newly independent state of Sulaco that emerges at the end of the novel is only a smaller, more tightly controlled and intolerant version of the larger state from which it has seceded and has now come to displace in wealth and importance. Conrad allows the reader to see that imperialism is a system. Life in one subordinate realm of experience is imprinted by the fictions and follies of the dominant realm. But the reverse is true, too, as experience in the dominant society comes to depend uncritically on natives and their territories perceived as in need of *la mission civilisatrice*. [6]

However it is read, *Nostromo* offers a profoundly unforgiving view, and it has quite literally enabled the equally severe view of Western imperialist illusions in Graham Greene's *The Quiet American* or V. S. Naipaul's *A Bend in the River*, novels with very different agendas. Few readers today, after Vietnam, Iran, the Philippines, Algeria, Cuba, Nicaragua, Iraq, would disagree that it is precisely the fervent innocence of Greene's Pyle or Naipaul's Father Huismans, men for whom the native can be educated into "our" civilization, that turns out to produce the murder, subversion, and endless instability of "primitive" societies. A similar anger pervades films like Oliver Stone's *Salvador*, Francis Ford Coppola's *Apocalypse Now*, and Constantin Costa-Gavras's *Missing*, in which unscrupulous CIA operatives and power-mad officers manipulate natives and well-intentioned Americans alike.

Yet all these works, which are so indebted to Conrad's anti-imperialist irony in *Nostromo*, argue that the source of the world's significant action and life is in the West, whose representatives seem at liberty to visit their fantasies and philanthropies upon a mind-deadened Third World. In this view, the outlying regions of the world have no life, history, or culture to speak of, no independence or integrity worth representing without the West. And when there is something to be described it is, following Conrad, unutterably corrupt, degenerate, irredeemable. But whereas Conrad wrote *Nostromo* during a period of Europe's largely uncontested imperialist enthusiasm, contemporary novelists and filmmakers who have learned his ironies so well have done their work *after* decolonization, *after* the massive intellectual, moral, and imaginative overhaul and deconstruction of Western representation of the non-Western world, *after* the work of Frantz Fanon, Amilcar Cabral, C. L. R. James, Walter Rodney, *after* the novels and plays of Chinua Achebe, Ngugi wa Thiongo, Wole Soyinka, Salman Rushdie, Gabriel Garda Márquez, and many others.

Thus Conrad has passed along his residual imperialist propensities, although his heirs scarcely have an excuse to justify the often subtle and unreflecting bias of their work. This is not just a matter of Westerners who do not have enough sympathy for or comprehension of foreign cultures—since there are, after all, some artists and intellectuals who have, in effect, crossed to the other side—Jean Genet, Basil Davidson, Alben Memmi, Juan Goytisolo, and others. What is perhaps more relevant is the political willingness to take seriously the alternatives to imperialism, among them the existence of other cultures and societies. Whether one believes that Conrad's extraordinary fiction confirms habitual Western suspicions about Latin America, Africa, and Asia, or whether one sees in novels like *Nostromo* and *Great Expectations* the lineaments of an astonishingly durable imperial worldview, capable of warping the perspectives of reader and author equally: *both* those ways of reading the real alternatives seem outdated. The world today does not exist as a spectacle about which we can be either pessimistic or optimistic, about which our "texts" can be either ingenious or boring. All such attitudes involve the deployment of power and interests. To the extent that we see Conrad both criticizing and reproducing the imperial ideology of his time, to that extent we can characterize our own present attitudes: the projection, or the refusal, of the wish to dominate, the capacity to damn, or the energy to comprehend and engage with other societies, traditions, histories.

The world has changed since Conrad and Dickens in ways that have surprised, and often alarmed, metropolitan Europeans and Americans, who now confront large non-white immigrant populations in their midst, and face an impressive roster of newly empowered voices asking for their narratives to be heard. The point of my book is that such populations and voices have been there for some time, thanks to the globalized process set in motion by modern imperialism; to ignore or otherwise discount the overlapping experience of Westerners and Orientals, the interdependence of cultural terrains in which colonizer and colonized co-existed and battled each other through projections as well as rival geographies, narratives, and histories, is to miss what is essential about the world in the past century.

For the first time, the history of imperialism and its culture can now be studied as neither monolithic nor reductively compartmentalized, separate, distinct. True, there has been a disturbing eruption of separatist and chauvinist discourse, whether in India, Lebanon, or Yugoslavia, or in Afrocentric, Islamocentric, or Eurocentric proclamations; far from invalidating the struggle to be free from empire, these reductions of cultural discourse actually prove the validity of a fundamental liberationist energy that animates the wish *to* be independent, to speak freely and without the burden of unfair domination. The only way to understand this energy, however, is historically: and hence the rather wide geographical and historical range attempted in this book. In our wish to make ourselves heard, we tend very often to forget that the world is a crowded place, and that if everyone were to insist on the radical purity or priority of one's own voice, all we would have would be the awful din of unending strife, and a bloody political mess, the true horror of which is beginning to be perceptible here and there in the reemergence of racist politics in Europe, the cacophony of debates over political correctness and identity politics in the United States, and—to speak about my own part of the world—the intolerance of religious prejudice and illusionary promises of Bismarckian despotism[7], *à* la Saddam Hussein and his numerous Arab epigones and counterparts.

What a sobering and inspiring thing it is therefore not just to read one's own side, as it were, but also to grasp how a great artist like Kipling[8] (few more imperialist and reactionary than he) rendered India with such skill, and how in doing so his novel *Kim* not only depended on a long history of Anglo-Indian perspective, but also, in spite of itself, forecast the untenability of that perspective in its insistence on the belief that the Indian reality required, indeed beseeched British tutelage more or less indefinitely. The great cultural archive, I argue, is where the intellectual and aesthetic investments in overseas dominion are made. If you were British or French in the 1860s you saw, and you felt, India and North Africa with a combination of familiarity and distance, but never with a sense of their separate sovereignty. In your narratives, histories, travel tales, and explorations your consciousness was represented as the principal authority, an active point of energy that made sense not just of colonizing activities but of exotic geographies and peoples. Above all, your sense of power scarcely imagined that those "natives" who appeared either subservient or sullenly uncooperative were ever going to be capable of finally making you give up India or Algeria. Or of saying anything that might perhaps contradict, challenge, or otherwise disrupt the prevailing discourse.

Imperialism's culture was not invisible, nor did it conceal its worldly affiliations and interests. There is a sufficient clarity in the culture's major lines for us to remark the often scrupulous notations recorded there, and also to remark how they have not been paid much attention. Why they are now of such interest as, for instance, to spur this and other books derives less from a kind of retrospective vindictiveness than from a fortified need for links and connections. One of imperialism's achievements was to bring the world closer together, and although in the process the separation between Europeans and natives was an insidious and fundamentally unjust one, most of us should now regard the historical experience of empire as a common one. The task then is to describe it as pertaining to Indians *and* Britishers, Algerians *and* French, Westerners *and* Africans, Asians, Latin Americans, and Australians despite the horrors, the bloodshed, and the vengeful bitterness.

My method is to focus as much as possible on individual works, to read them first as great products of the creative or interpretative imagination, and then to show them as part of the relationship between culture and empire. I do not believe that authors are mechanically determined by ideology, class, or economic history, but authors are, I also believe, very much in the history of their societies, shaping and shaped by that history and their social experience in different measure. Culture and the aesthetic forms it contains derive from historical experience, which in effect is one of the main subjects of this book. As I discovered in writing *Orientalism*, you cannot grasp historical experience by lists or catalogues, and no matter how much you provide by way of coverage, some books, articles, authors, and ideas are going to be left out. Instead, I have tried to look at what I consider to be important and essential things, conceding in advance that selectivity and conscious choice have had to rule what I have done. My hope is that readers and critics of this book will use it to further the lines of inquiry and arguments about the historical experience of imperialism put forward in it. In discussing and analyzing what in fact is a global process, I have had to be occasionally both general and summary; yet no one, I am sure, would wish this book any longer than it is!

Moreover, there are several empires that I do not discuss: the Austro-Hungarian, the Russian, the Ottoman, and the Spanish and Portuguese. These omissions, however, are not at all meant to suggest that Russia's domination of Central Asia and Eastern Europe, Istanbul's rule over the Arab world, Portugal's over what are today's Angola and Mozambique, and Spain's domination in both the Pacific and Latin America have been either benign (and hence approved of) or any less imperialist. What I am saying about the British, French, and American imperial experience is that it has a unique coherence and a special cultural centrality. England of course is in an imperial class by itself, bigger, grander, more imposing than any other; for almost two centuries France was in direct competition with it. Since narrative plays such a remarkable part in the imperial quest, it is therefore not surprising that France and (especially) England have an unbroken tradition of novel-writing, unparalleled elsewhere. America began as an empire during the nineteenth century, but it was in the second half of the twentieth, after the decolonization of the British and French empires, that it directly followed its two great predecessors.

注释:

1. 参见 Robert Hughes, *The Fatal Shore: The Epic of Australia's Founding* (New York: Knopf, 1987), p. 586。

2. 边沁主义，即指功利主义。边沁（1748—1832），英国功利主义哲学家。功利主义，是指一种行为的对错取决于人们认为其结果是善还是恶，而所谓的善就是指它给人带来的快乐，恶则是指它给人带来的痛苦。边沁从趋乐避苦的人性假设出发，阐述个人主义的利己主义幸福论和功利主义的幸福观，对现代社会福利思想产生了深远的影响。

3. Paul Carrer, *The Road to Botany Bay: An Exploration of Landscape and History* (New York: Knopf, 1988), pp. 202-60. As a supplement to Hughes and Caner, see Sneja Gunew, "Denaturalizing Cultural Nationalisms: Multicultural Readings of 'Australia,'" in *Nation and Narration*, ed. Homi K. Bhabha (London: Routledge, 1990), pp. 99-120.

4. 约瑟夫·康拉德的小说《诺斯特罗莫》，见 Joseph Conrad, *Nostromo: A Tale of the Seaboard* (1904; Garden City: Doubleday, Page, 1925), p. 77. Tan Watt，是康拉德作品的最著名的评论家，曾评论到，在《诺斯特罗莫》这部著作中阐释了美国的帝国主义，参见他的专著《康拉德的〈诺斯特罗莫〉》(*Conrad*: "*Nostromo*", 1988)。在大卫·辛普森的专著《拜物教和想象：狄更斯、梅尔维尔和康拉德》中也暗示出地理、贸易和拜物教之间的关系，其中论及康拉德的作品。参见 David Simpson, *Fetishism and Imagination: Dickens, Melville, Conrad* (Baltimore: Johns Hopkins University Press, 1981), pp. 93-116.

5. 世界和平民主论，20 世纪 90 年代初，克林顿政府推行的外交政策。

6. 斜体短语意思为文明的使命。

7. 俾斯麦式专制主义。奥托·冯·俾斯麦（1815—1898），德意志帝国首任宰相（1871—1890），人称"铁血宰相"，依靠"铁血政策"自上而下地统一了德国，确立了德国在欧洲的霸权。.

8. 拉迪亚德·吉卜林（1865—1936），英国小说、诗人，出生于印度孟买。

Gayatri Chakravorty Spivak

佳亚特里·斯皮瓦克（1942— ），出生于印度，在美国康奈尔大学获得博士学位。早年师承美国解构主义大师保罗·德曼，20 世纪 70 年代曾将解构大师德里达的《论文字学》引入英语世界而蜚声北美理论界，是当今世界首屈一指的文学理论家和文化批评家，西方后殖民主义思潮的重要代表人物。现为美国哥伦比亚大学阿维龙基金会人文学科讲座教授、比较文学与社会中心主任。她的主要著作包括《底层研究：解构历史编撰学》《后殖民批评》《底层能说话吗？》《阐释的政治》等。

Three Women's Texts and a Critique of Imperialism

(Spivak, Gayatri Chakravorty. Three Women's Texts and a Critique of Imperialism. *Critical Inquiry*, Vol. 12, No. 1, pp. 243-261.)

《三个女性文本与对帝国主义批判》是斯皮瓦克的经典文章。该文选取经典女性主义文本《简·爱》《藻海无边》《弗兰肯斯坦》，考察被称作"第三世界"的"世界化"这个概念的情况。她认为，帝国主义思想一直存在于文化领域，尤其是在文学作品中，但在英语文学的阅读中经常被读者遗忘。新兴的女权主义批评开始复制帝国主义公理，对女性主题的尊崇仅限于欧洲与英美国家，女权主义范围也大致是在这样的一个领域，而"第三世界"却成为帝国主义意识的牺牲品。斯皮瓦克运用马克思主义、解构主义以及女权主义理论框架来分析文学文本，指出这三个经典的女性主义文本中隐含着强烈的帝国主义霸权叙述话语。

It should not be possible to read nineteenth-century British literature without remembering that imperialism, understood as England's social mission, was a crucial part of the cultural representation of England to the English. The role of literature in the production of cultural representation should not be ignored. These two obvious "facts" continue to be disregarded in the reading of nineteenth-century British literature. This itself attests to the continuing success of the imperialist project, displaced and dispersed into more modern forms.

If these "facts" were remembered, not only in the study of British literature but in the study of the literatures of the European colonizing cultures of the great age of imperialism, we would produce a narrative, in literary history, of the "worlding" of what is now called "the Third World." To consider the Third World as distant cultures, exploited but with rich intact literary heritages waiting to be recovered, interpreted, and curricularized in English translation fosters the emergence of "the Third World" as a signifier that allows us to forget that "worlding," even as it expands the empire of the literary discipline.[1]

It seems particularly unfortunate when the emergent perspective of feminist criticism reproduces the axioms of imperialism. A basically isolationist admiration for the literature of the female subject in Europe and Anglo-America establishes the high feminist norm. It is supported and operated by an information-retrieval approach to "Third World" literature which often employs a deliberately "nontheoretical" methodology with self-conscious rectitude.

In this essay, I will attempt to examine the operation of the "worlding" of what is today "the Third World" by what has become a cult text of feminism: *Jane Eyre*.[2] I plot the novel's reach and grasp, and locate its structural motors. I read *Wide Sargasso Sea* as *Jane Eyre's* reinscription and *Frankenstein* as an analysis—even a deconstruction—of a "worlding" such as Jane Eyre's.[3]

I need hardly mention that the object of my investigation is the printed book, not its "author." To make such a distinction is, of course, to ignore the lessons of deconstruction. A deconstructive critical approach would loosen the binding of the book, undo the opposition between verbal text and the bio-graphy of the named subject "Charlotte Brontë," and see the two as each other's "scene of writing." In such a reading, the life that writes itself as "my life" is as much a production in psychosocial space (other names can be found) as the book that is written by the holder of that named life—a book that is then consigned to what *is* most often recognized as genuinely "social": the world of publication and distribution.[4] To touch Brontë's "life" in such a way, however, would be too risky here. We must rather strategically take shelter in an essentialism which, not wishing to lose the important advantages won by U. S. mainstream feminism, will continue to honor the suspect binary oppositions—book and author, individual and history—and start with an assurance of the following sort: my readings here do not seek to undermine the excellence of the individual artist. If even minimally successful, the readings will incite a degree of rage against the imperialist narrativization of history, that it should produce so abject a script for her. I provide these assurances to allow myself some room to situate feminist individualism in its historical determination rather than simply to canonize it as feminism as such.

Sympathetic U. S. feminists have remarked that I do not do justice to Jane Eyre's subjectivity. A word of explanation is perhaps in order. The broad strokes of my presuppositions are that what is at stake, for feminist individualism in the age of imperialism, is precisely the making of human beings, the constitution and "interpellation" of the subject not only as individual but as "individualist."[5] This stake is represented on two registers: childbearing and soul making. The first is domestic-society-through-sexual-reproduction cathected as "companionate love"; the second is the imperialist project cathected as civil-society-through-social-mission. As the female individualist, not-quite/not-male, articulates herself in shifting relationship to what is at stake, the "native female" as such (*within* discourse, *as* a signifier) is excluded from any share in this emerging norm.[6] If we read this account from an isolationist perspective in a "metropolitan" context, we see nothing there but the psychobiography of the militant female subject. In a reading such as mine, in contrast, the effort is to wrench oneself away from the mesmerizing focus of the "subject-constitution" of the female individualist.

To develop further the notion that my stance need not be an accusing one, I will refer to a passage from Roberto Fernández Retamar's "Caliban."[7] José Enrique Rodó had argued in 1900 that the model for the Latin American intellectual in relationship to Europe could be Shakespeare's Ariel.[8] In 1971 Retamar, denying the possibility of an identifiable "Latin American Culture," recast the model as Caliban. Not surprisingly, this powerful exchange still excludes any specific consideration of the civilizations of the Maya, the Aztecs, the Incas, or the smaller nations of what is now called Latin America. Let us note carefully that, at this stage of my argument, this "conversation" between Europe and Latin America (without a specific consideration of the political economy of the "worlding" of the "native") provides a sufficient thematic description of our attempt to confront the ethnocentric and reverse-ethnocentric benevolent double bind (that is, considering the "native" as object for enthusiastic information-retrieval and thus denying its own "worlding") that I sketched in my opening paragraphs.

In a moving passage in "Caliban," Retamar locates both Caliban and Ariel in the postcolonial intellectual:

> There is no real Ariel-Caliban polarity: both are slaves in the hands of Prospero, the foreign magician. But Caliban is the rude and unconquerable master of the island, while Ariel, a creature of the air, although also a child of the isle, is the intellectual.
>
> The deformed Caliban—enslaved, robbed of his island, and taught the language by Prospero—rebukes him thus: "You taught me language, and

my profit on't / Is, I know how to curse." ["C," pp. 28, 11]

As we attempt to unlearn our so-called privilege as Ariel and "seek from [a certain] Caliban the honor of a place in his rebellious and glorious ranks," we do not ask that our students and colleagues should emulate us but that they should attend to us ("C," p. 72). If, however, we are driven by a nostalgia for lost origins, we too run the risk of effacing the "native" and stepping forth as "the real Caliban," of forgetting that he is a name in a play, an inaccessible blankness circumscribed by an interpretable text.[9] The stagings of Caliban work alongside the narrativization of history: claiming to *be* Caliban legitimizes the very individualism that we must persistently attempt to undermine from within.

Elizabeth Fox-Genovese, in an article on history and women's history, shows us how to define the historical moment of feminism in the West in terms of female access to individualism.[10] The battle for female individualism plays itself out within the larger theater of the establishment of meritocratic individualism, indexed in the aesthetic field by the ideology of "the creative imagination." Fox-Genovese's presupposition will guide us into the beautifully orchestrated opening of *Jane Eyre*.

It is a scene of the marginalization and privatization of the protagonist: "There was no possibility of taking a walk that day.... Out-door exercise was now out of the question. I was glad of it," Brontë writes (*JE*, p. 9). The movement continues as Jane breaks the rules of the appropriate topography of withdrawal. The family at the center withdraws into the sanctioned architectural space of the withdrawing room or drawing room; Jane inserts herself—"I slipped in"—into the margin—"A small breakfast-room *adjoined* the drawing room" (*JE*, p. 9; my emphasis).

The manipulation of the domestic inscription of space within the upwardly mobilizing currents of the eighteenth-and nineteenth-century bourgeoisie in England and France is well known. It seems fitting that the place to which Jane withdraws is not only not the withdrawing room but also not the dining room, the sanctioned place of family meals. Nor is it the library, the appropriate place for reading. The breakfast room "contained a book-case" (*JE*, p. 9). As Rudolph Ackerman wrote in his *Repository* (1823), one of the many manuals of taste in circulation in nineteenth-century England, these low bookcases and stands were designed to "contain all the books that may be desired for a sitting-room without reference to the library." Even in this already triply off-center place, "having drawn the red moreen curtain nearly close, I [Jane] was shrined in double retirement"(*JE*, pp. 9-10).

Here in Jane's self-marginalized uniqueness, the reader becomes her accomplice: the reader and Jane are united—both are reading. Yet Jane still preserves her odd privilege, for she continues never quite doing the proper thing in its proper place. She cares little for reading what is *meant* to be read: the "letter-press." *She* reads the pictures. The power of this singular hermeneutics is precisely that it can make the outside inside. "At intervals, while turning over the leaves of my book, I studied the aspect of that winter afternoon." Under "the clear panes of glass," the rain no longer penetrates, "the drear November day" is rather a one-dimensional "aspect" to be "studied," not decoded like the "letter-press" but, like pictures, deciphered by the unique creative imagination of the marginal individualist (*JE*, p. 10).

Before following the track of this unique imagination, let us consider the suggestion that the progress of *Jane Eyre* can be charted through a sequential arrangement of the family/counter-family dyad. In the novel, we encounter, first, the Reeds as the legal family and Jane, the late Mr. Reed's sister's daughter, as the representative of a near incestuous counter-family; second, the Brocklehursts, who run the school Jane is sent to, as the legal family and Jane, Miss Temple, and Helen Burns as a counter-family that falls short because it is only a community of women; third, Rochester and the mad Mrs. Rochester as the legal family and Jane and Rochester as the illicit counter-family. Other items may be added to the thematic chain in this sequence: Rochester and Céline Varens as structurally functional counter-family; Rochester and Blanche Ingram as dissimulation of legality—and so on. It is during this sequence that Jane is moved from the counter-family to the family-in-law. In the next sequence, it is Jane who restores full family status to the as-yet-incomplete community of siblings, the Riverses. The final sequence of the book is a *community of families*, with Jane, Rochester, and their children at the center.

In terms of the narrative energy of the novel, how is Jane moved from the place of the counter-family to the family-in-law? It is the active ideology of imperialism that provides the discursive field.

(My working definition of "discursive field" must assume the existence of discrete "systems of signs" at hand in the socius, each based on a specific axiomatics. I am identifying these systems as discursive fields. "Imperialism as social mission" generates the possibility of one such axiomatics. How the individual artist taps the discursive field at hand with a sure touch, if not with transhistorical clairvoyance, in order to make the narrative structure move I hope to demonstrate through the following example. It is crucial that we extend our analysis of this example beyond the minimal diagnosis of "racism.")

Let us consider the figure of Bertha Mason, a figure produced by the axiomatics of imperialism. Through Bertha Mason, the white Jamaican Creole, Brontë renders the human/animal frontier as acceptably indeterminate, so that a good greater than the letter of the Law can be broached. Here is the celebrated passage, given in the voice of Jane:

> In the deep shade, at the further end of the room, a figure ran backwards and forwards. What it was, whether beast or human being, one could not... tell: it grovelled, seemingly, on all fours; it snatched and growled like some strange wild animal: but it was covered with clothing, and a quantity of dark, grizzled hair, wild as a mane, hid its head and face. [*JE*, p. 295]

In a matching passage, given in the voice of Rochester speaking to Jane, Brontë presents the imperative for a shift beyond the Law as divine injunction rather than human motive. In the terms of my essay, we might say that this is the register not of mere marriage or sexual reproduction but of Europe and its not-yet-human Other, of soul making. The field of imperial conquest is here inscribed as Hell:

> One night I had been awakened by her yells... it was a fiery West Indian night....
>
> "'This life,' said I at last, 'is hell! —this is the air—those are the sounds of the bottomless pit! I *have a right* to deliver myself from it if I can.... Let me break away, and go home to God!'...
>
> "A wind fresh from Europe blew over the ocean and rushed through the open casement: the storm broke, streamed, thundered, blazed, and the air grew pure.... It was true Wisdom that consoled me in that hour, and showed me the right path....

"The sweet wind from Europe was still whispering in the refreshed leaves, and the Atlantic was thundering in glorious liberty....

"'Go,' said Hope, 'and live again in Europe.... You have done all that God and Humanity require of you.'" [*JE*, pp. 310-11; my emphasis]

It is the unquestioned ideology of imperialist axiomatics, then, that conditions Jane's move from the counter-family set to the set of the family-in-law. Marxist critics such as Terry Eagleton have seen this only in terms of the ambiguous *class* position of the governess.'" Sandra Gilbert and Susan Gubar, on the other hand, have seen Bertha Mason only in psychological terms, as Jane's dark double.[13]

I will not enter the critical debates that offer themselves here. Instead, I will develop the suggestion that nineteenth-century feminist individualism could conceive of a "greater" project than access to the closed circle of the nuclear family. This is the project of soul making beyond "mere" sexual reproduction. Here the native "subject" is not almost an animal but rather the object of what might be termed the terrorism of the categorical imperative.

I am using "Kant" in this essay as a metonym for the most flexible ethical moment in the European eighteenth century. Kant words the categorical imperative, conceived as the universal moral law given by pure reason, in this way: "In all creation every thing one chooses and over which one has any power, may be used *merely as means*; man alone, and with him every rational creature, is an *end in himself*." It is thus a moving displacement of Christian ethics from religion to philosophy. As Kant writes: "With this agrees very well the possibility of such a command as: *Love God above everything, and thy neighbor as thyself*. For as a command it requires respect for a law which *commands love* and does not leave it to our own arbitrary choice to make this our principle."[14]

The "categorical" in Kant cannot be adequately represented in determinately grounded action. The dangerous transformative power of philosophy, however, is that its formal subtlety can be travestied in the service of the state. Such a travesty in the case of the categorical imperative can justify the imperialist project by producing the following formula: make the heathen into a human so that he can be treated as an end in himself.[15] This project is presented as a sort of tangent in *Jane Eyre*, a tangent that escapes the closed circle of the *narrative* conclusion. The tangent narrative is the story of St. John Rivers, who is granted the important task of concluding the *text*.

At the novel's end, the *allegorical* language of Christian psychobiography-rather than the textually constituted and seemingly *private* grammar of the creative imagination which we noted in the novel's opening—marks the inaccessibility of the imperialist project as such to the nascent "feminist" scenario. The concluding passage of *Jane Eyre* places St. John Rivers within the fold of *Pilgrim's Progress*. Eagleton pays no attention to this but accepts the novel's ideological lexicon, which establishes St. John Rivers' heroism by identifying a life in Calcutta with an unquestioning choice of death. Gilbert and Gubar, by calling *Jane Eyre* "Plain Jane's progress," see the novel as simply replacing the male protagonist with the female. They do not notice the distance between sexual reproduction and soul making, both actualized by the unquestioned idiom of imperialist presuppositions evident in the last part of *Jane Eyre* :

> Firm, faithful, and devoted, full of energy, and zeal, and truth, [St. John Rivers] labours for his race.... His is the sternness of the warrior Greatheart, who guards his pilgrim convoy from the onslaught of Apollyon.... His is the ambition of the high master-spirit[s]... who stand without fault before the throne of God; who share the last mighty victories of the Lamb; who are called, and chosen, and faithful. [*JE*, p. 455]

Earlier in the novel, St. John Rivers himself justifies the project: "My vocation? My great work?... My hopes of being numbered in the band who have merged all ambitions in the glorious one of bettering their race—of carrying knowledge into the realms of ignorance—of substituting peace for war—freedom for bondage—religion for superstition—the hope of heaven for the fear of hell?" (*JE*, p. 376). Imperialism and its territorial and subject-constituting project are a violent deconstruction of these oppositions.

When Jean Rhys, born on the Caribbean island of Dominica, read *Jane Eyre* as a child, she was moved by Bertha Mason: "I thought I'd try to write her a life."[16] *Wide Sargasso Sea*, the slim novel published in 1965, at the end of Rhys' long career, is that "life."

I have suggested that Bertha's function in *Jane Eyre* is to render indeterminate the boundary between human and animal and thereby to weaken her entitlement under the spirit if not the letter of the Law. When Rhys rewrites the scene in *Jane Eyre* where Jane hears "a snarling, snatching sound, almost like a dog quarrelling" and then encounters a bleeding Richard Mason (*JE*, p. 210), she keeps Bertha's humanity, indeed her sanity as critic of imperialism, intact. Grace Poole, another character originally in *Jane Eyre*, describes the incident to Bertha in *Wide Sargasso Sea*: "So you don't remember that you attacked this gentleman with a knife?... I didn't hear all he said except 'I cannot interfere legally between yourself and your husband'. It was when he said 'legally' that you flew at him" (*WSS*, p. 150). In Rhys' retelling, it is the dissimulation that Bertha discerns in the word "legally"—not an innate bestiality—that prompts her violent *re*action.

In the figure of Antoinette, whom in *Wide Sargasso Sea* Rochester violently renames Bertha, Rhys suggests that so intimate a thing as personal and human identity might be determined by the politics of imperialism. Antoinette, as a white Creole child growing up at the time of emancipation in Jamaica, is caught between the English imperialist and the black native. In recounting Antoinette's development, Rhys reinscribes some thematics of Narcissus.

There are, noticeably, many images of mirroring in the text. I will quote one from the first section. In this passage, Tia is the little black servant girl who is Antoinette's close companion: "We had eaten the same food, slept side by side, bathed in the same river. As I ran, I thought, I will live with Tia and I will be like her.... When I was close I saw the jagged stone in her hand but I did not see her throw it.... We stared at each other, blood on my face, tears on hers. It was as if I saw myself. Like in a looking glass" (*WSS*, p. 38).

注释：

1. 这里的世界化是将海德格尔的观点通俗化。见"The Origin of the Work of Art," *Poetry*, *Language*, *Thought*, trans. Albert Hofstadter (New York, 1977), pp. 17-87。

2. 见夏洛蒂·勃朗特《简·爱》，文章中的《简·爱》简写为 *JE*，Charlotte Brontë, *Jane Eyre* (New York, 1960)。

3. 见简·里斯《藻海无边》，文章中的《藻海无边》简写为 *WSS*。see Jean Rhys, *Wide Sargasso Sea* (Harmondsworth, 1966)；玛丽·雪莱《弗兰肯斯坦》，在文章中简写为 *F*，see Mary Shelley, *Frankenstein; or, The Modern Prometheus* (New York, 1965)。

4. 作者在她的文章中试图说明这一点，参见"Unmaking and Making in To the Lighthouse," in *Women and Language in Literature and Society*, ed. Sally McConnell-Ginet, Ruth Borker, and

Nelly Furman (New York, 1980), pp. 310-27。

5. 参见路易·阿尔都塞的《意识形态与国家机器》，见 "Ideology an Ideological State Apparatuses (Notes towards an Investigation)," "*Lenin and Philosophy*" *and Other Essays*, trans. Ben Brewster (New York, 1971), pp. 127-86。个人与个人主义的区别见 V. N. Volosinov, *Marxism and the Philosophy of Language*, trans. Ladislav Matejka and I. R. Titunik, *Studies in Language*, *vol*. 1 (New York, 1973), pp. 93-94 and 152-53。关于英国个人主义的根源与影响见 C. B. MacPherson, *The Political Theory of Possessive Individualism*: *Hobbes to Locke* (Oxford, 1962)。

6. 这里借用了霍米·巴巴《论模拟与人：殖民话语的模糊性》的观点"不完美/非白"，参见 "Of Mimicry and Man: The Ambiguity of Colonial Discourse," *October* 28 (Spring 1984): 132。这里作者用"土著"回应"第三世界女性"，因为，前者当然不能以同样的历史公正性用于西印度群岛以及印度的语境中，也无法用于帝国主义放逐的语境中。

7. 见 Roberto Fernandez Retamar, "Caliban: Notes towards a Discussion of Culture in Our America," trans. Lynn Garafola, David Arthur McMurray, and Robert Marquez, *Massachusetts Review* 15 (Winter-Spring 1974): 7-72；全文用缩写 *C* 来代替。

8. 见 Jose Enrique Rod6, *Ariel*, ed, Gordon Brotherston (Cambridge, 1967)。

9. 关于这篇文章"An Inaccessible Blankness Circumscribed by an Interpretable Text"的详细阐释，见斯皮瓦克的文章 "Can the Subaltern Speak?" *Marxist Interpretations of Culture*, ed, Cary Nelson (Urbana, Ill., forthcoming), 10。见 Elizabeth Fox-Genovese, "Placing Women' s History in History," New Left Review 133 (May-June 1982): 5-29。

10. 见 Rudolph Ackerman, *The Repository of Arts*, *Literature*, *Commerce*, *Manufactures*, *Fashions*, *and Politics*, (London, 1823), p. 310。

11. 见特里伊格尔顿《权力的神话：对勃朗特姐妹作品的马克思主义研究》, Terry Eagleton, *Myths of Power*: *A Marxist Study of the Brontës* (London, 1975)。

12. 见桑德拉·吉尔伯特和苏珊·古芭著《阁楼上的疯女人》, Sandra M. Gilbert and Susan Gubar, *The Madwoman in the Attic*: *The Woman Writer and the Nineteenth-Century Literary Imagination* (New Haven, Conn., 1979), pp. 360-62.

13. 见康德《实践理性批判》, Immanuel Kant, *Critique of Practical Reason*;《纯粹理性批判》, *The* "*Critique of Pure Reason*"；《实践理批判与其他伦理学论文集》, "*Critique of Practical Reason*" *and Other Ethical Treatises*, *the* "*Critique of Judgement*," trans. J. M. D. Meiklejohn et al. (Chicago, 1952), pp. 328, 326。

14. 斯皮瓦克在论文《底层能说话吗？》中试图证明将复杂的社会历史问题做出归纳和陈述是可行的，此处的"滑稽模仿"并非一个偶然事件发生在伦理学的纯粹性上，而是作为一个可能补充特征而存在的。我的关于人类属上帝的臣民而非异教徒的论点可以在康德以下的著作中找到：《何为启蒙》"*What Is Enlightenment*?"。

Chapter Thirteen **Gender Studies**

性别研究，是指在文学批评中将性与性别作为关注焦点的一种跨学科批评模式。性别研究包括男同性恋研究、女同性恋研究以及酷儿（通常是双性恋和跨性别者）研究或批评，其批评范式类似于少数族裔研究或女性研究，旨在通过研究为同性恋运动和酷儿运动提供思想支撑，消除对同性恋的歧视和憎恶，抵制异性恋霸权行为，从而为同性恋者和酷儿谋求利益和福祉。性别研究涵盖一系列的议题，其中最突出的是性别认同的建立，即人的性别认同是如何被资本主义经济和医疗话语所塑造的。其他议题还包括挖掘历史上被主流文学批评和官方话语体系所遮蔽的同性恋和酷儿文本及历史，比如一战期间的诗歌中充斥着的同性恋情或是布鲁姆斯伯里团体成员的少数性取向等。此外，性别研究还关注同性恋和酷儿现象的文学和文化表征，比如从主流文本中探测隐藏着的同性恋欲望，或批评被认为是同性恋或酷儿叙事的文本。性别研究从多个思想潮流中汲取理论营养：首先，同性恋女性主义从女性主义中发展出来，在 20 世纪 70 年代成为独立的理论体系；其次，新历史主义和文化唯物主义揭示出性别作为历史和社会建构的真相，昭示出性别异见人士对文本进行差异化阅读的路径；最后，酷儿理论对于性和性别的反本质主义式的阐释受到了后结构主义的启发。

性别研究起源于 20 世纪六七十年代的同性恋解放运动，这一运动提出了抵制异性恋霸权的口号，即反对异性恋者对同性恋者的歧视和社会压迫行为。在理论上，性别研究有三个分支：男同性恋研究、女同性恋研究和酷儿理论。男同性恋研究主要受到弗洛伊德和福柯的影响。弗洛伊德的精神分析理论挑战了传统上把同性恋作为疾病的认知。而福柯里程碑式的巨著《性史》则揭示出权力话语在历史上对同性恋现象的操纵。受福柯的启发，英国学者乔纳森·多利莫尔（Jonathan Dollimore）和阿兰·辛菲尔德（Alan Sinfield）在文化诗学和文化政治学的范畴内发展了同性恋研究，致力于考察文学史中的同性恋文本和文学文本中的同性恋书写，揭示权力、欲望和性别认同之间相互交缠的复杂关系。女同性恋研究，尤其是女同性恋女性主义理论，既批判主流文化中的异性恋霸权，也批判男性主导的男权社会意识形态，主张通过其研究揭示出男权社会和异性恋霸权背后相同的压迫机制，主要理论家有莫妮克·威蒂格(Monique Wittig)、朱迪斯·巴特勒(Judith Butler)、芭芭拉·史密斯(Barbara Smith)、露丝·伊利格瑞(Luce Irigaray)、玛格丽特·克鲁伊申克(Margaret Cruikshank)、曼迪·默克(Mandy Merck)、特蕾莎·德·劳丽蒂斯(Teresa de Lauretis)等人。酷儿理论主要关注性、性别和欲望之间的非常态匹配及其产生的酷儿状态，它不仅包括同性恋、双性恋等少数性取向现象，也包括异装癖、跨性别身体和性别认知、性别模糊和变性手术等议题。酷儿理论发端于20世纪90年代，主要受到后结构主义思想的启发，反对对性别认知和性取向的本质主义认知，把性别看作是一种流动的状态，因此同其他两种理论相比观点更加激进，对于性别身份认同的解构也更加彻底。

Monique Wittig

莫妮克·威蒂格(1935—2003)，法国先锋女作家和女性主义思想家，也是著名的女性主义运动家，尤其以女同性恋女性主义思想和投身于女同性恋运动著称。她出生在法国阿尔萨斯，后进入位于巴黎的索邦大学求学。1964年，她出版的第一部小说《没药》(*L'Opoponax*)以先锋的叙事风格和激进的女性主义思想获得文学界的关注，并获得法国著名文学奖"美第西斯奖"。她的第二部小说《女游击队员》(*Les Guérillères*)产生了更大的影响力，被誉为是女同性恋女性主义的标志性作品。1976年，她移居美国，之后主要从事学术研究和教学工作，对女性主义思想酷儿理论的发展做出了重要贡献。

One Is Not Born a Woman

(Wittig, Monique. One Is Not Born a Woman. Henry Abelove, et al., eds. *The Lesbians and Gay Studies Reader*. New York: Routledge,1993,pp. 103-109.)

威蒂格是一位女同性恋女性主义思想家，在本文中她阐述了唯物主义女性主义的主要观点，同时指出了在唯物主义女性主义的视角下女同性恋的存在对于推翻男权制度和性别霸权的意义。从思想脉络上看，唯物主义女性主义是女同性恋女性主义同历史唯物主义的融合，而女同性恋女性主义又明显受到了后结构主义的影响。威蒂格首先反对男女性别二元对立的思维范式，指出性别差异似乎是自然的身体生成，但实际上是一种复杂的人为建构和想象，目的是对女性实施压迫。而要实现女性的彻底解放，要突破二元对立的范式，把女性群体作为一个社会阶级而非性别存在，彻底摆脱性别的标签和性别霸权，实现真正的男女平等和人格自由。

A materialist feminist approach to women's oppression destroys the idea that women are a "natural group": "a racial group of a special kind, a group perceived *as natural*, a group of men considered as materially specific in their bodies." What the analysis accomplishes on the level of ideas, practice makes actual at the level of facts: by its very existence, lesbian society destroys the artificial (social) fact constituting women as a "natural group." A lesbian society pragmatically reveals that the division from men of which women have been the object is a political one and shows that we have been ideologically rebuilt into a "natural group". In the case of women, ideology goes far since our bodies as well as our minds are the product of this manipulation. We have been compelled in our bodies and in our minds to correspond, feature by feature, with the *idea* of nature that has been established for us. Distorted to such an extent that our deformed body is what they call "natural", what is supposed to exist as such before oppression. Distorted to such an extent that in the end oppression seems to be a consequence of this "nature" within ourselves (a nature which is only an *idea*). What a materialist analysis does by reasoning, a lesbian society accomplishes practically: not only is there no natural group "women" (we lesbians are living proof of it), but as individuals as well we question "woman," which for us, as for Simone de Beauvoir,[1] is only a myth. She said: "One is not born, but becomes a woman. No biological, psychological, or economic fate determines the figure that the human female presents in society: it is civilization as a whole that produces this creature, intermediate between male and eunuch, which is described as feminine."

However, most of the feminists and lesbian-feminists in America and elsewhere still believe that the basis of women's oppression *is biological as well as* historical. Some of them even claim to find their sources in Simone de Beauvoir. The belief in mother right and in a "prehistory" when women created civilization (because of a biological predisposition) while the coarse and brutal men hunted (because of a biological predisposition) is symmetrical with the biologizing interpretation of history produced up to now by the class of men. It is still the same method of finding in women and men a biological explanation of their division, outside of social facts. For me this could never constitute a lesbian approach to women's oppression, since it assumes that the basis of society or the beginning of society lies in heterosexuality. Matriarchy is no less heterosexual than patriarchy: it is only the sex of the oppressor that changes. Furthermore, not only is this conception still imprisoned in the categories of sex (woman and man), but it holds onto the idea that the capacity to give birth (biology) is what defines a woman. Although practical facts and ways of living contradict this theory in lesbian society, there are lesbians who affirm that "women and men are different species or races (the words are used interchangeably): men are biologically inferior to women; male violence is a biological inevitability..." By doing this, by admitting that there is a "natural" division between women and men, we naturalize history, we assume that "men" and "women" have always existed and will always exist. Not only do we naturalize history, but also consequently we naturalize the social phenomena which express our oppression, making change impossible. For example, instead of seeing giving birth as a forced production, we see it as a "natural," "biological" process, forgetting that in our societies births are planned (demography), forgetting that we ourselves are programmed to produce children, while this is the only social activity "short of war" that presents such a great danger of death. Thus, as long as we will be "unable to abandon by will or impulse a lifelong and centuries-old commitment to childbearing as *the* female creative act," gaining control of the production of children will mean much more than the mere control of the material means of this production: women will have to abstract themselves from the definition "woman" which is imposed upon them.

A materialist feminist approach shows that what we take for the cause or origin of oppression is in fact only the *mark* imposed by the oppressor: the "myth of woman," plus its material effects and manifestations in the appropriated consciousness and bodies of women. Thus, this mark does not predate oppression: Colette Guillaumin[2] has shown that before the socioeconomic reality of black slavery, the concept of race did not exist, at least not in its modern meaning, since it was applied to the lineage of families. However, now, race, exactly like sex, is taken as an "immediate given," a "sensible given," "physical features," belonging to a natural order. But what we believe to be a physical and direct perception is only a sophisticated and mythic construction, an "imaginary formation," which reinterprets physical features (in themselves as neutral as any others but marked by the social system) through the network of relationships in which they are perceived. (They are seen as *black*, therefore they *are* black, they are seen as *women*, therefore, they *are* women. But before being *seen* that way, they first had to be *made* that way.) Lesbians should always remember and acknowledge how "unnatural," compelling, totally oppressive, and destructive being "woman" was for us in the old days before the women's liberation movement. It was a political constraint, and those who resisted it were accused of not being "real" women. But then we were proud of it, since in the accusation there was already something like a shadow of victory: the avowal by the oppressor that "woman" is not something that goes without saying, since to be one, one has to be a "real" one. We were at the same time accused of wanting to be men. Today this double accusation has been taken up again with enthusiasm in the context of the women's liberation movement by some feminists and also, alas, by some lesbians whose political goal seems somehow to be becoming more and more "feminine." To refuse to be a woman, however, does not mean that one has to become a man. Besides, if we take as an example the perfect "butch," the classic example which provokes the most horror, whom Proust[3] would have called a woman/man, how is her alienation different from that of someone who wants to become a woman? Tweedledum and Tweedledee. At least for a woman, wanting to become a man proves that she has escaped her initial programming. But even if she would like to, with all her strength, she cannot become a man. For becoming a man would demand from a woman not only a man's external appearance but his consciousness as well, that is, the consciousness of one who disposes by right of at least two "natural" slaves during his life span. This is impossible, and one feature of lesbian oppression consists precisely of making women out of reach for us, since women belong to men. Thus a lesbian *has* to be something else, a not-woman, a not-man, a product of society, not a product of nature, for there is no nature in society.

The refusal to become (or to remain) heterosexual always meant to refuse to become a man or a woman, consciously or not. For a lesbian this goes further than the refusal of the *role* "woman." It is the refusal of the economic, ideological, and political power of a man. This, we lesbians, and nonlesbians as well, knew before the beginning of the lesbian and feminist movement. However, as Andrea Dworkin[4] emphasizes, many lesbians recently "have increasingly tried to transform the very ideology that has enslaved us into a dynamic, religious, psychologically compelling celebration of female biological potential." Thus, some avenues of the feminist and lesbian movement lead us back to the myth of woman which was created by men especially for us, and with it we sink back into a natural group. Having stood up to fight for a sexless society, we now find ourselves entrapped in the familiar deadlock of "woman is wonderful." Simone de Beauvoir underlined particularly the false consciousness which consists of selecting among the features of the myth (that women are different from men) those which look good and using them as a definition for women. What the concept "woman is wonderful" accomplishes is that it retains for defining women the best features (best according to whom?) which oppression has granted us, and it does not radically question the categories "man" and "woman," which are political categories and not natural givens. It puts us in a position of fighting within the class "woman" not as the other classes do for the disappearance of our class, but for the defense of "woman" and its reenforcement. It leads us to develop with complacency "new" theories about our specificity: thus, we call our passivity "nonviolence," when the main and emergent point for us is to fight our passivity (our fear, rather, a justified one). The ambiguity of the term "feminist" sums up the whole situation. What does "feminist" mean? Feminist is formed with the word "femme," "woman," and means: someone who fights for women. For many of us it means someone who fights for women as a class and for the disappearance of this class. For many others it means someone who fights for woman and her defense—for the myth, then, and its reenforcement. But why was the word "feminist" chosen if it retains the least ambiguity? We chose to call ourselves "feminists" ten years ago, not in order to support or reenforce the myth of woman, nor to identify ourselves with the oppressor's definition of us, but rather to affirm that our movement had a history and to emphasize the political link with the old feminist movement.

It is, then, this movement that we can put in question for the meaning that it gave to feminism. It so happens that feminism in the last century could never resolve its contradictions on the subject of nature/culture, woman/society. Women started to fight for themselves as a group and rightly considered that they shared common features as a result of oppression. But for them these features were natural and biological rather than social. They went so far as to adopt the Darwinist theory of evolution. They did not believe like Darwin, however, "that women were less evolved than men, but they did believe that male and female natures had diverged in the course of evolutionary development and that society at large reflected this polarization." "The failure of early feminism was that it only attacked the Darwinist charge of female inferiority, while accepting the foundations of this charge—namely, the view of woman as 'unique.'" And finally it was women scholars—and not feminists—who scientifically destroyed this theory. But the early feminists had failed to regard history as a dynamic process which develops from conflicts of interests. Furthermore, they still believed as men do that the cause (origin) of their oppression lay within themselves. And therefore after some astonishing victories the feminists of this first front found themselves at an impasse out of a lack of reasons to fight. They upheld the illogical principle of "equality in difference," an idea now being born again. They fell back into the trap which threatens us once again: the myth of woman.

Thus it is our historical task, and only ours, to define what we call oppression in materialist terms, to make it evident that women are a class, which is to say that the category "woman" as well as the category "man" are political and economic categories not eternal ones. Our fight aims to suppress men as a class, not through a genocidal, but a political struggle. Once the class "men" disappears, "women" as a class will disappear as well, for there are no slaves without masters. Our first task, it seems, is to always thoroughly dissociate "women" (the class within which we fight) and "woman," the myth. For "woman" does not exist for us: it is only an imaginary formation, while "women" is the product of a social relationship. We felt this strongly when everywhere we refused to be called a "*woman*'s liberation movement." Furthermore, we have to destroy the myth inside and outside ourselves. "Woman" is not each one of us, but the political and ideological formation which negates "women" (the product of a relation of exploitation). "Woman" is there to confuse us, to hide the reality "woman." In order to be aware of being a class and to become a class we first have to kill the myth of "woman" including its most seductive aspects (I think about Virginia Woolf[5] when she said the first task of a woman writer is to kill "the angel in the house"). But to become a class we do not have to suppress our individual selves, and since no individual can be reduced to her/his oppression we are also confronted with the historical necessity of constituting ourselves as the individual subjects of our history as well. I believe this is the reason why all these attempts at "new" definitions of woman are blossoming now. What is at stake (and of course not only for women) is an individual definition as well as a class definition. For once one has acknowledged oppression, one needs to know and experience the fact that one can constitute oneself as a subject (as opposed to an object of oppression,) that one can become *someone* in spite of oppression, that one has one's own identity. There is no possible fight for someone deprived of an identity, no internal motivation for fighting, since, although I can fight only with others, first I fight for myself.

The question of the individual subject is historically a difficult one for everybody. Marxism, the last avatar of materialism, the science which has politically formed us, does not want to hear anything about a "subject." Marxism has rejected the transcendental subject, the subject as constitutive of knowledge, the "pure" consciousness. All that thinks per se, before all experience, has ended up in the garbage can of history, because it claimed to exist outside matter, prior to matter, and needed God, spirit, or soul to exist in such a way. This is what is called "idealism." As for individuals, they are only the product of social relations, therefore their consciousness can only be "alienated." (Marx, in *The German Ideology*, says precisely that individuals of the dominating class are also alienated, although they are the direct producers of the ideas that alienate the classes oppressed by them. But since they draw visible advantages from their own alienation they can bear it without too much suffering.) There exists such a thing as class consciousness, but a consciousness which does not refer to a particular subject, except as participating in general conditions of exploitation at the same time as the other subjects of their class, all sharing the same consciousness. As for the practical class problems—outside of the class problems as traditionally defined—that one could encounter (for example, sexual problems), they were considered "bourgeois" problems that would disappear with the final victory of the class struggle. "Individualistic," "subjectivist," "petit bourgeois," these were the labels given to any person who had shown problems which could not be reduced to the "class struggle" itself.

Thus Marxism has denied the members of oppressed classes the attribute of being a subject. In doing this, Marxism, because of the ideological and political power this "revolutionary science" immediately exercised upon the workers' movement and all other political groups, has prevented all categories of oppressed peoples from constituting themselves historically as subjects(subjects of their struggle, for example). This means that the "masses" did not fight for themselves but for *the* party or its organizations. And when an economic transformation took place (end of private property, constitution of the socialist state), no revolutionary change took place within new society, because the people themselves did not change.

For women, Marxism had two results. It prevented them from being aware that they are a class and therefore from constituting themselves as a class for a very long time, by leaving the relation "women/men" outside of the social order, by turning it into a natural relation, doubtless for Marxism the only one, along with the relation of mothers to children, to be seen this way, and by hiding the class conflict between men and women behind a natural division of labor (*The German Ideology*). This concerns the theoretical (ideological) level. On the practical level, Lenin,[6] *the* party, all the communist parties up to now, including all the most radical political groups, have always reacted to any attempt on the part of women to reflect and form groups based on their own class problem with an accusation of divisiveness. By uniting, we women are dividing the strength of the people. This means that for the Marxists women *belong* either to the bourgeois class or to the proletariat class, in other words, to the men of these classes. In addition, Marxist theory does not allow women any more than other classes of oppressed people to constitute themselves as historical subjects, because Marxism does not take into account the fact that a class also consists of individuals one by one. Class consciousness is not enough. We must try to understand philosophically (politically) these concepts of "subject" and "class consciousness" and how they work in relation to our history. When we discover that women are the objects of oppression and appropriation, at the very moment that we become able to perceive this, we become subjects in the sense of cognitive subjects, through an operation of abstraction. Consciousness of oppression is not only a reaction to (fight against) oppression. It is also the whole conceptual reevaluation of the social world, its whole reorganization with new concepts, from the point of view of oppression. It is what I would call the science of oppression created by the oppressed. This operation of understanding reality has to be undertaken by every one of us: call it a subjective, cognitive practice. The movement back and forth between the levels of reality (the conceptual reality and the material reality of oppression, which are both social realities) is accomplished through language.

It is we who historically must undertake the task of defining the individual subject in materialist terms. This certainly seems to be an impossibility since materialism andsubjectivity have always been mutually exclusive. Nevertheless, and rather than despairing of ever understanding, we must recognize the *need* to reach subjectivity in the abandonment by many us to the myth "woman" (the myth of woman being only a snare that holds us up). This real necessity for everyone to exist as an individual, as well as a member of a class, is perhaps the first condition for the accomplishment of a revolution, without which there can be no real fight or transformation. But the opposite is also true; without class and class consciousness there are no real subjects, only alienated individuals. For women to answer the question of the individual subject in materialist terms is first to show, as the lesbians and feminists did, that supposedly "subjective," "individual," "private" problems are in fact social problems, class problems; that sexuality is not for women an individual and subjective expression, but a social institution of violence. But once we have shown that all so-called personal problems are in fact class problems, we will still be left with the question of the subject of each singular woman—not the myth, but each one of us. At this point, let us say that a new personal and subjective definition for all humankind can only be found beyond the categories of sex (woman and man) and that the advent of individual subjects demands first destroying the categories of sex, ending the use of them, and rejecting all sciences which still use these categories as their fundamentals (practically all social sciences).

To destroy "woman" does not mean that we aim, short of physical destruction, to destroy lesbianism simultaneously with the categories of sex, because lesbianism provides for the moment the only social form in which we can live freely. Lesbian is the only concept I know of which is beyond the categories of sex (woman and man), because the designated subject (lesbian) is *not* a woman, either economically or politically, or ideologically. For what makes a woman is a specific social relation to a man, a relation that we have previously called servitude, a relation which implies personal and physical obligation as well as economic obligation ("forced residence," domestic corvée,[7] conjugal duties, unlimited production of children, etc.), a relation which lesbians escape by refusing to become or to stay heterosexual. We are escapees from our class in the same way as the American runaway slaves were when escaping slavery and becoming free. For us this is an absolute necessity; our survival demands that we contribute all our strength to the destruction of the class of women within which men appropriate women. This can be accomplished only by the destruction of heterosexuality as a social system which is based on the oppression of women by men and which produces the doctrine of the difference between the sexes to justify this oppression.

注释：

1. 西蒙娜·德·波伏娃（1908—1986），法国作家、存在主义哲学家、女性主义思想家和女权运动的创始人之一。

2. 柯里特·圭洛敏（1934—2017），法国社会学家、女性主义思想家。

3. 马塞尔·普鲁斯特（1871—1922），法国现代主义小说家，以长篇意识流小说《追忆似水年华》著称。

4. 安德丽娅·德沃金（1947—2005），美国激进的女权主义运动者，女同性恋女性主义思想家和作家。

5. 弗吉尼亚·伍尔芙（1882—1941），英国现代主义女作家、文学批评家和思想家，意识流小说的代表人物之一，也是女性主义的先锋人物，代表作有《达洛维夫人》《到灯塔去》等。

6. 列宁（1870—1924），俄国无产阶级革命领袖。

7. 指家庭内部的强迫劳役。

Judith Butler

朱迪斯·巴特勒（1956—　），美国哲学家、性别研究理论家，被广泛认为是当代最有影响力的文化理论家之一，在女性主义、文学理论、文化理论、政治学和伦理学等领域都颇有建树，尤其是其关于性与性别的操演性的思想成为酷儿理论发展的重要思想基础。巴特勒出生于美国俄亥俄州的医生家庭，后在耶鲁大学求学并获得哲学博士学位，现任教于加州大学伯克利分校，担任修辞学与比较文学系的讲席教授。巴特勒的思想深受后结构主义的影响，提出著名的性别操演理论用以解释性别的社会建构性，刷新了人们对于性别身份认同的认知。她的主要著作有《性别麻烦：女性主义与身份的颠覆》《身体之重：论"性别"的话语界限》《消解性别：欲望的主体》等。

Conclusion: From Parody to Politics

(Butler, Judith. *Gender Trouble: Feminism and the Subversion of Identity*. New York: Routledge, 1990, pp. 142-149.)

本文节选自朱迪斯·巴特勒的成名作《性别麻烦：女性主义与身份的颠覆》，是对该著作主要理论观点的梳理和总结。朱迪斯首先反对对于女性主体的本质主义认知，认为主体始终处于文化和话语的塑造之中，人们的性别身份不仅是一种后天的建构，更是在一套不断重复的、受到话语规则约束的意指行为中不断地生成的，这便是巴特勒著名的"性别操演理论"的内核。性别操演理论彻底颠覆了性别二元对立的认知模式，自然也改变了传统上人们思考性、性别、欲望和性别身份认同的方式。在此基础上，巴特勒呼吁抛弃性别本体论，建立一套性别政治学，从根本上消解男权社会中的性别霸权，实现真正意义上的女性解放。

I began with the speculative question of whether feminist politics could do without a "subject" in the category of women. At stake is not whether it still makes sense, strategically or transitionally, to refer to women in order to make representational claims in their behalf. The feminist "we" is always and only a phantasmatic construction, one that has its purposes, but which denies the internal complexity and indeterminacy of the term and constitutes itself only through the exclusion of some part of the constituency that it simultaneously seeks to represent. The tenuous or phantasmatic status of the "we," however, is not cause for despair or, at least, it is not *only* cause for despair. The radical instability of the category sets into question the *foundational* restrictions on feminist political theorizing and opens up other configurations, not only of genders and bodies, but of politics itself.

The foundationalist reasoning of identity politics tends to assume that an identity must first be in place in order for political interests to be elaborated and, subsequently, political action to be taken. My argument is that there need not be a "doer behind the deed," but that the "doer" is variably constructed in and through the deed. This is not return to an existential theory of the self as constituted through its acts, for the existential theory maintains a prediscursive structure for both the self and its acts. It is precisely the discursively variable construction of each in and through the other that has interested me here.

The question of locating "agency" is usually associated with the viability of the "subject," where the "subject" is understood to have some stable existence prior to the cultural field that it negotiates. Or, if the subject is culturally constructed, it is nevertheless vested with an agency, usually figured as the capacity for reflexive mediation, that remains intact regardless of its cultural embeddedness. On such a model, "culture" and "discourse" *mire* the subject, but do not constitute that subject. This move to qualify and enmire the preexisting subject has appeared necessary to establish a point of agency that is not fully *determined* by that culture and discourse. And yet, this kind of reasoning falsely presumes (a) agency can only be established through recourse to a prediscursive "I," even if that "I" is found in the midst of a discursive convergence, and (b) that to be *constituted* by discourse is to be *determined* by discourse, where determination forecloses the possibility of agency.

Even within the theories that maintain a highly qualified or situated subject, the subject still encounters its discursively constituted environment in an oppositional epistemological frame. The culturally enmired subject negotiates its constructions, even when those constructions are the very predicates of its own identity. In Beauvoir, for example, there is an "I" that does its gender, that becomes its gender, but that "I," invariably associated with its gender, is nevertheless a point of agency never fully identifiable with its gender. That *cogito* [1] is never fully *of* the cultural word that in negotiates, no matter the narrowness of the ontological distance that separates that subject from its cultural predicates. The theories of feminist identity that elaborate predicates of color, sexuality, ethnicity, class, and able-bodiedness invariably close with an embarrassed "etc." at the end of the list. Through this horizontal trajectory of adjectives, these positions strive to encompass a situated subject, but invariably fail to be complete. This failure, however, is instructive: what political impetus is to be derived from the exasperated "etc." that so often occurs at the end of such lines? This is a sign of exhaustion as well as of the illimitable process of signification itself. It is the *supplément*, the excess that necessarily accompanies any effort to posit identity once and for all. This illimitable *et cetera*, however, offers itself as a new departure for feminist political theorizing.

If identity is asserted through a process of signification, if identity is always already signified, and yet continues to signify as it circulates within various interlocking discourses, then the question of agency is not to be answered through recourse to an "I" that preexists signification. In other words, the enabling conditions for an assertion of "I" are provided by the structure of signification, the rules that regulate the legitimate and illegitimate invocation of that pronoun, the practices that establish the terms of intelligibility by which that pronoun can circulate. Language is not an *exterior medium or instrument* into which I pour a self and from which I glean a reflection of that self. The Hegelian model of self-recognition that has been appropriated by Marx, Lukacs,[2] and a variety of contemporary liberatory discourses presupposes a potential ad equation between the "I" that confronts its world, including its language, as an object, and the "I" that finds itself as an object in that world. But the subject/object dichotomy, which here belongs to the tradition of Western epistemology, conditions the very problematic of identity that it seeks to solve.

What discursive tradition establishes the "I" and its "Other" in an epistemological confrontation that subsequently decides where and how questions of knowability and agency are to be determined? What kinds of agency are foreclosed through the positing of an epistemological subject precisely because the rules and practices that govern the invocation of that subject and regulate its agency in advance are ruled out as sites of analysis and critical intervention? That the epistemological point of departure is in no sense inevitable is naively and pervasively confirmed by the mundane operations of ordinary language—widely documented within anthropology—that regard the subject/object dichotomy as a strange and contingent, if not violent, philosophical imposition. The language of appropriation, instrumentality, and distanciation germane to the epistemological mode also belong to a strategy of domination that pits the "I" against an "Other" and, once that separation is effected, creates an artificial set of questions about the knowability and recoverability of that Other.

As part of the epistemological inheritance of contemporary political discourses of identity, this binary opposition is a strategic move within a given set of signifying practices, one that establishes the "I" in and through this opposition and which reifies that opposition as a necessity, concealing the discursive apparatus by which the binary itself is constituted. The shift from an *epistemological* account of identity to one which locates the problematic within practices of *signification* permits an analysis that takes the epistemological mode itself as one possible and contingent signifying practice. Further, the question of *agency* is reformulated as a question of how signification and resignification work. In other words, what is signified as an identity is not signified at a given point in time after which it is simply there as an inert piece of entitative language. Clearly, identities *can* appear as so many inert substantives; indeed, epistemological models tend to take this appearance as their point of theoretical departure. However, the substantive "I" only appears as such through a signifying practice that seeks to conceal its own workings and to naturalize its effects. Further, to qualify as a substantive identity is an arduous task, for such appearances are rule-generated identities, ones which rely on the consistent and repeated invocation of rules that condition and restrict culturally intelligible practices of identity. Indeed, to understand identity as a *practice*, and as a signifying practice, is to understand culturally intelligible subjects as the resulting effects of a rule-bound discourse that inserts itself in the pervasive and mundane signifying acts of linguistic life. Abstractly considered, language refers to an open system of signs by which intelligibility is insistently created and contested. As historically specific organizations of language, discourses present themselves in the plural, coexisting within temporal frames, and instituting unpredictable and inadvertent convergences from which specific modalities of discursive possibilities are engendered.

As a process, signification harbors within itself what the epistemological discourse refers to as "agency." The rules that govern intelligible identity, i. e., that enable and restrict the intelligible assertion of an "I," rules that are partially structured along matrices of gender hierarchy and compulsory heterosexuality, operate through *repetition*. Indeed, when the subject is said to be constituted, that means simply that the subject is a consequence of certain rule-governed discourses that govern the intelligible invocation of identity. The subject is not *determined* by the rules through which it is generated because signification is *not a founding act, but rather a regulated process of repetition* that both conceals itself and enforces its rules precisely through the production of substantializing effects. In a sense, all signification takes place within the orbit of the compulsion to repeat; "agency," then, is to be located within the possibility of a variation on that repetition. If the rules governing signification not only restrict, but enable the assertion of alternative domains of cultural intelligibility, i. e., new possibilities for gender that contest the rigid codes of hierarchical binarisms, then it is only *within* the practices of repetitive signifying that a subversion of identity becomes possible. The injunction *to be* a given gender produces necessary failures, a variety of incoherent configurations that in their multiplicity exceed and defy the injunction by which they are generated. Further, the very injunction to be a given gender takes place through discursive routes: to be a good mother, to be a heterosexually desirable object, to be a fit worker, in sum, to signify a multiplicity of guarantees in response to a variety of different demands all at once. The coexistence or convergence of such discursive injunctions produces the possibility of a complex reconfiguration and redeployment; it is not a transcendental subject who enables action in the midst of such a convergence. There is no self that is prior to the convergence or who maintains "integrity" prior to its entrance into this conflicted cultural field. There is only a taking up of the tools where they lie, where the very "taking up" is enabled by the tool lying there.

What constitutes a subversive repetition within signifying practices of gender? I have argued ("I" deploy the grammar that governs the genre of the philosophical conclusion, but note that it is the grammar itself that deploys and enables this "I," even as the "I" that insists itself here repeats, redeploys, and—as the critics will determine—contests the philosophical grammar by which it is both enabled and restricted) that, for instance, within the sex/gender distinction, sex poses as "the real" and the "factic," the material or corporeal ground upon which gender operates as an act of cultural *inscription*. And yet gender is not written on the body as the torturing instrument of writing in Kafka's[3] "In the Penal Colony" inscribes itself unintelligibly on the flesh of the accused. The question is not: what meaning does that inscription carry within it, but what cultural apparatus arranges this meeting between instrument and body, what interventions into this ritualistic repetition are possible? The "real" and the "sexually factic" are phantasmatic constructions—illusions of substance—that bodies are compelled to approximate, but never can. What, then, enables the exposure of the rift between the phantasmatic and the real whereby the real admits itself as phantasmatic? Does this offer the possibility for a repetition that is not fully constrained by the injunction to reconsolidate naturalized identities? Just as bodily surfaces are enacted *as* the natural, so these surfaces can become the site of a dissonant and denaturalized performance that reveals the performative status of the natural itself.

Practices of parody can serve to reengage and reconsolidate the very distinction between a privileged and naturalized gender configuration and one that appears as derived, phantasmatic, and mimetic—a failed copy, as it were. And surely parody has been used to further a politics of despair, one which affirms a seemingly inevitable exclusion of marginal genders from the territory of the natural and the real. And yet this failure to become "real" and to embody "the natural" is, I would argue, a constitutive failure of all gender enactments for the very reason that these ontological locales are fundamentally uninhabitable. Hence, there is a subversive laughter in the pastiche-effect of parodic practices in which the original, the authentic, and the real are themselves constituted as effects. The loss of gender norms would have the effect of proliferating gender configurations, destabilizing substantive identity, and depriving the naturalizing narratives of compulsory heterosexuality of their central protagonists: "man" and "woman." The parodic repetition of gender exposes as well the illusion of gender identity as an intractable depth and inner substance. As the effects of a subtle and politically enforced performativity, gender is an "act," as it were, that is open to splittings, self-parody, self-criticism, and those hyperbolic exhibitions of "the natural" that, in their very exaggeration, reveal its fundamentally phantasmatic status.

I have tried to suggest that the identity categories often presumed to be foundational to feminist politics, that is, deemed necessary in order to mobilize feminism as an identity politics, simultaneously work to limit and constrain in advance the very cultural possibilities that feminism is supposed to open up. The tacit constraints that produce culturally intelligible "sex" ought to be understood as generative political structures rather than naturalized foundations. Paradoxically, the reconceptualization of identity as an *effect*, that is, as *produced* or *generated*, opens up possibilities of "agency" that are insidiously foreclosed by positions that take identity categories as foundational and fixed. For an identity to be an effect means that it is neither fatally determined nor fully artificial and arbitrary. That the *constituted* status of identity is misconstrued along these two conflicting lines suggests the ways in which the feminist discourse on cultural construction remains trapped within the unnecessary binarism of free will and determinism. Construction is not opposed to agency; it is the necessary scene of agency, the very terms in which agency is articulated and becomes culturally intelligible. The critical task for feminism is not to establish a point of view outside of constructed identities; that conceit is the construction of an epistemological model that would disavow its own cultural location and, hence, the imperialist strategies that feminism ought to criticize. The critical task is, rather, to locate strategies of subversive repetition enabled by those constructions, to affirm the local possibilities of intervention through participating in precisely those practices of repetition that constitute identity and, therefore, present the immanent possibility of contesting them.

This theoretical inquiry has attempted to locate the political in the very signifying practices that establish, regulate, and deregulate identity. This effort, however, can only be accomplished through the introduction of a set of questions that extend the very notion of the political. How to disrupt the foundations that cover over alternative cultural configurations of gender? How to destabilize and render in their phantasmatic dimension the "premises" of identity politics?

This task has required a critical genealogy of the naturalization of sex and of bodies in general. It has also demanded a reconsideration of the figure of the body as mute, prior to culture, awaiting signification, a figure that cross-checks with the figure of the feminine, awaiting the inscription-as-incision of the masculine signifier for entrance into language and culture. From a political analysis of compulsory heterosexuality, it has been necessary to question the construction of sex as binary, as a hierarchical binary. From the point of view of gender as enacted, questions have emerged over the fixity of gender identity as an interior depth that is said to be externalized in various forms of "expression." The implicit construction of the primary heterosexual construction of desire is shown to persist even as it appears in the mode of primary bisexuality. Strategies of exclusion and hierarchy are also shown to persist in the formulation of the sex/gender distinction and its recourse to "sex" as the prediscursive as well as the priority of sexuality to culture and, in particular, the cultural construction of sexuality as the prediscursive. Finally, the epistemological paradigm that presumes the priority of the doer to the deed establishes a global and globalizing subject who disavows its own locality as well as the conditions for local intervention.

If taken as the grounds of feminist theory or politics, these "effects" of gender hierarchy and compulsory heterosexuality are not only misdescribed as foundations, but the signifying practices that enable this metaleptic misdescription remain outside the purview of a feminist critique of gender relations. To enter into the repetitive practices of this terrain of signification is not a choice, for the "I" that might enter is always already inside: there is no possibility of agency or reality outside of the discursive practices that give those terms the intelligibility that they have. The task is not whether to repeat, but how to repeat or, indeed, to repeat and, through a radical proliferation of gender, to *displace* the very gender norms that enable the repetition itself. There is no ontology of gender on which we might construct a politics, for gender ontologies always operate within established political contexts as normative injunctions, determining what qualifies as intelligible sex, invoking and consolidating the reproductive constraints on sexuality, setting the prescriptive requirements whereby sexed or gendered bodies come into cultural intelligibility. Ontology is, thus, not a foundation, but a normative injunction that operates insidiously by installing itself into political discourse as its necessary ground.

The deconstruction of identity is not the deconstruction of politics; rather, it establishes as political the very terms through which identity is articulated. This kind of critique brings into question the foundationalist frame in which feminism as an identity politics has been articulated. The internal paradox of this foundationalism is that it presumes, fixes, and constrains the very "subjects" that it hopes to represent and liberate. The task here is not to celebrate each and every new possibility *qua* 4 possibility, but to redescribe those possibilities that *already* exist, but which exist within cultural domains designated as culturally unintelligible and impossible. If identities were no longer fixed as the premises of a political syllogism, and politics no longer understood as set of practices derived from the alleged interests that belong to a set of ready-made subjects, a new configuration of politics would surely emerge from the ruins of the old. Cultural configurations of sex and gender might the proliferate or, rather, their present proliferation might then become articulable within the discourses that establish intelligible cultural life, confounding the very binarism of sex, and exposing its fundamental unnaturalness. What other local strategies for engaging the "unnatural" might lead to the denaturalization of gender as such?

注释:

1. 拉丁文，意思是"我思"。
2. 格奥尔格·卢卡奇（1885—1971），匈牙利著名的马克思主义文艺评论家和哲学家。
3. 弗兰兹·卡夫卡（1883—1924），捷克德语小说家，20世纪最伟大的作家之一，著有小说《审判》《城堡》《变形记》等。
4. 作为：以……的身份。

Chapter Fourteen **Cultural Studies**

文化研究起源于20世纪50年代末的英国学界，但后来为世界范围内多学科领域的学者所改造和运用。文化研究是对当代文化的政治关系、历史语境、特征和冲突等进行理论或实证分析的研究。文化研究学者们通常考察文化行为是如何同其背后的权力体系相互交织，以及文化是怎样通过意识形态、阶级结构、国家、种族、性别和代际等社会现象进行运作的。文化研究认为，文化不是固定、有边界的特定实体，而是一系列相互作用和不断变化的文化实践和过程。文化研究的领域涵盖相当广泛，由多种理论视角和实践方法组成。将文化研究应用于文学批评突破了纯文学研究的藩篱，具有明显的跨学科特征，吸纳了社会学、人类学、政治学等学科的研究方法和视角。文化研究关注的核心是组织和构建人们日常生活的背后力量，其批评路径包括符号学、马克思主义、女性主义、民族志、后结构主义、后殖民主义、后现代主义、社会理论、政治理论、历史学、哲学、文学理论、种族批评理论、媒介理论、影视研究、传媒研究、政治经济学、翻译研究、博物馆学、艺术史和艺术批评等，关注和研究不同社会和历史时期的各种文化现象。具体说来，文化研究考察在特定的社会结构下社会经济和政治领域内文化符号意义的生产、传播及其如何同权力控制体系相互作用。文化研究领域的重要理论包括文化霸权理论和文化传播理论。

文化研究的对象是当代文化中复杂庞博的文化形式和文化现象，尤其是当代大众文化中的女性文化、工人阶级文化、少数族裔文化等处于边缘地位的非主流文化。文化研究所言的“文化”不再是传统意义上文化产品和文化活动，而是日常生活中多种多样的文化形式。把文化研究应用到文学批评中意味着文学研究突破了纯粹的高雅文学研究范畴，通俗小说、影视剧等大众文化形式也进入了研究视野。文化研究把影视、时尚、建筑等日常生活中方方面面的文化形式都视作由符号组成的文本，并力图从文本和话语背后探测出权力意识形态的身影。

文化研究最早始于英国的伯明翰学派，代表性人物有雷蒙·威廉斯、理查德·霍加特和斯图亚特·霍尔等。伯明翰学派的学者们从马克思、卢卡奇、阿尔都塞和葛兰西等马克思主义和西方马克思主义思想家那里汲取大量的理论营养，把文化视为统治阶级实现文化霸权的意识形态工具。同时，他们又受到了符号学、结构主义、女性主义等理论的启发，把文化视为意义符号的生产和传播，认为文化符号形成了权力话语和知识话语，维持着统治阶层对于社会大众的意识形态控制。文化霸权是文化研究的中心议题，文化研究学者们关心社会边缘阶层是如何回应或者抵抗统治阶层的文化统治的。文化研究的一个重要分支是媒介研究，媒介研究关注各类媒介尤其是大众媒介的内容、历史以及影响，在媒介研究的发展历程中也受到了传播学的强烈影响。此外，受到文化研究同时期的女权主义运动和民族解放运动的影响，文化研究也关心性别和种族议题，形成了性别文化研究和少数族裔文化研究两个领域。

Raymond Williams

雷蒙·威廉斯(1921—1988)，英国著名的马克思主义思想家和文化理论家，文化研究的主要奠基人之一。威廉斯出生于威尔士工人阶级家庭，后在剑桥求学并任教。他是英国新左派运动的中流砥柱，也是整个欧美左翼文化界的标杆。他关于政治、文化、大众媒介和文学的著作对当代马克思主义文艺批评做出了重要贡献。他创造性提出的文化唯物主义理论已经成为文艺批评的重要理论。威廉斯的主要著作有《文化与社会：1780—1950》《漫长的革命》《乡村与城市》《电视：科技与文化形式》《关键词：文化与社会的词汇》《政治与文学》等。他的著作在出版多年后仍十分畅销，其思想的影响力经久不衰。

Base and Superstructure in Marxist Cultural Theory

(Williams, Raymond. Base and Superstructure in Marxist Cultural Theory. *The Norton Anthology of Theory and Criticism*, *2nd ed*. Vincent B. Leitch, et al, eds. New York: Norton, 2010, pp. 1420-1437.)

本文节选自威廉斯的重要论文《马克思主义文化理论中的基础和上层建筑》，文章集中反映了威廉斯的文化研究思想和唯物主义文化分析方法。文章的主旨是对马克思主义中的经典命题“基础和上层建筑之关系”做出新的解读，并由此构建出一套马克思主义文化分析方法。从文中我们可以看到文化研究的一些关键议题：首先葛兰西提出的文化霸权理论有助于我们透析文化背后的权力运作和阶级冲突。威廉斯对残余文化和新兴文化的讨论使我们看到文化研究致力于阐释统治阶级意识形态之外的非主流文化的意义。此外，威廉斯还指出对包括文学在内的文化形式的考察应当将其置于大的历史语境和社会生产关系背景中进行，毕竟在文化研究看来，文化本质上是一种社会实践。

The Complexity of Hegemony

It is Gramsci's[1] great contribution to have emphasized hegemony, and also to have understood it at a depth which is, I think, rare. For hegemony supposes the existence of something which is truly total, which is not merely secondary or superstructural, like the weak sense of ideology, but which is lived at such a depth, which saturates the society to such an extent, and which, as Gramsci put it, even constitutes the limit of common sense for most people under its sway, that it corresponds to the reality of social experience very much more clearly than any notions derived from the formula of base and superstructure. For if ideology were merely some abstract imposed notion, if our social and political and cultural ideas and assumptions and habits were merely the result of specific manipulation, of a kind of overt training which might be simply ended or withdrawn, then the society would be very much easier to move and to change than in practice it has ever been or is. This notion of hegemony as deeply saturating the consciousness of a society seems to be fundamental. And hegemony has the advantage over general notions of totality, that it at the same time emphasizes the facts of domination.

Yet there are times when I hear discussions of hegemony and feel that it too, as a concept, is being dragged back to the relatively simple, uniform and static notion which 'superstructure' in ordinary use had become. Indeed I think that we have to give a very complex account of hegemony if we are talking about any real social formation. Above all we have to give an account which allows for its elements of real and constant change. We have to emphasize that hegemony is not singular; indeed that its own internal structures are highly complex, and have continually to be renewed, recreated and defended; and by the same token, that they can be continually challenged and in certain respects modified. That is why instead of speaking simply of 'the hegemony', 'a hegemony', I would propose a model which allows for this kind of variation and contradiction, its sets of alternatives and its processes of change.

But one thing that is evident in some of the best Marxist cultural analysis is that it is very much more at home in what one might call *epochal* questions than in what one has to call *historical* questions. That is to say, it is usually very much better at distinguishing the large features of different epochs of society, as between feudal and bourgeois, or what might be, than at distinguishing between different phases of bourgeois society, and different moments within the phases: that true historical process which demands a much greater precision and delicacy of analysis than the always striking epochal analysis which is concerned with main lineaments and features.

Now the theoretical model which I have been trying to work with is this. I would say first that in any society, in any particular period, there is a central system of practices, meanings and values, which we can properly call dominant and effective. This implies no presumption about its value. All I am saying is that it is central. Indeed I would call it a corporate system, but this might be confusing, since Gramsci uses 'corporate' to mean the subordinate as opposed to the general and dominant elements of hegemony. In any case what I have in mind is the central, effective and dominant system of meanings and values, which are not merely abstract but which are organized and lived. That is why hegemony is not to be understood at the level of mere opinion or mere manipulation. It is a whole body of practices and expectations; our assignments of energy, our ordinary understanding of the nature of man and of his world. It is a set of meanings and values which as they are experienced as practices appear as reciprocally confirming. It thus constitutes a sense of reality for most people in the society, a sense of absolute because experienced reality beyond which it is very difficult for most members of the society to move, in most areas of their lives. But this is not, except in the operation of a moment of abstract analysis, in any sense a static system. On the contrary we can only understand an effective and dominant culture if we understand the real social process on which it depends: I mean the process of incorporation.[2] The modes of incorporation are of great social significance, and incidentally in our kind of society have considerable economic significance. The educational institutions are usually the main agencies of the transmission of an effective dominant culture, and this is now a major economic as well as cultural activity; indeed it is both in the same moment. Moreover, at a philosophical level, at the true level of theory and at the level of the history of various practices, there is a process which I call the *selective tradition* : that which, within the terms of an effective dominant culture, is always passed off as 'the tradition', '*the* significant past'. But always the selectivity is the point; the way in which from a whole possible area of past and present, certain meanings and practices are chosen for emphasis, certain other meanings and practices are neglected and excluded. Even more crucially, some of these meanings and practices are reinterpreted, diluted, or put into forms which support or at least do not contradict other elements within the effective dominant culture. The processes of education; the processes of a much wider social training within institutions like the family; the practical definitions and organisation of work; the selective tradition at an intellectual and theoretical level: all these forces are involved in a continual making and remaking of an effective dominant culture, and on them, as experienced, as built into our living, its reality depends. If what we learn there were merely an imposed ideology, or if it were only the isolable meanings and practices of the ruling class, or of a section of the ruling class, which gets imposed on others, occupying merely the top of our minds, it would be—and one would be glad—a very much easier thing to overthrow.

It is not only the depths to which this process reaches, selecting and organizing and interpreting our experience. It is also that it is continually active and adjusting; it isn't just the past, the dry husks of ideology which we can more easily discard. And this can only be so, in a complex society, if it is something more substantial and more flexible than any abstract imposed ideology. Thus we have to recognize the alternative meanings and values, the alternative opinions and attitudes, even some alternative senses of the world, which can be accommodated and tolerated within a particular effective and dominant culture. This has been much under-emphasized in our notions of a superstructure, and even in some notions of hegemony. And the under-emphasis opens the way for retreat to an indifferent complexity. In the practice of politics, for example, there are certain truly incorporated modes of what are nevertheless, within those terms, real oppositions, that are felt and fought out. Their existence within the incorporation is recognizable by the fact that, whatever the degree of internal conflict or internal variation, they do not in practice go beyond the limits of the central effective and dominant definitions. This is true, for example, of the practice of parliamentary politics, though its internal oppositions are real. It is true about a whole range of practices and arguments, in any real society, which can by no means be reduced to an ideological cover, but which can nevertheless be properly analysed as in my sense corporate, if we find that, whatever the degree of internal controversy and variation, they do not exceed the limits of the central corporate definitions.

But if we are to say this, we have to think again about the sources of that which is not corporate; of those practices, experiences, meanings, values which are not part of the effective dominant culture. We can express this in two ways. There is clearly something that we can call alternative to the effective dominant culture, and there is something else that we can call oppositional, in a true sense. The degree of existence of these alternative and oppositional forms is itself a matter of constant historical variation in real circumstances. In certain societies it is possible to find areas of social life in which quite real alternatives are at least left alone. (If they are made available, of course, they are part of the corporate organization.) The existence of the possibility of opposition, and of its articulation, its degree of openness, and so on, again depends on very precise social and political forces. The facts of alternative and oppositional forms of social life and culture, in relation to the effective and dominant culture, have then to be recognized as subject to historical variation, and as having sources which are very significant, as a fact about the dominant culture itself.

Residual and Emergent Cultures

I have next to introduce a further distinction, between *residual* and *emergent* forms, both of alternative and of oppositional culture. By 'residual' I mean that some experiences, meanings and values which cannot be verified or cannot be expressed in the terms of the dominant culture, are nevertheless lived and practised on the basis of the residue—cultural as well as social—of some previous social formation. There is a real case of this in certain religious values, by contrast with the very evident incorporation of most religious meanings and values into the dominant system. The same is true, in a culture like Britain, of certain notions derived from a rural past, which have a very significant popularity. A residual culture is usually at some distance from the effective dominant culture, but one has to recognize that, in real cultural activities, it may get incorporated into it. This is because some part of it, some version of it—and especially if the residue is from some major area of the past—will in many cases have had to be incorporated if the effective dominant culture is to make sense in those areas. It is also because at certain points a dominant culture cannot allow too much of this kind of practice and experience outside itself, at least without risk. Thus the pressures are real, but certain genuinely residual meanings and practices in some important cases survive.

By 'emergent' I mean, first, that new meanings and values, new practices, new significances and experiences, are continually being created. But there is then a much earlier attempt to incorporate them, just because they are part—and yet not part—of effective contemporary practice. Indeed it is significant in our own period how very early this attempt is, how alert the dominant culture now is to anything that can be seen as emergent. We have then to see, first, as it were a temporal relation between a dominant culture and on the one hand a residual and on the other hand an emergent culture. But we can only understand this if we can make distinctions, that usually require very precise analysis, between residual-incorporated and residual not incorporated, and between emergent-incorporated and emergent not incorporated. It is an important fact about any particular society, how far it reaches into the whole range of human practices and experiences in an attempt at incorporation. It may be true of some earlier phases of bourgeois society, for example, that there were some areas of experience which it was willing to dispense with, which it was prepared to assign as the sphere of private or artistic life, and as being no particular business of society or the state. This went along with certain kinds of political tolerance, even if the reality of that tolerance was malign neglect. But I am sure it is true of the society that has come into existence since the last war, that progressively, because of developments in the social character of labour, in the social character of communications, and in the social character of decision, it extends much further than ever before in capitalist society into certain hitherto resigned areas of experience and practice and meaning. Thus the effective decision, as to whether a practice is alternative or oppositional, is often now made within a very much narrower scope. There is a simple theoretical distinction between alternative and oppositional, that is to say between someone who simply finds a different way to live and wishes to be left alone with it, and someone who finds a different way to live and wants to change the society in its light. This is usually the difference between individual and small-group solutions to social crisis and those solutions which properly belong to political and ultimately revolutionary practice. But it is often a very narrow line, in reality, between alternative and oppositional. A meaning or a practice may be tolerated as a deviation, and yet still be seen only as another particular way to live. But as the necessary area of effective dominance extends, the same meanings and practices can be seen by the dominant culture, not merely as disregarding or despising it, but as challenging it.

Now it is crucial to any Marxist theory of culture that it can give an adequate explanation of the sources of those practices and meanings. We can understand, from an ordinary historical approach, at least some of the sources of residual meanings and practices. These are the results of earlier social formations, in which certain real meanings and values were generated. In the subsequent default of a particular phase of a dominant culture, there is then a reaching back to those meanings and values which were created in real societies in the past, and which still seem to have some significance because they represent areas of human experience, aspiration and achievement, which the dominant culture undervalues or opposes, or even cannot recognise. But our hardest task theoretically, is to find a non-metaphysical and a non-subjectivist explanation of emergent cultural practice. Moreover, part of our answer to this question bears on the process of persistence of residual practices.

Class and Human Practice

We do have indeed one source to hand from the central body of Marxist theory. We have the formation of a new class, the coming to consciousness of a new class. This remains, without doubt, quite centrally important. Of course, in itself, this process of formation complicates any simple model of base and superstructure. It also complicates some of the ordinary versions of hegemony, although it was Gramsci's whole object to see and to create by organization the hegemony of a proletarian kind which is capable of challenging the bourgeois hegemony. We have then one central source of new practice, in the emergence of a new class. But we have also to recognize certain other kinds of source, and in cultural practice some of these are very important. I would say that we can recognize them on the basis of this proposition: that no mode of production, and therefore no dominant society or order of society, and therefore no dominant culture, in reality exhausts human practice, human energy, human intention. Indeed it seems to me that this emphasis is not merely a negative proposition, allowing us to account for certain things which happen outside the dominant mode. On the contrary, it is a fact about the modes of domination that they select from and consequently exclude the full range of human practice. The difficulties of human practice outside or against the dominant mode are, of course, real. It depends very much whether it is in an area in which the dominant class and the dominant culture have an interest and a stake. If the interest and the stake are explicit, many new practices will be reached for, and if possible incorporated, or else extirpated with extraordinary vigour. But in certain areas, there will be in certain periods practices and meanings which are not reached for. There will be areas of practice and meaning which, almost by definition from its own limited character, or in its profound deformation, the dominant culture is unable in any real terms to recognize. This gives us a bearing on the observable difference between, for example, the practices of a capitalist state and a state like the contemporary Soviet Union in relation to writers. Since from the whole Marxist tradition literature was seen as an important activity, indeed a crucial activity, the Soviet state is very much sharper in investigating areas where different versions of practice, different meanings and values, are being attempted and expressed. In capitalist practice, if the thing is not making a profit, or if it is not being widely circulated, then it can for some time be overlooked, at least while it remains alternative. When it becomes oppositional in an explicit way, it does, of course, get approached or attacked.

I am saying then that in relation to the full range of human practice at any one time, the dominant mode is a conscious selection and organization. At least in its fully formed state it is conscious. But there are always sources of real human practice which it neglects or excludes. And these can be different in quality from the developing and articulate interests of a rising class. They can include, for example, alternative perception of others, in immediate personal relationships, or new perceptions of material and media, in art and science, and within certain limits these new perceptions can be practised. The relations between the two kinds of source—the class and the excluded human area—are by no means necessarily contradictory. At times they can be very close, and on the relations between them, much in political practice depends. But culturally and as a matter of theory the areas can be seen as distinct.

Now if we go back to the cultural question in its most usual form—what are the relations between art and society, or literature and society? —in the light of the preceding discussion, we have to say first that there are no relations between literature and society in that abstracted way. The literature is there from the beginning as a practice in the society. Indeed until it and all other practices are present, the society cannot be seen as fully formed. A society is not fully available for analysis until each of its practices is included. But if we make that emphasis we must make a corresponding emphasis: that we cannot separate literature and art from other kinds of social practice, in such a way as to make them subject to quite special and distinct laws. They may have quite specific features as practices, but they cannot be separated from the general social process. Indeed one way of emphasizing this is to say, to insist, that literature is not restricted to operating in any one of the sectors I have been seeking to describe in this model. It would be easy to say, it is a familiar rhetoric, that literature operates in the emergent cultural sector, that it represents the new feelings, the new meanings, the new values. We might persuade ourselves of this theoretically, by abstract argument, but when we read much literature, over the whole range, without the sleight-of-hand of calling Literature only that which we have already selected as embodying certain meanings and values at a certain scale of intensity, we are bound to recognize that the act of writing, the practices of discourse in writing and speech, the making of novels and poems and plays and theories, all this activity takes place in all areas of the culture.

Literature appears by no means only in the emergent sector, which is always, in fact, quite rare. A great deal of writing is of a residual kind, and this has been deeply true of much English literature in the last half-century. Some of its fundamental meanings and values have belonged to the cultural achievements of long-past stages of society. So widespread is this fact, and the habits of mind it supports, that in many minds 'literature' and 'the past' acquire a certain identity, and it is then said that there is now no literature: all that glory is over. Yet most writing, in any period, including our own, is a form of contribution to the effective dominant culture. Indeed many of the specific qualities of literature, its capacity to embody and enact and perform certain meanings and values, or to create in single particular ways what would be otherwise merely general truths, enable it to fulfill this effective function with great power. To literature, of course, we must add the visual arts and music, and in our own society the powerful arts of film and of broadcasting. But the general theoretical point should be clear. If we are looking for the relations between literature and society, we cannot either separate out this one practice from a formed body of other practices, nor when we have identified the particular practice can we give it a uniform, static and ahistorical relation to some abstract social formation. The arts of writing and the arts of creation and performance, over their whole range, are parts of the cultural process in all the different ways, the different sectors, that I have been seeking to describe. They contribute to the effective dominant culture and are a central articulation of it. They embody residual meanings and values, not all of which are incorporated, though many are. They express also and significantly some emergent practices and meanings, yet some of these may eventually be incorporated, as they reach people and begin to move them. Thus it was very evident in the sixties, in some of the emergent arts of performance, that the dominant culture reached out to transform them or seek to transform them. In this process, of course, the dominant culture itself changes, not in its central formation, but in many of its articulated features. But then in a modern society it must always change in this way, if it is to remain dominant, if it is still to be felt as in real ways central in all our many activities and interests.

...

Objects and Practices

Now I think the true crisis in cultural theory, in our own time, is between this view of the work of art as object and the alternative view of art as a practice. Of course it is at once objected that the work of art *is* an object: that various works have survived from the past, particular sculptures, particular paintings, particular buildings, and these are objects. This is of course true, but the same way of thinking is applied to works which have no such specific material existence. There is no *Hamlet*,[3] no *Brothers Karamazov*,[4] no *Wuthering Heights*,[5] in the sense that there is a particular great painting. There is no *Fifth Symphony*,[6] there is no work in the whole area of music and dance and performance, which is an object in any way comparable to those works in the visual arts which have survived. And yet the habit of treating all such works as objects has persisted because this is a basic theoretical and practical presupposition. But in literature, especially in drama, in music and in a very wide area of the performing arts, what we have are not objects but *notations*. These notations have to be interpreted in an active way, according to particular conventions. But indeed this is true over an even wider field. The relationship between the making of a work of art and the reception of a work of art, is always active, and subject to conventions, which in themselves are forms of social organization and relationship, and this is radically different from the production and consumption of an object. It is indeed an activity and a practice, and in its accessible forms, although it may in some arts have the character of a material object, it is still only accessible through active perception and interpretation. This makes the case of notation, in arts like drama and literature and music, only a special case of a much wider truth.

What this can show us here about the practice of analysis is that we have to break from the notion of isolating the object and then discovering its components. On the contrary we have to discover the nature of a practice and then its conditions. Often these two processes may in part resemble each other: in many other cases they are of radically different kinds. And I would conclude with an observation on the way this distinction bears on the Marxist tradition of the relation between primary economic and social practices, and cultural practices. If we suppose that what is produced in cultural practice is a series of objects, we shall, as in most current forms of sociological-critical procedure, set about discovering their components. Within a Marxist emphasis these components will be from what we have been in the habit of calling the base. We shall isolate certain features which we can so to say recognize *in component form*, or we will ask what processes of transformation or mediation these components have gone through before they arrived in this accessible state. But I am saying that we should look not for the components of a product but for the conditions of a practice. When we find ourselves looking at a particular work, or group of works, often realizing, as we do so, their essential community as well as their irreducible individuality, we should find ourselves attending first to the reality of their practice and the conditions of the practice as it was then executed. And from this I think we ask essentially different questions. Take for example the way in which an object is related to a genre, in orthodox criticism. We identify it by certain leading features, we then assign it to a larger category, the genre, and then we may find the components of the genre in a particular social history (although in some variants of Marxist criticism not even that is done, and the genre is supposed to be some permanent category of the mind). It is not that way of proceeding that seems to be required. The recognition of the relation of a collective mode and an individual project—and these are the only categories that we can initially presume—is a recognition of related practices. That is to say, the irreducibly individual projects that particular works are, may come in experience and in analysis to show resemblances which allow us to group them into collective modes. These are by no means always genres. They may exist as resemblances within and across genres. They may be the practice of a group in a period, rather than the practice of a phase in a genre. But as we discover the nature of a particular practice, and the nature of the relation between an individual project and a collective mode, we find that we are analysing, as two forms of the same process, both its active composition and its conditions of composition, and in either direction this is a complex of extending active relationships. This means, of course, that we have no built-in procedure of the kind which is indicated by the fixed character of an object. We have the principles of the relations of practices, within a discoverably intentional organization, and we have the available hypotheses of dominant, residual and emergent. But what we are actively seeking is the true practice which has been alienated to an object, and the true conditions of practice—whether as literary conventions or as social relationships—

which have been alienated to components or to mere background. As a general proposition this is only an emphasis, but it seems to me to suggest at once the point of break and the point of departure, in practical and theoretical work, within an active and self-renewing Marxist cultural tradition.

注释:

1. 安东尼奥·葛兰西（1891—1937），意大利共产党创始人，马克思主义思想家。
2. 意为融入或收编，指大众文化对于个体的同化或塑造作用。
3. 《哈姆雷特》，英国剧作家莎士比亚的著名悲剧。
4. 《卡拉马佐夫兄弟》，俄罗斯文学巨匠陀思妥耶夫斯基的长篇小说。
5. 《呼啸山庄》，英国女作家艾米莉·勃朗特的长篇小说。
6. 贝多芬的《命运交响曲》。

Dick Hebdige

迪克·赫伯迪格(1951—),英国文化研究学者、媒介理论家和社会学家,伯明翰学派的代表性理论家和重要成员。他对文化研究的最大贡献是其对亚文化现象的研究,他在1979年出版的著作《亚文化:风格的意义》被认为是亚文化研究的里程碑式的作品,也是文化研究的经典之作。在该著作中,赫伯迪格以文化研究的视角揭示了青年亚文化是怎样通过其独特的文化风格抵抗社会主流文化价值观对青年收编的。赫伯迪格的学术生涯起步于英国伯明翰大学当代文化研究中心,后移居美国,在加州大学圣芭芭拉分校任教。除《亚文化:风格的意义》外,赫伯迪格的其他著作还有《切割与混合:文化、认同和加勒比海音乐》《躲在亮中:形象和物品的研究》等。

From Culture toHegemony

(Hebdige, Dick. From Culture to Hegemony. *The Cultural Studies Reader*. Simon During ed. New York: Routledge, 1993, pp. 357-367.)

在本文中,赫伯迪格简明扼要地论述了文化研究的几个核心概念,其实也是在简述自己从事亚文化研究的学术理路。文化研究首先把文化的概念扩展为人们的生产和生活方式中的所有现象,把文化从精英群体中解放出来,这就极大地拓宽了文化研究和文艺批评的学术视野。接着,赫伯迪格解释了巴尔特的符号学理论对于文化研究的影响,巴尔特将符号学分析方法应用到日常文化现象的分析为文化研究提供了基本的理论方法。文化研究就是要运用这一方法揭示日常文化形式背后的话语模式及其权力意志。这些话语构成了社会意识形态,与统治阶层的阶级压迫形成共谋,共同维护社会阶级秩序。而亚文化研究的重要任务就是分析亚文化是如何抵制社会主流意识形态对人的收编的。

CULTURE

> Culture: cultivation, tending, in Christian authors, worship; the action or practice of cultivating the soil; tillage, husbandry; the cultivation or rearing of certain animals (e. g. fish); the artificial development of microscopic organisms, organisms so produced; the cultivating or development (of the mind, faculties, manners), improvement or refinement by education and training; the condition of being trained or refined; the intellectual side of civilization; the prosecution or special attention or study of any subject or pursuit. (*Oxford English Dictionary*)

Culture is a notoriously ambiguous concept as the above definition demonstrates. Refracted through centuries of usage, the word has acquired a number of quite different, often contradictory, meanings. Even as a scientific term, it refers both to a process (artificial development of microscopic organisms) and a product (organisms so produced). More specifically, since the end of the eighteenth century, it has been used by English intellectuals and literary figures to focus critical attention on a whole range of controversial issues. The 'quality of life', the effects in human terms of mechanization, the division of labour and the creation of a mass society have all been discussed within the larger confines of what Raymond Williams has called the 'Culture and Society' debate. It was through this tradition of dissent and criticism that the dream of the 'organic society'—of society as an integrated, meaningful whole—was largely kept alive. The dream had two basic trajectories. One led back to the past and to the feudal ideal of a hierarchically ordered community. Here, culture assumed an almost sacred function. Its 'harmonious perfection' was posited against the Wasteland of contemporary life.

The other trajectory, less heavily supported, led towards the future, to a socialist Utopia where the distinction between labour and leisure was to be annulled. Two basic definitions of culture emerged from this tradition, though these were by no means necessarily congruent with the two trajectories outlined above. The first—the one which is probably most familiar to the reader—was essentially classical and conservative. It represented culture as a standard of aesthetic excellence: 'the best that has been thought and said in the world', and it derived from an appreciation of 'classic' aesthetic form (opera, ballet, drama, literature, art). The second, traced back by Williams to Herder[1] and the eighteenth century, was rooted in anthropology. Here the term 'culture' referred to a

> ...particular way of life which expresses certain meanings and values not only in art and learning, but also in institutions and ordinary behaviour. The analysis of culture, from such a definition, is the clarification of the meanings and values implicit and explicit in a particular way of life, a particular culture. (Williams 1958)

This definition obviously had a much broader range. It encompassed, in T. S. Eliot's words,

> ...all the characteristic activities and interests of a people. Derby Day, Henley Regatta, Cowes, the 12th of August, a cup final, the dog races, the pin table, the dartboard, Wensleydale cheese, boiled cabbage cut into sections, beetroot in vinegar, 19th Century Gothic churches, the music of Elgar...

As Williams noted, such a definition could only be supported if a new theoretical initiative was taken. The theory of culture now involved the 'study of relationships between elements in a whole way of life'(William 1958). The emphasis shifted from immutable to historical criteria, from fixity to transformation:

> ...an emphasis [which] from studying particular meaning and values seeks not so much to compare these, as a way of establishing a scale, but by studying their modes of change to discover certain general causes or 'trends' by which social and cultural developments as a whole can be better understood. (William 1958)

Williams was, then, proposing an altogether broader formulation of the relationships between culture and society, one which through the analysis of 'particular meanings and values' sought to uncover the conceived fundamentals of history; the 'general causes' and broad social 'trends' which lie behind the manifest appearances of an 'everyday life'.

In the early years, when it was being established in the Universities, Cultural Studies sat rather uncomfortably on the fence between these two conflicting definitions—culture as a standard of excellence, culture as a 'whole way of life'—unable to determine which represented the most fruitful line of enquiry. Richard Hoggart[2] and Raymond Williams portrayed working-class culture sympathetically in wistful accounts of pre-scholarship boyhoods (Leeds for Hoggart (1957), a Welsh mining village for Williams (1958)) but their work displayed a strong bias towards literature and literacy and an equally strong moral tone. Hoggart deplored the way in which the traditional working-class community—a community of tried and tested values despite the dour landscape in which it had been set—was being undermined and replaced by a 'Candy Floss World' of thrills and cheap fiction which was somehow bland *and* sleazy. Williams tentatively endorsed the new mass communications but was concerned to establish aesthetic and moral criteria for distinguishing the worthwhile products from the 'trash'; the jazz—'a real musical form'—and the football—'a wonderful game'—from the 'rape novel, the Sunday strip paper and the latest Tin Pan drool'(Williams 1961). In 1966 Hoggart laid down the basic premises upon which Cultural Studies were based:

> First, without appreciating good literature, no one will really understand the nature of society, second, literary critical analysis can be applied to certain social phenomena other than 'academically respectable' literature (for example, the popular arts, mass communications) so as to illuminate their meanings for individuals and their societies.

The implicit assumption that it still required a literary sensibility to 'read' society with the requisite subtlety, and that the two ideas of culture could be ultimately reconciled was also, paradoxically, to inform the early work of the French writer, Roland Barthes,[3] though here it found validation in a method—semiotics—a way of reading signs(Hawkes 1977).

BARTHES: MYTHS AND SIGNS

Using models derived from the work of the Swiss linguist Ferdinand de Saussure[4] Barthes sought to expose the *arbitrary* nature of cultural phenomena, to uncover the latent meanings of an everyday life which, to all intents and purposes, was 'perfectly natural'. Unlike Hoggart, Barthes was not concerned with distinguishing the good form the bad in modern mass culture, but rather with showing how *all* the apparently spontaneous forms and ritual of contemporary bourgeois societies are subject to a systematic distortion, liable at any moment to be dehistoricized, 'naturalized', converted into myth:

> The whole of France is steeped in this anonymous ideology: our press, our films, our theatre, our pulp literature, our rituals, our Justice, our diplomacy, our conversations, our remarks about the weather, a murder trial, a touching wedding, the cooking we dream of, the garments we wear, everything in everyday life is dependent on the representation which the bourgeoisie *has and makes us have* of the relations between men and the world. (Barthes 1972)

Like Eliot, Barthes's notion of culture extends beyond the library, the opera-house and the theatre to encompass the whole of everyday life. But this everyday life is for Barthes overlaid with a significance which is at once more insidious and more systematically organized. Starting from the premise that 'myth is a type of speech', Barthes set out in *Mythologies* to examine the normally hidden set of rules, codes and conventions through which meanings particular to specific social groups (i. e. those in power) are rendered universal and 'given' for the whole of society. He found in phenomena as disparate as a wrestling match, a writer on holiday, a tourist guide-book, the same artificial nature, the same ideological core. Each had been exposed to the same prevailing rhetoric (the rhetoric of common sense)and turned into myth, into a mere element in a 'second-order semiological system' (Barthes 1972). (Barthes uses the example of a photograph in *Pairs-Match* of a Negro soldier saluting the French flag, which has a first and second order connotation: (1) a gesture of loyalty, but also (2) 'France is a great empire, and all her sons, without colour discrimination, faithfully serve under her flag'.)

Barthes's application of a method rooted in linguistics to other systems of discourse outside language (fashion, film, food, etc.) opened up completely new possibilities for contemporary cultural studies. It was hoped that the invisible seam between language, experience and reality could be located and prised open through a semiotic analysis of this kind: that the gulf between the alienated intellectual and the 'real' world could be rendered meaningful and, miraculously, at the same time, be made to disappear. Moreover, under Barthes's direction, semiotics promised nothing less than the reconciliation of the two conflicting definitions of culture upon which Cultural Studies was so ambiguously posited—a marriage of moral conviction (in this case, Barthes's Marxist beliefs) and popular themes: the study of a society's total way of life .

This is not to say that semiotics was easily assimilable within the Cultural Studies project. Though Barthes shared the literary preoccupations of Hoggart and Williams, his work introduced a new Marxist 'problematic' which was alien to the British tradition of concerned and largely untheorized 'social commentary'. As a result, the old debate seemed suddenly limited. In E. P. Thompson's[5] words it appeared to reflect the parochial concerns of a group of 'gentlemen amateurs'. Thompson sought to replace Williams's definition of the theory of culture as 'a theory of relations between elements in a whole way of life' with his own more rigorously Marxist formulation: 'the study of relationships in a whole way of *conflict* '. A more analytical framework was required; a new vocabulary had to be learned. As part of this process of theorization, the word 'ideology' came to acquire a much wider range of meanings than had previously been the case. We have seen how Barthes found an 'anonymous ideology' penetrating every possible level of social life, inscribed in the most mundane of rituals, framing the most casual social encounters. But how can ideology be 'anonymous', and how can it assume such a broad significance? Before we attempt any reading of subcultural style, we must first define the term 'ideology' more precisely.

IDEOLOGY: A LIVED RELATION

In the *German Ideology*, Marx shows how the basis of the capitalist economic structure (surplus value, neatly defined by Godelier[6] as 'Profit... is unpaid work' (Godelier 1970)) is hidden from the consciousness of the agents of production. The failure to see through appearances to the real relations which underlie them does not occur as the direct result of some kind of masking operation consciously carried out by individuals, social groups or institutions. On the contrary, ideology by definition thrives *beneath* consciousness. It is here, at the level of 'normal common sense', that ideological frames of reference are most firmly sedimented and most effective, because it is here that their ideological nature is most effectively concealed. As Stuart Hall[7] puts it:

> It is precisely its 'spontaneous' quality, its transparency, its 'naturalness', its refusal to be made to examine the premises on which it is founded, its resistance to change or to correction, its effect of instant recognition, and the closed circle in which it moves which makes common sense, at one and the same time, 'spontaneous', ideological and *unconscious*. You cannot learn, through common sense, *how things are* : you can only discover *where they fit* into the existing scheme of things. In this way, its very taken-for-grantedness is what establishes it as a medium in which its own premises and presuppositions are being rendered *invisible* by its apparent transparency. (Hall 1977)

Since ideology saturates everyday discourse in the form of common sense, it cannot be bracketed off from everyday life as a self-contained set of 'political opinions' or 'biased views'. Neither can it be reduced to the abstract dimensions of a 'world view' or used in the crude Marxist sense to designate 'false consciousness'. Instead, as Louis Althusser[8] has pointed out:

> ... ideology has very little to do with 'consciousness'... It is profoundly *unconscious*... Ideology is indeed a system of representation, but in the majority of cases these representations have nothing to do with 'consciousness': they are usually images and occasionally concepts, but it is above all as *structures* that they impose on the vast majority of men, not via their 'consciousness'. They are perceived-accepted-suffered cultural objects and they act functionally on men via a process that escapes them. (Althusser 1969)

Although Althusser is here referring to structures like the family, cultural and political institutions, etc. , we can illustrate the point quite simple by taking as our example a physical structure. Most modern institutes of education, despite the apparent neutrality of the materials from which they are constructed (red brick, white tile, etc.) carry within themselves implicit ideological assumptions which are literally structured into the architecture itself. The categorization of knowledge into arts and sciences is reproduced in the faculty system which houses different disciplines in different buildings, and most colleges maintain the traditional divisions by devoting a separate floor to each subject. Moreover, the hierarchical relationship between teacher and taught is inscribed in the very lay-out of the lecture theatre where the seating arrangements—benches rising in tiers before a raised lectern—dictate the flow of information and serve to 'naturalize' professorial authority. Thus, a whole range of decisions about what is and what is not possible within education have been made, however unconsciously, before the content of individual courses is even decided.

These decisions help to set the limits not only on what is taught but on *how* it is taught. Here the buildings literally *reproduce* in concrete terms prevailing (ideological) notions about what education is and it is through this process that the educational structure, which can, of course, be altered, is placed beyond question and appears to us as a 'given' (i. e. as immutable). In this case, the frames of our thinking have been translated into actual bricks and mortar.

Social relations and processes are then appropriated by individuals only through the forms in which they are represented to those individuals. These forms are, as we have seen, by no means transparent. They are shrouded in a 'common sense' which simultaneously validates and mystifies them. It is precisely these 'perceived-accepted-suffered cultural objects' which semiotics sets out to 'interrogate' and decipher. All aspects of culture possess a semiotic value, and the most taken-for-granted phenomena can function as signs: as elements in communication systems governed by semantic rules and codes which are not themselves directly apprehended in experience. These signs are, then, as opaque as the social relations which produce them and which they represent. In other words there is an ideological dimension to every signification.

To uncover the ideological dimension of signs we must first try to disentangle the codes through which meaning is organized. 'Connotative' codes are particularly important. As Stuart Hall has argued, they '... cover the face of social life and render it classifiable, intelligible, meaningful'(Hall 1977). He goes on to describe these codes as 'maps of meaning' which are of necessity the product of selection. They cut across a range of potential meanings, making certain meanings available and ruling others out of court. We tend to live inside these maps as surely as we live in the 'real' world: they 'think' us as much as we 'think' them, and this in itself is quite 'natural'. All human societies *reproduce* themselves in this way through a process of 'naturalization'. It is through this process—a kind of inevitable reflex of all social life—that *particular* sets of social relations, *particular* ways of organizing the world appear to us as if they were universal and timeless. This is what Althusser means when he says that 'ideology has no history' and that ideology in this general sense will always be an 'essential element of every social formation'(Althusser and Balibar 1968).

However, in highly complex societies like ours, which function through a finely graded system of divided (i. e. specialized) labour, the crucial question has to do with which specific ideologies, representing the interests of which specific groups and classes will prevail at any given moment, in any given situation. To deal with this question, we must first consider how power is distributed in our society. That is, we must ask which groups and classes have how much say in defining, ordering and classifying out the social world. For instance, if we pause to reflect for a moment, it should be obvious that access to the means by which ideas are disseminated in our society (i. e. principally the mass media) is *not* the same for all classes. Some groups have more say, more opportunity to make the rules, to organize meaning, while others are less favourably placed, have less power to produce and impose their definitions of the world on the world.

Thus, when we come to look beneath the level of 'ideology-in-general' at the way in which specific ideologies work, how some gain dominance and others remain marginal, we can see that in advanced Western democracies the ideological field is by no means neutral. To return to the 'connotative' codes to which Stuart Hall refers we can see that these 'maps of meaning' are charged with a potentially explosive significance because they are traced and re-traced along the lines laid down by the *dominant* discourses about reality, the *dominant* ideologies. They thus tend to represent, in however obscure and contradictory a fashion, the interests of the *dominant* groups in society.

To understand this point we should refer to Marx:

> The ideas of the ruling class are in every epoch the ruling ideas, i. e. the class which is the ruling *material* force of society is at the same time its

ruling *intellectual* force. The class which has the means of material production at its disposal, has control at the same time over the means of mental production, so that generally speaking, the ideas of those who lack the means of mental production are subject to it. The ruling ideas are nothing more than the ideal expression of the dominant material relationships grasped as ideas; hence of the relationships which make the one class the ruling class, therefore the ideas of its dominance. (Marx and Engels 1970)

This is the basis of Antonio Gramsci's[9] theory of *hegemony* which provides the most adequate account of how dominance is sustained in advanced capitalist societies.

HEGEMONY: THE MOVING EQUILIBRIUM

Society cannot share a common communication system so long as it is split into warring classes. (Brecht, *A Short Organum for the Theatre*)

The term hegemony refers to a situation in which a provisional alliance of certain social groups can exert 'total social authority' over other subordinate groups, not simply by coercion or by the direct imposition of ruling ideas, but by 'winning and shaping consent so that the power of the dominant classes appears both legitimate and natural'(Hall 1977). Hegemony can only be maintained so long as the dominant classes 'succeed in framing all competing definitions within their range', so that subordinate groups are, if not controlled, then at least contained within an ideological space which does not seem at all 'ideological': which appears instead to be permanent and 'natural', to lie outside history, to be beyond particular interests.

This is how, according to Barthes, 'mythology' performs its vital function of naturalization and normalization and it is in his book *Mythologies* that Barthes demonstrates most forcefully the full extension of these normalized forms and meanings. However, Gramsci adds the important proviso that hegemonic power, precisely *because* it requires the consent of the dominated majority, can never be permanently exercised by the same alliance of 'class fractions'. As has been pointed out, 'Hegemony... is not universal and "given" to the continuing rule of a particular class. It has to be won, reproduced, sustained. Hegemony is, as Gramsci said, a "moving equilibrium" containing relations of forces favourable or unfavourable to this or that tendency'(Hall and Jefferson 1976).

In the same way, forms cannot be permanently normalized. They can always be deconstructed, demystified, by a 'mythologist' like Barthes. Moreover commodities can be symbolically 'repossessed' in everyday life, and endowed with implicitly oppositional meanings, by the very groups who originally produced them. The symbiosis in which ideology and social order, production and reproduction, are linked is then neither fixed nor guaranteed. It can be prised open. The consensus can be fractured, challenged, overruled, and resistance to the groups in dominance cannot always be lightly dismissed or automatically incorporated. Although, as Lefebvre[10] has written, we live in a society where '... objects in practice become signs and signs objects and a second nature takes the place of the first—the initial layer of perceptible reality'(Lefebvre 1971), there are, as he goes on to affirm, always 'objections and contradictions which hinder the closing of the circuit' between sign and object, production and reproduction.

We can now return to the meaning of youth subcultures, for the emergence of such groups has signalled in a spectacular fashion the breakdown of consensus in the post-war period. It is precisely objections and contradictions of the kind which Lefebvre has described that find expression in subculture. However, the challenge to hegemony which subcultures represent is not issued directly by them. Rather it is expressed obliquely, in style. The objections are lodged, the contradictions displayed (and 'magically resolved') at the profoundly superficial level of appearances: that is, at the level of signs. For the sign-community, the community of myth-consumers, is not a uniform body. As Volosinov has written, it is cut through by class:

> Class does not coincide with the sign community, i.e. with the totality of users of the same set of signs of ideological communication. Thus various different classes will use one and the same language. As a result, differently oriented accents intersect in every ideological sign. Sign becomes the arena of the class struggle. (Volosinov 1973)

The struggle between different discourses, different definitions and meanings within ideology is therefore always, at the same time, a struggle within signification: a struggle for possession of the sign which extend to even the most mundane areas of everyday life. 'Humble objects' can be magically appropriated; 'stolen' by subordinate groups and made to carry 'secret' meanings: meanings which express, in code, a form of resistance to the order which guarantees their continued subordination.

Style in subculture is, then, pregnant with significance. Its transformations go 'against nature', interrupting the process of 'normalization'. As such, they are gestures, movements towards a speech which offends the 'silent majority', which challenges the principle of unity and cohesion, which contradicts the myth of consensus. Our task becomes, like Barthes's, to discern the hidden messages inscribed in code on the glossy surfaces of style, to trace them out as 'maps of meaning' which obscurely re-present the very contradictions they are designed to resolve or conceal.

注释:

1. 赫尔德（1744—1803），德国哲学家、神学家和诗人。他被认为是德国浪漫主义的先驱，其《论语言的起源》等著作对后来的狂飙运动、浪漫主义文学和历史哲学都产生了深远的影响。

2. 理查德·霍加特（1918—2014），英国当代著名的文化批评理论家，文化研究的早期奠基者之一。他在1964年创立了著名的伯明翰大学当代文化研究中心。

3. 罗兰·巴特（1915—1980），法国哲学家、作家和文学评论家、符号学家。其对文论最大的贡献是将符号学的分析方法应用到文艺批评中，这对结构主义、符号学、人类学、后结构主义都产生了巨大的影响。

4. 费尔迪南·德·索绪尔（1857—1913），瑞士语言学家，被后世学者公认为结构主义的创始人，现代语言学理论的奠基者。

5. E. P. 汤普森（1924—1993），英国著名的历史学家、作家、社会主义者、和平活动家。

6. 莫里斯·戈德利尔（1934— ），法国人类学家，开创性地将马克思主义应用于人类学研究，对推动人类学的发展做出了杰出贡献。

7. 斯图亚特·霍尔（1932—2014），英国著名的文化研究学者、媒介研究批评家、社会学家和思想家，曾任英国伯明翰大学当代文化研究中心主任。

8. 路易·阿尔都塞（1918—1990），法国著名的马克思主义哲学家。

9. 安东尼奥·葛兰西（1891—1937），意大利马克思主义思想家。

10. 亨利·列菲弗尔（1901—1991），法国著名的马克思主义理论家、哲学家、城市社会学家。

Chapter Fifteen **Ecological Literary Criticism**

生态文学批评作为一种文学批评方法始于20世纪80年代，是研究文学作品中的生态意识的思想理论。它源于对环境现实的深切忧思，以保护生态为重心，着重分析文学和自然环境之间关系，其最重要的目的是唤醒人们的生态保护意识。

1978年，当生态批评作为一个概念被威廉·鲁克尔特引入文学批评后，便以星火燎原之势，迅速席卷理论界。生态学被应用于文学研究，成为一种文学批评的崭新范式。生态文学批评迅速扩展到人文、社会和自然等多个学科和领域，显示出强劲的渗透力，成为理论界最为广泛的跨学科研究领域之一。迄今为止，生态批评的发展大致分为三个阶段。第一个阶段的生态文学批评以"自然书写"为重心，欧文、梭罗、爱默生和约翰·巴勒斯、奥尔多·利奥波德等美国自然文学作品成为生态批评思想的来源，人们在文学作品中重新发现、评估自然的价值，寻归自然的怀抱，以激发人类对自然的重视，呼唤对工业文明的抗拒、对生态平衡的关注与行动。第二个阶段的批评视角开始远离平静的田野，城市景观成为关注的焦点，它的重要主题是人类福祉和环境正义，生态批评也开始了由自然书写转向人类社会生活内部的批判，诸如消费机器、女性运动以及种族问题等。正是在这个时期，生态女性主义、社会生态学、深生态学等生态学分支开始形成并独立发展。第三个阶段的生态文学批评呈现多元化发展趋势，主要特征为以环境视角为出发点，探索人类生活经验的各个方面，同时，在肯定种族和国家特殊性的基础上，超越种族、国家以及民族之间的界限。

总体来讲，生态文学批评理论主要探究的是文学与生态环境之间的互动关系，它重新审视传统经典文学作品，从中挖掘人与自然、人与社会、人与地球之间的多重关系，旨在开启文学研究的一种新的视角和思路。这种文学与生态学的跨学科研究，以生态的整体性思维指导人类社会的发展，引起人们对文学作品中的生态环境描写的关注，以生态视角解读文学作品，反思生态危机与人类自身的文化和生存方式之间的关系。其研究范围不仅涉及自然环境，还涵盖科学技术观、环境伦理、社会伦理以及社会文化等各个方面。它反对人类中心主义，反对等级制度和二元对立的西方传统思维方式，主张人是整个宏大的生态系统、生物圈和生态活动过程中的有机组成部分，因此，人的各种活动都应该而且必须遵守生物共同体行为规则。目前，生态文学批评在当代文学批评理论之中仍特别活跃，它不断与时俱进，吸收新的思想，生态文学批评的后现代转向、物质转向，都是它在当下的最新发展，其强大的生命力彰显的正是人类对自然的关注，纠正社会生活模式弊端的信心。

Arne Naess

阿恩·纳斯(1912—2009)，生于挪威奥斯陆，于奥斯陆大学获得硕士学位，后继续在巴黎和维也纳求学，他参加了德国哲学家莫里茨·石里克(Moritz Schilick)创立的逻辑实证主义小组。1939 年被任命为奥斯陆大学哲学教授，参加挪威反击第二次世界大战的战役，是著名的哲学家和环境学家。他创立的现代环境伦理学新理论，是当代西方环境主义思潮中最具革命性和挑战性的生态哲学。他也是深生态学理论的创始人，深生态学是要突破浅生态学的认识局限，对所面临的环境事务提出深层的问题并寻求深层的解决答案。

The Shallow and the Deep, Long-Range Ecology Movement: A Summary

(Naess, Arne. The Shallow and the Deep, Long-Range Ecology Movement: A Summary. *Inquiry*, 16 (1), pp. 95-100.)

深生态学不仅是西方众多生态批评思潮中最令人瞩目的新思想，而且已成为当代西方环境运动中起先导作用的环境价值理念。深生态学主张重塑人类文明的秩序，使之成为自然整体中的一个有机部分。在这篇文章中，纳斯首次提出“深生态学”一词，批判了将大自然工具化的人类中心主义，以及与之对应的“浅生态学”，系统总结了深生态学的几个主要特征，是生态文学批评中的宝贵思想资源之一。

Ecologically responsible policies are concerned only in part with pollution and resource depletion. There are deeper concerns which touch upon principles of diversity, complexity, autonomy, decentralization, symbiosis, egalitarianism, and classlessness.

The emergence of ecologists from their former relative obscurity marks a turning-point in our scientific communities. But their message is twisted and misused. A shallow, but presently rather powerful movement, and a deep, but less influential movement, compete for our attention. I shall make an effort to characterize the two.

1. *The Shallow Ecology movement*:

Fight against pollution and resource depletion. Central objective: the health and affluence of people in the developed countries.

2. *The Deep Ecology movement*:

(1) Rejection of the man-in-environment image[1] in favour of *the relational, total-field image*. Organisms as knots in the biospherical net or field of intrinsic relations. An intrinsic relation between two things *A* and *B* is such that the relation belongs to the definitions or basic constitutions of *A* and *B*, so that without the relation, *A* and *B* are no longer the same things. The total-field model dissolves not only the man-in-environment concept, but every compact thing-in-milieu concept — except when talking at a superficial or preliminary level of communication.

(2) *Biospherical egalitarianism* — in principle[2]. The 'in principle' clause is inserted because any realistic praxis necessitates some killing, exploitation, and suppression. The ecological field-worker acquires a deepseated respect, or even veneration, for ways and forms of life. He reaches an understanding from within, a kind of understanding that others reserve for fellow men and for a narrow section of ways and forms of life. To the ecological field-worker, *the equal right to live and blossom* is an intuitively clear and obvious value axiom. Its restriction to humans is an anthropocentrism with detrimental effects upon the life quality of humans themselves. This quality depends in part upon the deep pleasure and satisfaction we receive from close partnership with other forms of life. The attempt to ignore our dependence and to establish a master-slave role has contributed to the alienation of man from himself.

Ecological egalitarianism implies the reinterpretation of the future research variable, 'level of crowding', so that *general* mammalian crowding and loss of life-equality is taken seriously, not only human crowding. (Research on the high requirements of free space of certain mammals has, incidentally, suggested that theorists of human urbanism have largely underestimated human life-space requirements. Behavioural crowding symptoms [neuroses, aggressiveness, loss of traditions...] are largely the same among mammals.)

(3) *Principles of diversity and of symbiosis.* Diversity enhances the potentialities of survival, the chances of new modes of life, the richness of forms. And the so-called struggle of life, and survival of the fittest, should be interpreted in the sense of ability to coexist and cooperate in complex relationships, rather than ability to kill, exploit, and suppress. 'Live and let live' is a more powerful ecological principle than 'Either you or me'[3].

The latter tends to reduce the multiplicity of kinds of forms of life, and also to create destruction within the communities of the same species. Ecologically inspired attitudes therefore favour diversity of human ways of life, of cultures, of occupations, of economies. They support the fight against economic and cultural, as much as military, invasion and domination, and they are opposed to the annihilation of seals and whales as much as to that of human tribes or cultures.

(4) *Anti-class posture.* Diversity of human ways of life is in part due to (intended or unintended) exploitation and suppression on the part of certain groups. The exploiter lives differently from the exploited, but both are adversely affected in their potentialities of self-realization. The principle of diversity does not cover differences due merely to certain attitudes or behaviours forcibly blocked or restrained. The principles of ecological egalitarianism and of symbiosis support the same anti-class posture. The ecological attitude favours the extension of all three principles to any group conflicts, including those of today between developing and developed nations. The three principles also favour extreme caution towards any over-all plans for the future, except those consistent with wide and widening classless diversity.

(5) Fight against *pollution and resource depletion.* In this fight ecologists have found powerful supporters, but sometimes to the detriment of their total stand. This happens when attention is focused on pollution and resource depletion rather than on the other points, or when projects are implemented which reduce pollution but increase evils of the other kinds. Thus, if prices of life necessities increase because of the installation of anti-pollution devices, class differences increase too. An ethics of responsibility implies that ecologists do not serve the shallow, but the deep ecological movement. That is, not only point (5), but all seven points must be considered together.

Ecologists are irreplaceable informants in any society, whatever their political colour. If well organized, they have the power to reject jobs in which they submit themselves to institutions or to planners with limited ecological perspectives. As it is now, ecologists sometimes serve masters who deliberately ignore the wider perspectives.

(6) *Complexity, not complication* [4]. The theory of ecosystems contains an important distinction between what is complicated without any Gestalt or unifying principles — we may think of finding our way through a chaotic city — and what is complex. A multiplicity of more or less lawful, interacting factors may operate together to form a unity, a system. We make a shoe or use a map or integrate a variety of activities into a workaday pattern. Organisms, ways of life, and interactions in the biosphere in general, exhibit complexity of such an astoundingly high level as to colour the general outlook of ecologists. Such complexity makes thinking in terms of vast systems inevitable. It also makes for a keen, steady perception of the profound *human ignorance* of biospherical relationships and therefore of the effect of disturbances.

Applied to humans, the complexity-not-complication principle favours division of labour, *not fragmentation of labour*. It favours integrated actions in which the whole person is active, not mere reactions. It favours complex economies, an integrated variety of means of living. (Combinations of industrial and agricultural activity, of intellectual and manual work, of specialized and non-specialized occupations, of urban and non-urban activity, of work in city and recreation in nature with recreation in city and work in nature...)

It favours soft technique and 'soft future-research'[6], less prognosis, more clarification of possibilities. More sensitivity towards continuity and live traditions, and — most importantly — towards our state of ignorance.

The implementation of ecologically responsible policies requires in this century an exponential growth of technical skill and invention — but in new directions, directions which today are not consistently and liberally supported by the research policy organs of our nation-states.

(7) *Local autonomy and decentralization* [7]. The vulnerability of a form of life is roughly proportional to the weight of influences from afar, from outside the local region in which that form has obtained an ecological equilibrium. This lends support to our efforts to strengthen local self-government and material and mental self-

sufficiency. But these efforts presuppose an impetus towards decentralization. Pollution problems, including those of thermal pollution and recirculation of materials, also lead us in this direction, because increased local autonomy, if we are able to keep other factors constant, reduces energy consumption. (Compare an approximately self-sufficient locality with one requiring the importation of foodstuff, materials for house construction, fuel and skilled labour from other continents. The former may use only five per cent of the energy used by the latter.) Local autonomy is strengthened by a reduction in the number of links in the hierarchical chains of decision. (For example a chain consisting of local board, municipal council, highest sub-national decision-maker, a state-wide institution in a state federation, a federal national government institution, a coalition of nations, and of institutions, e. g. E. E. C. top levels, and a global institution, can be reduced to one made up of local board, nation-wide institution, and global institution.) Even if a decision follows majority rules at each step, many local interests may be dropped along the line, if it is too long.

Summing up, then, it should, first of all, be borne in mind that the norms and tendencies of the Deep Ecology movement are not derived from ecology by logic or induction. Ecological knowledge and the life-style of the ecological field-worker have *suggested, inspired, and fortified* the perspectives of the Deep Ecology movement. Many of the formulations in the above seven-point survey are rather vague generalizations, only tenable if made more precise in certain directions. But all over the world the inspiration from ecology has shown remarkable convergencies. The survey does not pretend to be more than one of the possible condensed codifications of these convergencies.

Secondly, it should be fully appreciated that the significant tenets of the Deep Ecology movement are clearly and forcefully *normative*. They express a value priority system only in part based on results (or lack of results, cf. point [6]) of scientific research. Today, ecologists try to influence policy-making bodies largely through threats, through predictions concerning pollutants and resource depletion, knowing that policy-makers accept at least certain minimum *norms* concerning health and just distribution. But it is clear that there is a vast number of people in all countries, and even a considerable number of people in power, who accept as valid the wider norms and values characteristic of the Deep Ecology movement. There are political potentials in this movement which should not be overlooked and which have little to do with pollution and resource depletion. In plotting possible futures, the norms should be freely used and elaborated.

Thirdly, in so far as ecology movements deserve our attention, they are *ecophilosophical* rather than ecological. Ecology is a *limited* science which makes *use* of scientific methods. Philosophy is the most general forum of debate on fundamentals, descriptive as well as prescriptive, and political philosophy is one of its subsections. By an *ecosophy* I mean a philosophy of ecological harmony or equilibrium. A philosophy as a kind of *sofia* wisdom, is openly normative, it contains *both* norms, rules, postulates, value priority announcements *and* hypotheses concerning the state of affairs in our universe. Wisdom is policy wisdom, prescription, not only scientific description and prediction.

The details of an ecosophy will show many variations due to significant differences concerning not only 'facts' of pollution, resources, population, etc., but also value priorities. Today, however, the seven points listed provide one unified framework for ecosophical systems.

In general system theory, systems are mostly conceived in terms of causally or functionally interacting or interrelated items. An ecosophy, however, is more like a system of the kind constructed by Aristotle or Spinoza. It is expressed verbally as a set of sentences with a variety of functions, descriptive and prescriptive. The basic relation is that between subsets of premises and subsets of conclusions, that is, the relation of derivability. The relevant notions of derivability may be classed according to rigour, with logical and mathematical deductions topping the list, but also according to how much is implicitly taken for granted. An exposition of an ecosophy must necessarily be only moderately precise considering the vast scope of relevant ecological and normative (social, political, ethical) material. At the moment, ecosophy might profitably use models of systems, rough approximations of global systematizations. It is the global character, not preciseness in detail, which distinguishes an ecosophy. It articulates and integrates the efforts of an ideal ecological team, a team comprising not only scientists from an extreme variety of disciplines, but also students of politics and active policy-makers.

Under the name of *ecologism*, various deviations from the deep movement have been championed — primarily with a one-sided stress on pollution and resource depletion, but also with a neglect of the great differences between under-and over-developed countries in favour of a vague global approach. The global approach is essential, but regional differences must largely determine policies in the coming years.

注释:

1. man-in-environment image，环境中人的形象。这里的环境中人是指，将人归于环境中的一部分，是一种环境整体论观。

2. in principle，原则上。这里加上原则上，是因为生物圈中不可能是一种绝对的公平、平等，而应该是一种相对的平等主义。

3. live and let live，相互宽容、相互依存的意思，either you or me，非你即我。这里相互宽容是一种相互联系、相互影响、共荣共存的普遍联系观，而非你即我则完全不同，它是一种孤立的世界观。

4. complexity, not complication，复杂而非杂乱。这里指明生态系统的确是一个非常复杂的生物圈，其具有多样性特征，但并非是一种杂乱的联系，而是一种系整体性的存在。

5. local autonomy and decentralization，地方自治与非中心化，加强地方部门对生态环境的职能。

6. soft future research，软未来研究。这里相对于软技术而言，软未来是指未来生态环境发展。

7. ecosophy，生态哲学，即研究生态平衡和生态和谐的一种崭新哲学。

8. ecologism，生态主义。

Karen J. Warren

凯伦·沃伦(1947—)，美国著名作家、学者，于明尼苏达大学获得学士学位，在马萨诸塞大学获得博士学位，执教于默士达大学。沃伦称自己为"街头哲学家"，一直致力于环境、伦理和女性思想领域的研究，此后发表多篇关于环境哲学的学术论文，著有《非传统西方哲学史:男性与女性的对话》《生态女性主义哲学:西方关于是什么和为什么重要之观点》《生态女性主义:女性、文化和自然》，沃伦对于生态文学批评的贡献在于她对生态女性主义理论的开拓性研究，推动了生态文学和女性批评理论的共同发展。

Introduction to Ecofeminism

(Warren, Karen. Introduction to Ecofeminism. *Environmental Philosophy*:

From Animal Rights to Radical Ecology. Michael E. Zimmerman, et al., eds. Upper Saddle River: Prentice-Hall, 1993, pp. 253-267.)

《生态女性主义简介》发表于1991年，对当时的文学理论界来讲，是第一篇介绍生态女性主义理论的文章。文章的开端系统梳理了生态女性主义的概念、主要特征，然后分析总结了女性和自然之间的联系，即在伦理、理论、政治、认识论、象征层面、实证和经验层面、历史层面都有深刻的联系，这也是生态主义和女性主义能够结合起来的重要原因。此外，该论文还探讨了生态批评与女性主义、环境主义和环境哲学以及哲学之间的联系。生态女性主义理论的提出，不仅是对生态哲学的又一重大贡献，同时也是对女性主义文学的一大贡献。

...

SOME ALLEGED CONNECTIONS BETWEEN FEMINISM AND THE ENVIRONMENT

There are at least eight sorts of connections that ecofeminists have identified. These alleged connections provide sometimes competing, sometimes mutually complementary or supportive, analyses of the nature of the twin dominations of women and nature. A casual, albeit philosophically uncritical, perusal of these eight alleged connections helps to identify the range and variety of ecofeminist positions on woman-nature connections.

1. *Historical, Typically Causal, Connections*. One alleged connection between women and nature is historical. When historical data are used to generate theories concerning the sources of the dominations of women and nature, it is also causal. So pervasive is the historical-causal theme in ecofeminist writing that Ariel Salleh practically defines ecofeminism in terms of it: "Eco-feminism is a recent development in feminist thought which argues that the current global environmental crisis is a predictable outcome of patriarchal culture."[1]

What are these alleged historical-causal connections? Some ecofeminists[2] trace these connections to prototypical patterns of domination begun with the invasion of Indo-European societies by nomadic tribes from Eurasia about 4500 B.C.[3]. Riane Eisler describes the time before these invasions as a "matrifocal, matrilineal, peaceful agrarian era." Others[4] trace historical connections to patriarchal dualisms and conceptions of rationality in classical Greek philosophy and the rationalist tradition. Still other feminists[5], this section focus on cultural and scientific changes that occurred more recently—during the scientific revolution of the sixteenth and seventeenth centuries: it was then that an older world order characterized by cooperation between humans and nature was replaced by a reductionist, "mechanistic world view of modern science," which sanctioned the exploitation of nature, unchecked commercial and industrial expansion, and the subordination of women.

What prompts and explains these alleged historical and causal woman-nature connections? What *else* was in place to permit and sanction these twin dominations? To answer these questions, ecofeminists have turned to the conceptual props that they claim keep these historical dominations in place.

2. *Conceptual Connections*. Many authors have argued that, ultimately, historical and causal links between the dominations of women and nature are located in conceptual structures of domination that construct women and nature in male-biased ways. Basically three such conceptual links have been offered.

One account locates a conceptual basis of the twin dominations of women and nature in *value dualisms*, i. e. , in disjunctive pairs in which the disjuncts are seen as oppositional (rather than as complementary) and as exclusive (rather than as inclusive), and *value hierarchies*, i. e. , perceptions of diversity organized by a spatial Up-Down metaphor, which attributes higher value (status, prestige) to that which is higher("Up"). Frequently cited examples of these hierarchically organized value dualisms include reason/emotion, mind/body, culture/nature, human/nature, and man/woman dichotomies. These theorists argue that whatever is historically associated with emotion, body, nature, and women is regarded as inferior to that which is (historically) associated with reason, mind, culture, human(i. e. , male) and men.

A second account expands on the first by housing the problematic value dualisms and value hierarchies in larger, oppressive conceptual frameworks--ones that are common to all social "isms of domination" (e. g. , sexism, racism, classism, heterosexism as well as "naturism, "i. e. , the unjustified domination of nonhuman nature. A conceptual framework is a socially constructed set of basic beliefs, values, attitudes and assumptions that shapes and reflects how one views oneself and others. It is oppressive when it explains, justifies, and maintains relationships of domination and subordination. An oppressive conceptual framework is *patriarchal* when it explains, justifies, and maintains the subordination of women by men.

Oppressive and patriarchal conceptual frameworks are characterized not only by value dualisms and hierarchies but also by "*power-over*" *conceptions of power* and relationships of domination and a *logic of domination*, i. e., a structure of argumentation that provides the moral premise that superiority justifies subordination[6]. On this view, it is oppressive and patriarchal conceptual frameworks, and the behaviors that they give rise to, that sanction, maintain, and perpetuate the twin dominations of women and nature.

A third account locates a conceptual basis in sex-gender differences, particularly in differentiated personality formation or consciousness. The claim is that female bodily experiences[7], not female biology *per se*, situate women differently with respect to nature than men. This sex-gender difference is (allegedly) revealed in a different consciousness in women than men toward nature; it is rooted conceptually in "paradigms that are uncritically oriented to the dominant western masculine forms of experiencing the world: the analytic, non-related, delightfully called 'objective' or 'scientific' approaches"[8]—just those value dualisms that are claimed to separate and inferiorize what is historically female-gender identified. These sociopsychological factors provide a conceptual link insofar as they are embedded in different conceptualization structures and strategies ("different ways of knowing"), coping strategies and way of relating to nature for women and men. A goal of ecofeminism then, is to develop gender-sensitive language, theory, and practices that do not further the exploitative experiences and habits of dissociated, male-gender identified culture toward women and nature.

One project of ecofeminism is to expose and dismantle the conceptual structures of domination which have kept various "isms of domination," particularly the dominations of women and nature, in place. If ecofeminists who allege various conceptual woman-nature connections are correct, this will involve reconceiving those mainstay philosophical notions which rely on them (e. g., notions of reason and rationality, knowledge, objectivity, ethics, and the knowing, moral self).

3. *Empirical and Experiential Connections*. Many ecofeminists have focused on uncovering empirical evidence linking women (and children, people of color, the underclass) with environmental destruction. Some point to various health and risk factors borne disproportionately by women children, racial minorities and the poor caused by the presence of low-level radiation, pesticides, toxics, and other pollutants. Others provide data to show that First World development policies result in policies and practices regarding food, forest, and water, which directly contribute to the inability of women to provide adequately for themselves and their families.

Feminist animal rights scholars argue that factory farming, animal experimentation, hunting, and meat eating are tied to patriarchal concepts and practices. Some connect rape and pornography with male-gender identified abuse of both women and nature. Appeal to such empirical data is intended both to document the very real, felt, lived "experiential" connections between the dominations of women and nature and to motivate the need for joining together feminist critical analysis and environmental concerns.

Sometimes, however, the empirical and experiential connections between women and nature are intended to reveal important cultural and spiritual ties to the earth honored and celebrated by (some) women and indigenous peoples. This suggests that some woman-nature connections are features of important symbol systems.

4. *Symbolic Connections*. Some ecofeminists have explored the symbolic association and devaluation of women and nature that appears in religion, theology, art, and literature. Documenting such connections and making them integral to the project of ecofeminism is often heralded as ecofeminism's most promising contribution to the creation of liberating, life-affirming, and postpatriarchal worldviews and earth-based spiritualties or theologies. Ecofeminism is then presented as offering alternative spiritual symbols[9], spiritualties or theologies, and even utopian societies. Appreciating such symbolic woman-nature connections involves understanding "the politics of women's spirituality"[10].

Some ecofeminist theorists draw on literature, particularly "nature writing," to unpack the nature of the woman-nature linguistic symbolic connections. Literary criticism of the sort offered by Patrick Murphy claims that patriarchal conceptions of nature and women have justified "a two-pronged rape and domination of the earth and the women who live on it"[11], often using this as background for developing an ecofeminist literary theory.

Some theorists focus on language, particularly the symbolic connections between sexist and naturist language, i. e., language that inferiorizes women and nonhuman nature by naturalizing women and feminizing nature. For example, there are concerns about whether ex-gendered language used to describe "Mother Nature" is, inYnestra King's words, "potentially liberating or simply a rationale for the continued subordination of women"[12]. There are concerns about connections between the languages used to describe women, nature, and nuclear weaponry. Women are often described in animal terms (e. g., as cows, foxes, chicks, serpents, bitches, beavers, old bats, pussycats, cats, bird-brains, hare-brains). Nature is often described in female and sexual terms: nature is raped, mastered, conquered, controlled, mined. Her "secrets" are "penetrated" and her "womb" is put into the services of the "man of science." "Virgin timber" is felled, cut down. "Fertile soil" is tilled and land that lies "fallow" is "barren," useless. The claim is that language that so feminizes nature and naturalizes women describes, reflects, and perpetuates the domination and inferiorization of both by failing to see the extent to which the twin dominations of women and nature (including animals) are, in fact, culturally (and not merely figuratively) analogous. The development of theory and praxis in feminism and environmental philosophy that does not perpetuate such sexist-naturist language and the power over systems of domination they reinforce is, therefore, a goal of ecofeminism.

5. *Epistemological Connections*. The various alleged historical, causal conceptual, empirical, and symbolic woman-nature connections (discussed above) have also motivated the need for new, ecofeminist epistemologies. Typically these emerging epistemologies build on scholarship currently under way in feminist philosophy, which challenges mainstream views of reason, rationality, knowledge, and the nature of the knower. As Val Plumwood suggests in this section, if one mistakenly construes environmental philosophy as only or primarily concerned with ethics, one will neglect "a key aspect of the overall problem, which is concerned with the definition of the human self as separate from nature, the connection between this and the instrumental view of nature, and broader *political* aspects of the critique of instrumentalism"[13]. For Plumwood, ecofeminist epistemologies must critique rationalism in the Western philosophical tradition and develop views of the ethical, knowing self that do not maintain and perpetuate harmful value dualisms and hierarchies, particularly human-nature ones.

Some feminists appeal to the critical theory of Horkheimer, Adorno, Balbus, and the Frankfurt circle, claiming that "their epistemology and substantive analysis both point to a convergence of feminist and ecological concerns, anticipating the more recent arrival of eco-feminism"[14]. For these feminists, "critical theory" provides a critique of the "nature versus culture" dichotomy and an epistemological structure for critiquing the relationships between the domination of women and the domination of nature.

6. *Political* (*Praxis*) *Connections*. Francoised Eaubonne introduced the term

"ecofeminisme" in 1974 to bring attention to women's potential for ecological revolution. Ecofeminism has always been a grassroots political movement motivated by pressing pragmatic concerns. These range from issues of women's and environmental health, to science, development and technology, the treatment of animals, and peace, antinuclear, antimilitarist activism. The varieties of ecofeminist perspectives on the environment are properly seen as an attempt to take seriously such grassroots activism and political concerns by developing analyses of domination that explain, clarify, and guide that praxis.

7. *Ethical Connections*. To date, most of the philosophical literature on woman-nature connections has appeared in the area of environmental philosophy known as "environmental ethics." The claim is that the interconnections among the conceptualizations and treatment of women, animals, and (the rest of) nature require a feminist ethical analysis and response. Minimally, the goal of ecofeminist environmental ethics is to develop theories and practices concerning humans and the natural environment that are not male-biased and provide a guide to action in the prefeminist present (Warren 1990). This may involve developing an ecofeminist ethic of care and appropriate reciprocity, ecofeminist kinship ethics, ecofeminist animal rights positions, an ecofeminist social ecology or ecofeminist bioregionalism. As Plumwood and Warren claim in their essays in this section, mainstream environmental ethics are inadequate to the extent that they are problematically anthropocentric or hopelessly androcentric.

8. *Theoretical Connections*. The varieties of alleged woman-nature connections discussed above have generated different, sometimes competing, theoretical positions in all areas of feminist and environmental philosophy. Nowhere is this more evident than in the field of environmental ethics. Primarily because of space limitations, the discussion of "theoretical connections" offered here is restricted to environmental ethics.

In many respects, contemporary environmental ethics reflects the range of positions in contemporary philosophical ethics. The latter includes traditional consequentialist (e. g., ethical egoist, utilitarian) and nonconsequentialist or deontotogical (e. g., Kantian, rights-based, virtue-based) positions, as well as challenges to them by nontraditional (e. g., some feminist, existentialist, Marxist, Afrocentric, non-Western) approaches. Such is also the case in environmental ethics. There are consequentialist (e. g., ethical egoist, eco-utilitarian, utilitarian-based animal liberation ethics) and nonconsequentailist (e. g., rights-based animal liberation, stewardship ethics) approaches that extend traditional ethical considerations to include animals and the nonhuman environment. (Some would argue that these are not *bona fide* environmental ethics, since they do not make then atural environment itself deserving of moral consideration.) There also are nontraditional approaches (e. g., holistic Leopoldian land ethics, social ecology, deep ecology, ecological feminism) that raise considerations underplayed or omitted entirely from mainstream philosophical ethics. Feminists who address environmental issues can be found advocating positions within this broad philosophical range. So where do ecological feminists fit in?

Where one thinks ecological feminists fit in will depend largely on what one means by "ecological feminism." If ecological feminism is an umbrella term for any feminism that raises feminist concerns about the environment, then presumably ecofeminists can be found along the continuum of feminist-inspired and advocated environmental ethics (or, environmental philosophy). If, however, the term "ecological feminism" is used as I am using the term and as it is used by the authors in this section, viz., as the name for a variety of positions expressly committed to exploring woman-nature connections (of the sort identified above) and to developing feminist and environmental philosophies based on these insights, then ecological feminism is best viewed as one of several nontraditional approaches to environmental ethics and philosophy. We are back to where we began: "ecological feminism" is the name of a variety of positions that make visible different sorts of woman-nature connections, claiming that an understanding of these connections is necessary for any adequate feminism, environmentalism, or environmental philosophy. Whether the connections alleged and the arguments advanced in support of them are accepted on feminist and philosophical grounds is a question the friendly critic must answer.

注释：

1. "生态女性主义是女性思想在当下的最新发展，当下的全球环境危机正是父权制文化的结果。" 见 Salleh，Ariel Kay 的文章《生产的隐喻和认识论：一种生态女性主义批评理论》，收录在《人文学科研究》，由 Patrick Murphy 主编，第 130 至 139 页。

2. (e. g., Spretnak 1990；Eisler 1988，1990) 见查伦·斯普瑞特奈克的文章《生态女性主义：我们的根和花》，收录在《重组世界：生态女性主义的出现》，由 Irene Diamond 和 Glorla Femen Orenstein 主编。

3. Lahar, Stephanie. 1991. Ecofeminist theory and grassroots politics, *Hypatia*, 6 (1): 28-45.

4. 这里其他学者指苏珊·格里芬（Susan Griffin），她在专著《女性和自然：她内心的呼喊》中提到类似的观点；还有其他学者，如 Plumwood，以及 Ruether Rosemary Radford。

5. 这里持有相同观点的学者还包括 Susan Griffin，Plumwood，Ruether Rosemary Radford。

6. Karen, Waren. 1987. Feminism and ecology: making connections, *Environmental Ethics* 9 (1): 3-20.

7. 这里特指女性生育和抚养孩子特有的经历。

8. 见 Salleh，Ariel Kay 的文章《生产的隐喻和认识论：一种生态女性主义批评理论》，收录在《人文学科研究》，由 Patrick Murphy 主编，第 130 页。

9. 比如盖亚和其他女神形象。

10. 见查伦·斯普瑞特奈克的专著《女性精神的政治维度》。

11. Murphy, Patrick. 1988. Introduction: feminism, ecology, and the future of the humanities *Studies in the Humanities*. Special issue on feminism, ecology, and the future of the humanities. 15 (2): 85-9.

12. "Feminism and the Revolt of Nature," in *Heresies* 13 *Feminism and Ecology* 4 (1): 12-16.

13. Plumwood, Val. 1991. Nature, self, and gender: feminism, environmental philosophy and the critique of rationalism, *Hypatia*, 6 (1): 3-37.

14. Epistemology and the Metaphors of Production: an eco-feminist reading of critical theory, in *Studies in the Humanities*. Special issue on feminism, ecology, and the future of the humanities, ed. Patrick Murphy. 15 (2): 130-39.

Chapter Sixteen **Ecological Postmodernism**

生态后现代主义是于20世纪末在美国兴起的一股崭新的后现代生态思想，是生态批评理论的后现代转向，也是后现代理论在当下的最新发展，其以斯普瑞特奈克的专著《真实之复兴：极度现代的世界中的身体、自然和地方》的出版为主要标志。主要代表人物包括查伦·斯普瑞特奈克（Charlene Spretnak）、大卫·格里芬（David Griffin）、理查德·罗蒂（Richard Rorty），以及大卫·霍伊（David Hoy）等。生态后现代主义理论批判了解构性后现代主义的时代局限性，它深度批判现代性危机，将现代性意识形态的表现总结为：经济人假设、工业主义、客观主义、理性主义、机械论世界观、标准化、官僚政治、人类中心论、与自然对立和轻视乡下人、分隔化、逃离宗教和宇宙论背景的缩小以及极度男性论。正是在解构性后现代主义和现代性的基础上，生态后现代主义才提出了解决现代性危机的救赎之路。

在汲取生态批评理论精髓的基础上，生态后现代主义拓展了理论内涵。首先，生态后现代主义主张建构尊重自然、关爱生命、融于地方的生态环境意识。它以相互联系的关系思维拓展了生命与物质之间的动态关系。该理论认为，在地球共同体中，每一个宇宙生命的形式尽管不同，它们之中没有一个是孤立地存在着，意识到这样一种生态整体观，人类应该树立一种"生态自我观"，颠覆传统的"人类中心主义"，将自我概念延伸到环境和地球层面，担负起地球生态守护神的重要职责。这就需要人类必须与现代性意识形态做斗争。重建真实的"身体"、"自然"和"地方"。"身体"是指统一的身心，具有认知能力、能够与周围环境相协调，并且为生存做积极的抗争；"自然"是孕育、滋养生命，具有主体性的"返魅"的自然，是人类生存的重要活动场所；"地方"是指人类赖以生存、实现情感依附的物理背景。

生态后现代主义理论的第二个维度指向技术，它积极引导现代技术应用的道德化、生态化和人性化发展。它反对人类对技术的一味膜拜所导致的人性异化，即所谓技术的复杂就是"幸福生活"，技术的革新就是"社会进步"，技术的应用就是"发展完善"，也批判了现代媒介技术对真实生活的歪曲以及对人类真实情感的压制。理想的技术发展观应该罢黜技术的统治地位，引导技术沿着富含人文情怀、造福人类的方向发展。

生态后现代主义第三个维度指向社会生存维度，它积极推进生态政府的建设，批判基于经济增长和物质生活水平提高为标准的衡量政府执政能力的误区，认为生态政府应该以生态普遍联系性为指导思想，全面拒绝对自然资源掠夺式的经济发展战略。生态政府的完善还有赖于草根民主建设，草根组织、绿色社团的存在都会对政府管理能力形成一种重要的鞭策力量。

生态后现代主义还涵盖人类生存的精神维度，它弘扬真实的传统文化，建构真实的世界观，敦促人们追寻后现代时期的生存意义。它以生态原则为基石的思想并未局限于生态系统，而是拓展了人类的精神世界，以一种关系思维来维护自我与他人、社会、环境以及各种共同体的关系，至此才能实现人类与自然的和谐发展、共存共荣。

生态后现代主义是一种健康的、积极的后现代生态观，是重构性后现代主义或者建设性后现代主义的重要组成部分。它源于对后工业社会中人类的生存状况与命运的反思，深刻批判现代性思维模式导致的异化世界，主张建立生态整体思想和真实的世界观，传承拯救人类的生命共同体精神。它试图重构一种和谐、民主和生命之间相互关爱的生态社会，恢复人与人、人与世界之间的相互联系。生态后现代主义主张的宇宙间万物的普遍联系性不仅丰富和推进了生态批评理论，构建了一种崭新的后现代生态思想，而且对于人类社会"共同福祉"蓝图的实现有着重要的时代意义。

Charlene Spretnak

查伦·斯普瑞特奈克(1946—)，出生于美国宾夕法尼亚州的匹兹堡，本科和研究生期间主修英语，同时兼修哲学和心理学。加州大学伯克利分校研究生毕业后留校，后转到圣名大学文化与创造精神研究所工作，现为美国加州整合研究院教授，讲授哲学与宗教课程。迄今为止，她已经参与组织、策划了5次有关生态后现代主义的国际研讨会。她的工作在精神性、文化史、女权主义和其他社会批评以及生态学思想(绿色政治、生态女权主义运动、生态哲学)等领域得到国际认可。主要著作包括《绿色政治：全球的许诺》《绿色政治的精神维度》《真实之复兴：极度现代的世界中的身体、自然和地方》等。

The Complex Sense of Place

(Spretnak, Charlene. *The Resurgence of the Real: Body, Nature, and Place in a Hypermodern World*. New York: Routledge, 1997, pp. 11-36.)

1997年,查伦·斯普瑞特奈克出版了她的著作《真实之复兴:极度现代的世界中的身体、自然和地方》,这是一部关于她创立的生态后现代主义理论的重要文献。斯普瑞特奈克在本书中分析了现代性思维模式导致的种种危机,如生态恶化、道德滑坡、技术霸权、精神颓废以及断裂的身心,这个星球中身体、自然和地方都成为极不真实的存在。不仅如此,她在书中细致梳理了人类历史上对技术一直以来的反对的呼声,分析总结了目前发达国家存在的社会发展问题。斯普瑞特奈克认为重建真实的身体、自然和地方是建构整体性生态社会意识形态,将人类的生存境况和前途命运同整个地球共同体的未来联系起来思考,通过生态整体性视角,救赎整个人类社会,摆脱现代性危机,开辟出一条具有划时代意义的生态复兴之路。

In the modern worldview, place[1] is not important except as a springboard from which the salvific ideology of progress would launch its grand trajectory. Place was associated with constraint: the binding ties of community, extended family, and tradition, as well as the local demands of nature. The heroic figures of modern literature boldly escape their place of origin and head for the new promised land: the city, with its sprawling urban *potential rising* from flattened hills and filled-in stream beds, offering anonymity and a heady autonomy in exchange for nearly everything else. Modernist architecture and design liberated itself from the local and the vernacular by a fierce reduction to sterile minimalism that is truly cosmopolitan, reflecting no place and no culture, only an ideology of freedom through denial. Examples of the International style of skyscrapers and kindred versions of the "dumb box"[2] are nearly interchangeable, having gone forcefully beyond the constraints of place. With a similar sophistication, modern political boundaries have often been drawn with disdain for the integrity of place—with disastrous consequences that are now intensifying.

In recent years a different sort of disengagement from place has emerged alongside the modern: The deconstructionist postmodern analysis asserts that we never actually know anything about our local patch of the biosphere because we can know only the concepts our particular society has invented (including language and science) to refer to the natural world. While the more dogmatic forms of this orientation have finally faded, a softer "constructionist" version remains influential among many intellectuals today. It spawns books and articles that perceive only a oneway creative power: the projection by humans of their "social constructions" onto nature.[3] All this seems exceedingly odd—and more than a little pathological—to traditional native peoples, for instance. From an early age, they pay a great deal of attention to the dynamics of the natural world, both individually and collectively. They observe with great sensitivity the dramas, rhythms, and *presence* of place.

Even children who have been schooled in modernity's radical discontinuity between humans and nature often have a profound engagement with a natural place—a summer camp, a grandparent's farm, or a hideaway spot near home. Throughout Their lives they carry in their minds that sense of place, a place they came to know with a child's deep capacity for personal response. The presence of a place evoked their interiority and shaped their unfolding, offering over the years refuge and sustenance, stability and grace.

A two-way process of communication[4], then, situates a people in place over hundreds or thousands of years. In fact, premodern and nonmodern cultures have no meaning or definition if their essential connection with place is denied. Yet their freedom to interact with place has most often been usurped and directed by conceptual inventions such as the modern nation-state. Even worse, their identity as a people-of-place has often been deliberately suppressed by the modern state in order to create a new cosmopolitan, modern society.

Viewed through the lens of the modem worldview, the contemporary crises and revolts that threaten the political status quo in many nationstates appear to be sporadic, unrelated occurrences that simply need to be brought under order and control. Modern institutions—nation-states, the media, corporations, the social sciences—cannot hear the "noise" of these rebellions as anything other than bothersome aberrations, lacking common ground or deep cause. Nonetheless, challenges to both the ideological assumptions and conditions of modern statehood are driving many of the crucial events of our time. If awareness of that dynamic eludes most people, it is because the news of the day is perceived, shaped, and presented to us through the filter of the modern worldview. One could hardly expect the modern media to do otherwise. Yet another perspective is possible, one that makes sense of seemingly baffling events by bringing attention to a broader and deeper context than the ideology of modernity allows.

The independence efforts of such peoples as the Kurds, Basques, Tibetans, Chechnyans, Slovenians, and Croatians can best be understood in the context of the thousands of *nations* (long-standing or indigenous cultural entities) whose ancient territory has been surrounded or divided by the boundaries of modern *nation-states*, either capitalist or communist. Since no level of autonomy below the state is recognized by die modern political system, these nations have no legal forum in which to present their case for sovereignty. The United Nations, the European Union, die North Atlantic Treaty Organization (NATO), and so forth are all clubs whose membership is open only to sovereign states. Consequently, 72 percent of the wars fought since World War II have been wars of independence initiated by ancient nations that have been gobbled up by modern states.[5] These independence efforts are invariably called "insurgencies," "ethnic uprisings," or regressive "tribalism" by diplomats and the media. They are usually viewed as disruptions of peace and stability that rightfully should be crushed by the state. That policy has created 23 million refugees worldwide, plus another 26 million displaced persons who have remained within the borders of their nation-state. A network called Unrepresented Nations and Peoples Organization (UNPO), headquartered in The Hague, estimates that there are some five thousand unrepresented nations, many of which are indigenous. Not all of them are pressing for total independence; some would prefer to be a largely autonomous unit within the surrounding state.

The yearning for freedom is not going to disappear among the "captive nations," as they have been dubbed by Richard Falk, a scholar of international law. Their deep love of place and tradition has not been replaced with the standardized culture imposed by a centralized modern state. The modern drive to homogenize cultural differences eventually overpowered the principle of tolerance that was foundational in the secular state. In hindsight, a confederal model would have been a wiser choice than the federal model whenever modem states were formed by the merging of ancient nations. In that way, ethnic and regional identity could have been formally honored at the same time the Enlightenment values of human rights and tolerance were adopted. Instead, the domination and elimination of difference has resulted in patterns of persecution and loss played out over generations.

The moral impulse propelling attempts to achieve self-determination has exposed a critical flaw in the very meaning of the modern state. That meaning is understood to derive from a mandate, or social contract, to defend territorial borders, exercise sovereignty, maintain domestic order, support the economic system of choice (capitalist or socialist), further prosperity, and, as Max Weber noted, legitimize all violence conducted by the state. Only recently has a full sense of state-sponsored violence come to wide attention through the voices of captive nations. Those whose geopolitical situations are sufficiently strategic to make "the news" tell of enforced suppression of their language, traditional culture, and religion. It has seemed perfectly correct, and indeed progressive, for the modern state to "phase out" such "backward" vestiges because its own origins are rooted in that very dynamic, that is, liberation from tradition. Leaping beyond the despotic rule of kings and cardinals, however, need not have included a sweeping contempt for all deeply rooted cultures of spirit and place[6]. In the name of efficiency (and control), a standardized dominant culture was enforced. Modern France, for example, insisted until quite recently that all children be named after figures in French history or the Judeo-Christian tradition, thereby rendering illegal the ancient Celtic names traditionally given to children in Brittany. The U. S. federal government forced several generations of Native American children to attend boarding schools where they were beaten if they spoke their own language, even privately. The communist attitude was similar: Forced assimilation into the modern mold, with no respect for traditional culture, was the rule for dozens of ancient nations within the borders of the Soviet Union and the People's Republic of China. Now that the flattening of diversity has assumed global proportions through mass media and ubiquitous marketing, the protection of particularity has taken on a poignant urgency—at least for all those cultural nations struggling to survive.

It is rarely made clear in news coverage of those struggles, however, that the outbreak of war is not *caused* by the captive nations seeking freedom. A *violent, military response is chosen* by the state in response to an independence vote or declaration. The captive nations merely want to leave, not engage in warfare, especially not with the comparatively huge military capabilities of the state's armed forces. The modern states *could* choose to bid the newly independent nations a fond farewell and begin negotiating regional compacts with them for trade, transportation, and so forth. However, modern states are under no pressure to do so because the dominant interpretation of the principle of self-determination in international law since World War Ⅱ considers secessionist efforts to be legitimate only in situations of colonized nations seeking to break free from an empire. Ancient nations who have been "colonized" at closer range have no standing. For that reason, modern nation-states are free to unleash devastating reprisals against their captive nations who attempt liberation.

In recent years an argument has been put forth by several legal scholars for expanding the category of legal independence efforts to include ancient nations surrounded or divided by modern states. A strong interpretation of this extension would make military or other reprisals by states clearly illegal, once a bona fide independence vote had been taken in the seceding nation. Had that been the case when the three independence votes were taken in the former Yugoslavia (first in Slovenia, then in Croatia, then in Bosnia), the federal government (by then mostly Serbian) would not have been permitted to call out its armed forces and retaliate with impunity—first by bombing the capital of Slovenia and later by bombing scores of villages, towns, and cities in Croatia and, still later, in Bosnia. Neither would the federal government have been permitted to incite and supply surrogate groups (Bosnian Serbs in Bosnia, Krajina Serbs in Croatia) with weapons and other material support. In the absence of international law that would recognize captive nations, the international community felt from the beginning that it could not intervene in a conflict taking place within the borders of a modern state. Consequently, federal and surrogate-federal bombings of civilian targets (including irreplaceable medieval churches and museums), plus the establishment of rape camps and concentration camps with starvation rations, were allowed to continue *for four years*.

There are scores of Slovenias, Croatias, and Bosnias all over the world, risking devastating retribution by their quest for freedom. The fact that these three independence wars took place in south-central Europe made them more newsworthy than the others, thereby focusing attention on the shocking paralysis, for a very long while, of the United Nations, NATO, the European Union, and the international community at large. It is possible that the wrong lesson will be learned from the protracted carnage in the former Yugoslavia—that the international community' should quickly supply all means of military aid to states facing secessionist efforts so that the "illegal" freedom-fighters will be crushed as soon as possible, resulting in minimum loss of life to all parties. This, after all, was the attitude expressed by the U. S. ambassador to Yugoslavia when it became clear that Belgrade would opt for a military response to the independence votes: The United States supports "stability in the region" at all costs.

"All costs" includes billions of dollars paid to the U. S. arms industry by governments around the world that are engaged in military responses to the independence efforts of captive nations. In 1994 and 1995, our country contributed $ 12 billion of exports annually to the global arms trade—four times more than

Germany or Russia, who are the second-and third-largest exporters of arms, respectively. Arms manufacturers in the United States received $ 7.6 billion of taxpayer subsidies in 1995, while 6395 arms salesmen employed by the Pentagon peddled their wares abroad. Many of die arms customers insist that production facilities and jobs be located in their own countries, with the result that American arms deals now produce more jobs overseas than in the United States.[7]

Half of U.S. arms sales are made to Third World governments, many of whom have "separatist problems" within their borders. Several Third World countries have themselves become suppliers of small arms for such conflicts. The enormous global arms industry today props up countless economies, in both the northern and southern hemispheres, and is largely dependent on the protraction of the independence wars.

The political emergence of the captive nations, even peacefully, raises questions, of course. The growing effort to restructure the United Nations, for instance, already includes several proposals to accommodate a much greater number of members, plus stronger regional organization. In addition, the principle of human rights, certainly the crown of modern political philosophy, could be combined with the actions to correct the modern subjugation of ancient nations: The newly independent nations would be granted diplomatic recognition by the international community only if their constitutions guarantee human rights to all residents. Harrassment of ethnic or religious minorities would result in various international sanctions. What this essentially means is a return to place as the focal point in territorial claims, rather than ownership based on the supposedly pure bloodlines of the majority group who have lived there for a long while. A plurality of peoples now inhabit most places on this earth. A peaceful future requires honoring that diversity, both culturally and legally, as the new orientation for the continuing unfolding of ecosocial communities in millions of places worldwide.

The problems are not insurmountable, but their solutions can grow only from *a post* modern recognition of the moral legitimacy of self-determination for ancient nations. The independence wars are not freak events but desperate efforts at cultural survival. They are unfathomable only to those who believe *pax moderna* to be the sole rational arrangement.

A second area in which place has become a focus is the emergent challenge to the destructive effects of the globalized economy. The assumption underlying the euphoric claims for the global market, now structured by the rules of the Global

Agreement on Tariffs and Trade (GATT), is that every nation will earn most of its income from exports. Nearly every conservative and every liberal party in every modern nation-state in the world today supports this model, in spite of the fact that basing one's future on conditions in distant markets is extraordinarily insecure. Advocates for the global economy, who until recently included most editorial writers in American newspapers, regard it as the bearer of unbounded potential, a rising tide that will lift all boats. True believers see it as an evolutionary triumph with spiritual overtones. Alas, it is difficult to accept that spiritual spin unless one truly feels that the universe harbors a teleological urge to have Planet Earth controlled by transnational corporations, for that is the outcome of global "free trade" as structured by GATT. Even books that tout the supposed decentralization of computerized trade as a boon for small entrepreneurs often let slip the truth about the new game: It is largely about market shares for the big boys. For example, John Naisbitt's almost delirious declaration of unlimited opportunities for anyone with a laptop— *Global Paradox: The Bigger the World Economy the More Powerful the Smallest Players* (1994)—admits that large portions of the market share for various products in, say, China are already controlled by transnational corporations.[8] When five firms control more than half of a global market, that market is considered to be highly monopolistic. In 1993, *The Economist* reported concentration ratios for twelve global industries. The greatest concentration was found in consumer durables, where the top five firms control nearly 70 percent of the entire world market in their industry. In the automotive, airline, aerospace, electronic components, electrical and electronic, and steel industries, the top five firms control more than 50 percent of the global market, clearly placing them in the monopoly category. In the oil, personal computer, and media industries, the top five firms control more than 40 percent of sales, thus showing strong monopolistic tendencies.[9]

Centralization of ownership through expansion of the biggest firms will increase under the renegotiated version of GATT, which now makes it illegal for any national, state, or local government to enforce its internal laws for environmental protection, labor protection, or community-based economics if any transnational corporation considers any of those laws to be burdensome or "prejudicial" to the sale of any of their products or services. In fact, shortly after GATT went into effect in 1994, three grievances were filed with the World Trade Organization (WTO) against the United States by foreign enterprises claiming that a U. S. law was a "restraint against free trade." Daimler-Benz argued that the American miles-per-gallon requirement is prejudicial to their most luxurious model of Mercedes-Benz; oil producers in Brazil and Venezuela asserted that the U. S. law requiring them to clean their raw oil before marketing it in this country is prejudicial against them; and the Mexican fishing industry argued that the U. S. law prohibiting the importation of tuna caught with the type of nets that also trap dolphins is an unfair restraint against their product. In each case, the grievance was decided in favor of the petitioners by the arbitration panel at the WTO in Geneva, which is neither elected nor accountable to anyone. When a country loses in a grievance decision, they must either change their internal law or pay the filer of the grievance the amount of money lost to them because of the "prejudicial" law. In short, GATT redefines "free trade" to mean that transnational corporations are free to do anything they want; no one else is.

All this was forewarned prior to Congress's approval of GATT and NAFTA (son of GATT) in a well-argued collection of essays by Ralph Nader, William Grieder, Margaret Atwood, Jerry Brown, Herman Daly, Wendell Berry, and others: *The Case against "Free Trade"* (1993). Not one newspaper or magazine in the United States reviewed that book. Nor did the media shine their spotlight on any opponents of the highly undemocratic trade agreements except for the most eccentric representative, Ross Perot. A critical examination of those trade treaties finally got a boost more than two years later, when Pat Buchanan made them an issue in his campaign for the Republican nomination for President in the spring of 1996; however, his right-wing views muddied the waters.

As the industrialized nations are gradually figuring out, the new world order imposed by the globalized economy means a race to the bottom for everyone, as jobs are eliminated in the name of global competitiveness or exported and the transnational corporations assume a level of power above any government. Even in a country like India, where 10 percent of the 980,000,000 residents comprise a new middle class that has benefited from the globalized presence of transnationals, the other 90 percent are simply not in the plan for the dazzling future. The 10 percent with disposable income constitute a large enough market to cause salivation among the global players: India is called a great success story!

Because the resources of the transnationals can crush any competition, especially with the carte blanche afforded by GATT, communities all over the world are now vulnerable to the insecurity and destructive effects of the global market. The alternative of community-based economics and regional trade, however, is rapidly gaining adherents. In the first half of the 1990s, many lending agencies, development programs, and foundations shifted their focus to micro-loans for very small-scale entrepreneurs, usually Third World women both in villages and among the urban poor. The demand for small-scale, sustainable economic development, in fact, emerged as a dominant concern at the Fourth United Nations Conference on Women in Beijing in 1995. The hypermodern dream of a globalized cyber-economy is also being challenged in the United States by a growing focus on community-based enterprises and organizations, including micro-loan programs, nonprofit corporations that build housing, and farmers' markets and other types of community-supported agriculture. The security, both economic and social, of *place* is now the countervalent focus as the global market continues to intensify.

注释:

1. 斯普瑞特奈克在本书中谈到的地方概念比较抽象。 首先，地方不同于空间，地方比空间更具体化、实体化；其次，地方更能够引起人们的遐想，地方也更容易与人类生存环境相联系。这里的地方可大可小，可以具体指某一场所，也可以指较大的人类生存的物理背景。 地方具有生态意义，产生重要话语，是集集体记忆与个人记忆于一体的重要场所。

2. 无声的盒子。 这里斯普瑞特奈克关注的是现代大城市中的建筑物，它们在现代性思维模式的束缚下，呈现出千篇一律的格式化风格，隔断了与地方原有的历史文化之间的联系，因此，“无声的盒子”这一比喻凸显了地方中历史文化感的缺失。 这一点在伊格尔顿的《人生的意义》中也有论述，即地方蜕变为意义流逝的帮凶。

3. 西蒙 · 沙玛在其专著《风景与记忆》中曾对自然与历史之间的关系展开论述，他有趣地对人类历史及文化层面向自然投射的各种方式都进行了研究，但是，这一关系中的另一方面——自然对人类言说及对人类行为的反应的方式——缺失了，这也是现代书评中作者没有注意到的忽视。

4. 这里的交流的双向过程即人类与地方之间的双向互动。

5. 这一数据统计见 Bernard Nietschmann, “Third World War,” *Cultural Survival Quarterly*, vol. 11, no. 3, 1987, 1-15. Also see *State of the Peoples: A Global Human Rights Reports on Societies in Danger*, by the Cultural Survival Center Staff (Boston: Beacon Press, 1993)。

6. 地方的复杂性还体现在地方文化面临着标准化的文化逐步加强的压力，从而将独特的地方文化逐步淘汰。

7. Jon Stewart, “Arms merchants as Welfare Kings”. 其中，所引数据来自世界政策研究所 William Hartung 最近的披露报告。 1996 年由国会研究中心 Richard Gimmett 所写的一个报告认为，俄罗斯 1995 年在把武器卖给发展中国家方面于美国之前徐徐前行；参见 “Russia Once Again

Is Top Seller of Arms to Developing Nations"，这份报告注明，从1992—1995年，美国对发展中国家销售武器的比例已达到45.3%。

8. John Naisbitt 的 Global Paradox: The Bigger the World Economy, the More Powerful Its Smallest Players, New York: Morrow, 1994, p. 74。

9. "A Survey of Multinationals: Everybody's Favorite Monsters", The Economist, London. March 27, 1993, p. 17;引自 David C. Koten, *When Corporations Rule the World*, West Hartford, CT and San Francisco: Kumarian Press and Berrett-Koehler, 1995, p. 233。

Relational Revelations

(Spretnak, Charlene. *Relational Reality: New Discoveries of Interrelatedness That Are Translating the Modern World*. Topsham, ME: Green Horizon Books, 2011, pp. 1-21.)

2011年，斯普瑞特奈克出版《关系现实：改变现代世界的相互联系性》这本重要专著。在这本书中，她指出，目前我们人类对现实自然世界之间的深度关系认识肤浅。她引用物理学和心理学的最新研究成果说明我们所处的自然世界之间联系的复杂性，这种相互联系性不仅是动态的，而且具有创造性，并且列举了许多现实生活中联系观的最新研究成果，这就颠覆了人们对自然世界的旧有观点，即它们太抽象了而不可能有任何关系。这些关系现实的发现改变了人类研究的每个领域，如教育、育儿、医疗、医疗机构的设计、政府建设、社区绿化以及经济活动。

Our hypermodern societies currently possess only a kindergarten-level understanding of the deeply relational nature of reality. It may seem unlikely that such advanced cultures could have missed "the way the world works," but it was simply a matter of habit. Out cultural tendency had been to perceive the physical world as an aggregate of separate entities. We noticed some relationships between and among things, of course, but those seemed of marginal significance compared to what things are made of and how they function.

The failure to notice that reality is inherently dynamic and interrelated at all levels-including substance and functioning-has caused a vast range of suffering: our medical system designed treatments as if our bodies were biomachines with independently functioning parts; our education systems regarded students as essentially isolate units into which learning can be implanted; our psychologists authoritatively conveyed to patients the Freudian notion that separating from core family relationships is the key to healthy maturation; and our workplaces and dwellings were designed with no inkling of the relationship between human health and natural light. Moreover, our communities have become fragmented and alienating, as the focus of modern life has largely contracted to the sphere by support for the social fabric. Even more tragically, the entire planet is now imperiled by climate destabilization and ecological degradation, resulting from the modern assumption that highly advanced societies could throw toxic substances "away" somewhere and could exude staggeringly unnatural levels of carbon dioxide and other greenhouse gases into our atmosphere without ill effect.

In recent years, however, the medical profession's general advice about staying healthy-eat nutritious food, get sufficient exercise, get a full night's sleep, avoid smoking, and wash hands often during could and flu season—was joined by an incongruous addition: have friends and socialize often with them. *Friends*? This amended list seemed to me at first like one of those children's puzzles that ask "which of these does not belong?" we were accustomed to hearing medical experts explain that illness results from quantifiable physical conditions, such as the malfunction of, say, the heart of the endocrine systems, or the presence of a nasty bacteria or virus—but personal relationships? Moreover, we were assured that this new finding is now firmly established in 21th-century medical knowledge because it has been replicated in numerous well-designed scientific studies and published in prestigious medical journals. All of which left me wondering, "How is possible that the vast analytical powers of modern medical research had missed this crucial fact for hundreds of years? And what else, by the way, have they missed?"

The answers to that question continue to unfold. As soon as it became respectable for medical researchers to study relational effects on human health and mental capabilities, a flood of discoveries and new basic knowledge emerged and entered the medical journal. For instance, it was found in 2002 that the presence of a small circle of good relationships in an elderly person' life is far more likely to prevent dementia than is the practice of doing mental calisthenics such as crossword puzzles. In fact, researchers ascertained in 2007 that for people of all ages ten minutes of talking with someone, in person or even by phone, boosts mental performance and memory as much as doing crossword puzzles of the same amount of time. Moreover, it was found that the more social contact people have, the higher their level of mental functioning. In 2009 a study of older adults found that those with fewer social interactions experienced a more rapid rate of decline in motor function such as walking, gripping, and balancing. Several studies have found that if one's social contact includes being of service to others, such as volunteering weekly, the volunteer experiences improved physical health and longevity[1].

Perhaps the most surprising discovery in what might be called "relational physiology", however, is that even our IQ, long held to be a measure of innate, fixed intelligence, is partially a malleable, relational matter. Earlier studies had found that one's IQ is influenced by one's place in the birth order, in that the eldest child generally scores a few IQ points higher on a standardized intelligence test. The startling finding of a study conducted in 2007, however, was that becoming the eldest because of the early death of an older sibling, or even two older siblings, still yields the additional IQ points at age 19 commonly seen in the scores earned by eldest children[2]. In short, the development and expression of intelligence (at least on a standardized test) is significantly affected by relational dynamics in the family. Is this because parents relate differently to their eldest child, giving her or him more responsibility (such as watching over the younger ones on occasion), which might cause the child to feel more capable and confident? Is it because the eldest child tends to identify more with the adult world (and being tested by it) than do the younger siblings? The researchers did not speculate, yet their findings are remarkable.

Even more surprisingly, a study in 2009 found that IQ scores within the United States, as well as cross-culturally, are influenced detrimentally by whether a child was spanked and how often. The more spanking the slower the mental development of the child, and even a small amount of spanking made a difference[3]. Apparently, corporal punishment is such a relational violation of a child' being that it is a trauma to the entire bodymind, which causes lasting damage to his or her capabilities of intelligence[4].

Any one of these discoveries would have been dismissed out of hand only a decade ago by nearly all physiologists. The evidence of the centrality of relational dynamics had always been right under the noses of the experts, but it did not fit into the frame of reference with which they had been trained to practice medicine, focusing solely on physical matter and quantifiable processes. In fact, it clashes directly with the foundational assumption that had shaped the entire body of modern medical knowledge since its beginnings in the 17th century: humans are essentially self-contained biomachines that operate on biomechianical principles. From the biomechanistic perspective, whether or not a patient had a number of enjoyable friends could not have been more irrelevant to physical health.

Less dramatic than the discoveries in "relational physiology," but also unexpected, have been the recent findings in studies of what could be called "relational behavior": aspects of our behavior, such as overeating or not and feeling happy or not, are apparently influenced by the behavior of others situated near us in our network of social interactions. Researchers in the social sciences call this phenomenon "connectivity" (or sometimes "social contagion"). In September 2009 *The New York Times Magazine* featured a cover story about the new studies in connectivity, "Is Happiness Catching?"-or, as the journalist put is, "The Way the World Works."[5] Well, certainly relational behavior is a part of the emerging sense of how inherently relational reality actually is, but it merely one example of a far larger phenomenon.

A growing stream of discoveries in recent years has begun to dislodge assumptions that have been in place for nearly four centuries about how we humans and the rest of the natural world function. With each new finding, it is becoming apparent that the established view was quite wrong about us in many respects, overlooking significant evidence that would have led to far more accurate systems of knowledge. Yet nearly all of us were schooled in the modern, mechanistic perspective, and those of us who have gone on frame of reference have been understandably resistant to acknowledging the mounting evidence to the contrary. Nonetheless, reality is far more relational and dynamic than various experts thought, though they have been able to deny the obvious throughout their career, just as the modern West has done for centuries. It is somewhat amusing, actually, to watch the medical profession, for instance, try to casually absorb the startling new relational findings by merely tacking them on to their usual way of reading the human body-Oh, yes, here's one more prescription: socialize with friends to stay healthy-when, in fact, that single relational discovery alone challenges the most basic assumptions of modern medical science.

One simple idea underlies the systems of knowledge that have shaped modernity: that all entities in the natural world, including us, are essentially separate and that they function through mechanistic ways of interacting. In contrast, a very different , yet elegantly simple, idea is now emerging and correcting the extremely limited mechanistic view: that all entities in the natural world, including us, are thoroughly relational beings of great complexity, who are both composed of and nested within contextual networks of dynamic and reciprocal relationships. We are made entirely of relationships, as is the whole of the natural world. Both the mechanistic and relational modes of perceptions are ways of seeing the world. They are each a foundational frame of reference, which results in a particular worldview, or paradigm. The relational worldview, however, is a close fit with the relational nature of reality, while the mechanistic worldview is not.

The most widely acknowledged example of the relational shift in thinking is the recognition that our health is determined to a significant extent by creative, dynamic relationships within the bodymind[6] as well as relationships among people and with other forms of life. However, numerous examples in fields other than physiology and medicine are also surfacing with increasing frequency. For instance, Malclm Gladwell made the case in The Tipping Point that collective change is best understood by paying attention to the relational "power of context," and he next demonstrated, in *Outliers*, that the full expression and cultivation of one's talents is very much situated in a web of either challenging or supportive relationships. That is, the long-standing assumption of the born genius, or the entirely self-made successful person, is being corrected by the relational perspective. Similarly, David Brooks analyzed recent discoveries in cognitive science and concluded in his book *The Social Animal: The Hidden Sources of Love, Character, and Achievement* that we emerge out of relationships and live to bond with each other and connect to larger ideas.

In a relate vein, Oxford University Press published a book in 2009 titled *Relational being: Beyond Self and Community* by Kenneth Gergen, which they described as presenting the "radical and potentially exciting landscape of relational thought and practice" that is sweeping through the field of psychology. Around the same time *The Empathic Civilization* by Jeremy Rifkin was published, making the case that we are "hardwired" for empathy, which he defines as the ability to show solidarity with others. Several other recent books have analyzed a particular current event, crisis, or situation by focusing on the relational dynamics, a perspective that yields a far more accurate sense of what is going on. Each of these works explores a significant aspect of the overview I propose here. Certainly there will be many books in the future explicating "the growing understanding in many disciplines about all things being fundamentally relational," as the British magazine *Resurgence* observed in 2009.[7]

For my part, I have long been intrigued with the emergent perception of relational reality, though my focus has not been limited to its effect on interhuman connections. All of reality is relational. I was puzzled-and still am-by the fact that it took only about 100 years for the mechanistic worldview to spread through nearly all social institutions and systems of knowledge in 18th-century Britain and France (beginning with the culmination of the Scientific Revolution in the late 17th century) yet it has now been more than 100 years since Einstein's first two articles established that the universe is best understood as highly relational, rather than mechanistic. Wouldn't one expect a (post-mechanistic) worldview to spread from science into society at a far more rapid pace in the 20th century than did the previous, comparable shift? Instead, the implications of the new physics have hardly affected society's ways of thinking, perhaps because people find them too abstract to e relevant to daily life. In the 1980s and 1990s complexity studies in biology and other areas of science discovered that dynamic interrelatedness is the key to understanding living systems. The implications of those discoveries, too, had some impact beyond science but did not really have a significant impact on the mainstream. Similarly , the emergence of alternative medicine(now called integral, or integrated, medicine)made some waves as it was grudgingly, but increasingly, accepted by the medical system. (Many of the recent discoveries of relational physiology, however, are surprising even to practitioners of integral medicine.)

Because of this partial progress, I was able to gather some examples of the relational perspective for my book *The Resurgence of the Real* (1997), although that book was focused mainly on cultural history. After finishing that project, my attention was drawn elsewhere. Perhaps, I thought, the Relational Shift would not become widespread in my lifetime. So I was surprised to begin noticing in mainstream media, around 2004, a growing stream of references to discoveries of the relational nature of reality in various fields, nearly all of which had successful application. Moreover, I was often amazed by the findings in many of the recent studies, even though I was no stranger to the phenomenon. Evidently, reality is far more deeply interrelated than even relational thinkers had previously supposed.

It seems to me that a coherence exists among the numerous, yet seemingly disparate relational discoveries and innovation. Taken together, to have engendered the Relational Shift. In my view, they can be recognized as one coherent phenomenon, with myriad versions, which is transforming the modern world. We are profoundly relational beings who have been living-with some difficulty-in anti-relational (mechanistic) systems of thought and ways of doing things. Finally, all that has begun to change.

In this book I seek to illuminate the largely unrecognized common ground among the relational discoveries within various fields-and also among various fields. My goal is to map the territory and present the Big Picture of this vast development. My hope is that readers of this book will emerge with a well grounded sense that we are now living through a transformation of a grand scale, as many of the most basic assumptions of the centuries-old modern worldview are being radically corrected, expanded, or replaced entirely. In many respects, it feels as if the blinders are coming off that had conditioned modern societies to overlook the profound significance of the relational dimension of life and living. Of course, modernity did not so much "overlook" the relational worldview as aggressively replace it. Hence the often difficult, and sometimes forced, transition to modernity from indigenous or traditional societies involved at its core the abandoning of a relational perception of the world for a more "sophisticated," mechanistic perspective.

Rather than try for an encyclopedic account of the extent of the relational transformation, I focus on four major areas as examples: education and parenting, health and healthcare, community design and architecture, and the economy. There are, however, many more. For instance, some of the old assumptions about criminal justice are yielding to the success of a relational approach called "restorative justice": communities across the country have found that arrested offenders, when given the chance to take responsibility for their actions in a relational manner and repair the harm they have done (such as apologizing, returning stolen money, or doing community service) in exchange for having the charges dropped, tend to avoid engaging in any further criminal activity in the future. That is, their rate of recidivism is only 10percent, compared to 70 percent among those who go through the traditional criminal justice system.[8]

In truth, no field of human endeavor lies beyond the revitalizing influence of this rising phenomenon. Having touched on some of the changes in physiology and medicine at the beginning of this chapter, I will now cite a few of the manifestations of the Relational Shift in three others fields, each of which is covered in one of the following chapters.

First, in the related areas of education and parenting, efforts to teach and learn have been severely compromised in recent decades by the detrimental effects on children's formative years of electronic immersion, vapid but mesmerizing media content, not-nutritive "food," lack of physical exercise, and a widespread condition that psychologists call "attachment displacement disorder," which orients many children away from their parents and leaves them hardened and "cool" but seriously adrift, as they struggle with deficits in their development. The frightening groundlessness that results in high levels of alienation and depression in so many adolescents is being addressed by several new approaches that cultivate the student's relational capabilities. In the younger grades, school gardens are one means by which a connection with nature, for instance, is nurtured. Additionally, young children learn about basic relationships (between plants and the sun, for instance) and gradually increase their knowledge of the network of relationships that constitute arithmetic, literature, science, social studies, art, and all other areas of human accomplishment. At the university level, relational thinking is rippling through all the disciplines, replacing the mechanistic assumptions underlying many foundational concepts with more realistic perspectives that pay attention to interrelatedness and dynamic context. Relational analysis quickly crosses the boundaries of traditional academic disciplines, as well, so it is increasingly evident in the mushrooming growth of interdisciplinary programs at universities. As various fields of knowledge have begun to adopt the relational perspective, the new thinking has begun to spread throughout society and to reshape our institutions.

Second, in architecture and city planning the ways in which we build houses and buildings and design our cities has shifted significantly because of relational insights and remarkable innovations with regard to various ecosocial realities. For example, not only are structures now built to meet standards of ecological efficiency but we have discovered that people remain healthier if the buildings in which they work allow natural light to come in. in the past, designers would have dismissed such a distinction on the grounds that "Light is light-as long as it illuminates the employee's desk sufficiently." That was an incorrect assumption. Our bodymind thrives in organic relationship with that which is vital and life-giving, such as the light of the sun.

Third, the science of modern economics, which has long been enthroned at the center of all industrialized societies regardless of their form of government, holds as a underlying premise that the expansion of material production and economic growth automatically bring sin its wake solutions to social problems and personal well-being for citizens. Yet event that foundational slab of modern economic theory-which drives governments to strive for continuous growth of their Gross Domestic Product and per capita income-has been challenged in recent years by various Quality of Life Indicators and by the new field of "happiness economics," or "happiness studies."

Combining the analytical tools of economics and psychological surveys, many of these socio-economic studies have found that in much of Europe in recent decades, happiness (or "contentment") has decreased while material prosperity has increased. What factors correlate with people's happiness in the high-scoring countries? The European Social Survey of thirty countries found in 2007 that high levels of trust in their governments, the police, and the justice system, as well as those around them were consistent factors in the happy societies, in addition to having plenty of friends and acquaintances and at least one very close friend, or "significant other." Denmark was the happiest country, followed by Sweden, Finland, and the Netherland. Women generally classed themselves as happier than did men, while the old and the young tended to be happier than people in mid-life.[9] On the global level the World Database of Happiness, which compiles the findings of several surveys in 148 nations, found that in 2009 the happiest counties were Costa Rica, Denmark, Iceland, Switzerland, and Canada, with the United States ranking 20th.[10] (When sustainability is also considered-via life enjoyment, life expectancy, and the country's "ecological footprint" on the environment-the Happy Planet Index of 143countries found in 2009 that Costa Rica comes in first and the Unites States ranks 114th.[11])

In general, such studies have found that beyond a basic level of material comfort and security, happiness does not appear to be a matter of having conspicuous material possessions of the latest design. Rather, happiness is largely a result of having a network of good relationships-with family, friends, co-workers, community, and with nature, as well as cultivating the mental qualities of gratitude, hope, and zest for life. In fact, we are significantly happier when we spend money on gifts or give to charity than when we spend it in ourselves.[12] Moreover, although most people experience loss as having amore intense and lasting effect in their lives than does gain, they are better able to adapt to loss in their finances than in the relational sphere, including family bonds, romantic relationships, and the social fabric of community.[13] Beyond a certain level of security, per capita income is not, after all, the key to happiness and well-bing, yet classical economic theory was oblivious to this relational reality.

注释:

1. 关于长寿原因这一点，斯普瑞特奈克曾在《真实之复兴：极度现代的世界中的身体、自然和地方》中也提到过，致力于奉献精神、为他人着想的人一般都长寿。

2. 2007 年《纽约时报》刊载一篇 Bendict Cary 的文章，题目是“长子的智商更高”，此文是基于对挪威年龄为 18 或 19 岁的有兵役经历的男性的研究。在其他国家更早的研究也有类似的报告，斯坦福大学的 Robert Zajonc 教授也提出出生顺序和智商之间的关系，但挪威学者进一步指出，即便是长子去世后，次子因而变为长子，出生顺序和智商之间仍然有这种联系。

3. 打屁股会损伤儿童智商，这一点在社会学家和家庭教育学者的研究报告中已经证实。研究者指出，父母打孩子确实会影响孩子的智力发展，挨打越多，心智成熟越慢，甚至程度轻的挨打也会造成智商发展缓慢。国际上，Straus 教授也发现在流行肉体惩罚孩子的国家，平均智商确实会低下，他的分析暗示出，孩子都到了青少年期还使用肉体惩罚，对他们的智商影响则更明显。鉴于此，目前许多国家已经出台法律坚决抵制父母对儿童的肉体惩罚。

4. 参见 Lisa Berlin et al.，“Correlates and Consequences of Spanking and Verbal Punishment for Low-Income White, African American, and Mexican American Toddlers, Child Development, vol. 80, issue 5, Sept./Oct. 2009, pp. 1403-20. 这一研究是基于 2573 个低收入的有家暴孩子或语言暴力情况的家庭，包括白人、非裔美国人、墨西哥裔美国人，涉及年龄在 1 岁、2 岁或 3 岁的孩子。研究表明，从 1 岁开始有体罚经历的孩子，在 2 岁时候极有可能有攻击行为，3 岁时候心智发展相对缓慢。

5. 参见 Clive Thompson,“Is Happiness Catching?”, New York Times Magazine, Sept. 13, 2009, pp. 28, 30-35, and 42。

6. 将“身体”与“心理”割裂是一种机械的投射，最近的心理学和生物学研究也认为这样做没有任何意义。感知、记忆和创造性回应都是身心协调一致的努力结果。

7. 见 Shakti Maira,“The Ananda Experience,” Resurgence Magazine, No. 256, Sept. Oct. 2009, p. 63。

8. 见“ A New Kind of Criminal Justice,” Parade Magazine, Oct. 25, 2009, p. 6。

9. 见“A New Kind of Criminal Justice,” Parade Magazine, Oct. 25,2009, p.6。

见网址（http: // www. esds. ac. uk/International/access/14732. asp [accessed on Jan. 8, 2010]）。

10. 世界幸福数据库：对生活的主观评价的连续性客观研究。此研究由荷兰鹿特丹大学的拉特维荷芬发起，参见 http: // worlddatabaseof happiness. eur. nl/index。

11. 幸福星球索引是由英国新经济发起的一项研究工程，见 www. happinessplanetindex. org。

12. 参见 Dorothy Foltz Gray，“What Really Makes Us Happy，” Prevention magazine，Feb. 2006，p. 158. 在这篇文章中，Foltz Gray 教授对 5000 人进行了追踪研究，他的研究结果是，幸福的人普遍心理特征是他们去爱、被爱，他们心怀感激、心存希冀。参见 Jen Angel，“10 Things Science Says Will Make You Happy，” Yes! Magazine，Winter 2009，p. 22；“Spend Yourself Happy，” AARP Magazine，Nov. /Dec. 2008，p. 20。

13. 见 Carol Graham，“The Economics of Happiness，” in The New Palgrave Dictionary of Economics，2nd edition（New York: Palgrave Macmillan，2008）。

Chapter Seventeen **Posthumanism**

后人文主义理论是继后结构主义、后现代主义、后现代文学伦理学批评之后的另一种重要的后学。后人类(posthuman)这个概念起源于科幻小说、未来学、当代艺术和哲学,其字面意义是指存在于超越人类状态的个人或实体。这一概念提出了伦理学与正义、语言与跨物种交流、社会制度与跨学科知识的问题。在批评理论中,后人类是一个思索性的存在,它代表或追求对人类的重新设想。后人文主义以人类作为自己批评的对象,批判地质疑人文主义。作为哲学的一个分支,人文主义声称人性是一种普遍的状态,人类就是从这种状态中出现的。人性是自主的、理性的、有自由意志的能力,将其自身统一为存在的顶点。因此,后人类承认其自身的不完美和不统一,而且在追求维护智力刚性和致力于客观观察的同时,通过多样化视角认识世界。

后人文主义思想是在对传统人文主义思想的反思和批判基础上发展起来的,在文学批评领域和文化研究领域分别发展出"批判性后人文主义"和"文化后人文主义"两条源流。到了20世纪90年代末,批判性后人文主义和文化后人文主义发展成为一种更聚焦在哲学上的探究,如今被称为"哲学后人文主义"。后人文主义经常被解释为后人类主义和后人类中心主义,因为它出现在人类概念之后和人文主义历史之后,这两者都是建立在分等级的社会建构和以人为中心的假设基础之上的。对物种歧视的批判是后人类批评方法整体构成的一个重要方面。

后人文主义超越后现代主义研究,被各种各样的文化理论家使用。对后人文主义思想做出重要贡献的理论家包括伊哈布·哈桑、福柯、巴特勒、格雷戈里·贝特森(Gregory Bateson)、沃伦·麦卡洛克(Warren McCulloch)、诺伯特·维纳(Norbert Wiener)、布鲁诺·拉图尔(Bruno Latour)、海尔斯、哈拉维、史路戴(Peter Stroday)、索格纳(Stefan Lorenz Sorgner)、埃文·汤普森(Evan Thompson)、瓦雷拉(Francisco Valera)、亨伯托·马图拉纳(Humberto Mathurana)、道格拉斯·凯尔纳(Douglas Kellner)等,也有哲学家,如罗伯特·佩珀雷尔(Robert Pepperell),他们在著作中探讨了经常被后人文主义这个术语所代替的后人类状况。

后人文主义话语旨在打开空间，依据当前文化和历史语境重新定义人类：人类是许多自然物种之一，是非统一的多元的存在。后人类不断地与智能机器一起共同进化，这种共同进化使人们超越了具体存在的边界，扩展了他们对真实经验的主观理解。后人文主义意味着以身体边界为基础的主体性的丧失，这种状态被经常用来与赛博格观念相联系。虽然后人文主义是一种开阔的、复杂的意识形态，但它蕴含着对现今和未来的相关暗示。它试图重新界定社会结构，不是根据固有的符合人性的或生物的起源，而是依据社会的和心理的系统，在这种系统里意识和沟通可能作为独特的无实质的实体而存在。在人们对语言、象征主义、主体性、现象学、伦理学、正义和创造性做了新的关注之后，又出现了有关人类存在中技术的目前使用及其未来的问题。从这个角度看，后人文主义理论不仅有助于揭示新兴技术的内在政治，同时也为我们重新看待人与技术、人与动物、人与环境等的关系提供了一个全新的出发点、一种新型的研究方式。

Francesca Ferrando

弗朗西斯卡·费兰多(1978—)，纽约大学人文学系助理哲学教授，后人文主义思想研究的开拓者和代表性学者之一。她是纽约后人类研究小组的发起者，也是全球后人文主义研究组织"全球后人类网络"(Global Network Posthuman)的创建者，该组织是世界范围内跨学科、多视角的后人文主义研究机构。费兰多教授出生于意大利并在意大利求学，后赴英美等多国访学，直至 2014 年起在纽约大学担任教师，所教授课程包括从人类到后人类、展望人类存在等。她是美国哲学学会和美国宗教学会会员，同时也是一位颇有成就的作家，学术成果曾获得多项文学和哲学奖项。她在后人文主义领域的代表性著作有《哲学后人文主义》(*Philosophical Posthumanism*，2019)。

Posthumanism, Transhumanism, Antihumanism, Metahumanism, and New Materialisms: Differences and Relations

(Ferrando, Francesca. Posthumanism, Transhumanism, Antihumanism, Metahumanism, and New Materialisms: Differences and Relations. *Existenz*, Vol. 8, No. 2, 2013, pp. 26-32.)

本文首先指出“后人类”是一个颇为复杂且相对宽泛的概念，其在哲学、文化研究和批评理论中都各有侧重。文章然后对“后人文主义”、“跨人文主义”、“反人文主义”、“元人文主义”和“新物质主义”这几个容易混淆且又存在一定关联的概念做了简单而清晰的辨析，点出后人文主义思想的准确含义、研究领域和思想意指。简而言之，后人文主义拥有明确的反人类中心主义立场，但同时也反对简单的人与非人对立的二元论。后人文主义把人类视作一种短暂的、流动的、多元的、开放包容的存在，是世界万物关系网中的一个节点。这样，后人文主义就使我们重新认识人在世界和现实中的地位，重新认识曾自以为是“万物的尺度”和“中心”的人，重新认识曾经以为是清楚已知的世界。

Introduction

In contemporary academic debate, "posthuman" has become a key term to cope with an urgency for the integral redefinition of the notion of the human, following the onto-epistemological as well as scientific and bio-technological developments of the twentieth and twenty-first centuries. The philosophical landscape, which has since developed, includes several movements and schools of thought. The label "posthuman" is often evoked in a generic and all-inclusive way, to indicate any of these different perspectives, creating methodological and theoretical confusion between experts and non-experts alike. "Posthuman" has become an umbrella term to include (philosophical, cultural, and critical) posthumanism, transhumanism (in its variants as extropianism, liberal and democratic transhumanism, among other currents), new materialisms (a specific feminist development within the posthumanist frame), and the heterogeneous landscapes of antihumanism, posthumanities, and metahumanities. The most confused areas of signification are the ones shared by posthumanism and transhumanism. There are different reasons for such confusion. Both movements arose more specifically in the late Eighties and early Nineties, with interests around similar topics. They share a common perception of the human as a non-fixed and mutable condition, but they generally do not share the same roots and perspectives. Moreover, within the transhumanist debate, the concept of posthumanism itself is interpreted in a specific transhumanist way, which causes further confusion in the general understanding of the posthuman: for some transhumanists, human beings may eventually transform themselves so radically as to become posthuman, a condition expected to follow the current transhuman era. Such a take on the posthuman should not be confused with the post-anthropocentric and post-dualistic approach of (philosophical, cultural, and critical) posthumanism. This essay clarifies some of the differences between these two independent, yet related movements, and suggests that posthumanism, in its radical onto-existential re-signification of the notion of the human, may offer a more comprehensive approach.

Transhumanism

The movement of transhumanism problematizes the current understanding of the human not necessarily through its past and present legacies, but through the possibilities inscribed within its possible biological and technological evolutions. Human enhancement is a crucial notion to the transhumanist reflection; the main keys to access such a goal are identified in science and technology, in all of their variables, as existing, emerging and speculative frames—from regenerative medicine to nanotechnology, radical life extension, mind uploading and cryonics,[1] among other fields. Distinctive currents coexist in transhumanism, such as: libertarian transhumanism, democratic transhumanism, and extropianism.[2] Science and technology are the main assets of interest for each of these positions, but with different emphases. Libertarian transhumanism advocates free market as the best guarantor of the right to human enhancement. Democratic transhumanism calls for an equal access to technological enhancements, which could otherwise be limited to certain socio-political classes and related to economic power, consequently encoding racial and sexual politics. The principles of extropianism have been delineated by its founder Max More as: perpetual progress, self-transformation, practical optimism, intelligent technology, open society (information and democracy), self-direction, and rational thinking. The emphasis on notions such as rationality, progress and optimism is in line with the fact that, philosophically, transhumanism roots itself in the Enlightenment, and so it does not expropriate rational humanism. By taking humanism further, transhumanism can be defined as "ultra-humanism." This theoretical location weakens the transhumanist reflection, as argued anon.

In the West, the human has been historically posed in a hierarchical scale to the non-human realm. Such a symbolic structure, based on a human exceptionalism well depicted in the Great Chain of Being,[3] has not only sustained the primacy of humans over non-human animals, but it has also (in)formed the human realm itself, with sexist, racist, classist, homophobic, and ethnocentric presumptions. In other words, not every human being has been considered as such: women, African-American descendents, gays and lesbians, differently-abled people, among others, have represented the margins to what would be considered human. For instance, in the case of chattel slavery, slaves were treated as personal property of an owner, to be bought and sold. And still, transhumanist reflections, in their "ultra-humanistic" endeavors, do not fully engage with a critical and historical account of the human, which is often presented in a generic and "fit-for-all" way.

Furthermore, the transhumanist perseverance in recognizing science and technology as the main assets of reformulation of the human runs the risk of techno-reductionism: technology becomes a hierarchical project, based on rational thought, driven towards progression. Considering that a large number of the world's population is still occupied with mere survival, if the reflection on desirable futures was reduced to an overestimation of the technological kinship of the human revisited in its specific technical outcomes, such a preference would confine it to a classist and techno-centric movement.

For these reasons, although offering inspiring views on the ongoing interaction between the biological and the technological realm, transhumanism is rooted within traditions of thought which pose unredeemable restrictions to its perspectives. Its reliance on technology and science should be investigated from a broader angle; a less centralized and more integrated approach would deeply enrich the debate. In this sense, posthumanism may offer a more suitable point of departure.

Posthumanist Technologies

If posthumanism and transhumanism share a common interest in technology, the ways in which they reflect upon this notion is structurally different. The historical and ontological dimension of technology is a crucial issue, when it comes to a proper understanding of the posthuman agenda; yet, posthumanism does not turn technology into its main focus, which would reduce its own theoretical attempt to a form of essentialism and techno-reductionism. Technology is neither the "other" to be feared and to rebel against (in a sort of neo-luddite attitude), nor does it sustain the almost divine characteristics which some transhumanists attribute to it (for instance, by addressing technology as an external source which might guarantee humanity a place in post-biological futures). What transhumanism and posthumanism share is the notion of technogenesis. Technology is a trait of the human outfit. More than a functional tool for obtaining (energy; more sophisticated technology; or even immortality), technology arrives at the posthumanist debate through the mediation of feminism, in particular, through Donna Haraway's[4] cyborg and her dismantling of strict dualisms and boundaries, such as the one between human and non-human animals, biological organisms and machines, the physical and the nonphysical realm; and ultimately, the boundary between technology and the self.

The non-separateness between the human and the techno realm shall be investigated not only as an anthropological and paleontological issue, but also as an ontological one. Technology, within a posthumanist frame, can be gleaned through the work of Martin Heidegger,[5] specifically in his essay "The Question Concerning Technology," where he stated: "Technology is therefore no mere means. Technology is a way of revealing." Posthumanism investigates technology precisely as a mode of revealing, thus re-accessing its ontological significance in a contemporary setting where technology has been mostly reduced to its technical endeavors. Additional relevant aspects to be mentioned in relation to posthumanism, are the technologies of the self, as defined by Michel Foucault.[6] The technologies of the self dismantle the separation self/others through a relational ontology, playing a substantial role in the process of existential revealing, and opening the debate to posthuman ethics and applied philosophy. Posthumanism is a praxis. The ways the futures are being conceived and imagined are not disconnected from their actual enactments: in the posthuman post-dualistic approach, the "what" is the "how." For instance, posthumanism takes into account space migration but, in its post-modern and post-colonial roots, cannot support space colonization, a concept which is often found in transhumanist literature. This is a good example how transhumanism and posthumanism may approach the same subject from different standpoints and theoretical legacies.

Posthumanism

Although the roots of posthumanism can be already traced in the first wave of postmodernism, the posthuman turn was fully enacted by feminist theorists in the Nineties, within the field of literary criticism— what will later be defined as critical posthumanism. Simultaneously, cultural studies also embraced it, producing a specific take which has been referred to as cultural posthumanism. By the end of the

1990s (critical and cultural) posthumanism developed into a more philosophically focused inquiry (now referred to as philosophical posthumanism), in a comprehensive attempt to re-access each field of philosophical investigation through a newly gained awareness of the limits of previous anthropocentric and humanistic assumptions. Posthumanism is often defined as a post-humanism and a post-anthropocentrism: it is "post" to the concept of the human and to the historical occurrence of humanism, both based, as we have previously seen, on hierarchical social constructs and human-centric assumptions. Speciesism has turned into an integral aspect of the posthuman critical approach. The posthuman overcoming of human primacy, though, is not to be replaced with other types of primacies (such as the one of the machines). Posthumanism can be seen as a post-exclusivism: an empirical philosophy of mediation which offers a reconciliation of existence in its broadest significations. Posthumanism does not employ any frontal dualism or antithesis, demystifying any ontological polarization through the postmodern practice of deconstruction.

Not obsessed with proving the originality of its own proposal, posthumanism can also be seen as a post-exceptionalism. It implies an assimilation of the "dissolution of the new," which Gianni Vattimo[7] identified as a specific trait of the postmodern. In order to postulate the "new," the centre of the discourse has to be located, so that the question "New to what?" shall be answered. But the novelty of human thought is relative and situated: what is considered new in one society might be common knowledge in another. Moreover, hegemonic perspectives do not explicitly acknowledge all the resistant standpoints which coexist within each specific cultural-historical paradigm, thus failing to recognize the discontinuities embedded in any discursive formation. What Posthumanism puts at stake is not only the identity of the traditional centre of Western discourse—which has already been radically deconstructed by its own peripheries (feminist, critical race, queer, and postcolonial theorists, to name a few). Posthumanism is a post-centralizing, in the sense that it recognizes not one but many specific centers of interest; it dismisses the centrality of the centre in its singular form, both in its hegemonic as in its resistant modes. Posthumanism might recognize centers of interests; its centers, though, are mutable, nomadic, ephemeral. Its perspectives have to be pluralistic, multilayered, and as comprehensive and inclusive as possible.

As posthumanism attracts more attention and becomes mainstream, new challenges arise. For example, some thinkers are currently looking to embrace the "exotic" difference, such as the robot, the biotechnological chimeras, the alien, without having to deal with the differences embedded within the human realm, thus avoiding the studies developed from the human "margins," such as feminism or critical race studies. But posthumanism does not stand on a hierarchical system: there are no higher and lower degrees of alterity, when formulating a posthuman standpoint, so that the non-human differences are as compelling as the human ones. Posthumanism is a philosophy which provides a suitable way of departure to think in relational and multi-layered ways, expanding the focus to the non-human realm in post-dualistic, post-hierarchical modes, thus allowing one to envision post-human futures which will radically stretch the boundaries of human imagination.

New Materialisms

New materialisms is another specific movement within the posthumanist theoretical scenario. Diana Coole[8] and Samantha Frost point out: "the renewed critical materialisms are not synonymous with a revival of Marxism," but, more literary, they re-inscribe matter as a process of materialization, in the feminist critical debate. Already traceable in the mid to late Nineties in the emphasis given to the body by corporeal feminism, such a rediscovered feminist interest became more extensively matter-oriented by the first decade of the twenty-first century. New materialisms philosophically arose as a reaction to the representationalist and constructivist radicalizations of late postmodernity, which somehow lost track of the material realm. Such a loss postulated an inner dualism between what was perceived as manipulated by the act of observing and describing, as pursued by the observers, and an external reality, that would thus become unapproachable. Even though the roots of new materialisms can be traced in postmodernism, new materialisms point out that the postmodern rejection of the dualism nature/ culture resulted in a clear preference for its nurtural aspects. Such a preference produced a multiplication of genealogical accounts investigating the constructivist implications of any natural presumptions, in what can be seen as a wave of radical constructivist feminist literature related to the major influence of Judith Butler's[9] groundbreaking works. This literature exhibited an unbalanced result: if culture did not need to be bracketed, most certainly nature did. In an ironic tone, Karen Barad, one of the main theorists of new materialisms, implicitly referring to Butler's book *Bodies that Matter*, has stated: "Language matters. Discourse matters. Culture matters. There is an important sense in which the only thing that does not seem to matter anymore is matter." New materialisms pose no division between language and matter: biology is culturally mediated as much as culture is materialistically constructed. New materialisms perceive matter as an ongoing process of materialization, elegantly reconciling science and critical theories: quantum physics with a post-structuralist and postmodern sensitivity. Matter is not viewed in any way as something static, fixed, or passive, waiting to be molded by some external force; rather, it is emphasized as "a process of materialization" (*BM* 9). Such a process, which is dynamic, shifting, inherently entangled, diffractional, and performative, does not hold any primacy over the materialization, nor can the materialization be reduced to its processual terms.

Antihumanism, Metahumanism, Metahumanities, and Posthumanities

There are significant differences within the posthuman scenario, each leading to a specialized forum of discourse. If modern rationality, progress and free will are at the core of the transhumanist debate, a radical critique of these same presuppositions is the kernel of antihumanism, a philosophical position which shares with posthumanism its roots in postmodernity, but differs in other aspects. The deconstruction of the notion of the human is central to antihumanism: this is one of its main points in common with posthumanism. However, a major distinction between the two movements is already embedded in their morphologies, specifically in their denotation of "post-" and "anti-." Antihumanism fully acknowledges the consequences of the "death of Man," as already asserted by some post-structuralist theorists, in particular by Michel Foucault. In contrast, posthumanism does not rely on any symbolic death: such an assumption would be based on the dualism dead/alive, while any strict form of dualism has been already challenged by posthumanism, in its post-dualistic process-ontological perspective. Posthumanism, after all, is aware of the fact that hierarchical humanistic presumptions cannot be easily dismissed or erased. In this respect, it is more in tune with Derrida's[10] deconstructive approach rather than with Foucault's death of Man. To complete a presentation of the posthuman scenario, metahumanism is a recent approach closely related to a Deleuzian legacy; it emphasizes the body as a locus for amorphic re-significations, extended in kinetic relations as a body-network. It should not be confused with metahumanity, a term which appeared in the 1980s within comics narratives and role-playing games, referring to superheros and mutants, and it has since been employed specifically in the context of cultural studies. Lastly, the notion of posthumanities has been welcomed in academia to emphasize an internal shift (from the humanities to the posthumanities), extending the study of the human condition to the posthuman; furthermore, it may also refer to future generations of beings evolutionarily related to the human species.

Conclusion

The posthuman discourse is an ongoing process of different standpoints and movements, which has flourished as a result of the contemporary attempt to redefine the human condition. Posthumanism, transhumanism, new materialisms, antihumanism, metahumanism, metahumanity and posthumanities offer significant ways to rethink possible existential outcomes. This essay clarifies some of the differences between these movements, and emphasizes the similarities and discrepancies between transhumanism and posthumanism, two areas of reflection that are often confused with each other. Transhumanism offers a very rich debate on the impact of technological and scientific developments in the evolution of the human species; and still, it holds a humanistic and human-centric perspective which weakens its standpoint: it is a "Humanity Plus" movement, whose aim is to "elevate the human condition." On the contrary, speciesism has become an integral part of the posthumanist approach, formulated on a post-anthropocentric and post-humanistic *episteme* based on decentralized and non-hierarchical modes. Although posthumanism investigates the realms of science and technology, it does not recognize them as its main axes of reflection, nor does it limit itself to their technical endeavors, but it expands its reflection to the technologies of existence.

Posthumanism (here understood as critical, cultural, and philosophical posthumanism, as well as new materialisms) seems appropriate to investigate the geological time of the anthropocene. As the anthropocene marks the extent of the impact of human activities on a planetary level, the posthuman focuses on de-centering the human from the primary focus of the discourse. In tune with antihumanism, posthumanism stresses the urgency for humans to become aware of pertaining to an ecosystem which, when damaged, negatively affects the human condition as well. In such a framework, the human is not approached as an autonomous agent, but is located within an extensive system of relations. Humans are perceived as material nodes of becoming; such becomings operate as technologies of existence. The way humans inhabit this planet, what they eat, how they behave, what relations they entertain, creates the network of who and what they are: it is not a disembodied network, but (also) a material one, whose agency exceeds the political, social, and biological human realms, as new materialist thinkers sharply point out. In this expanded horizon, it becomes clear that any types of essentialism, reductionism, or intrinsic biases are limiting factors in approaching such multidimensional networks. Posthumanism keeps a critical and deconstructive standpoint informed by the acknowledgement of the past, while setting a comprehensive and generative perspective to sustain and nurture alternatives for the present and for the futures. Within the current philosophical environment, posthumanism offers a unique balance between agency, memory, and imagination, aiming to achieve harmonic legacies in the evolving ecology of interconnected existence.

注释:

1. 指把人体死亡后冷冻起来以期在未来起死回生的人体冷冻技术。
2. 负熵主义，指相信科技的发展能够给人带来永生的一种超越性哲学思想。
3. 伟大的存在之链是自古希腊时期以来对西方思想产生巨大影响的概念之一，它认为世界万物都是一个发展和联系的自然阶梯。
4. 唐娜·哈拉维（1944— ），美国著名后现代主义和女性主义学者，哲学家。
5. 马丁·海德格尔（1889—1976），德国哲学家，其思想对现象学、存在主义、解构主义、诠释学、后现代主义等哲学领域产生了重要影响。
6. 米歇尔·福柯（1926—1984），法国哲学家、社会思想家，著有《疯癫与文明》《性史》《规训与惩罚》《知识考古学》《词与物》等诸多革命性的思想巨著。
7. 基阿尼·瓦蒂莫（1936— ），意大利当代哲学家和政治家，代表作有《现代性的终结》。
8. 戴安娜·库尔（1952— ），英国伦敦大学政治与社会理论教授，新物质主义思想的代表性学者之一。
9. 朱迪斯·巴特勒（1956— ），美国后现代主义思想家，女性主义批评家和性别研究、政治哲学学者。
10. 雅克·德里达（1930—2004），法国著名哲学家，解构主义的代表人物。

N. Katherine Hayles

N. 凯瑟琳·海尔斯(1943—)，著名的后人文主义学者和理论家，也是一位文学批评学者,现任美国杜克大学文学系讲席教授。海尔斯对后人文主义思想的研究以跨学科为特色,她以最新的科学进展反思人类当下的生存状态,同时结合文学文本探讨人之存在本质,思想充满了具有穿透力的洞见。她的研究曾获包括古根海姆奖在内的多项奖励。海尔斯的代表作有《我们何以成为后人类:文学、信息科学和控制论中的虚拟身体》《我们如何思考:数字媒体与当代科技》《无意识:认知无意识的力量》等。

Conclusion: What Does It Mean to Be Posthuman?

(Hayles, N. Katherine. *How We Became Posthuman: Virtual Bodies in Cybernetics, Literature, and Informatics*. Chicago: University Of Chicago Press, 1999, pp. 283-291.)

本文节选自海尔斯的名作《我们何以成为后人类:文学、信息科学和控制论中的虚拟身体》,是对该著作观点的集中呈现。在文中,海尔斯的主要观点是:后人文主义并非要像科幻作品那样展望人的终结,而是要在科技已经进步到能够用人工生命替代人类身体和意识的后人类时代对人之存在提出一种崭新的理解方式,这样人类才能够更加坚实地继续在后人类时代中找寻自我。后人文主义对人的新型理解方式迥异于传统自由人文主义对于人的自足、自生、自主的存在状态的理解,而是从认知科学、神经科学、控制论和系统科学等新型科学中汲取思想营养,把人看作一种同外在共生和共同进化的主体的生成过程。海尔斯因而指出,人类并不会在后人类时代终结,因为人类一直以来就都已经是后人类。

What, finally, are we to make of the posthuman? At the beginning of this book, I suggested that the prospect of becoming posthuman both evokes terror and excites pleasure. At the end of the book, perhaps I can summarize the implications of the posthuman by interrogating the sources of this terror and pleasure. The terror is relatively easy to understand. "Post," with its dual connotation of superseding the human and coming after it, hints that the days of "the human" may be numbered. Some researchers (notably Hans Moravec[1] but also my UCLA colleague Michael Dyer and many others) believe that this is true not only in a general intellectual sense that displaces one definition of "human" with another but also in a more disturbingly literal sense that envisions humans displaced as the dominant form of life on the planet by intelligent machines. Humans can either go gently into that good night, joining the dinosaurs as a species that once ruled the earth but is now obsolete, or hang on for a while longer by becoming machines themselves. In either case, Moravec and like-minded thinkers believe, the age of the human is drawing to a close. The view echoes the deeply pessimistic sentiments of Warren McCulloch[2] in his old age. As noted earlier, he remarked: "Man to my mind is about the nastiest, most destructive of all the animals. I don't see any reason, if he can evolve machines that can have more fun than he himself can, why they shouldn't take over, enslave us, quite happily. They might have a lot more fun. Invent better games than we ever did." Is it any wonder that faced with such dismal scenarios, most people have understandably negative reactions? If this is what the posthuman means, why shouldn't it be resisted?

Fortunately, these views do not exhaust the meanings of the posthuman. As I have repeatedly argued, human being is first of all embodied being, and the complexities of this embodiment mean that human awareness unfolds in ways very different from those of intelligence embodied in cybernetic machines. Although Moravec's dream of downloading human consciousness into a computer would likely come in for some hard knocks in literature departments (which tend to be skeptical of any kind of transcendence but especially of transcendence through technology), literary studies share with Moravec a major blind spot when it comes to the significance of embodiment. This blind spot is most evident, perhaps, when literary and cultural critics confront the fields of evolutionary biology. From an evolutionary biologist's point of view, modem humans, for all their technological prowess, represent an eye blink in the history of life, a species far too recent to have significant evolutionary impact on human biological behaviors and structures. In my view, arguments like those that Jared Diamond[3] advances in *Guns, Germs, and Steel: The Fates of Human Societies* and *Why Sex Is Fun: The Evolution of Human Sexuality* should be taken seriously. The body is the net result of thousands of years of sedimented evolutionary history, and it is naive to think that this history does not affect human behaviors at every level of thought and action.

Of course, the reflexivity that looms large in cybernetics also inhabits evolutionary biology. The models proposed by evolutionary biologists have encoded within them cultural attitudes and assumptions formed by the same history they propose to analyze; as with cybernetics, observer and system are reflexively bound up with one another. To take only one example, the computer module model advanced by Jerome H. Barkow, Leda Cosmides, and John Tooby in *The Adapted Mind: Evolutionary Psychology and the Generation of Culture* to explain human evolutionary psychology testifies at least as much to the importance of information technologies in shaping contemporary worldviews as it does to human brain function. Nevertheless, these reflexive complexities do not negate the importance of the sedimented history incarnated within the body. Interpreted through metaphors resonant with cultural meanings, the body itself is a congealed metaphor, a physical structure whose constraints and possibilities have been formed by an evolutionary history that intelligent machines do not share. Humans may enter into symbiotic relationships with intelligent machines (already the case, for example, in computer-assisted surgery); they may be displaced by intelligent machines (already in effect, for example, at Japanese and American assembly plants that use robotic arms for labor); but there is a limit to how seamlessly humans can be articulated with intelligent machines, which remain distinctively different from humans in their embodiments. The terror, then, though it does not disappear in this view, tends away from the apocalyptic and toward a more moderate view of seriated social, technological, political, and cultural changes.

What about the pleasures? For some people, including me, the posthuman evokes the exhilarating prospect of getting out of some of the old boxes and opening up new ways of thinking about what being human means. In positing a shift from presence/absence to pattern/randomness, I have sought to show how these categories can be transformed *from the inside* to arrive at new kinds of cultural configurations, which may soon render such dualities obsolete if they have not already. This process of transformation is fueled by tensions between the assumptions encoded in pattern/randomness as opposed to presence/absence. In Jacques Derrida's performance of presence/absence, presence is allied with Logos, God, teleology—in general, with an originary plenitude that can act to ground signification and give order and meaning to the trajectory of history. The work of Eric Havelock, among others, demonstrates how in Plato's *Republic* this view of originary presence authorized a stable, coherent self that could witness and testify to a stable, coherent reality. Through these and other means, the metaphysics of presence front-loaded meaning into the system. Meaning was guaranteed because a stable origin existed. It is now a familiar story how deconstruction exposed the inability of systems to posit their own origins, thus ungrounding signification and rendering meaning indeterminate. As the presence/

absence hierarchy was destabilized and as absence was privileged over presence, lack displaced plenitude, and desire usurped certitude. Important as these moves have been in late-twentieth-century thought, they still took place within the compass of the presence/absence dialectic. One feels lack only if presence is posited or assumed; one is driven by desire only if the object of desire is conceptualized as something to be possessed. Just as the metaphysics of presence required an originary plenitude to articulate a stable self, deconstruction required a metaphysics of presence to articulate the destabilization of that self.

By contrast, pattern/randomness is underlaid by a very different set of assumptions. In this dialectic, meaning is not front-loaded into the system, and the origin does not act to ground signification. As we have seen for multiagent simulations, complexity evolves from highly recursive processes being applied to simple rules. Rather than proceeding along a trajectory toward a known end, such systems evolve toward an open future marked by contingency and unpredictability. Meaning is not guaranteed by a coherent origin; rather, it is made possible (but not inevitable) by the blind force of evolution finding workable solutions within given parameters. Although pattern has traditionally been the privileged term (for example, among the electrical engineers developing information theory), randomness has increasingly been seen to play a fruitful role in the evolution of complex systems. For Chris Langton[4] and Stuart Kauffman[5], chaos accelerates the evolution of biological and artificial life; for Francisco Varela[6], randomness is the froth of noise from which coherent microstates evolve and to which living systems owe their capacity for fast, flexible response; for Henri Atlan[7], noise is the body's murmuring from which emerges complex communication between different levels in a biological system. Although these models differ in their specifics, they agree in seeing randomness not simply as the lack of pattern but as the creative ground from which pattern can emerge.

Indeed, it is not too much to say that in these and similar models, randomness rather than pattern is invested with plenitude. If pattern is the realization of a certain set of possibilities, randomness is the much, much larger set of everything else, from phenomena that cannot be rendered coherent by a given system's organization to those the system cannot perceive at all. In Gregory Bateson's[8] cybernetic epistemology, randomness is what exists outside the confines of the box in which a system is located; it is the larger and unknowable complexity for which the perceptual processes of an organism are a metaphor. Significance is achieved by evolutionary processes that ensure the surviving systems are the ones whose organizations instantiate metaphors for this complexity, unthinkable in itself. When Varela and his coauthors argue in *Embodied Mind* that there is no stable, coherent self but only autonomous agents running programs, they envision pattern as a limitation that drops away as human awareness expands beyond consciousness and encounters the emptiness that, in another guise, could equally well be called the chaos from which all forms emerge.

What do these developments mean for the posthuman? When the self is envisioned as grounded in presence, identified with originary guarantees and teleological trajectories, associated with solid foundations and logical coherence, the posthuman is likely to be seen as antihuman because it envisions the conscious mind as a small subsystem running its program of self-construction and self-assurance while remaining ignorant of the actual dynamics of complex systems. But the posthuman does not really mean the end of humanity. It signals instead the end of a certain conception of the human, a conception that may have applied, at best, to that fraction of humanity who had the wealth, power, and leisure to conceptualize themselves as autonomous beings exercising their will through individual agency and choice. What is lethal is not the posthuman as such but the grafting of the posthuman onto a liberal humanist view of the self. When Moravec imagines "you" choosing to download yourself into a computer, thereby obtaining through technological mastery the ultimate privilege of immortality, he is not abandoning the autonomous liberal subject but is expanding its prerogatives into the realm of the posthuman. Yet the posthuman need not be recuperated back into liberal humanism, nor need it be construed as antihuman. Located within the dialectic of pattern/randomness and grounded in embodied actuality rather than disembodied information, the posthuman offers resources for rethinking the articulation of humans with intelligent machines.

To explore these resources, let us return to Bateson's idea that those organisms that survive will tend to be the ones whose internal structures are good metaphors for the complexities without. What kind of environments will be created by the expanding power and sophistication of intelligent machines? As Richard Lanham has pointed out, in the information-rich environments created by ubiquitous computing, the limiting factor is not the speed of computers, or the rates of transmission through fiber-optic cables, or the amount of data that can be generated and stored. Rather, the scarce commodity is human attention. It makes sense, then, that technological innovation will focus on compensating for this bottleneck. An obvious solution is to design intelligent machines to attend to the choices and tasks that do not have to be done by humans. For example, there are already intelligent-agent programs to sort email, discarding unwanted messages and prioritizing the rest. The programs work along lines similar to neural nets. They tabulate the choices the human operators make, and they feed back this information in recursive loops to readjust the weights given to various kinds of email addresses. After an initial learning period, the sorting programs take over more and more of the email management, freeing humans to give their attention to other matters.

If we extrapolate from these relatively simple programs to an environment that, as Charles Ostman likes to put it, supplies synthetic sentience on demand, human consciousness would ride on top of a highly articulated and complex computational ecology in which many decisions, invisible to human attention, would be made by intelligent machines. Over two decades ago, Joseph Weizenbaum[9] foresaw just such an ecology and passionately argued that judgment is a uniquely human function and must not be turned over to computers. With the rapid development of neural nets and expert programs, it is no longer so clear that sophisticated judgments cannot be made by machines and, in some instances, made more accurately than by humans. But the issue, in Weizenbaum's view, involves more than whether or not the programs work. Rather, the issue is an ethical imperative that humans keep control; to do otherwise is to abdicate their responsibilities as autonomous independent beings. What Weizenbaum's argument makes clear is the connection between the assumptions undergirding the liberal humanist subject and the ethical position that humans, not machines, must be in control. Such an argument assumes a vision of the human in which conscious agency is the essence of human identity. Sacrifice this, and we humans are hopelessly compromised, contaminated with mechanic alienness in the very heart of our humanity. Hence there is an urgency, even panic, in Weizenbaum's insistence that judgment is a uniquely human function. At stake for him is nothing less than what it means to be human.

In the posthuman view, by contrast, conscious agency has never been "in control." In fact, the very illusion of control bespeaks a fundamental ignorance about the nature of the emergent processes through which consciousness, the organism, and the environment are constituted. Mastery through the exercise of autonomous will is merely the story consciousness tells itself to explain results that actually come about through chaotic dynamics and emergent structures. If, as Donna Haraway, Sandra Harding, Evelyn Fox Keller, Carolyn Merchant, and other feminist critics of science have argued, there is a relation among the desire for mastery, an objectivist account of science, and the imperialist project of subduing nature, then the posthuman offers resources for the construction of another kind of account. In this account, emergence replaces teleology; reflexive epistemology replaces objectivism; distributed cognition replaces autonomous will; embodiment replaces a body seen as a support system for the mind; and a dynamic partnership between humans and intelligent machines replaces the liberal humanist subject's manifest destiny to dominate and control nature. Of course, this is not necessarily what the posthuman *will* mean—only what it *can* mean if certain strands among its complex seriations are highlighted and combined to create a vision of the human that uses the posthuman as leverage to avoid reinscribing, and thus repeating, some of the mistakes of the past.

Just as the posthuman need not be antihuman, so it also need not be apocalyptic. Edwin Hutchins[10] addresses the idea of distributed cognition through his nuanced study of the navigational systems of oceangoing ships. His meticulous research shows that the cognitive system responsible for locating the ship in space and navigating it successfully resides not in humans alone but in the complex interactions within an environment that includes both human and nonhuman actors. His study allows him to give an excellent response to John Searle's[11] famous "Chinese room." By imagining a situation in which communication in Chinese can take place without the actors knowing what their actions mean, Searle challenged the idea that machines can think. Suppose, Searle said, that he is stuck inside a room, he who knows not a word of Chinese. Texts written in Chinese are slid through a slot in the door. He has in the room with him baskets of Chinese characters and a rulebook correlating the symbols written on the texts with other symbols in the basket. Using the rulebook, he assembles strings of characters and pushes them out the door. Although his Chinese interlocutors take these strings to be clever responses to their inquiries, Searle has not the least idea of the meaning of the texts he has produced. Therefore, it would be a mistake to say that machines can think, he argues, for like him, they produce comprehensible results without comprehending anything themselves. In Hutchins's neat interpretation, Searle's argument is valuable precisely because it makes clear that it is not Searle but the entire room that knows Chinese. In this distributed cognitive system, the Chinese room knows more than do any of its components, including Searle. The situation of modem humans is akin to that of Searle in the Chinese room, for every day we participate in systems whose total cognitive capacity exceeds our individual knowledge, including such devices as cars with electronic ignition systems, microwaves with computer chips that precisely adjust power levels, fax machines that warble to other fax machines, and electronic watches that communicate with a timing radio wave to set themselves and correct their date. Modern humans are capable of more sophisticated cognition than cavemen not because moderns are smarter, Hutchins concludes, but because they have constructed smarter environments in which to work.

Hutchins would no doubt disagree with Weizenbaum's view that judgment should be reserved for humans alone. Like cognition, decision-making is distributed between human and nonhuman agents, from the steam-powered steering system that suddenly failed on a navy vessel Hutchins was studying to the charts and pocket calculators that the navigators were then forced to use to calculate their position. He convincingly shows that these adaptations to changed circumstances were evolutionary and embodied rather than abstract and consciously designed (pp. 347-51). The solution to the problem caused by this sudden failure of the steering mechanism was "clearly discovered by the organization [of the system as a whole] before it was discovered by any of the participants" (p. 361). Seen in this perspective, the prospect of humans working in partnership with intelligent machines is not so much a usurpation of human right and responsibility as it is a further development in the construction of distributed cognition environments, a construction that has been ongoing for thousands of years. Also changed in this perspective is the relation of human subjectivity to its environment. No longer is human will seen as the source from which emanates the mastery necessary to dominate and control the environment. Rather, the distributed cognition of the emergent human subject correlates with—in Bateson's phrase, becomes a metaphor for—the distributed cognitive system as a whole, in which "thinking" is done by both human and nonhuman actors. "Thinking consists of bringing these structures into coordination so they can shape and be shaped by one another," Hutchins wrote (p. 316). To conceptualize the human in these terms is not to imperil human survival but is precisely to enhance it, for the more we understand the flexible, adaptive structures that coordinate our environments and the metaphors that we ourselves are, the better we can fashion images of ourselves that accurately reflect the complex interplays that ultimately make the entire world one system.

This view of the posthuman also offers resources for thinking in more sophisticated ways about virtual technologies. As long as the human subject is envisioned as an autonomous self with unambiguous boundaries, the human-computer interface can only be parsed as a division between the solidity of real life on one side and the illusion of virtual reality on the other, thus obscuring the far-reaching changes initiated by the development of virtual technologies. Only if one thinks of the subject as an autonomous self independent of the environment is one likely to experience the panic performed by Norbert Wiener's[12] *Cybernetics* and Bernard Wolfe's *Limbo*. This view of the self authorizes the fear that if the boundaries are breached at all, there will be nothing to stop the self's complete dissolution. By contrast, when the human is seen as part of a distributed system, the full expression of human capability can be seen precisely to *depend* on the splice rather than being imperiled by it. Writing in another context, Hutchins arrives at an insight profoundly applicable to virtual technologies: "What used to look like internalization [of thought and subjectivity] now appears as a gradual propagation of organized functional properties across a set of malleable media" (p. 312). This vision is a potent antidote to the view that parses virtuality as a division between an inert body that is left behind and a disembodied subjectivity that inhabits a virtual realm, the construction of virtuality performed by Case in William Gibson's[13] *Neuromancer* when he delights in the "bodiless exultation of cyberspace" and fears, above all, dropping back into the "meat" of the body. By contrast, in the model that Hutchins presents and that the posthuman helps to authorize, human functionality expands because the parameters of the cognitive system it inhabits expand. In this model, it is not a question of leaving the body behind but rather of extending embodied awareness in highly specific, local, and material ways that would be impossible without electronic prosthesis.

As we have seen, cybernetics was born in a froth of noise when Norbert Wiener first thought of it as a way to maximize human potential in a world that is in essence chaotic and unpredictable. Like many other pioneers, Wiener helped to initiate a journey that would prove to have consequences more far-reaching and subversive than even his formidable powers of imagination could conceive. As Bateson, Varela, and others would later argue, the noise crashes within as well as without. The chaotic, unpredictable nature of complex dynamics implies that subjectivity is emergent rather than given, distributed rather than located solely in consciousness, emerging from and integrated into a chaotic world rather than occupying a position of mastery and control removed from it. Bruno Latour[14] has argued that we have never been modern; the seriated history of cybernetics—emerging from networks at once materially real, socially regulated, and discursively constructed—suggests, for similar reasons, that we have always been posthuman. The purpose of this book has been to chronicle the journeys that have made this realization possible. If the three stories told here—how information lost its body, how the cyborg was constructed in the postwar years as technological artifact and cultural icon, and how the human became the posthuman—have at times seemed to present the posthuman as a transformation to be feared and abhorred rather than welcomed and embraced, that reaction has everything to do with how the posthuman is constructed and understood. The best possible time to contest for what the posthuman means is now, before the trains of thought it embodies have been laid down so firmly that it would take dynamite to change them. Although some current versions of the posthuman point toward the antihuman and the apocalyptic, we can craft others that will be conducive to the long-range survival of humans and of the other life-forms, biological and artificial, with whom we share the planet and ourselves.

注释:

1. 汉斯·莫拉维克（1948— ），卡内基梅隆大学移动机器人实验室主任，同时也是一位未来学和后人文主义学者。他关于机器人、人工智能和技术给人类带来的影响等方面的论述产生了广泛的影响。

2. 沃伦·麦卡洛克（1898—1969），美国神经科学家和控制论学者，以其在大脑理论基础上的工作和对控制论的贡献而闻名。

3. 贾雷德·戴蒙德（1937— ），美国演化生物学家、生理学家、生物地理学家以及非小说类作家。他最著名的作品《枪炮、病菌与钢铁》发表于1997年，获1998年美国普利策奖和英国科普图书奖。

4. 克里斯托弗·朗顿（1949— ），美国计算机科学家，人工生命领域的创始人之一，是“人工生命”这一名词的创造者。

5. 斯图亚特·考夫曼（1939— ），美国医学博士、理论生物学家和复杂系统研究员，主要研究人类生命的起源。

6. 弗朗西斯克·瓦雷拉（1946—2001），智利生物学家、哲学家和神经科学家，最著名的成就是提出生物学上的自生性概念。

7. 亨利·阿特朗（1931— ），法国生物学家和哲学家。

8. 格雷戈里·贝特森（1904—1980），英国人类学家、语言学家、心理学家和控制论学者。

9. 约瑟夫· 维森鲍姆（1923—2008），美国计算机科学家，麻省理工学院荣休教授。

10. 埃德温·哈钦斯（1948— ），美国神经科学家和认知人类学家，分布式认知理论的主要贡献者。

11. 约翰·塞尔（1932— ），美国哲学家，研究专长为语言哲学和心灵哲学。

12. 诺伯特·维纳（1894—1964），美国应用数学家，控制论的创始人。

13. 威廉·吉布森（1948— ），美国科幻小说作家。

14. 布鲁诺·拉图尔（1947— ），法国著名哲学家、社会学家、人类学家。

Chapter Eighteen **Postmodern Ethical Literary Criticism**

伦理同社会生活息息相关，也应随着社会的变化不断改变，这样才能更好地发挥伦理道德的功用，规范人们的伦理关系和道德行为，指导人的全面发展，促进社会和谐。进入后现代主义时期，现代西方伦理学已经变得不再合乎时宜，反而把人类带入了伦理失范和道德危机、社会危机的深渊。后现代主义伦理学应运而生。作为后现代主义时期的一种特定的意识形态，后现代伦理学呼吁人们关注后现代时期人类生存和发展的价值和意义，解构和批判现代性和现代伦理，试图重新建立后现代道德和价值体系，重构自我与他者之间的道德关系，强调自我必须承担对他者的绝对责任，并以此来重塑人与人之间、人与群体之间的道德关系，实现人类社会的和谐运行，从而推动经济、社会和环境的全面、协调、可持续发展。

后现代文学伦理学批评从后现代西方伦理学视角阐释后现代主义文学文本，通过虚构的人与社会所表现的后现代被接受和认可的伦理关系，以及在这种关系的基础上形成的道德秩序和维系这种秩序的各种规范，揭示文学文本所描写的后现代伦理关系和道德秩序的变化及其引发的各种问题和导致的不同结果，为后现代人类文明进步提供后现代伦理教诲和道德经验。

后现代西方伦理学家主张重新确立自我与他者之间的一种新的牢固的道德关系——承认差异，尊重他者，担负对他者的绝对责任，建构为他者的自我和“为他者的人道主义”，建构超越民族、种族、国家、文化等最低限度的后现代伦理共同体。列维纳斯认为，人类的天性和主体性是对他者的责任，自我与他者之间的关系是一种尊重他者并对他者担负绝对责任的道德关系。后现代伦理学在呼唤责任、呼唤友善、呼唤自我担负对他者绝对责任的同时，也反思和批判造成社会不公的集权和暴力。德里达认为，“在无条件地对他人负责的绝对律令下，谈论博爱、友谊、平等、未来的民主才是有意义的。也就是说，在最低限度共同体之内的‘友爱’才不是一种空虚的许诺”。

“未来的民主”开放经验之中对美好生活的价值理想的许诺，意味着无条件地尊重个体性，无条件地体现“无名的主体间”的平等，无条件地兼容别人。

后现代伦理学不仅倡导人类社会建立尊重差异、相互包容、相互关爱的伦理关系，同时也聚焦人与自然之间的道德关系，反对现代性的人与自然的主奴关系，强调人与自然的伙伴关系、相互依存的关系，呼吁人类与自然同生共荣、协同进步，反对人类采取算计、盘剥和掠夺自然的生产方式和生活方式建立生态的意识形态，建构可持续发展的生态的人类关系。

在对后现代文学作品的主题思想进行深刻探讨的同时，后现代文学伦理学批评还关注后现代文学作品的叙事手法。后现代文学伦理的叙事取消作者的权威和文本的叙述中心，尊重差异和他者，采用多角度观察、多叙述者、多声音的叙述、多样杂糅的结构、多元变化的表现技巧，使用平行结构、戏谑模仿、直接引用等构成后现代伦理狂欢化的互文叙事。这些叙事手法同后现代伦理道德价值观完全一致。

Zygmunt Bauman

齐格蒙特·鲍曼（1925—2017），波兰裔英国社会学家和哲学家。他出生于波兰并在波兰求学，但在 1968 年波兰政治危机中被迫放弃波兰国籍，经辗转后定居英国，任教于利兹大学。鲍曼是当代最知名的社会理论家和思想家之一，他的学术关注领域广泛，涵盖同当代社会性质的变迁及其对群体和个人之影响相关的方方面面的议题，但影响力最大的要数他关于现代性和大屠杀、后现代消费主义以及流动的现代性的探讨。他也是后现代主义思想的主要贡献者之一。鲍曼的主要著作有《后现代伦理学》《现代性与大屠杀》《流动的现代性》《共同体》《个体化社会》等。他于 1990 年被授予雅马尔费奖，1998 年被授予阿多尔诺奖，2010 年被授予阿斯图里亚斯王子人文奖。

Introduction: Morality in Modern and Postmodern Perspective

（Bauman, Zygmunt. *Postmodern Ethics*. Cambridge: Wiley-Blackwell, 1993, pp. 1-14.）

本文节选自鲍曼的名著《后现代伦理学》，是全书的开篇总纲。在选段中，鲍曼首先指出了现代伦理所犯的两个致命错误——追寻道德的普遍性以及为道德设立理性根基。这两点现代伦理奉行的根本性原则不仅不符合道德的原初面目，而且使道德沦为权力的帮凶，正如在集权体制下威权打着道德的名义清除异己所做的那样。鲍曼接着强调了后现代道德的特点：后现代道德认为道德的本来面目是含混，不是非黑即白的；道德是非理性的，而且并不存在先验性的道德原则；没有普遍性的道德准则。后现代伦理提倡的道德是人们必须遵守的一种绝对的道德责任感，即对他者的关爱。这种道德责任是无法被解释的、非理性的义务。只有无条件地遵守这一道德责任，社会才能和谐地运行，保障所有个体的福祉。

Modern ethical thought in co-operation with modern legislative practice fought its way through to such a radical solution under the twin banners of *universality* and *foundation*.

In the practice of legislators, *universality* stood for the exceptionless rule of one set of laws on the territory over which their sovereignty extended. Philosophers defined universality as that feature of ethical prescriptions which compelled every human creature, just for the fact of being a human creature, to recognize it as right and thus to accept it as obligatory. The two universalities winked and beckoned to each other without really merging. But they did co-operate, closely and fruitfully, even if no contract was entered, signed and lodged in the state archives or university libraries. The legislators' coercive practices (or intentions) of uniformization supplied the 'epistemological ground' on which philosophers could build their models of universal human nature: while the philosophers' success in 'naturalizing' the legislators' cultural (or, rather, administrative) artifice helped to represent the legally constructed model of the state-subject as the embodiment and epitome of human destiny.

In the practice of the legislators, *foundations* stood for the coercive powers of the state that rendered obedience to the rules a sensible expectation; the rule was 'well founded' in as far as it enjoyed the support of such powers, and the foundation was strengthened with the effectiveness of the support. For the philosophers, rules would be well founded when the persons expected to follow them believed, or could be convinced, that for one reason or another following them was the right thing to do. 'Well-founded' are such rules as offer a cogent answer to the question 'Why should I obey them?' The laying of such a foundation was seen as imperative, since autonomous individuals faced with heteronomous legal/ethical demands were likely to ask such questions—and above all, the question 'why should I be moral?' At any rate, the philosophers and legislators alike did expect them to ask such questions—as both thought or acted on the same assumption that good rules must be artificially designed rules, on the same premise that individuals when free would not necessarily volunteer to embrace good rules if unassisted, and on the same principle that in order to act morally, individuals must first accept the rules of moral behavior, and that this would not happen were they not persuaded first that acting morally is more agreeable than acting without morals, and that the rules they are called to accept spell out indeed what moral acting is. Again—as in the case of 'universality'—the two versions of 'foundations', without ever blending, co-operated and complemented each other. Popular belief that the rules are well justified in what they do would ease the task of coercive agencies, while the relentless pressure of legal sanctions would pour blood into the dry veins of philosophical argument.

All in all, the persevering and unyielding search for rules that 'will stick' and foundations that 'won't shake' drew its animus from the faith in the feasibility and ultimate triumph of the humanist project. A society free from irremovable contradictions, a society pointing the way, as logic does, to correct solutions only, can be built eventually, given enough time and good will. The right design and final argument can be, must be, and will be found. With such a faith, singed fingers would not hurt too much, there would be no last straws and failure of yesterday's hopes would only spur the explorers to a yet greater effort today. Any allegedly 'foolproof' recipe[1] could be proved wrong, disavowed and rejected—but not the very search for a truly foolproof recipe, one that will, as one of them surely must, put paid to all further search. In other words, the moral thought and practice of modernity was animated by the belief in the possibility of a *non-ambivalent*, *non-aporetic ethical code*. Perhaps such a code has not been found yet. But it surely waits round the next corner. Or the corner after next.

It is the *disbelief* in such a possibility that is *post*modern-'post' not in the 'chronological' sense (not in the sense of displacing and replacing modernity, of being born only at the moment when modernity ends or fades away, of rendering the modern view impossible once it comes into its own), but in the sense of implying (in the form of conclusion, or mere premonition) that the long and earnest efforts of modernity have been misguided, undertaken under false pretenses and bound to—sooner or later—run their course; that, in other words, it is modernity itself that will demonstrate (if it has not demonstrated yet) and demonstrate beyond reasonable doubt its impossibility, the vanity of its hopes and the wastefulness of its works. The foolproof—universal and unshakably founded—ethical code will never be found;

having singed our fingers once too often, we know now what we did not know then, when we embarked on this journey of exploration: that a non-aporetic, non-ambivalent morality, an ethics that is universal and 'objectively founded', is a practical impossibility; perhaps also an *oxymoron*, a contradiction in terms.

It is the exploration of consequences of this postmodern critique of modern ambitions that constitutes the subject-matter of this study.

I suggest that the following are the marks of moral conditions, as they appear once contemplated from the postmodern perspective.

1. The assertions (mutually contradictory, yet stated all too often with the same force of conviction) 'Humans are essentially good, and they only have to be assisted to act according to their nature', and 'Humans are essentially bad, and they must be prevented from acting on their impulses', are both wrong. In fact, humans are morally ambivalent: ambivalence resides at the heart of the 'primary scene'[2] of human face-to-face. All subsequent social arrangements—the power—assisted institutions as well as the rationally articulated and pondered rules and duties—deploy that ambivalence as their building material while doing their best to cleanse it from its original sin of being an ambivalence. The latter efforts are either ineffective or result in exacerbating the evil they wish to disarm. Given the primary structure of human togetherness, a non-ambivalent morality is an existential impossibility. No logically coherent ethical code can 'fit' the essentially ambivalent condition of morality. Neither can rationality 'override' moral impulse; at the utmost, it can silence it and paralyse, thereby rendering the chances of the 'good being done' not stronger, perhaps weaker, than they otherwise would have been. What follows is that moral conduct cannot be guaranteed; not by better designed contexts for human action, nor by better formed motives of human action. We need to learn how to live without such guarantees, and with the awareness that guarantees will never be offered—that a perfect society, as well as a perfect human being, is not a viable prospect, while attempts to prove the contrary result in more cruelty than humanity, and certainly less morality.

2. Moral phenomena are inherently 'non-rational'. Since they are moral only if they precede the consideration of purpose and the calculation of gains and losses, they do not fit the 'means-end' scheme. They also escape explanation in terms of the utility or service they render or are called to render to the moral subject, a group or a cause. They are not regular, repetitive, monotonous and predictable in a way that

would allow them to be represented as *rule-guided*. It is mainly for this reason they cannot be exhausted by any 'ethical code'. Ethics is thought of after the pattern of Law. As Law does, it strives to define the 'proper' and 'improper' actions in situations on which it takes a stand. It sets for itself an ideal (rarely if ever reached in practice) of churning up exhaustive and unambiguous definitions; such as would provide clear-cut rules for the choice between proper and improper and leave no 'grey area' of ambivalence and multiple interpretations. In other words, it acts on the assumption that in each life-situation one choice can and should be decreed to be good in opposition to numerous bad ones, and so acting in all situations can be rational while the actors are, as they should be, rational as well. But this assumption leaves out what is properly moral in morality. It shifts moral phenomena from the realm of personal autonomy into that of power-assisted heteronomy. It substitutes the learnable knowledge of rules for the moral self constituted by responsibility. It places answerability to the legislators and guardians of the code where there had formerly been answerability to the Other and to moral self-conscience, the context in which moral stand is taken.

3. Morality is incurably *aporetic*. Few choices (and only those which are relatively trivial and of minor existential importance) are unambiguously good. The majority of moral choices are made between contradictory impulses. Most importantly, however, virtually every moral impulse, if acted upon in full, leads to immoral consequences (most characteristically, the impulse to care for the Other, when taken to its extreme, leads to the annihilation of the autonomy of the Other, to domination and oppression); yet no moral impulse can implement itself unless the moral actor earnestly strives to stretch the effort to the limit. The moral self moves, feels and acts in the context of ambivalence and is shot through with uncertainty. Hence the ambiguity-free moral situation has solely an utopian existence of the perhaps indispensable horizon and stimulus for a moral self, but not a realistic target of ethical practice. Seldom may moral acts bring complete satisfaction; responsibility that guides the moral person is always ahead of what has been and what can be done. All the efforts to the contrary notwithstanding, uncertainty is bound to accompany the condition of the moral self forever. Indeed, one can recognize the moral self by its uncertainty whether all that should have been done, has been.

4. Morality is *not universalizable*. This statement does not necessarily endorse moral relativism, expressed in the frequently voiced and apparently similar

proposition, that any morality is but a local (and temporary) custom, that what is believed to be moral in one place and time is certain to be frowned upon in another, and so all kinds of moral conduct practised so far happen to be relative to the time and place, affected by vagaries of local or tribal histories and cultural inventions; that proposition is more often than not correlated with an injunction against all comparisons between moralities, and above all against all exploration of other than purely accidental and contingent sources of morality. I will argue against this overtly relativistic and in the end nihilistic view of morality. The assertion 'morality is un-universalizable' as it appears in this book carries a different meaning: it opposes a concrete version of moral universalism which in the modern era served as but a thinly disguised declaration of intent to embark on *Gleichschaltung*,[3] on an arduous campaign to smother the differences and above all to eliminate all 'wild'—autonomous, obstreperous[4] and uncontrolled—sources of moral judgement. While acknowledging the present diversity of moral beliefs and institutionally promoted actions, and the past and persistent variety of individual moral postures, modern thought and modern practice considered it an abomination and a challenge and tried hard to overcome it. But it did not do so openly, not in the name of extending one's own preferred ethical code over populations which abide by different codes and tightening up the grip in which it held populations already under its rule—but surreptitiously, in the name of one all-human ethics bound to evict and supplant all local *distortions*. Such efforts, as we see it now, may take no other form than that of the substitution of heteronomous, enforced-from-outside, ethical rules for the autonomous responsibility of the moral self (and that means nothing less than the incapacitation, even destruction, of the moral self). Thus, their overall effect is not so much the 'universalization of morality', as the silencing of moral impulse and channelling of moral capacities to socially designed targets that may, and do, include immoral purposes.

5. From the perspective of the 'rational order', morality is and is bound to remain *irrational*. For every social totality bent on uniformity and the soliciting of disciplined, co-ordinated action, the stubborn and resilient autonomy of the moral self is a scandal. From the control desk of society, it is viewed as the germ of chaos and anarchy inside order; as the outer limit of what reason (or its self-appointed spokesmen and agents) can do to design and implement whatever has been proclaimed as the 'perfect' as the arrangement of human cohabitation. Moral impulses are,

however, also an indispensable resource in the administration of any such 'really existing' arrangement: they supply the raw material of sociality and of commitment to others in which all social orders are moulded. They have to be, therefore, tamed, harnessed, and exploited, rather than merely suppressed or outlawed. Hence the endemic ambivalence in the treatment of moral self by societal administration: the moral self needs to be cultivated without being given a free rein; it needs to be constantly trimmed and kept in the desire shape without its growth being stifled and its vitality desiccated. The social management of morality is a complex and delicate operation which cannot but precipitate more ambivalence than it manages to eliminate.

6. Given the ambiguous impact of the societal efforts at ethical legislation, one must assume that moral responsibility—being *for* the Other before one can be *with* the Other—is the first reality of the self, a starting point rather than a product of society. It precedes all engagement with the Other, be it through knowledge, evaluation, suffering or doing. It has therefore no 'foundation'—no cause, no determining factor. For the same reason for which it cannot be wished or maneuvered out of existence, it cannot offer a convincing case for the necessity of its presence. In the absence of a foundation, the question 'How possible?' makes no sense when addressed to morality. Such a question calls morality to justify itself—yet morality has no excuse, as it precedes the emergence of the socially administered context inside which the terms in which justifications and excuses are couched appear and make sense. That question demands that morality show the certificate of its origin—yet there is no self before the moral self, morality being the ultimate, non-determined presence; indeed an act of creation *ex nihilo*,[5] if there ever was one. That question, finally, assumes tacitly that moral responsibility is a mystery contrary to reason, that selves would not be 'normally' moral if not for some special and powerful cause; to become moral, selves have first to give up or curtail some other constituent of themselves (the most common being the premise that—with moral action being uncharacteristically unselfish—the element surrendered is self-interest; what is assumed here is that being-for-the-Other rather than for-itself is 'contrary to nature'; and that two modalities of being are in opposition). Yet moral responsibility is precisely the act of self-constitution. The surrender, if any, occurs on the road leading from the moral to the social self, from being-for to being 'merely' with. It took centuries of power-assisted legal drill and philosophical indoctrination to make

the opposite seem evidently true.

7. What follows is that contrary to both the popular opinion and hot-headed 'everything goes'[6] triumphalism of certain postmodernist writers, the postmodern perspective on moral phenomena *does not reveal the relativism* of morality. Neither must it call for, or obliquely recommend, a 'nothing we can do about it' disarmament in the face of an apparently irreducible variety of ethic codes. The contrary is the case. Modern societies practice moral parochialism under the mask of promoting universal ethics. By exposing the essential incongruity between any power-assisted ethical code on the one hand and the infinitely complex condition of the moral self on the other, and by exposing the falsity of society's pretence to be the ultimate author and the sole trustworthy guardian of morality, the postmodern perspective shows the relativity of ethical codes and of moral practices they recommend or support to be the outcome of the *politically* promoted parochiality of *ethical codes* that pretend to be universal, and not of the 'uncodified' moral condition and moral conduct which they decried as parochial. It is the ethical codes which are plagued with relativism, that plague being but a reflection or a sediment of tribal parochialism of institutional powers that usurp ethical authority. The overcoming of variety through the extension of the scope and the reach of a given institutional power, political or cultural (as the modern fighters against moral relativism demanded virtually in unison) can only lead to a yet more thorough substitution of ethics for morality, a code for the moral self, heteronomy for autonomy. What the postmodern perspective succeeded in doing, having cast aside the prophesies of the imminent arrival of the power-assisted brand of universality, was to pierce through the thick veil of myths down to the common moral condition that precedes all diversifying effects of the social administration of moral capacity, not to mention the felt need of similarly administered 'universalization'. The humankind-wide moral unity is thinkable, if at all, not as the end-product of globalizing the domain of political powers with ethical pretensions, but as the utopian horizon of deconstructing the 'without us the deluge'[7] claims of nation-states, nations-in-search-of-the-state, traditional communities and communities-in-search-of-a-tradition, tribes and neo-tribes, as well as their appointed and self-appointed spokesmen and prophets; as the remote (and, so be it, utopian) prospect of the emancipation of the autonomous moral self and vindication of its moral responsibility; as a prospect of the moral self facing up, without being tempted to escape, to the inherent and incurable ambivalence in which

that responsibility casts it and which is already its fate, still waiting to be recast into its destiny.

注释:

1. 指安全可靠，永远不会出错的办法。
2. “第一现场”，这里指道德原本的性质就是其模糊性。
3. 该词原本是纳粹党术语，后用来指极权政体之下社会、经济或机构的统一化、标准化。
4. 无序的，难以管控的。
5. 拉丁语，英译为 out of nothing，意指事物的绝对存在性。
6. 某些自诩的后现代主义者常喊出的口号，意思是“什么都行”。
7. 指道德冷漠者常说的口头禅:“只要与我们无关，哪怕洪水滔天。”

Emmanuel Levinas

伊曼努尔·列维纳斯(1906—1995),是法国现当代哲学界中最具创见和影响力的哲学家之一。列维纳斯出生于立陶宛的犹太人家庭,后赴法国求学并在法国任教。列维纳斯的思想深受犹太哲学的影响,同时也受到海德格尔、胡塞尔、布朗肖等人的启发,他试图打通犹太哲学和大陆哲学的脉络,对存在主义、伦理学、现象学和本体论等领域都有所涉猎。他的主要学术思路是对西方哲学中的本体论进行批判,指出西方哲学传统总是试图建立一个总体性的框架,因而抹杀了异质性的他者之存在。而同本体论相比,伦理学应该是第一哲学,因为伦理学对承认差异、尊重他者提出了绝对的要求。他的代表作有《总体与无限:论外在性》《从存在到存在者》等。

Sense and Ethics

(Levinas, Emmanuel. *Humanism of the Other*, Nidra Poller trans, Chicago: University of Illinois Press, 2005, pp. 29-36.)

列维纳斯哲学思想的最大特点是其把伦理学作为第一哲学,而其伦理学思想的核心是他者伦理,即他把自我同他者之间的伦理关系作为社会伦理建构的基础。在列维纳斯看来,他者的存在具有绝对性,他者的绝对存在要求主体自我面向他者,响应他者向自我发出的呼唤,承担对他者的绝对责任。列维纳斯也指出,这种自我对他者应负的责任并不能被传统西方哲学中的推理所论证，而是一种超越性的存在，指向无限。本文节选自列维纳斯的著作《他者的人道主义》，是对自我同他者之伦理关系的一段简要却雄辩的阐述，在其中列维纳斯指出他者对自我有一种原初的吸引力，而他者对自我发出不夹杂任何意志的、赤裸的律令，要求自我面向他者，为他者而存在。

Sense as the liturgical orientation of the work does not proceed from need. Need opens onto a world that is *for me*; it returns to self. Even when it is sublime, like the need for salvation, it is still nostalgia, homesickness. Need is precisely return, the Ego's anxiety for self, egoism, the original form of identification, assimilation of the world in view of coincidence with self, in view of happiness.

In *Cantique des Colonnes*, Valéry[1] speaks of "desire without deficiency." This is surely a reference to Plato's analysis of pure pleasures, where he finds aspiration conditioned by no prior need. We will take up this term of desire. To a subject turned in on itself and characterized, according to the Stoicist[2] expression, by ορμη or the tendency to persist in its being or, according to Heidegger's[3] formulation "one whose existence is an issue for that existence itself," to a subject who so defines himself by concern for self and who, in happiness, fulfils his *for-himself*, we oppose the Desire of the Other that proceeds from a being already satisfied and in that sense independent, and who does not desire for himself. Need of someone who has no more needs, recognized in the need of an Other who is Others, who is not (as in Hobbes and Hegel) my enemy, and not my "complement" as he remains in Plato's *Republic*, constituted because something is lacking in the subsistence of each individual. The Desire for Others—sociality—arises in a being who lacks nothing or, more exactly, arises beyond all that could be lacking or satisfying to him. In Desire the Ego goes out to Others in a way that compromises the sovereign identification of the Ego with oneself whose need is just nostalgia, and that the consciousness of need anticipates. Instead of completing or contenting me, the movement toward Others involves me in a contingency that in one aspect didn't concern me and should leave me indifferent: what am I doing in this mess? Where does the shock come from, when I pass by, indifferent, under the gaze of Others? The relation with Others challenges me, empties me of myself and keeps on emptying me by showing me ever new resources. I did not know I was so rich, but I don't have the right to keep anything anymore. Is the Desire for Others appetite or generosity? The Desirable does not satisfy my Desire, it hollows me, nourishing me somehow with new hungers. Desire turns out to be bounty. There is a scene in *Crime and Punishment* where Dostoyevsky[4] describes Sonia Marmeladova looking with "insatiable compassion" at Raskolnikov in his despair. He does not say "inexhaustible compassion." As if the compassion that goes from Sonia to Raskolnikov were a hunger that Raskolnikov's presence nourished beyond all saturation, by increasing that hunger, infinitely.

The Desire for Others that we feel in the most common social experience is fundamental movement, pure transport, absolute orientation, sense. All analysis of language in contemporary philosophy emphasizes, and rightfully so, its hermeneutic structure and the cultural effort of the embodied being who expresses himself. Hasn't the third dimension been forgotten? The direction toward the Other who is not only collaborator and neighbor of our cultural work of expression or client of our artistic production, but interlocutor: the one to whom expression expresses, for whom celebration celebrates, he who is both term of an orientation and first signification. In other words, before it is celebration of being, expression is a relation with the one to whom I express the expression and whose presence is already required so that my cultural gesture of expression can be produced. The Other who faces me is not included in the totality of being that is expressed. He arises behind all collection of being, as the one to whom I express what I express. I find myself facing the Other. He is neither a cultural signification nor a simply given. He is, primordially, *sense* because he lends it to expression itself, because only through him can a phenomenon such as signification introduce itself, of itself, into being.

The analyses of Desire, which we first carefully distinguished from need, Desire, which traces sense in being, will be clarified by an analysis of the otherness toward which Desire tends.

The manifestation of the Other is of course produced, first of all, in the way all signification is produced. The Other is present in a cultural whole, illuminated by that whole just as a text by its context. The manifestation of the whole ensures its presence. It is illuminated by the light of the world. Comprehension of the Other is therefore a hermeneutic, an exegesis. The Other gives itself in the concrete of the totality to which it is immanent and that—corresponding to the remarkable analyses of Merleau-Ponty[5] on which we have widely drawn in the first sections of this study—our cultural initiatives—artistic, linguistic, or corporeal gesture—expresses and unveils.

But the epiphany of the Other bears its own significance, independent of the signification received from the world. The Other not only comes to us from a context but signifies by itself, without that mediation. The cultural signification that is in a way revealed, reveals, *horizontally*; that reveals itself from the historical world to which it belongs; and, as phenomenology expresses it, reveals the horizon of this world; this mundane signification is disturbed and upset by another presence, abstract (or more exactly, absolute), non-integrated in the world. That presence consists in coming to us, *making an entry*. Which can be stated thus: the *phenomenon* that is the apparition of the Other is also *face*; or again (to show this entry at every instant new in the immanence and essential historicity of the phenomenon), the epiphany of the face is *visitation*. Whereas the phenomenon is already, on whatever score, image, captive manifestation of its mute plastic form, the epiphany of the face is alive. Its life consists in undoing the form where every *being* [*étant*], when it enters into immanence—that is, when it exposes itself as theme—is already dissimulated.

The Other who manifests himself in the face pierces, in a way, his own plastic essence, like a being who opens the window where, nevertheless, his face is already traced. His presence consists in divesting himself of the form that nevertheless already manifested him. His manifestation is a surplus on the inevitable paralysis of manifestation. This is what we describe with the words: the face speaks. The manifestation of the face is the first discourse. Speaking is first and foremost this way of coming from behind one's appearance, behind one's form; an opening in the opening.

So the visitation of the face is not the unveiling of a world. In the concreteness of the world, the face is abstract or naked. It is denuded of its own image. By the nudity of the face, nudity in itself is simply possible in the world.

The nudity of the face is a stripping with no cultural ornament—an absolution—a detachment of its form in the heart of production of form. The face *enters* our world from an ab-solutely foreign sphere, that is, precisely, from an absolute, which is in fact the name of the completely foreign. The signification of the face in its abstraction is, in the literal sense of the term, extraordinary, exterior to all order, to all world. How is such a construction possible? How is it that the coming of the Other, the visitation of the face, the absolute, cannot convert—in any way—into revelation, be it symbolism or suggestion? How can the face not be simply *true representation* where the Other renounces his otherness? To answer that we must study, in concluding, the exceptional significance of the trace and the personal "order" where such a signification is possible.

For the moment let us emphasize the sense entailed by the abstraction or nudity of the face that pierces the order of the world, and the upheaval of consciousness that responds to this "abstraction." Stripped of its form, the face is chilled to the bone in its nakedness. It is a desolation. The nakedness of the face is destitution and already supplication in the rectitude that sights me. But this supplication is an obligation. Humility unites with elevation. And announces thereby the ethical dimension of visitation. Whereas true *representation* remains the possibility of appearance, whereas the world that collides with thought can do nothing against *free thinking* able to refuse itself from within, taking refuge in itself, remaining precisely *free thinking* in face of the true, able to go back to itself, reflect on itself and claim to be the origin of that which it receives, able to master by memory that which precedes it, whereas free thinking *stays the Same*, the face imposes on me and I cannot stay deaf to its appeal, or forget it, what I mean is I cannot stop being responsible for its desolation. Consciousness loses its first place.

Thus, the presence of the face signifies an irrefutable order—a commandment—that arrests the availability of consciousness. Consciousness is challenged [*mise en question*] by the face. The challenge does not come from awareness of that challenge. The "absolutely other" is not reflected in consciousness. It resists to such an extent that even its resistance is not converted into contents of consciousness. The visitation is the upset of the very egoism of the Ego that upholds that conversion. The face disorients the intentionality that sights it.

This is a challenge of consciousness, not a consciousness of the challenge. The Ego loses its sovereign coincidence with self, its identification where consciousness comes back triumphantly to itself to reside in itself. In the face of the obligation of the Other, the Ego is banished from that repose, is not the already glorious consciousness of this exile. All complacency destroys the rectitude of the ethical movement.

But the challenge to that naïve savage liberty for self, sure of its refuge in itself, is not reduced to a negative movement. The challenge to self is precisely reception of the absolutely other. The epiphany of the absolutely other is face where the Other hails me and signifies to me, by its nakedness, by its destitution, an order. Its presence is this summons to respond. The Ego does not only become conscious of this necessity to respond as if it were a demand or a particular duty it must decide on. The Ego is through and through, in its very position, responsibility, or diacony, as in chapter 53 or Isaiah.[6]

To be Me/Ego thenceforth signifies being unable to escape from responsibility, as if the whole edifice of creation stood on my shoulders. But the responsibility that empties the Ego of its imperialism and egoism—be it egoism of salvation—does not transform it into a moment of the universal order; it confirms the uniqueness of the Ego. The uniqueness of the Ego is the fact that no one can answer in my stead.

Discovering such an orientation for the Ego means identifying Ego and morality. The Ego is infinitely responsible in face of the Other. The Other who incites this ethical movement of consciousness, who deregulates the good conscience of the coincidence of Same with self, includes a surplus that is inadequate to intentionality. This is Desire, burning with a fire that is not need extinguished by saturation, thinking beyond what one thinks. Because of this unassimilable surplus, because of this *beyond*, we call the relation that attaches the Ego to Other: the idea of Infinity.

The idea of Infinity is Desire. It consists, paradoxically, in thinking more than is thought while keeping it immeasurable with regard to thought, and entering into relation with the ungraspable while maintaining its status as ungraspable. Infinity is not correlative to the idea of Infinity, as if that idea were an intentionality *accomplishing itself* in its "objects." The marvel of infinity in the finitude of thought is an upheaval of intentionality, an upheaval of this appetite for light that is intentionality; contrary to saturation where intentionality is pacified, Infinity disorients its Idea. The Ego, in relation with Infinity, is the impossibility of stopping the forward march, the impossibility, as Plato expressed it in the *Phaedo*, of deserting one's post; it is, literally, no time to look back, no way to escape responsibility, no inner hiding place to go back into self; it is marching straight ahead without concern for self. Increase of obligations with regard to self: the more I face up to my responsibilities the more I am responsible. Power made of "powerlessness"—that is the challenge to consciousness and its entry into a contingency of relations that clash with unveiling.

There, in the relation with the face—the ethical relation—the rectitude of an orientation or sense is traced. The *consciousness* of philosophers is essentially reflective. Or at least consciousness is grasped by philosophers in the moment of its return, which is taken for its birth. In its spontaneous pre-reflexive movements it already casts a sidelong glance, they believe, toward its origin, and measures the path covered. That is where its initial essence would reside: critique, mastery of self, analysis and decomposition of all signification that overflows itself. Well, responsibility is definitely not blind or amnesiac; through all the movements of thought where it unfurls it is carried by an extreme urgency or, more exactly, coincides with it. What was just described as a "no time to look back" is not the happenstance of an awkward or unfortunate consciousness "overflowed by events," or that "can't manage." It is the absolute rigor of an attitude without reflection, a primordial rectitude, a *sense* of being. "Where does it come from, this resistance of the unreflected to reflection?" Merleau-Ponty asked at Royaumont in April 1957, referring to problems posed by Husserl's[7] theory of phenomenological reduction. Our analysis of *sense* may well answer this fundamental question that Merleau-Ponty refused to settled by simple recourse to the finitude of the subject, incapable of total reflection. "Turn to the truth with all one's soul"—Plato's recommendation is not simply a lesson in common sense, preaching effort and sincerity. Is it not aimed at the ultimate most underhand reticence of a soul that, in the face of the Good, would persist in reflecting on Self, thereby arresting the movement toward Others? Is not the force of that "resistance of the unreflected to reflection" the Will itself, anterior and posterior, alpha and omega to all Representation? Then is the will not thorough humility rather than will to power? Humility not to be confused with an ambiguous negation of Self, already prideful of its virtue which, on reflection, it immediately recognizes in itself. But humility of one who "has no time" to turn back to self, who takes no steps to "deny" the self, if not the abnegation of the Work's rectilinear movement towards the infinity of the Other.

To affirm such an orientation and such a sense, to place a consciousness without reflection above and below all reflections, to surprise in the depth of the Ego an unambiguous sincerity and a servant's humility that no transcendental method could either corrupt or absorb, is to ensure the necessary conditions of the "beyond the given" that shows up in all signification, of the *meta*-phor that animates it, a marvel of language whose "verbal origin" will be endlessly denounced by philosophic analysis, without destroying the evident intention that penetrates it. Whatever its philological, social, or psychological history, the *beyond* that the metaphor produces has a sense that transcends that history; the illusionist power with which language is endowed must be recognized; lucidity does not abolish the beyond of those illusions.

It is of course the role of reflection to bring significations back to their subjective sources, subconscious or social or verbal, to tally their transcendental inventory. However, this method, legitimate for destroying many prestiges, already precludes an essential result: it prohibits in advance all transcendent sight [*visée*] in signification. Before research begins, the method converts all *Other* into *Same*, through Reflection in its own purifying work will employ these notions—if only the *beyond* with regard to which immanence is situated—which, in the absence of the sincerity and rectitude of "consciousness with no return," have no signification. Nothing that is sublime can do without verbal, social, or psychological sources, except enhancement [*sublimation*] itself.

But this consciousness "without reflection" is not simply pre-reflexive, naïve, spontaneous consciousness; it is not pre-critical. Discovering the orientation and unique sense in the moral relation is precisely placing the Ego as already challenged by the Other it desires and, consequently, as criticized in the rectitude of its movement. That is why the challenge of consciousness is not, initially, consciousness of this challenge. That conditions this. How would spontaneous thought turn back if the Other, the Exterior, did not challenge it? And how, in a concern for total Critique entrusted to reflection, would the new naïveté of reflection rise up, lifting the premier naïveté? Well, the Ego erodes its dogmatic naïveté in the face of the Other who demands more than it can spontaneously give.

注释：

1. 保尔·瓦雷里（1871—1945），法国象征派诗人，代表作有《年轻的命运女神》《旧诗稿》《幻美集》等。

2. 斯多葛主义，又称斯多葛学派，由芝诺创立，是古希腊最具影响力的哲学流派之一。该学派主张在其逻辑学说和自然观之上建立起一套个人伦理准则。

3. 马丁·海德格尔（1889—1976），德国现代著名哲学家，20 世纪存在主义哲学的创始人和主要代表之一。

4. 陀思妥耶夫斯基（1821—1881），俄罗斯作家，代表作有长篇小说《卡拉马佐夫兄弟》《罪与罚》《白痴》《群魔》等。

5. 梅洛·庞蒂（1908—1961），法国现象学哲学家，主要著作有《行为的结构》《知觉现象学》《意义与无意义》等。

6. 以赛亚，犹太教和基督教中的先知。

7. 埃德蒙德·胡塞尔（1859—1938），德国著名哲学家，现象学的奠基人。

后记

本书工作量较大，编者要从大量的理论文献中精选、编写和压缩为短篇幅作为学者自主阅读的文献资料。因此，我邀请了4名英美文学、西方文论研究方向博士史岩林、张东芹、王小会和黄贺作为副主编，协助我完成《文论选读》的文献精选和编写工作。尽管他们各自都很忙，但他们都欣然加入我的工作团队，给予了大力支持。因此，我要衷心地感谢他们！

本书编写分工如下：陈世丹主编，史岩林、张东芹、王小会、黄贺副主编。

上卷由陈世丹、史岩林、张东芹负责；下卷由陈世丹、王小会、黄贺负责。

本书得到中国人民大学“中央高校建设世界一流大学（学科）和特色发展引导专项资金”经费支持，特向中国人民大学外国语学院表示衷心的感谢！本书还得到了华中科技大学出版社的大力支持，特向华中科技大学出版社领导、张馨芳编辑表示衷心的感谢！

陈世丹

2020年4月16日